The Fever of the World

Phil Rickman lives on the Welsh border where he writes and presents the book programme *Phil the Shelf* on BBC Radio Wales. He is the acclaimed author of *Midwinter of the Spirit* (now a major ITV series), the Merrily Watkins series and the John Dee Papers. Visit his website at www.philrickman.co.uk.

Also by Phil Rickman

THE MERRILY WATKINS SERIES

The Wine of Angels
Midwinter of the Spirit
A Crown of Lights
The Cure of Souls
The Lamp of the Wicked
The Prayer of the Night Shepherd
The Smile of a Ghost
The Remains of an Altar
The Fabric of Sin
To Dream of the Dead
The Secrets of Pain
The Magus of Hay
Friends of the Dusk
All of a Winter's Night
The Fever of the World

THE JOHN DEE PAPERS

The Bones of Avalon
The Heresy of Dr Dee

OTHER TITLES

Candlenight
Curfew
The Man in the Moss
December
The Chalice
Night After Night
The Cold Calling
Mean Spirit

OTHER TITLES

The House of Susan Lulham

Phil Rickman

The Fever of the World

Published in hardback in Great Britain in 2022 by Corvus,
an imprint of Atlantic Books Ltd.

This paperback edition published in 2023 by Corvus.

10 9 8 7 6 5 4 3 2 1

A CIP catalogue record for this book is available from the British Library.

Hardback ISBN: 978 1 78649 459 7
E-book ISBN: 978 1 78649 460 3
Paperback ISBN: 978 1 78649 461 0

Printed in Great Britain by Clays Ltd, Elcograf S.p.A.

Corvus
An imprint of Atlantic Books Ltd
Ormond House
26–27 Boswell Street
London
WC1N 3JZ

www.atlantic-books.co.uk

The Fever of the World

. . . when the fretful stir
Unprofitable, and the fever of the world,
Have hung upon the beatings of my heart –
How oft, in spirit, have I turned to thee,
O sylvan Wye! Thou wanderer thro, the woods,
How often has my spirit turned to thee!'

WILLIAM WORDSWORTH
Lines composed a few miles above Tintern Abbey, on
revisiting the banks of the Wye during a tour
JULY 13, 1798

Part One

Lampe and Cupitt proposed that 'exorcism should have no official status in the Church at all...'

... they argued that encouraging belief in 'occult evil powers' could lead to dire social consequences... and implied that exorcism was a kind of Christian magic...

About a public letter from theologians
Geoffrey Lampe and Don Cupitt in 1975, quoted in
A History of Anglican Exorcism by Francis Young

1

The lolly and the stick

THE SKY HAD grown darker, small lights had begun bobbing below the forestry, and a chainsaw's whine fell away into the evening wind. David Vaynor didn't like any of it, though the Home Office pathologist with him didn't appear particularly fazed, contemplating the newly dead man in the beam of his lamp and nodding.

'I've seen this, I think, twice before. There's a name for it, though I can't remember for the moment what it is.'

He moved closer, flashlight shining brutally into the lifeless face and the dark silver hair.

'Stone dead after falling... what, forty metres... two hundred? Who knows?'

Behind him, avoiding the light and the face, Vaynor smothered a shudder. Working detectives were supposed to have left shuddering far behind.

'But it's him, all right,' Dr Billy Grace said. 'Peter Portis. You can certainly confirm that to Bliss.'

Billy's face, with its lavish white moustache, was lit up by Vaynor's own lamplight. He raised both hands and gazed up as if waiting to receive something substantial from a crane.

'Ending up on one's feet, supported only by bushes, is *not*, as might be thought, any kind of aid to survival.' He lowered his arms. 'When someone comes down with some velocity, like this chap, the upper vertebrae may pass quite neatly through a ring fracture of the occipital bone. You see?'

Vaynor forced himself to move closer. He'd need to tell DI Bliss he'd viewed the damage, but couldn't remember where the occipital bone was.

Then, avoiding the dead man's open eyes, he somehow knew.

Oh, God…

'Like, uh…' he turned away again, coughed '…the stick getting pushed through the lollipop?'

Billy Grace turned and beamed at him.

'The lolly and the stick. Ha. Yes, indeed.' Billy's mouth was a lavish gash under the moustache he'd probably first grown in the army more than twenty years earlier. 'Perhaps put that in my report for the coroner. He'll pretend to the police he thought of it himself, but that's a coroner's prerogative.'

'You said Portis,' Vaynor said. 'This is Portis the estate agent?'

'*And* the region's leading rock-climber… And now, I'm afraid, *ex*-rock-climber.'

In a fatal fall, Vaynor was thinking, from a rock where climbing was no longer permitted. Unsafe, unstable. In all kinds of ways.

'He was climbing alone?'

'Nothing to immediately indicate he wasn't,' Billy Grace said. Though I expect that's why you're here. We'll be checking for signs of struggle, of course.'

'I think the DI is just covering his back in case it turns out to be more sinister,' Vaynor said. 'I can probably think of a few people who'd like to help an estate agent off a cliff, but…'

Billy Grace might have smiled. Over his plastic protective suit, he wore a plaid jacket so conspicuously dated that he'd probably bought it from a rack labelled *windjammers*. But even up here there was very little wind, and the dusk was folding the surrounding hills, into a luminous mid-March night.

Spring, then. But nobody was in the mood for spring this year, Vaynor thought, thanks to the virus, which seemed to be rampaging everywhere.

'*Could*'ve been suicide,' Billy said. 'Though he never struck me as the type. Thought too highly of himself.'

'You knew him?'

'Not well, but I saw him less than a month ago, at a rotary lunch.' He sniffed.

Vaynor said, 'I didn't know you—'

'I'm not. I was their guest after-lunch speaker. You find rotarians all keep their food down if you don't go into too much detail.' Billy Grace kind of laughed as he prepared to march off. 'Let's hope you keep yours.' He clapped Vaynor on the shoulder. 'Don't really like this sort of thing, do you? Unsightly death?'

'Heights,' Vaynor said guardedly. 'I don't really like heights. But I was the only one who knew how to reach this place quickly.' He raised a hand to the projecting rocks. 'The Seven Sisters, anyway.'

He let his gaze glide down from the Sisters' faces to the water-top and the rising oaks that hid the cave.

Between the trees on the left, Vaynor could just see where the rocks arose from stony soil, where the poet Wordsworth had once walked. Apart from the lights and the chainsaw, not much had changed since William Wordsworth was here, having fled from the blood-pooled streets of Paris, heads bouncing under the guillotine blade behind him. Seeking peace again where he thought he'd once known it.

Again I hear those waters rolling from their mountain springs.

Vaynor thought he could hear the water, too, where the bank of trees ended above the Wye. Must have been about five years since *he* was last here. Very little had changed since then, and the forestry roads, lit by sparse headlights, were no safer.

Now Billy, cutting a figure bulkier than Wordsworth's, was striding ahead into the dusk, and Vaynor called to him, not looking at the body.

'Follow you down then, doc?'

Dr Billy Grace stretched out an arm towards the river, obscured by the bank of trees below the bony crag.

'"*O sylvan Wye…*"'

'"*…how often has my spirit turned to thee?*"' Vaynor murmured instinctively.

Billy Grace nodded.

'English at Oxford, David? In fact shouldn't *I* be calling *you* doc?

'No way! Please don't.'

No way did Vaynor want to be one of those people who insisted on being addressed as *doctor* on the strength of one poxy thesis.

It had been published online under the pseudonym Al Fox – after the house Alfoxden, where the poet and his sister had lived in Somerset. He – or rather, Al – had been invited to give a talk at Hereford Library on the poet's 250th anniversary next month. A big relief, therefore, for the reticent Vaynor, when Hereford's proposed Wordsworth weekend festival had been abandoned because of the virus and he could go on being seen just as a cop.

He followed the Home Office pathologist to an old, black Jaguar parked at the edge of the field. Of course, Billy Grace *would* have an ageing Jag, letting in an echo of Eve's disparaging voice from last night at the bedroom door.

You know, I can just imagine you in twenty years' time – one of those sad old Inspector Morse cops, full of regrets.

Which was how the destructive stuff had started, right on bedtime, going on for dismal hours and climaxing in the morning, with Eve quietly following the taxi driver and her suitcases out of the door, having barely spoken to him since first light. Given a last chance to put things right with her, he'd thrown it all away and walked off to work at Gaol Street, thinking he could deal with it later. But he'd sensed… relief, could it have been that, coming from Eve? Could this be her relief at having left him, at getting it over so quickly?

'Didn't really need a lamp tonight, David,' Billy Grace said, unlocking the Jag's boot. 'Not with the lovely Venus doing her best for us.'

He jabbed a thumb towards the single bright planet which dominated the darkening sky. Some years you were hardly aware of Venus at all and other times, night after night, you couldn't avoid Wordsworth's evening star.

To watch thy course when Day-light, fled from earth,
In the grey sky hath left his lingering Ghost.

Vaynor looked away, thinking he should be going to try and repair things with Eve before it really was too late. Should have stopped himself from instinctively responding when Bliss had first asked the small gathering in the CID room if anybody knew where the Seven Sisters rocks were. Unless there was something Bliss hadn't told them, it was just a routine climbing accident which, even on a quiet day like this, would surely have nothing for CID. Nobody particularly wanted to negotiate those treacherous forestry tracks at this time of day.

Vaynor sighed into the early night breeze. He remembered the Seven Sisters rocks rising from a bend of the River Wye. If you happened to fall off the wrong sister you could drop directly into the river.

'This is where I encountered my first corpses after moving

here,' Billy said. 'Similar kind of atmosphere, with the planet Venus just as obvious.'

'Venus is always showing off, coming up to spring,' Vaynor said. 'And then she disappears and the nights are quieter and slowly get warmer.'

'It was a much warmer night than this,' Billy said, 'when they perished.' He pointed. 'Just about *there*, as I recall. Venus should have vanished from the sky by then. I remember thinking that. Wondering why this dramatic evening star was still on show so far into the new year. Was it her part in this drama, to stick around, so that she could illuminate death?'

Billy Grace conclusively zipped up his windjammer.

'Venus appears to like death,' he said.

2

Cold fire

YOU HOPED FOR bright, frosty days and got floods and gales, nature's end-of-winter debris collecting under unhealthy skies of pink and grey like dead, peeling skin. This sky was clear now, though: no sun to set, no moon, only the dominant planet that Merrily thought was Venus or maybe Jupiter.

She'd been laying the kitchen wood stove for the evening ahead when he came banging on the door urgently, as though he had a writ to serve. Then he retreated to a partly visible Land Rover. In a corner of the window, she saw the ancient Defender blocking the drive in the last light and steaming like an exhausted bull. Shutting the stove, she went into the hall, slipping the front-door catch.

The cool evening smacked her face as she went outside, calling over to Huw Owen.

'Just happened to be passing… thought you'd drop in for a brew before lockdown?'

Lockdown: a new word that suddenly everybody was using. It was your life that was locked down, apparently to prevent it getting lost.

Merrily registered that Huw had shaved off his beard. His skin looked as raw as the sky and as mournful as that night under a limp moon, a few years ago, when he'd walked her up a stony track in the Beacons to warn her about wankers in the pews, psychotic grinders of the dark satanic mills, little rat-eyes in the dark. All the horrors awaiting a woman exorcist. Even in a lockdown, God knew.

Did God know? Did God have a role in all this drama? She'd read in a Sunday paper that one effect of the pandemic was a worldwide increase in spirituality, a feeling that only God could stop the spread of this illness. Or that the illness had been *started* by God to cull a population that was getting way out of control.

God. Her old mate. Merrily caught sight of herself in the mirror near the door: tangled dark hair, cursory make-up… was she finally starting to look tired and middle-aged? Bloody hoped not.

'Make it a strong 'un, lass,' Huw said, leaving his Land Rover behind and shaking himself like a ragged mongrel. 'And three sugars?'

She smiled. Brought up in Yorkshire by his Welsh mother, he *was* a ragged mongrel. Who apparently could speak primitive, basic Welsh, only with a Yorkshire accent.

*

Pulling off his boots to follow her into the vicarage kitchen, shedding his old charity-shop RAF greatcoat, Huw was rubbing his hands above the stove then stopping in dismay.

'You've let this bugger go out!'

'Hasn't been lit yet. Been out of the house most of the day, seeing people I now may not see for weeks in their homes, and Jane's at work.'

Huw shrugged his coat back on.

'Thought the kid were away at college.'

'Still on the gap year. It's complicated.' Merrily opened the stove and prised two logs apart with the poker. 'She's back in the village now. When the dig ended she went to the festival shop she'll be running for Barry from the Swan. How she swung that

I still don't know, but she spends most days setting it up, and I'm not making a fuss. Not yet, anyway. These are strange days.'

'Just on me way back from London,' Huw said. 'Church House, Merrily. You forgot?'

'Oh.' Merrily let the poker fall. Behind the stove glass, yellow flames gushed. 'I did. Went down the street to make a fire for my old organist, see a couple of people who've lost their jobs.'

'And you were right about the C of E,' he said. 'This is becoming serious.'

'Is it?'

'Never been the same since they let the Wizard Merlin out of Canterbury,' Huw said. 'Bad sign when he went. We thought him becoming archbishop were the start of summat new and promising, but it could be that him leaving so fast, that were the start of... the end game.'

He'd evidently been to a meeting of the Christian Deliverance Study Group, an offshoot of the clergy who organized exorcisms. First meeting of the year and a significant one for future dealings with the Unseen but not always Untarnished. The one she'd been hoping he'd attend but hadn't liked to remind him about.

'Even worse than we thought,' he said. 'Buggers might finally pull it off, too, the way things are going. So we've no time to waste.'

'How many of them *are* there now?'

'We won't know till they're in the majority. And then it'll be too bloody late – wi' God turned into a celestial social worker, deliverance study group'll have nowt to study. And unless we stop 'em now, you, lass, will be an ordinary vicar again. For as long as ordinary vicars last.'

While Huw sat down at the kitchen table to drink his tea Merrily considered how life would be so much simpler if she was an ordinary vicar.

'Is that what you want?' Huw said. 'Caring and compassionate? Sending your congregation home on a Sunday night – all six of 'em – believing there's nowt bad out there as knows their name?'

Apart from the stove, the kitchen was almost dark. She asked if her bishop had been anywhere near Church House today. He said nothing.

'Or his pal, Crowden?'

Merrily opened the stove, picturing Crowden: stocky, shaven-headed, pumped-up. Could still hear his plummy voice at the gathering of Welsh Border exorcists she'd hosted last year at the Black Swan, where he'd proclaimed – looking directly at Merrily – that exorcism had nothing to do with faith.

It has some of us hunting for spurious evidence of an active, supernatural evil.

Crowden was the sceptical deliverance minister for an English diocese beyond the north-eastern fringe of Hereford. He seemed committed to putting himself and Merrily – especially Merrily – out of a job. He was, unsurprisingly, in favour with the Bishop.

As we've no means of understanding what, if anything's, actually happening, he'd said, *we should regard it all as potentially evil, in the sense that we could be opening doors to the growth of mental illness.*

Merrily arranged a heavy log in the stove. It kept her hands steady. She looked up at Huw to make sure he wasn't displaying any obvious symptoms of the virus. He looked fatigued, certainly, but not conspicuously ill.

'Took me back many years, to the days of Lampe and Cupitt – long before your time, lass.'

'I've read about their campaign to get exorcism dumped by the Church. But they clearly failed.'

'Aye. At the time. And that were well before your time. Back in the 1970s, when understanding the Unseen and, when necessary, facing up to an active evil, were still accepted as part of the Church's job. Now t'Church is groping for credibility in an increasingly secular society by reducing what it admits to believing in. Demonic possession… that's become a mental health issue.'

Yes, she thought. And ghosts were officially considered to be illusion or scientific anomalies. Because the Church, increasingly, took a realistic stance.

'End of the day, none of it's our business,' Huw said. 'That's what we're being told. And they'll consign us to history.'

He leaned back. Outside the kitchen window, the day glowered into evening. He'd been in this room for fewer than ten minutes, and already was asking the big questions. This was going to take some time.

Huw pulled off his woolly hat. His hair looked like old straw left out in a blizzard.

'Some basics, lass. Can I take it you still want to go on peering into the Unknown? Listening to folk who think they're getting glimpses of the Unseen? I need to ask because I need to get this right. You've a decision to make and this is the time to make it. Either don't resist, just go quietly or… How are *you* coping wi' Innes's new rules?'

He meant the Bishop Craig Innes's decree that any enquiries involving the paranormal must now be run past his office, so they could, when possible, be quietly dumped. Or referred to social services – or the NHS, if it had time for any of this rubbish. Or, more likely, dealt with by what remained of the local clergy, using various forms of counselling and always avoiding the now-discredited E-word.

'All right, then.' Merrily pushed hair back from her eyes and stopped avoiding the big question. 'People like me, Huw… are they actually winding us down? Is that the way it's going – all clergy offered a basic one- or two-day deliverance course... grounded in psychology? And that'll be an end to it?'

There was silence and then Huw nodded soberly.

'They're saying the clergy are here to help, not investigate, and shouldn't ask too many questions to which they know they won't get answers. But... if the Church is phasing out your role, who's left to assist parish priests facing summat genuinely iffy?' Huw threw a small log on the cringing fire. 'Tell me – when are you finding that nervous vicars are coming to you these days?'

Merrily stared into the smouldering logs.

'When the Bishop says they can.'

And the Bishop didn't have to explain himself. Deliverance advisors, who used to be called exorcists, weren't licensed. A bishop could simply stop making use of his, if he wanted to. When he was told about something he thought could be dealt with under the heading of mental health or dismissed as superstition, wishful-thinking or hocus-pocus, Innes no longer passed it down to Sophie in the gatehouse so a decision could be taken on whether further action was necessary. Taking action, now, was less of an option. Sophie was reduced to working two days a week.

'When Bernie Dunmore was Bishop, *all* the spooky stuff eventually landed on Sophie's desk and we were the ones who decided priorities.'

Huw said nothing. She wondered if he'd seen Sophie today – and, if he had, whether this would be for the last time.

'I've had just two routine bereavement apparitions since Christmas,' she said. 'Listening sympathetically to new widows who desperately want to believe the fireside chair is still occupied.'

She watched small flames flickering hopefully as they tried to reach the latest log.

'Bereavement apparitions, we've always quietly accepted that imagination has a part to play. But they're a part of the grieving process. And if we have a policy of rejecting it, we'll soon be rejecting other stuff, like...'

Like the call from Sophie an hour ago, saying that the new vicar of Whitchurch, in the Wye Valley, wanted to talk to the diocesan deliverance advisor about an alleged haunting reported by a female parishioner in a holiday home.

Merrily was watching Huw closely. He knew more about this than he was chasing.

'Sophie indicated that, as the Whitchurch guy hasn't informed the Bishop's office, as all vicars are now expected do, I should be taking a look at it and, if necessary, quietly pursuing it. "Quietly" meaning *me* not telling the Bishop either. Which, as you know, is a bit risky right now.'

Sophie had said mysteriously that she and Merrily needed more time to discuss it – *and not on the phone.*

Merrily had tried not to get too interested. It could be a trap. And, if she didn't report it to the Bishop's office because it looked genuine, she'd step right into it.

The fire glimmered silently in the woodstove's windows, as the phone rang behind her in the scullery.

'And your two widows,' Huw said. 'Do you just politely discourage their... delusions?'

'Perhaps I should suggest to them that they ought to pull themselves together and take their old wedding pictures off the piano for a while?'

'And how would that seem to you?'

'Erm... quite brutal, Huw? Don't you think?'

Huw said nothing. The phone in the next room went on

ringing, and she went on not answering it, letting the answering machine cut in.

It was the new vicar of Whitchurch.

They'd never met, but she recognized his voice. From television. Huw must have known that this man would be ringing Merrily – Sophie must have told him. She wanted to know if Merrily was up for the summons, if she was prepared to disregard the Bishop's instructions.

In her head, Merrily heard the theme music rising and saw the thin, pale face of the Whitchurch vicar tightening as he bent over a loaded syringe.

3

Bringer of Light. Also…

On the way out of the building, the head of CID called in at Bliss's office, pulling on a dark green trench coat.

'It's Peter Portis, the property man,' she said. 'Did you know?'

Bliss nodded.

'Found dead near a well-known beauty-spot.' He went back to his desk. 'Panoramic views. Fine open aspects over the famous River Wye. Close to all amenities and the renowned Symonds Yat.'

Detective Chief Inspector Annie Howe sighed.

'There was me vainly hoping you'd resist the property gags.'

'Actually, that was an exaggeration,' Bliss said. 'It doesn't seem to be close to any obvious amenities. Only Vaynor knew where it was exactly, so I sent him up there for a poke around in case it was suspicious.'

'Quite a big death in Hereford,' Annie Howe said.

'According to the NHS guys there could be a lorra little ones soon. If you can call them little.'

'Eleven cases of the virus in the hospital,' Annie said, 'but nobody's died yet.'

'This could be early days.'

They'd talk about it tonight, discreetly. They never left together or drove the same road out of Hereford at the same time, although they'd been quietly turning out the light over the same bed for more than a year now.

'Never actually met him,' Bliss said, 'Portis. Though me and Kirsty did buy a house off his firm.'

The CID room outside the office door was deserted. Annie stopped, turning back to face him.

'This is your house at Marden? The one with...'

Bliss nodded.

'His son did the business. Royce, his name. Seemed a bit of a cocky twat.'

Annie tucked very pale blonde hair into her collar, came into the office and stood with her back to the door.

'Peter Portis's death appears to be linked to his rock-climbing activities – which is how *I* met him, as it happens.'

'Recently?'

'No, would have been several years ago. He was involved in some climbing-safety publicity exercise supported by my father in return for the work he was doing with young offenders on the rocks. Any particular reason for CID to take an interest in this?'

'Possibly.' Bliss shrugged. 'Portis scared the life out of some of them hard kids, gerrin' them up the rocks on bits of rope.'

'They didn't *have* to go up, did they?'

'They were all volunteers,' Bliss said. 'Better than detention – they thought. And they all came back down, one way or another. Anyway, Vaynor's looking into it. He volunteered, too. I'm sending him to talk to a young woman, possibly the only witness to the fall.'

'Where, exactly?'

'Seven Sisters rocks in the Wye Valley. Portis fell off one. Didn't actually land at this girl's feet, but it was near enough to spoil her walk.'

'Francis, Portis was a serious rock climber. They don't just *fall*.'

'No. Not often. This has overtones of possible suicide as well as... the other thing. But Billy Grace reckons Portis wasn't the kind to top himself. He lived not far from where he landed, which might mean something. Anyway, I thought it'd be worth gerrin' Darth to have a quick poke around. He seems to have left his PhD up there.'

Annie used a tissue to dust Bliss's chair before perching on the edge of it.

'What did he get a PhD in, then? I should know, but...'

'Involved the poet Wordsworth,' Bliss said. 'Who spent weeks around there at the end of the eighteenth century, thinking up fancy rhymes and stuff.'

'Vaynor came down from Oxford with a dissertation on English romantic poetry?' Annie said. 'And now he's working for *you?*'

'Life's strange like that, isn't it, ma-am?'

Annie stood, pulled up the collar of her trench coat and tightened her belt.

'People've been saying that to me since panic first set in over this virus. And they might be right. Unusual things do appear to be happening everywhere. Except, of course, that crime's been coming down.'

*

'Who found the body?' Vaynor asked.

'A client of his, as it happens,' Billy Grace replied. A lot of houses and former farms round here. This was a young woman his firm's rented a village house to, someone said. Must've been quite a shock for her, taking a stroll before dark and a body almost lands on you. Well, couldn't have been long after it happened. I wonder if he *wanted* to land in the river.'

'So he jumped?'

Vaynor looked up to where the nearest of the Seven Sisters was summit-butting a night cloud, and shuddered. A grey van drew up and Slim Fiddler, Hereford crime scene boss, staggered out. Then there was a traffic car containing two uniformed cops. Headlight beams intersected across the grass.

Only a mile or two from the normally crowded A40 dual carriageway, there was a separateness about this slice of the England–Wales border, an aloof beauty unlike anywhere else Vaynor knew in southern Britain. Yet there were places where the Wye Valley wildtrack included the low rumble of not-so-distant industrial traffic. After a while, he became aware of the moving paleness of a plastic-covered stretcher. Too dark now to see how many people were supporting it.

A timeless scene, Vaynor thought. Could have been the body of some Celtic chieftain borne from a battlefield in the Dark Ages.

It stopped.

'Always attracted picturesque drama, this area,' Billy Grace said, as van doors rattled open. 'Despite the remains of industry, the lower Wye was probably Britain's first actual tourist area, did you know that?'

Vaynor did. It had been a theme in the introduction to his PhD thesis: the combination of steep rocks, crumbling walls and partly overgrown castle ruins that had gradually become part of the landscape.

The river was on their right, visible through the wooden bones of the Biblins footbridge. He'd crossed it just the once, didn't like the way the slats swayed under you. It was said that someone died in the Wye every year.

'Tourism, as we know it, was only just starting when Wordsworth came here,' he told Billy Grace as a uniform and one of the crime scene team bore the body to the rear of the van.

'Meanwhile, death never stops happening,' Billy said. 'Or maybe I just notice it more in this job.'

Wherever you met him, there was a story attached to the place, some mortality tale, told with professional relish. Vaynor should have known there was going to be a memory held in this deep valley. Billy's neon teeth were projecting a smile like a death-ray.

'Moonbathers,' he said.

'Here?'

'Man and wife. Both drowned.'

'When would that have been? Before my time, I imagine. And after Wordsworth's or I'd've read about it.'

'*Well* before your time. She was naked, he was fully clothed apart from plimsolls and socks. Indicating she'd gone swimming – on impulse, perhaps – and pretty soon got into difficulties. He'd plunged in to try and save her, but evidently wasn't as strong a swimmer as he'd thought. And it was too near the rapids – down there. You'll hear them in a minute.'

'I've never heard that story.'

'David, you wouldn't've even've started school back then.' Billy waved an empty sleeve towards high crags piercing the last light, as the van pulled away. 'Not that much older than the baby, if at all.'

'Baby?'

'I believe they had one with them.'

'*In the river?*'

'One assumes not, as it certainly survived, but I do seem to remember something.'

He was staring up at the fading rocks. The first, or maybe the seventh of the sisters was in hard view, a limestone outcrop high above the river. Even in full daylight you'd only see three of them from here, peering out like giant skulls, as if the rest of the bodies were entangled in the forestry and the feet were in the water.

'You're not a climbing man, then, David?'

'I get vertigo on tall bar-stools.'

Someone at Gaol Street had once asked Vaynor if he didn't get vertigo just standing up. You attracted these predictable remarks when you were six and a half feet tall. Bliss had immediately dubbed him Darth, and it had stuck. *Darth Vaynor*, from *Star Wars*. At least there was no reference in that to anything academic.

'But you've obviously spent some time up here, even if you don't like heights,' Billy Grace said. 'You know your way around.'

'The um…' Vaynor hesitated. Might as well get it over. '… the thesis brought me. I was born in Hereford, so this was quite local, and it was the setting for a relatively unexplored side of William Wordsworth. Changed him a lot, the time he spent down here, and I thought I'd try and find out why.'

'And did you?'

'Um… not to my complete satisfaction. He left some elements of mystery behind. Which I failed to solve. I wasn't a copper then.'

'If you got the PhD, it must've made sense to somebody. But you became a copper in the end.'

'If this *is* the end.' Vaynor went on walking towards the lights, letting go a long breath. 'My girlfriend thought I'd made a… bad decision and I'd eventually go back to academia.'

'But you won't?'

'Bit late now.'

'Is it? How old are you?'

'Coming up to twenty-eight. Soon.'

Around the same age Wordsworth had been when he was here for the second time, having returned from post-revolution France, disillusioned by the violence and blood. Seemed to have seen more death than Vaynor.

'Extraordinary sight, that, isn't it?' Billy Grace looked up at the spectacular planet, pulling off his windjammer. 'So dominant that it's still often reported as a UFO.'

'"*It cheers the lofty spirit most,*" Vaynor said, "*to watch thy course when daylight, fled from earth, in the grey sky hath left his lingering ghost*".'

'Wordsworth again?'

'He wrote at least two poems about Venus. One as an evening star, one about when it appears in the early morning.'

'And changes its name,' Billy said.

'Also its sex. Known as Lucifer in the early morning sky.'

'Bringer of light.' Billy began to unzip his protective coversuit, shedding it like a shiny snakeskin. 'And, ah... also Satan. Who the hell...?' Pulling his mobile out of a hip pocket. 'Better get this. Yes, he is...'

Thrusting his phone at Vaynor, he shrugged on his jacket.

Vaynor sighed. If someone had found even the smallest indication that Peter Portis had been assisted down from one of the Seven Sisters, they'd be here all night.

'You've gorra gerra more powerful phone, Darth,' DI Bliss said.

'It's a bad place for signal, boss, the Wye Valley.'

'What about Goodrich?' Bliss said. 'That's not far from you, is it? Walking distance?'

'Well... if you know where you're going.'

'The woman who may have seen Portis's body come down. You'll find her at a house called Churchyard Cottage,' Bliss said. 'Near the church, as you might imagine.'

4

Reopening an old door

THE WALLS THAT had been white yesterday were now dark blue, and still gleaming wet in the thin light. They'd all be matte when dry, like night sky. Jane scanned the surface for gaps, holding up her paintbrush so that any drips would fall on her fingers or one of the two frayed sweaters she was wearing against the cold.

Yes, yes, yes. The voice of Lucy Devenish. *That's perfectly acceptable, but by the time you open for business – are you listening to me, Jane? – by the time you open, I want* none *of those walls visible, do you understand? You need shelving everywhere, and all the shelves packed.*

'Sure.' Jane knelt down to press the lid back into the top of the paint can. 'Just don't expect any little pot fairies. I'll do apples. Pot fairies, forget it.'

You know very well they were all I could get at the time.

'Yeah, well, times have changed. I'll preserve the ethos, where possible, but there's no room for too much compromise. I want to keep out the whimsy factor. I get one chance at this, and if I fuck up it's over.'

***I** do the swearing, Jane.*

Lucy conveyed a frown that you could almost see imprinted on the gloomy air. Jane laughed and then smothered it when she saw Lol through the shop window, about to come in.

Never locked the door when she was working in here. It was about appearing open to potential customers who might come back when there were actually things to buy. Lol wouldn't buy anything, but Lol was different.

He stood there in the last light, jacket hanging open over what was surely the last of the *Alien* sweatshirts commemorating his first album. Time spun back like a revolving door and suddenly Jane was fifteen again, meeting him for the first time in this very shop, then belonging to Lucy. He'd worn a nervy, hunted look then, too.

'Jane, are you sleeping here these days?'

'I'm off home soon, but I do like being here in the dark. Watching the walls absorb it. Sharing space with Lucy.' She put the brush down on the paint can, which sat on the stair above hers. 'What's up?'

He didn't reply. Jane held up the can so she could be sure the lid was tight.

'We did Mum's office in the scullery at home a couple of weeks ago, and there was some left over, so I got a small tin of black and mixed it in because… I felt something should be restored.'

It was about banishing the blandness of Ledwardine Fine Arts – what the new owners had called this shop after Lucy Devenish died, filling it with glacial tat that had sod-all to do with Ledwardine. Jane had stood here in the total dark a couple of nights ago and asked Lucy if it would be OK to paint all the white away, and Lucy… well, Lucy hadn't given any indication that it wouldn't be.

Lol seemed to shrug.

'If Barry's happy with it…'

'Haven't asked him. If he doesn't like it, I suppose he'll just kill me very quietly.'

Strictly speaking, it was now Barry's shop, a few doors from Barry's hotel, the Black Swan. Barry was a significant presence in Ledwardine, now he'd retired from the SAS still youngish, having earned the right, like so many of them, never to get accused of being from Off. It was good that Barry and Lol – they couldn't be more different – were mates and organizing the folk festival together: Lol a musician, inherently neurotic, while Barry, an ex-SAS guy, saw the necessity of good prep.

Lol closed the shop door.

'So, uh, who were you talking to when I came in? Not that it's my—'

'It's your ears. All musos go deaf.'

'That's Iron Maiden, Jane, not tinkly little acoustic guys.'

'All I'm going to say,' Jane said, 'is that we do have to recognize that Lucy was the soul of this shop. She might be dead but she's never going to be gone.'

'And when you talk to her… does she reply?'

Jane frowned.

'It's just that I'd hate her to miss you when you've left,' Lol said. 'Bearing in mind that the shop's only going to be ours – yours – till the Ledwardine festival's over. And talking of festivals, I've got a bit of news. I had a call from Prof Levin this morning.'

'About *Glasto*?'

Jane was on her feet. Lol shrugged.

'Assuming it doesn't get called off because of the lockdown…'

'Wow! I knew they'd finally ask you. And you'll be on TV again.'

'Unlikely.'

'Let's not start off defeatist, Lol. It *might* happen. And then you've got the *Ledwardine* festival soon afterwards…'

'Even that may not happen, the way things are going.'

Lol figured he'd done his last local gig for a good while and there was no other source of income unless he could produce a commercial album faster than he'd ever done before.

And nothing Jane could do. The one thing that definitely wouldn't help was going off to university to prepare for a job that was iffy at best.

For a couple of weeks, she'd been planning how to say some of this to Mum. There'd be rows. Bitter rows. Crockery-smashing, close to eye-clawing rows, but she'd have to say it soon. To them all.

Feeling hot, suddenly, in her two sweaters, she drew a big breath.

'I'm not sure how to put this, Lol, but like could you and Barry start thinking of me as in this for the duration?'

'Duration of what?'

She said nothing.

'You're going to university soon, Jane.'

'Yeah, well... possibly. At some stage.'

'Unless I've got this wrong, gap years aren't any longer than ordinary years?'

'Well... actually, they are... can be. You can have, like, two gap years if you want? Or more? Just means that when you eventually go to university, you check in as a mature student and get treated with more respect.'

Actually, he wasn't the first she'd kind of told. She'd begun by explaining it to Eirion, when he was just out of hospital and they were all over one another. Eirion had still warned her, as he'd probably thought Mum would want him to, against doing anything radical. Not pushing it, mind, because he'd realize their resumed relationship was still fairy dust.

Lol said, 'Let me get this right. You really *don't* want to go to university in the autumn?'

Looking maybe a little worried now. He and Jane had been

mates for a while before he'd succumbed to Mum's charms. But even if he and Mum ever tied the official knot he was never going to cut it as a stepfather.

'What difference would it make?' Jane said. 'We both know how many qualified archaeologists there are who haven't a hope in hell of getting a proper job. And don't tell me that's just a phase. And further education really *costs*. Look at it this way. If Mum can't afford the fees, and I've no money… no money *yet*, that is…'

'Ah.'

'However, if I can make this shop take off as an actual business…'

'Selling what?'

'Music, books. And mysterious stuff. Not Goth exactly, that was more Mum's era. Nothing obviously New Agey, nothing tacky. But, like, proper books on Welsh Border history and folklore next to the dowsing rods and pendulums. And make a special feature of *this guy*.'

She pulled a book from the table and held it up as she sat down again. *Alfred Watkins' Herefordshire.*

'The man half of Herefordshire tried to forget because he discovered ley lines. Which the archaeologists tried to dismiss, but now they're finding out he was right!'

'Are they?' Lol said.

'Oh yeah, they're coming round to it. So we'll have all *his* books. And maybe some Border Morris kit. Lucy will understand. And…' She moved over to the cast-iron spiral stairway. 'I'd like to open up the attic, as well, for retail. You remember the attic?'

This shop was also part of his history. He'd hidden in that attic once, to avoid meeting a guy who'd wanted to re-form the band they'd both been in.

'Listen,' she said, 'it makes sense. All of this. It's a good thing to do. Lucy was important to this village, still is.'

'Jane, she's—'

'Dead, sure. And the *guardian* now, however you want to take that. Don't you feel her presence?'

He ought to, living in her old cottage. But this shop had been more important to Lucy. He was surely ready to believe she was still more accessible here.

'This is going to be like… reopening an old door, Lol.'

She could barely see him now. Her mission, inherited from Lucy, was to kick open doors into the past. Be here when archaeologists excavated what she was convinced would turn out to be a neolithic henge around the centre of the village where the old orchard used to be. The henge which, like Lucy, was still here. And she wanted to be a part of all that… which was not quite the same as wanting a career in archaeology. More personal. More mystical.

Lol said, 'You talked about this to your… to Merrily?'

'She's got enough problems right now. But you can tell her if you want.'

Lol laughed. Jane shrugged.

'Worth a try. Look, *I'll* get round to telling her. When the time's right.' She sat down on the second iron step. 'Now it's your turn. What's on your mind? It's half past five. Why aren't you still working?'

It was how his day usually went. Songwriting was a profession, demanding proper working hours. No getting up around half-eleven, walking around, smoking a joint, waiting for the vibe to set in, and then off to the pub. It was his job.

He sat down on the wooden stool.

'When Huw Owen turns up at the vicarage at last light on a winter's day, is that ever good?'

'I don't know. You mean he…'

'Is there now. So I just came to ask if you know why, because—'

'No, I don't.' Disturbed. She'd been avoiding long, serious

chats with Mum about the future in case the word university got introduced. So she hadn't learned much lately. 'Something about the Bishop?'

Jane hooked an arm around the spiral staircase rail. Mum was still convinced she was on borrowed time here, with this bishop. And this was one of the issues she'd only ever really discuss with her so-called spiritual adviser, the guy who'd guided her into exorcism.

'Mum's always afraid she might get forced out of this vicarage – and therefore the Night Job – and she knows what living here means to me... and you. Right? Right?'

'Jane, it means a lot me, of course it does, but—'

'Don't give me all that shit about Mum meaning more. I'm even prepared to accept that. But if she got pushed out of Ledwardine, she wouldn't be the same person. Neither would you. As for someone like me...'

'Look, maybe we're overreacting. Maybe Huw—'

'Like Huw ever does social calls this side of the border? What if he's come to tell her he's finally going to retire? Then she's really on her own. Got to happen sometime, Lol. He's not getting any younger.'

Lol said nothing. He was genuinely worried, and Jane could see why. The future of his relationship with Mum was something he never took for granted.

'OK... Why don't you go and wait for him to come out of the vicarage? He won't leave too late, he never does. Just put yourself behind the gate and then step out as his Land Rover comes out of the drive. Don't let *her* see you, obviously. Just, like, do an ambush and get the truth out of him.'

Jane pointed towards the door, somehow sensing Lucy's spectral forefinger aligned with hers.

5

Burnout

WHEN THE PHONE rang for the third time, Huw was on his feet. Merrily switched on the lamp on the dresser.

'You don't have to go yet.'

'I've taken up too much of your time, lass.' He put up both hands, mid blink, as if fending off flying bricks. 'Just wanted to let you know you're not entirely surrounded by mates. Don't trust everybody. I'll see meself out. You get that phone, it might be significant.'

If it was, he knew it. Propping up a limp smile, she went stumbling through to the scullery with its new deep blue ceiling between the beams. When they'd painted it she'd been thinking serenity. Jane had done the wry look: why not be realistic, have blood-red slashed with black? She grabbed the phone, dragging the tangled wire round the desk and flopping down in the old captain's chair.

'Ledwardine Vicarage.'

Too late. Dead line. She had to track the number.

Whitchurch vicar, village in the south of the county. She switched on the computer to remind herself who she'd be ringing. Found his name at the top of the search results and clicked.

Ripley. Arlo. There was a link to an early episode of *Burnout* they'd missed but she'd found on YouTube. It opened on an ill-lit bedroom and a sob. Two people; you weren't sure which of them the sob had been ripped from, but the girl spoke next.

'You don't have to go on doing this. We could just get out. Even if it's only Ireland or somewhere. Just disappear. You don't owe these bastards anything.'

'You're not getting this.' Simon Wilding trying to shout through pressing tears. Florid stitches where his jaw had been slashed. Hand-held camerawork, gliding shadows. *'You're just not getting it, Sandy. All the people I shared that house with...'*

'Are dead, yeah. That's the problem with smack. One day you think you can handle it, the next you're kissing the sky and realizing you're never coming down. And if the drugs don't get you...'

'I said I'd give it till the end of the year.'

'And you know what? When you're killed, that'll be the best piece of evidence the cops could wish for, so they'll just stand back and let it fucking happen. A win for them. Another dead user they can forget they once owned. Who'll never have to talk about what they did with him. Go on, tell me I'm wrong.'

The screen blacked out. A moment of silence before the credits came up in shades of grey. No music. Another episode was trailed on YouTube.

British noir. Cutting-edge Channel Four. Simon Wilding, a former junkie, had been more or less blackmailed into helping the Metropolitan police take down an international drug syndicate. Must've been three or four years ago when Merrily had watched most of series one with Jane. She clicked on another link, and the Net reminded her why there was no series two.

> *...with three episodes written, the second*
> *series of the BAFTA-nominated* Burnout *was*
> *cancelled after Arlo Ripley quit suddenly,*
> *amid talk of a nervous breakdown. He was*

later divorced from his wife of five years and announced his intention of being ordained into the Church. 'Simon Wilding was not, in the end, good for me,' Ripley would admit later.

Before becoming an actor, he'd obtained a respectable degree in theology, doing am-dram in his college days, a few scenes as a TV extra. But extras who looked like him got noticed. Pale, sensitive face, cool name. There were bit parts, then, after leaving college, a few months as a minor character in *EastEnders* before *Burnout* had been built around him. After that BAFTA nomination, he must have been looking at a pile of money. Maybe more in another year or so than he'd get from the Church over the rest of his life.

There was a news picture of him in a dog collar with some sullen kids outside a grimy urban church.

As a curate in Bristol, Ripley became involved in helping drug users and says he felt like a fraud, fearing that his poetically-wasted Burnout *character, Simon Wilding, had only glamorized hard drugs. 'I was in the grip of a very twisted kind of guilt,' Ripley said in an interview with the* Observer.

The phone rang again. Merrily picked it up. She had most of the picture.

In the phone, a male voice was emerging cautiously, like someone tentatively peering around a door.

'It's… Arlo Ripley.'

'Hello. Merrily Watkins. I'm sorry, I missed your first call.'

'I don't think we've ever met,' he said, 'and... I'm sure you're imagining Simon Wilding. Quite sophisticated people seem to see me only as a heroin addict.'

She recognized the Rev. Arlo Ripley's slightly tired Londonish voice as it turned into the images she knew from the TV titles: a syringe and a sleeve rolled up. Or creamy powder on a saucer, two smeared spoons. Now the spare, pale-skinned junkie was no more, because, after nine episodes, the actor who played him had become a priest.

There'd been a piece about him in the *Hereford Times* a few weeks ago, followed up the next day by national papers. Then a trickle of tabloid publicity, most of which she'd missed because Ripley had arrived in the middle of the Kilpeck problem at the end of last year. Without the needles.

Lol ran into the road as the old Land Rover reversed out of the vicarage drive and levelled up on the edge of the pavement with a snort of blue exhaust. When he tapped on the driver's window, it was lowered the old way, with a handle inside. Lol leaned in.

'Quick drink?'

'Bit early for me, lad.'

'Tea? Coffee?'

'Too much caffeine frazzles me brain.'

Lol breathed in diesel fumes and shivered; the last of his *Alien* sweatshirts was wearing thin and the zip on his fleece had broken.

'You feel like watching me frazzle *my* brain?'

Huw sniffed.

'Quiet in the Swan, is it, this time of day?'

He wound his window up and the Defender went rattling away towards the square, Lol trotting along the cobbles behind the exhaust. Black and white Ledwardine was rising around him as if old beams and rafters were stretching up to any last sun. In the lounge bar of the Black Swan the tang of fresh polish was biting into the kindling.

Barry tossed a log on top of the fire and looked over his shoulder.

'Seen what Jane's doing in that shop, Laurence? Cos I couldn't. Not without a torch.'

'Should we be worried?'

'Depends.' Barry dusting bark fragments from his hands. 'All you Devenish disciples are half-baked. Me, I just wish I hadn't ended up with Lucy's old shop. Not sure I want to see a new Ledwardine Lore, bits of spooky tat everywhere.' He ducked under the bar-flap. 'Tea, is it?'

'And a couple of slices of toast? No, make it three.'

'That bloke's with you?'

Huw was taking a seat at the table for two, down by the long mullioned window with the milky glass. He wore an old RAF greatcoat and a fraying grey scarf. Looked like a pilgrim who was starting to wonder if his faith would withstand the miles. Lol leaned across the bar to Barry, whispering.

'It's Merrily's mentor, from the Beacons. You remember?'

'What happened to the beard?'

Huw glanced up. Without his beard, he looked less in control, more mental than mentor. Lol walked down the bar, past empty tables, wondering how he was going to approach this. Did Huw owe him anything?

He sat down. There was a rattle of crockery from behind the bar. Huw ran a hand over his disconcertingly naked jaw.

'Lovely woman, your lass, Laurence. Pity she comes wi' all this baggage, eh?'

Lol said nothing for a while. For a long time the situation had been like a pressure behind his eyes.

'Baggage,' Huw said.

Lol sighed. Then he was coming out with it – first time; he didn't know how it would sound to Huw: how the baggage didn't weigh so much any more. How he and Merrily had been living close to one another... *kind of* together... for a few crowded years. How it no longer seemed to matter as much any more that he didn't go to church services, only to some of Merrily's Sunday evening meditations, which, he pointed out, were now overtaking the traditional services and keeping the parish church alive.

'You do understand why she's doing this job?' Huw said. 'Why she thinks it's necessary for a village to have a vicar?'

'Maybe it's just that she was an otherwise normal person who seemed to have been given access to another layer of experience. No, that wasn't right.'

'She just accepts summat else's there wi'out embarrassment.' Huw rocked his chair back against the deep-set window frame. 'And happen she's told you about some buggers in the C of E closing ranks against the woo-woo.'

'That's what they're calling it?'

'Meant to be disparaging, but I've always liked woo-woo better than the words some folk come up with. Exorcism gets reduced to Deliverance. Which could mean owt. Buggers've even toned that down now to *Healing* and Deliverance. She tell you what she's planning to do? Because she knows she can't go on like this.'

Lol shook his head.

'Me neither,' Huw said glumly. 'I called in tonight, warned her things could be coming to a head and I need to know if she's staying the course. Sophie needs to know, too, so I went there first. Ta, lad.'

Barry had brought the tea and toast but no conversation; he knew something was moving. With Barry back behind the bar, Lol cautiously listened to Huw talking about his meeting at Church House in London: many people in the Church apparently happy with the Bishop of Hereford's no-nonsense, Bible-as-blunt-instrument approach to the paranormal.

'What's Sophie saying, Huw?'

'She's saying we don't know – *can't* know – the way the Church of England's going. But we've got to keep asking questions. Keep lifting curtains, trying the handles of locked doors. And don't let no bishops tell us which doors to leave alone for the sake of our sanity.'

Lol said, 'Merrily reckons they're talking about unofficially appointing Craig Innes as the Archbishop's special advisor on deliverance. What's that mean, exactly?'

Huw took a piece of buttered toast and opened the little jar of Herefordshire honey.

'It don't give Innes actual authority over anybugger, but it does make him a key tool for winding it all down. Handing the dicey stuff to the shrinks. Let the vicars concentrate on what's essentially social work. And there's a test case coming up – the first in a while. What I learned from Sophie, Laurence, is the lass'll be hearing about it tonight. From a new vicar, who wants her to take it off his hands.'

'This is deliverance?'

'Happen. And she's supposed to clear it wi' the Bishop before she gets herself involved.'

'Oh.'

'Only the way things are, if she reports it to the Bishop, he'll tell her to leave it alone, let the vicar handle it himself and then they'll make sure the vicar either counsels this woman out of it or gives it a zap-job then backs off. But Sophie reckons there might be some unfinished business in it. And if the lass doesn't take it on, it won't get looked into at all.'

'Do *you* think it should be looked into? At the risk of giving the Bishop ammunition he might use?'

Huw poured himself some tea.

'Laurence, you ever tell her this you're dead, all right?'

Lol shrugged.

'But she's the best deliverance student I've ever had.' Huw took a sip from his mug. 'Don't know why I'm saying that. She's no theologian, doesn't have a scary amount of knowledge like most of the new clergy these days. Goes to bed, on and off, wi' a failed rock-star, who—'

'If they see me as anything at all it's as a failed folkie,' Lol said. 'Can't get lower than that.'

'I were being charitable.' Huw put his mug down. 'You actually settled here?'

'What?'

It wasn't something he'd let himself consider for a while. He liked Ledwardine and he was comfortable with a few of the locals.

'You know what I'm asking.'

'Huw, I honestly don't know. Maybe if Merrily—'

'No, lad… I mean *you*.'

'Well, I… I want to *feel* settled here.'

Huw obviously wanted to know if he was prepared to join Merrily in relocating. Maybe inflict his little folk-festival on the village this summer then make a new start somewhere else. He wasn't, after all, local, or famous enough to have become any kind of asset.

Huw pushed his plate away, rose to his feet.

'Wi' this bloody virus around, nobody feels entirely settled. But I'm telling you that this lass won't survive for long in Craig Innes's backyard.'

'You really think she needs to leave here?'

'She's increasingly an embarrassment to him. Entirely incompatible with his career plan – and bishops tend to have them now.' He finished his tea in four swift gulps, wiped his lips. 'Life's a pool of shite, Laurence. All you get to decide is who you swim with. Or drown, choking.'

6

Dead children

As Arlo Ripley spoke, she could almost see his sweat-shiny skin, his eyes half-closed in resignation and an ingrained regret. She saw one of his sleeves rolled up. Creamy powder on a saucer, two smeared spoons.

He said quietly, 'You've Googled me, right?'

Merrily hurriedly put the laptop with its incriminating search history back to sleep, felt in her pocket for the vape stick and fired it up.

'We... watched the first series. Me and my daughter. I thought if you'd done another one, you might've won that BAFTA.'

'You let a child watch it?'

'Not so long ago. She's twenty now.'

'I, in turn, Googled you last night,' Ripley said. 'If your daughter's twenty, I can't help thinking something illegal happened to you.'

'Nice of you to say so, but I expect it was an old picture. Can I ask who referred you to Sophie?'

He laughed.

'I have an old friend in the diocese.'

She waited but he didn't identify the friend.

'To be honest I was glad to get out of Bristol,' he said. 'Too many people thought I'd been an actual addict. If you ever *were* an addict, you never quite leave it behind. You'll always be "recovering". Actors too, I've learned that. I'm a recovering actor. Looking for somewhere I can recover out of sight.'

She didn't have the heart to tell him that if he was looking to sink discreetly into the countryside, he was in the wrong place.

'I need to stay out of the press, when possible,' he said. 'And also social media. I'd like to help this woman, and she does seem to need help. But not from me. She's not even in my parish. She's in the next village – Goodrich, which I'm minding while they're waiting for a new priest-in-charge.'

She wasn't too familiar with Goodrich or Whitchurch, in the south of the county, where the River Wye and the A40 swooped into rural Monmouthshire and the less-fashionable part of Gloucestershire.

'They're between vicars,' Ripley said. 'I've done occasional services there. Last Sunday evening, a young woman approached me outside the church and asked for my help. Told me this extraordinary story, and I… I've never done this kind of thing before, Mrs Watkins, but I know what would happen very quickly if I did.'

Merrily waited, white vapour wreathing her fingers.

'So I went home and thought about it,' he said. 'Deciding I ought to report it to the Bishop, even though I'd been told that if I did that I'd be invited to deal with it myself.'

Merrily said, 'The Bishop likes to suggest that… deliverance cases… are part of the routine. And should be treated that way.' Being careful. 'You said you knew what would happen if you responded to this. *What* would happen?'

'It would attract more publicity than it's worth. Because – I'm afraid – because of me. I can imagine the tabloid headlines about, ah, Simon Wilding going ghost-hunting.'

'They'd do that?'

'Obviously. And they wouldn't let go of it. You, on the other hand… it really *is* routine for you.'

Not any more. Merrily thought about it.

'The woman's house is haunted? Or she says it is?'

'More the garden. The cottage she's renting is close to Goodrich church and she thinks some of the former garden used to be part of what is now churchyard. And as such must be full of old bones.'

'Well, that's possible, but means nothing in my experience.'

'Also, she… this is almost laughable…'

He didn't sound amused. Merrily waited. Ripley cleared his throat.

'I offered her a blessing,' he said. 'As we were told to do initially on the two-day deliverance course.'

'You could do that quickly. And it might be all that's needed.'

He sighed.

'It was clear she expected more. And she – her name is Maya Madden – she works in television, I'm afraid. Another problem for me.'

Merrily said nothing.

'It's why she's here,' Ripley said. 'Says she's putting together a documentary programme. As you can imagine, with my history, I'm suspicious if approached by TV people. They seem not to understand I'm no longer part of their world. I've been to see her once, but I'd prefer it if someone else dealt with her problem. With that in mind, I rang Mrs Hill at her office, as a friend advised, and she gave me your number.'

'Erm… you do know she's supposed to give you the number of the Bishop's office?'

'Yes.' A short laugh. 'Mrs Hill has told me about the new rules in this diocese. People who bring these matters to our attention should be reassured and talked down, if possible. If I didn't instinctively trust Sophie Hill I wouldn't have called you, as she suggested. If I'm asked, you can count on me not saying I've talked to you… as an exorcist?'

'Deliverance consultant,' Merrily said. 'And if you've heard that the Bishop doesn't like deliverance specialists, that's true. He thinks we should all be phased out ASAP. But he can't *say* that, because if the media get hold of it he'll be accused of…'

'Persecuting people like you?' Arlo Ripley laughed. 'And they'll all have a picture of you from the Internet. Probably the one I've seen.'

He wasn't wrong. And this wasn't the road she wanted to go down. She snatched a hit from the vape stick.

'Erm… so what's this woman's problem? Even if I do encourage her to see what the bishop might regard as reason, I'd like to know a little in advance.'

'All right. It concerns…' he hesitated '…the TV programme she's involved with, relating to the poet Wordsworth, who spent some time here. Where he wrote a poem called, "We Are Seven". Which, ah, deals with dead children.'

'She thinks she's seeing the spirit of a child?'

'I'd assume something like that. I didn't spend long with her.'

'And she lives… where, exactly?'

'On a small housing estate near Goodrich church. Churchyard Cottage is her address. It's actually named in the Wordsworth poem. The poem about the dead children.'

'OK.' Merrily stood up the vape stick on the desk next to the computer. What could she say? 'I'll go, then. If the lock-down doesn't prevent me.'

'Children don't appear to be greatly at risk from the virus,' Ripley said drily.

'And ghosts,' Merrily said, 'even less.'

7

Doctor's badge

NEXT MORNING, BLISS climbed the stairs to the newly-silent CID room to find Vaynor in there, finishing his report on the estate agent's fall. The lights were all on. He pointed to his office door and followed Vaynor through. The lad was nearly a foot taller than Bliss, therefore easier to talk to when he was sitting down.

Bliss said, 'What's a yat, Darth?'

Still not sure why he got on well with this overeducated bastard. Vaynor sometimes wore a waistcoat under his jacket. And had all those letters after his name, if only a D and a C in front of it.

Not for long, though, surely? Vaynor would be on a track so fast he'd be a DS by the end of the year, probably ACC within the next ten, and then nobody would be calling him Darth any more.

Except for Bliss: matter of principle. He shut the door, took his seat near the window with its view across the flat roof towards St Peter's Church.

'It's either the thirtieth or the thirty-second letter of the Cyrillic alphabet, boss,' Vaynor said.

'Huh?'

'Although in the case of *Symonds* Yat, it probably just means an entrance. Gateway to the Wye gorge, perhaps. Anyway, Portis landed a mile or so downriver from there. Near the Doward.'

'That's a hill, right?'

'There's the Great Doward and the Little Doward, both wrapped in big, dark trees. The Little Doward ends with the Seven Sisters rocks overlooking the Wye. And that was where he fell.'

'Born near there, were you?'

'The other side of town, actually. Just spent a lot of time, as a teenager, walking and biking around the lower Wye. And camping. Once. While I was working on my, um...'

Bliss stared at him.

'Thesis? It's norra dirty word, Darth.'

Vaynor said nothing.

Iain Brent, PhD, now a detective superintendent up at headquarters in Worcester, had been heard to say *his* thesis was an exercise entirely compatible with higher police work.

'What was it about, exactly? The thesis.'

'Wordsworth again,' Vaynor said tiredly. 'The poet? Eighteenth, nineteenth centuries?'

'From the Lake District, right? Host of golden daffs?'

'His muse also took him across Europe – mainly on foot.' Vaynor looked out of the window, at still-dim Hereford. 'Passed through here, a few times. In fact, the lower Wye Valley was the most significant tour he ever did, according to some experts. Brought out his genius.' He looked regretful. 'That thesis was me trying to explain why.'

'You must've pulled it off if you gorra doctor's badge for it.'

'Not necessarily.' Vaynor shuffled about. 'Not to my satisfaction. But a thesis is not so much about nailing something as convincing people you *might* have.'

Bliss nodded. *Higher police work*. Frigging Brent.

'Taught me things about the Wye Valley,' Vaynor said. 'Like

that it hadn't changed much since Wordsworth was here in the 1790s. Might actually be quieter now, with no industry left on the banks.'

'All knocked down to boost tourism?'

'But some parts of the valley are still in the Dark Ages,' Vaynor said. 'Narrow lanes, dense woods…'

'And this is where Portis lived, right? And died.'

'A renovated farmhouse up there. Only a couple of miles from the A40, but you wouldn't know it. A little world of its own. Portis did his recreational climbing on the rocks a short walk from his house. Hadn't done as much in recent years, but it seemed to be important to him to prove he still could.'

'You go inside the house?'

'Uniform did. With the, er… with the son when he arrived. He'd been valuing a house the other side of Hereford. It's all in my report.'

'You didn't go into his dad's house with him, then?'

'I was a few miles away by then, talking to the woman who found the body, boss… after seeing where it landed.'

'Bit scary for her, seeing it come down.'

'Especially with it landing about fifty yards away, on its feet. As if he'd jumped.'

Bliss put his head on one side.

'And did he?'

'Nobody thinks that. I'm afraid it doesn't happen often, boss.'

Vaynor turned away, but he still felt Bliss's eyes resting on him.

'We're not gonna drop it, Darth. I've gorra feeling.'

'Just… just a feeling, boss?'

Bliss said nothing. All right, he knew there wasn't much competing with this for CID time, but…

'It did occur to me you'd know Portis junior,' he said eventually. 'From your schooldays – both of you at the Cathedral School, wasn't it?'

'He was a year or two ahead of me, boss,' Vaynor said mildly. 'Didn't really know him that well.'

'And did you gerron with him?'

'It didn't matter,' Vaynor said.

Which meant *no*. Bliss knew Vaynor had been at the Cathedral School on a scholarship, whereas Portis was charged the full fee. And that they'd gone home to different parts of town. And that Portis, who'd sold him a duff property, had had this vibe he'd felt certain times before. A vibe which – and there was no getting round this – could only convey a definite repressed violence.

'Where's the son living now, Darth?'

'Here, I think,' Vaynor said. 'In the city. Near their main office. Quite a posh house. I believe Peter Portis's Wye Valley place has flag floors, bare stone walls and not much furniture. Apparently, his mountaineering mates would spend hard-man weekends with him there. And possibly the occasional passing girlfriend.'

'His wife died in an RTC, right?'

'Ex-wife by then. When he accepted she wasn't coming back he seems to have thrown himself into his climbing.'

'Literally, in the end, it seems. Any near neighbours?'

'Next house along is a second home, nearly half a mile away, Nobody there most of the year, apparently. A lot of houses in the area are empty until the weather starts to improve.'

'And nobody saw him up on the rocks yesterday?'

'Not that we've found so far.'

'Son doesn't climb?'

Vaynor shook his head.

'I'm told Royce has been more or less running the estate agency for a couple of years, since his dad went back to the wild.'

Bliss spotted Sonia Seagull landing on the flat roof of the police station and found out the remains of a doughnut in a bag in his desk. Stood up and opened the window, crumbling the doughnut as Sonia came waddling over.

'Boss, it... you know, it really doesn't look like anything interesting. No indication of murder or suicide. I realise an open verdict is never entirely satisfactory, but...'

'Maybe. Or maybe not.' Bliss shook the doughnut crumbs off his hands and shut the window. 'But let's not get caught out. I've heard one or two things that leave a few questions. Coupla days ago I was talking to somebody who... doesn't work here any more, but when he did he was fairly hot on what we used to think of as local intelligence.'

'Former-inspector Ford?' Darth asked.

Bliss smiled.

'You're a smart boy, Darth. Yeh, Rich Ford's looking for somewhere to move, out of the city. The place he had in mind, up by the Black Mountains, the deal fell through, so he wound up talking to Portis about a house at Symonds Yat. And he said it was like he was dealing with a different Portis – a countryman. Portis had moved to the sticks and the climber seemed to have taken over from the cynical city businessman. So...'

Bliss shrugged, opened out his hands.

'When Royce's mother-in-law sold up, his wife took over her house at Crocker's Ash, just down the valley. They're doing it up now, apparently, maybe to live in. In fact, if anything becomes vacant thereabouts, they'll have it, according to Rich. Now, why're they doing that? The coroner's officer is meeting Royce this morning at their Ross shop. In about an hour. Why don't you go with him? Give him a ring and fix it.'

Vaynor nodded without much interest.

Bliss said, 'The lad inherits the firm, I'm assuming. Or is there somebody else to share?'

'I think he gets the lot,' Vaynor said. 'And his dad's house, too?'

Bliss nodded and strolled to the end of their social distance. 'You definitely need to see him. Um… did you *fit in* at the Cathedral School, Darth?'

'It's not exactly Eton, boss.'

'Close as you'll get in Hereford.'

Vaynor didn't look up, mumbled at the floor.

'I was at that place on a scholarship.'

'Due to you being clever but not having particularly well-off parents. And then, unlike most of them, you went on to Oxford.'

Vaynor nodded, told Bliss that quite a few coppers had PhDs these days.

Bliss said, 'While this probably *looks* like an accident… if there's any reason to think this lad may have helped his old feller down from a high rock—'

'We should get the PM results later today, boss. Dr Grace told me last night that he doesn't expect to find any signs of foul play.'

Seeing again the image of a man dying on his feet. It had been inside his head when he awoke this morning. Probably the scariest fatality he'd ever seen. And then it all went away because he'd noticed Eve had gone from the bed, and that was scarier.

'So the son had moved back to Hereford city,' Bliss said, 'with his wife, who he met in the Wye Valley when his dad bought a house there and decided he wanted to become a countryman.'

'Royce's wife was *born* in the Wye Valley,' Vaynor said. 'He took up with her soon after the Portises moved in. Peter Portis gave her a job at the new office he'd opened in Whitchurch, and within a year she was manager and engaged to Royce.'

'Where'd you learn all that?'

'From the woman who saw the body land. Maya Madden. She's renting a house in Goodrich from the Portises who seem to own a few holiday homes round there. She, um, works in television.'

'How'd she see Portis fall?'

'It was the light. And she wasn't far away when Portis's body came down. He apparently wasn't crying out or anything. Shocked *her* quite a bit, obviously. When she realized what she'd seen, she called 999 on her mobile.'

Bliss swung his legs from the desk. He obviously knew this.

'How far away was she?'

'Fifty yards? She does a lot of walking, checking out locations. Places that, um, William Wordsworth once visited.'

'*Him* again?'

'It's the 250th anniversary of his birth next month,' Vaynor said reluctantly. 'She's a producer with the Bristol-based TV production company that's doing a programme about his time in these parts. He was born in the Lake District but, as I said, this is where some people think he found his genius.'

And then mislaid it.

'So... are you involved with this programme?' Bliss asked.

'I'm a cop,' Vaynor said, almost resentfully. 'Why should I be?'

One of those sad old Inspector Morse cops, Eve said in his head. *Full of regrets.*

8

Woad

BACK AT THE old shop, Lol watched Jane sitting down on the lower steps of the spiral stairway, brushing hair back from her eyes and leaving a blue smear that looked like woad, as worn by Celtic warriors. She must have known it was there, but made no attempt to wipe it off.

'Sorry,' Lol said. 'But you did want to know.'

'So the Bishop wants every priest to be an exorcist,' Jane said. 'But not much of one.'

'According to Huw, the exorcism part won't go much further than priests getting trained to recognize symptoms – distinguish between bipolar and schizophrenia. Decide who should be referred to the psychiatric services.'

Jane's eyes hardened, the woad appearing to go darker.

'And if psychiatry doesn't work?'

'Things don't change,' Lol said. 'If you don't get cured, you get chemically controlled. Mostly, you don't get cured.'

He looked down at the flagstones, not wanting to discuss his own experiences on a psychiatric ward, what *that* had done to his mind, how lucky he'd been to get most of it back, thanks to Merrily Watkins… and, it had to be admitted, Lucy Devenish.

'So exorcism within the Church is being dismantled,' Jane rose slowly, as if she was absorbing the forcefield of Lucy Devenish. 'What will priests actually do when it no longer exists?'

Lol had to smile. He'd been having these nothing-barred conversations with her since she'd been a precocious kid. An adult now; at her age, Merrily had been pregnant with her.

'Offer to pray with you,' he said. 'Hold your hand. Even now, people who think they're possessed by evil have to be seen by a psychiatrist before the Church even considers acting on it. In the future that'll probably extend to hauntings and similar disturbances. That's what Huw thinks will happen.'

'They won't acknowledge that anything paranormal exists?'

'Nobody's actually going to say that. And maybe a certain amount will go on behind the scenes, just like it always has... but the Church won't be taking responsibility for it.'

Jane wiped her hands on the paint rag, and carried the bucket to the sink behind the stairs.

'And you think Mum'll be able to live with that? Maybe at one time she might have. But now she's seen too much. More things in heaven and earth... At first, I thought that when she accepted this deliverance job she was joining some kind of spiritual police to deter people from exploring their inner selves. "*The blue and the gold and the lamplit path*".' Jane smiled helplessly. 'She used to say that. The lamplit path – I've always loved that, though I've never told her. I should have, because that— Jesus, look at me!'

Half her face was blue. She turned on the cold tap and started squeezing the paint rag hard under the gush of water.

'The important part of Mum's job goes down the toilet, right?'

Lol didn't know what to say.

'And now it really *is* the important part. The last link with what those experiences the establishment tells us to ignore it because, like, *it didn't really happen*. What's left to hold onto when you wake up in the early hours? You know what name Mum gives exorcism?'

'The Night Job?'

'Prescient, huh? You can't be seen to do it in the light of day.'

'Huw's thinking…' Lol hesitated '…that in the future, there'll be situations she might want to look into, which they'll block, tell her it's not a priest's job. In fact that's already started.'

'*Can* they block it?'

'They can make things difficult for her. Force her underground. Kind of.'

'Until she quits,' Jane said. 'And loses the vicarage. And the village. We *all* lose the village. It becomes just this pretty bolthole for rich gits. Mum's not going to be moving in across the road with you, is she? Watching some new priest shambling in and out of the vic?'

Lol said nothing. He turned as the shop door opened and a woman came in, slowly unwinding a long, green and white collegiac scarf.

'Not closed, are you?'

'We're not even open yet,' Jane said. 'Maybe in a few weeks.'

'Oh, I'm sorry. Someone said Ledwardine Lore was reopening, so I said I'd look in and ask if—' She blinked, putting up her hands as if protectively. '*Jane Watkins? Is* it?'

Lol saw Jane trying to place someone she hadn't immediately recognized. And then she did and her expression became slightly rueful, and Lol thought he might be in the way of something. He lifted a hand to Jane and moved to the door, where the woman stood behind a wispy smile.

'Well, good God.'

Jane's smile was wispier.

'What happened,' she murmured, 'to *good Goddess*?'

9

Abodes of darkness

THE WINGS OF the goddess had half-opened, awakening, for a moment, that old tremulous excitement in Jane. Flashback to a wintry day, not unlike this one. She was sixteen and standing at her bedroom window at the vic, opening her arms.

> *Hail to thee, eternal spiritual sun*
> *Whose symbol now rises in the heavens.*
> *Hail to thee from the abodes of morning.*

Relations with Mum at the time had been so unstable that Jane had been slightly thrilled at the idea of a pagan summons invoked at early dawn, from a fractionally opened window in a vicarage. Though she was never going to say it out loud, she knew she'd only become a pagan because Mum had been ordained. She was only sixteen, after all.

Still, she'd felt empowered by the warmth of her welcome from the Hereford women's pagan group that had met over Pod's, the healthfood shop in Bridge Street.

Run by Sorrel. Sorrel Podmore.

'Hey…' Jane grinned at her and mimed a hug. 'How are you? Is it still… I mean, the group, is it still going?'

'Oh.' Sorrel pulled her scarf loose. 'We're still friends, and we still gather sometimes, for the old festivals. We make rather nice greetings cards for Imbolc and Beltane, though not Samhain – nobody wants to send cards to the dead.'

Sorrel stayed near the door, leaving it slightly open.

'That's really why I called in – to see if you might be a possible outlet. I had no idea this was you. It was just I'd heard that Ledwardine Lore was coming back. Which sounded quite exciting.'

Sorrel didn't look capable of much excitement any more, Jane thought. All too often the heat of magic was transitory. She'd lost weight, her hair was shorter, less lustrous, her eyes sunken. Jane hadn't recognized her at first, remembered her as about the same age as Mum, but she looked older now, quite dowdy in her mustard-coloured padded raincoat.

'I didn't know you knew Lucy.'

'Only by reputation,' Sorrel said. 'Hedge-witch? That the right term?'

'Folklorist. Wise-woman.'

Jane momentarily remembered Lucy sitting at the table, slicing an apple crossways to reveal the secret seed-pentagram at its core that hardly anyone ever saw because they always cut downwards from the stalk. *Let no one talk of the humble apple to me.*

Sorrel looked a bit regretful.

'We all used to think we were wise-women, but it was just a phase.'

'I wish I could make you some tea or coffee or hot chocolate or something. But I don't think you're supposed to accept anything from me. Or anybody.'

'I won't be staying. I didn't think you'd be open, I was just going to look in the window. I'll come in again, when you're...'

'I want to bring Ledwardine alive again, you see,' Jane said. 'To resist the heart-of-the-New-Cotswolds gloss with regimented rows of executive homes. It was a sacred place once. There was a ritual henge here, preserved by the old orchard.'

She mapped a circle with hands.

'A lot of it's built over now, but if we can prove it was there, we can get some of the vibration back. *Apple-power.* Starting with this shop.'

Sorrel began to rewind her scarf.

'We all had hopes for you, Jane. Patricia – she might've seemed severe, but she always said there was a rare energy in you, which, if you were able to direct it—'

'*Patricia* said that?'

'She'd never have dreamed of telling you. How old are you now?'

'Pushing twenty-one. From above.'

Made her feel despondent just saying that. You were supposed to be an adult at eighteen. By twenty you should be a *fully motivated* adult. Hell, she'd felt a stronger sense of direction at fifteen. Maybe this was what happened as you grew away from the clear certainties of childhood.

Only there had been no certainties then either. Mum's marriage cracking up. Dad dying on the motorway. Mum drifting into the Church – the same Church that was now about to shaft her.

'Has it been worth it?' Jane said.

Sorrel looked startled, let go of her scarf.

'Paganism.' Jane was now remembering a night in the vicarage garden under an icy full moon. 'Invoking the goddess.'

> *Hail to thee, Lady Moon*
> *Whose light reflects our most secret hopes*
> *Hail to thee from the abodes of darkness.*

'I suppose things wax and wane,' Sorrel said. 'Like the moon. Patricia moved to East Anglia to be near her daughter, and sadly died of heart failure soon afterwards, as you know.'

'Oh God, I *didn't* know. I'm… really sorry.'

'It was quite sudden. Hit me hard when I was told. I'd ring her sometimes, for advice. If we'd known, we could have… I'd thought we *would* know when one of us was ailing. I'd thought we had access to reserves of healing energy and we could direct it. We'd always encouraged each other to think we could make things happen.'

'You *can*.'

'I still believe *some* people can,' Sorrel said. 'But they're rarely the good people, are they? Achieving something good is so much harder. And you often get invaded by people in search of personal power who'll use you. It's so much easier to be destructive. Anyway… I've often wondered how *you* were getting on… and your mother.'

'Things have been better, I guess,' Jane said. 'But mostly we work things out. And we've become more open. I wouldn't quite say we're like sisters, now, but…'

'We were afraid for you amidst all those rumours of dark things at the Cathedral. And shocked at the way we were used – to get at your mother through you. After all that, we became frightened of what we might be on the edge of. And who we might be harbouring without knowing.'

Jane remembered the deceptively considerate woman who'd read the tarot for her. Planting ideas about her future, her potential. Directing her to the Pod for training – to these well-meaning women who thought they were practising a healthy form of native paganism. Which was what paganism meant – the Latin, *paganus* – a villager, rustic. It had not been that simple. The tarot woman who'd become connected with them hadn't been what she seemed. Everything could be infiltrated, darkened. Even the Church, as Mum was now finding out.

Trust nobody.

'We stopped looking for new members after that,' Sorrel said. 'We rather closed in. All our rituals were protective. It had really taken the heart out of us.'

'The tarot woman's gone now.'

'Along with Patricia who was disciplined enough to bring us through all that.' Sorrel shuddered and picked up the end of her scarf. 'I have to say, Jane, that if I've learned one thing, from all my studies and my experience, it's that nobody is ever truly gone. They've left an imprint that will always be visible. Even when people pretend it isn't there.'

Jane, who wished she could see Lucy Devenish again, found a nod.

'Look, I'd better go.' Sorrel was buttoning her raincoat. 'One of my shop assistants has to take the afternoon off. Perhaps I'll come in again and show you a selection of our cards. No obligation.'

Yes there was. Seeing Sorrel again had brought too much back, too quickly. It felt as if she'd only called to show how rapidly the wings of the goddess could fold themselves away. To get a feel for potent spirituality, surely you had to accept that a better future was at least possible.

Jane listened for Lucy's distant voice. Heard nothing.

Because Lucy was dead. Patricia was dead. How many more? Both had been old. Most people who died *were* old.

Standing in the window, Jane thought about her oldest friend, Gomer Parry – everybody's old friend – and realized that her sweat was turning colder.

'There's more to come,' Sorrel said at the door. 'I spent four hours last night with the star charts. All this began years ago when Pluto went into Capricorn and the stock market crashed. Pluto meets Jupiter in April. There'll be violence and damage in the cities, even Hereford—'

Jane suddenly needed to go and see Gomer Parry who never seemed out of control, who never lived in fear and, you had to admit it, had outlived many people who did.

*

When they suddenly came face to face at the top of the vicarage drive, Lol instinctively moved to Merrily. And then both were backing away, nervous.

Lol was aware that most people in the village now knew about them, but they weren't a recognized item, even here. And they wouldn't want rumours to fall into the hands of the Bishop, who wouldn't hesitate to use them.

They were alone at the entrance, nobody else in sight.

'I know we can't go on like this,' Merrily said, 'but what I just *don't* know…'

'Is when… Or how. Huw Owen thinks—'

'You've spoken to Huw?'

'Yesterday. We went in the pub. He says we should think about getting out, possibly starting again somewhere.'

'He actually said *that*?'

'I think he meant get out of this diocese.'

'He wants you to leave Lucy's cottage?'

'We didn't go into that kind of detail. He just wants you working under a more liberal bishop.'

Merrily looked perturbed.

'He thinks I should run away from Innes?'

'Maybe.'

'What do *you* think?'

'You must know what I think,' Lol said.

Merrily moved closer but didn't touch him. He felt he was caressing her inside his aura, whatever that was. She lowered her voice.

'What if we found a way of staying here and I moved in with you at Lucy's cottage? Having found another job. I dunno what… stacking Jim Prosser's shelves? Am I serious? Maybe.' She held his arm. 'Listen, I need to ask you something. Something relating to a possible deliverance job.'

'Innes has actually let you do one?'

'He doesn't know about it yet. But he hasn't formally fired me, any more than he formally took me on. This job… is about William Wordsworth. A poem he wrote in this area. "*A simple Child, that lightly draws its breath, And feels its life in every limb…*"'

'"*What should it know of death?*"' Lol asked.

Merrily smiled.

'I *thought* you'd know it.'

'Very simply written,' Lol said, remembering. 'Almost like a nursery rhyme. Yet somehow uncanny.'

'Inspired by a little girl he met in the Wye Valley. Where she grew up.'

'Or didn't,' Lol said. 'We only know she'd made it to the age of eight, when Wordsworth encountered her near Goodrich Castle ruins. Where she told him she was from a family of seven, but some were dead.'

'Left me wondering what Wordsworth thought this kid was trying to convey to him about the meaning of death that he, as an adult, didn't get.'

'It was about what happened after death,' Lol said. 'In those days people were beginning to decide that dead meant gone – and that was it. A bit like your bishop. Whereas this kid…'

'Thought her dead siblings might still be open to conversation?'

'Wordsworth thought it was quite significant that a little kid should be talking like this,' Lol said. 'As if she knew something she shouldn't know. I read he kept coming back to try and find her again. Which he seems to have failed to do. The last time possibly fifty years after that first meeting. I always remember that, because at first I thought he must've invented her for the poem.'

'*That* long after?' Merrily's eyes widened. 'She'd have been well into middle age and *he*...' She stepped back. 'She must have made quite an impact on him. How did he know she was still even alive?'

'Do you know *exactly* where the kid grew up?' Lol asked. 'If she ever left – Goodrich village, was it? – where did she go?'

'Don't know anything about her,' Merrily said. 'But I think she was only in that one poem.'

'And he never even found out her name.'

'So nobody else has. Which would be a handicap if I had to exorcize her,' Merrily said.

Lol's eyes widened.

'*Do* you?'

'Or bring some peace and quiet to wherever she lived. According to the poem, it was a certain Churchyard Cottage.'

'At Goodrich?'

'Which is where my dwindling role as deliverance consultant is probably taking me before the end of the week.'

'You haven't done a... what you used to call a *clearance*... in quite a while.'

'I don't know whether this is one. I hope not.'

'An eight-year-old girl,' Lol said. 'Isn't that...'

'Post mortem child-abuse?' Merrily frowned. 'It's probably better if you don't ask Jane.'

10

Confuse a tortured spirit

THERE WAS A blurred sense of the half-forgotten in the part of Ross-on-Wye uphill from the town centre. Buildings which had lost their original identity long ago – the old school, the old magistrates' court – existed now as hints of history amongst streets whose names were tinted with sepia backstories. Only Ross police station was still functioning, somehow, in Old Maid's Walk, from which Vaynor found his way to Copse Cross Street – the first word of which he always seem to read as *Corpse*.

Not necessarily a mistake, as he learned from Roger Hamer, the coroner's officer, when they met, as arranged, on a quiet corner in the early afternoon.

'I may be wrong, David,' Roger said, 'but, as I understand it, here, cross means cross*roads*, and this was where they used to bury suicides. Without a priest.'

'It actually *was corpse*-cross?'

'The idea was to confuse a tortured spirit,' Roger said. 'It was thought that it wouldn't know which way to turn at a crossroads, so it stayed put and didn't come back to frighten the residents.'

Roger Hamer, tubby, deliberate and old-fashioned, right up to his Victorian moustache, probably knew more about the etiquette of unnatural death than anybody in town, Vaynor thought. The motto of the Coroners' Officers and Staff Association was *Advocates for the dead to safeguard the living.* He was still trying to work that one out.

Roger put on leather gloves, clicking the poppers at the wrists, rolling his lower lip over his murderer's moustache.

'Now then, David, let me just get something right before we go in. What are you hoping to take away from this? What's your issue with this death? A big death, I'll grant you... but CID?'

Roger explained that Bliss had phoned him on his mobile to let him know they weren't allowing the grass to grow, but he hadn't explained why.

'Think of me as an observer,' Vaynor said to Roger. 'I might want to apply for your job when you retire.'

'You'd find my job very disappointing, David. Every other day a corpse, and some are on lavatories. Am I right in thinking you don't want to say what this is about?'

'Just that we've had some information we're following up.'

'Well, I wouldn't rule out suicide. Obviously, it doesn't mean anything that he died on his feet – but that does drive the spine through—'

'Yes, I know,' Vaynor said.

They walked down the street towards the office at the end of a building that was part stone, part brick, age indeterminate. *PPP,* it said: Peter Portis Property.

'Met Mr Royce Portis before, have we, David?'

'Well... not for—'

'He's changed. No bad thing. Bit of a hell-raiser in his youth. Fast cars till a drink-driving conviction had him off the road for a year. Father was furious. People round yere don't buy houses from irresponsible young men in fast cars.'

'I can understand that.'

'Proper car now. And properly married to a local woman, for whom people still have a lot sympathy. Diana, her name. Royce is on Hereford City council, now, could be mayor in a year or two. Here we are.'

A traditional slowly revolving display was quietly illuminated in the PPP window. The sort that would usually feature costly-looking houses, but not today. All the photos showed the late Peter Portis smiling from sheer cliff-faces, secure as a barnacle.

The too-late snow had thickened, imposing a shrinelike silence on the former Corpse Cross Street.

*

'What I *can* tell you, Royce,' Roger Hamer said, 'is that it very much looks like an accident but, in the absence of witnesses, I'm sorry to say that the coroner will have to consider other possibilities.'

'And let *me* tell you *this*, mate,' Royce replied. 'If my old man had wanted to quit this world, he'd've gone off some rock famous for being unclimbable. Not one of the Seven fucking Sisters.'

Royce had thickened out, probably looked like Peter in his climbing prime. Hacked from the same cliff, except that there was more of him. He was moist-lipped, like Vaynor remembered, with dark hair, razored at the sides, so powerfully thick that you could almost watch it growing back. For some reason, Vaynor found himself thinking of the bronze Hereford bull in High Town, scrotum the size of a handbag.

They were talking in what clearly had been Peter Portis's own office – photos on the walls not of properties but mountains and jagged rock faces. One was of the Seven Sisters which looked entirely unclimbable to Vaynor.

'Was your dad doing *much* rock climbing these days, Royce?' Roger Hamer asked.

'That's why he was semi-retired – more time for his rocks. Might've been fifty-nine but he kept himself acutely well-tuned. His doctor will tell you.'

'I'm sure we'll be checking that. And the pathologist's report will fill in any gaps. Except, of course, those relating to your dad's state of mind. Which you'll probably be asked about.'

'State of—?' Portis sat up hard in his black leather swivel chair. 'You think he was one of those chaps who wanders off into the night, all dressed for his last climb?'

Although he'd been born and educated here, Vaynor couldn't hear much Hereford in Royce's big voice. He was one of those guys for whom sorrow got quickly mixed into anger. During Vaynor's short time in uniform, learning how to break tragic news, he'd met a few like this, usually men, whose first thought was to blame the emergency services for letting it happen.

'As you know, he was found before dark,' Roger Hamer said. 'Immediately after falling from the Seven Sisters – one of them. The pathologist thinks he died instantly. Although I believe, Royce, that you told the police you hadn't seen him at all yesterday.'

'That's not unusual. I knew he had a property to view in the afternoon. As it turns out, that was postponed, which probably explains why he ended up going climbing. Which he sometimes did on dry days with no wind, before it went dark.'

'He'd often go on his own?'

'Only on rocks he knew well. I mean, he wasn't a loner. He liked climbing with other people. He was popular. Wide range of friends. Lately, he'd often go with this TV guy, Smiffy Gill. He'd been an advisor on rock climbing for an edition of *The Octane Show* a couple of years ago.' Royce stared at him. 'Remind me. Who're you, again?'

'David Vaynor, Hereford CID.' Vaynor accepted it wasn't unusual not to recognize blokes who'd once been younger boys at your school, though he didn't believe Royce had completely forgotten him. 'I don't climb, Mr Portis, but I know the lower Wye fairly well. Did your father still have many climbing friends?'

'Dozens, obviously. All ages. Some of them were—'

'Women,' Mrs Diana Portis said. 'He wasn't too old for women, yet, either.'

First time she'd spoken. One of those candy-sweet voices you heard in American cartoons but with a Gloucestershire roll. Something sharply turned inside Vaynor. He knew her. Too well. He didn't know her as Royce's wife, but...

She smiled at him. She had what he thought of as ironic eyes under a weight of dark curls. A firm, young body in a smoky-pink suit. Having insisted on giving up her chair to Roger, she was leaning back on her hands on the edge of Royce's desk. Split skirt, one leg bent and a fair bit of it on show. She was younger than he'd expected, a few years younger than Royce, but very much a woman and... and *oh, God...*

'But if we're being honest,' she said, 'he loved climbing alone on rocks that were familiar to him. Yes, he did know he officially was not supposed to climb the Seven Sisters. Used to say they were his secret girlfriends. Could've gone up them in the dark.'

Royce Portis was expressionless, but Vaynor sensed he didn't like borderline smutty stuff from his wife.

His wife? This was his *wife*?

'Always knew where to put his hands,' Mrs Portis purred.

'Climbing's this whole sub-culture round the Yat,' Royce said. 'Which you must know only too well, Hamer, all the times he was sometimes used by your people as an expert witness when some poor bastard took the quick way down.'

'Yes.' Roger grabbing at this. 'Yes, he was, Royce. Always ready to help us. Which is why *I* never thought it would come to this... not for *him*. A man who's been running climbing-safety courses for years.'

'The Seven Sisters are... not far from his home,' Vaynor said.

Roger Hamer said, 'Didn't he buy that house on the Doward specifically because of its proximity to those rocks?'

'Partly,' Royce said. 'When he sold our family home at Whitchurch, he wanted somewhere smaller and more remote.'

Vaynor said, 'And neither of you knew he might be going up there yesterday.'

Royce: 'Once again, no, we didn't.'

'Would you have tried to stop him?'

'What, tell him he was too fucking old?'

Royce was clearly getting tired of this. A business to pull together, Vaynor thought. Houses to sell. More important things than the sudden death of his father.

'The more *I* think about it...' Mrs Portis fingered her jawline, showcasing a neat nose-ring with a green stone '...the more I reckon that if you'd asked Peter how he wanted to go – though not for some years, obviously – he might have said he'd like to exit the way he did. Off the rocks overlooking the Wye. The river was part of it for Peter. Greatest river there is, he used to say.'

'You can't see it from the house, though,' Vaynor said. 'Can you?'

He looked at Mrs Portis the way he thought a policeman should if he was a stranger.

'You can feel it, though,' she said. 'It calls to you and you go to it. Climbing gave Peter views of it you couldn't see any other way. Great wide views that only climbers know. The last thing he saw would've been the Wye coming up at him, faster and faster, to...' spreading her arms, hands vibrating '...welcome him home.'

Her voice was whispery. She was fantasizing, Vaynor thought. If, as Billy Grace had suggested, Portis had been falling vertically, staring straight ahead, all he'd've seen would have been bare trees and sky.

'I'll tell you one other thing,' Mrs Portis said. 'You know that old legend about the Wye taking an annual sacrifice?'

'Diana...' Some pain in Roger Hamer's smile. 'I like to think that, as coroner's officer, I'm in a position to say that when you examine the records you'll probably find that this particular folk-tale doesn't quite hold water.'

'Oh, really?' She was peering at him under the tangle of curls. 'Long river. Your patch is just a bit of it. I can hear Peter saying – in his matter-of-fact way – "Well, that's this year's sorted. Save some other poor sod."' She laughed. 'Look, what's so wrong with that? I'm the kind of person who likes to find the good in bad things. He's had a more distinctive death than all the virus victims...'

Vaynor quickly asked Royce Portis if he'd done any climbing himself, and Royce sniffed and said it had never interested him.

'I've done a bit,' Diana said. 'When you're born in that immediate area, you tend to want to give it a shot. Cheaper than a gym and better views. You should try it. You've got the reach for it.'

'Right,' Royce said, 'so if there's nothing else you guys want to know…'

'There *is* something I'm obliged to ask,' Vaynor said. 'As this is a sudden death in a public place with – given your father's skills – no obvious explanation, we do have to eliminate some things, and I have to ask… did he have any enemies? Had he been involved in any recent disputes?'

'You seem determined to have a fucking murder inquiry!'

'No, we're here simply to obtain closure, Royce,' Roger Hamer said. 'To get it all finished and sorted. Everybody satisfied.'

'Coffee, I think.' Diana Portis coming down from the desk, skirt rising. 'Or tea?'

'Not for me, thank you,' Roger said. 'Too soon after lunch.'

'Well, I'm having some. If *anyone* wants to join me.'

An eyebrow raised at Vaynor, and he found himself standing up and following her out of the room and down the stairs until he was sunk into a deep sofa in a small room, with muted lighting, behind the main office. House-hunters could sit here and view fantasy homes in the fantasy Wye Valley on a large television over the coal-effect gas fire. Thin snow was gathering on the leaded window but, on the screen, sunshine was filtered through mature trees, reflected in swimming pools and garden ponds and wine bottles on the wicker tables in dappled conservatories.

'You OK, there?'

Mrs Portis with a tray.

'Just dreaming about living there,' Vaynor made himself say. 'One day.'

'Good time of year to buy, Inspector Vaynor.' She bent with the tray, proffered coffee. 'Before the spring.'

'Not on my money. And it's, um, Detective Constable.'

'Won't be for long.' She sat next to him on the sofa. 'If you can't handle a big mortgage yet, you will, sooner than you think.'

Vaynor didn't reply. He slowly turned his head to Mrs Portis.

'So your husband takes over the business now?'

'He's been more or less in charge for a few years.' She watched him sugaring his coffee. 'I suppose you do need a bit of a reputation to get taken on by the Met. Can't see this case doing it for you, however.'

'Sorry?'

'Not a crime to jump off a high rock, is it?'

'You think that's what he did?'

'Unlike Royce, I probably do think that. If he was starting to lose his grip on the rocks, if his feet were failing to find that essential cleft… But we'll never know, will we?'

Won't we?

The pictures on the TV had switched from individual homes to wide views of the area, and then it went aerial, as if shot from a drone taking off like one of the peregrine falcons that apparently nested in the tower-block cliffs. The screen was suddenly full of a precipitous view of the Wye under a dizzying wild blue sky. Like the view you'd get if you came off one of the Seven Sisters on a summer morning. He felt his stomach clench, looked away.

'Your signs are everywhere in the lower Wye Valley.'

'It's our best area. We know what works it.'

Vaynor wondered what exactly she meant by that, but he didn't ask her.

'Mrs Portis, when a mature, experienced rock climber falls to his death, with no known witnesses, there mustn't be too many questions left hanging around in the air. If you see what I mean.'

'Perhaps it was part of his make-up. If he was out for a walk and it turned into what most people would consider a climb, he wouldn't turn back.'

'No matter how dangerous?'

'"Challenging" would be his term for it. What exactly are you looking for? Or is this a case of "We ask the questions, lady..."' She was leaning back against an arm of the sofa, eyes flickering mischief. 'I could see you wanted to ask my husband something that you thought might offend him. Well, you don't always have to ask Royce. I can be much more forthcoming... and less sensitive.'

Vaynor had a long, slow sip to take the dryness from his mouth. On the TV, the drone camera was racing through a chasm that made his gut throb, before cutting to a shot of what looked like a sequence of giant keyholes in the side of a low cliff.

'Is that King Arthur's Cave?' he said.

It *would* appear on the screen now.

She said, 'You know it?'

He hesitated.

'I... slept in it once.' Voice sounded unsteady even to him. 'Almost.'

'You're serious?'

'It was raining hard and getting dark, and my tent had got ripped. Not a very high quality tent, and there were no lights to show me the way back. This was when I was a post-graduate student.'

'You *do* know,' she said, 'that there are some stories about that cave?'

'I know a few things about it,' Vaynor said. 'I'm sure you do, too, growing up not far away.'

Thinking, *This could be the time, if it happened.* But where had he seen her if it hadn't?

She didn't rise to it. Perhaps she'd never been in that cave. Perhaps he'd never seen her before.

But having grown up in this small county, he couldn't say that about anybody with any certainty. You saw people time and time again without knowing their names. Returning from Oxford, he'd realised what a small city Hereford was.

At least he was sure of that. Wasn't he?

On his way back to the car, he walked out of Corpse Cross Street and up towards Ross's dominant church steeple. He looked down to the bottom of the graveyard, saw where he guessed scores of people had been buried, uncoffined, a few centuries ago: all plague victims, apparently. And now it was all happening again. Wholesale death from a new kind of plague. No certainty that the pandemic wouldn't spread here, and soon.

Vaynor stopped, leaning back hard against the churchyard wall, breathing faster and aware of a growing confinement involving both space and time. He gazed down towards where he guessed the river was. It occurred to him that very little had changed recently in this old town, where whole centuries had shrunk but the same horizons remained.

'Are you all right?'

Someone else he knew. A voice. He snapped back against the wall to avoid bumping into a young woman in a cream puffer jacket, holding a phone.

'Oh...' Her hand holding the mobile dropped to her side. 'The policeman. From last night.'

Dark-brown hair blew across her face, and he at once remembered her as the finder of the body of Peter Portis.

'Maya Madden,' she said.

Vaynor said, 'Sorry that you saw him land. At your feet, more or less. Hell of a shock.'

She shuddered.

'I don't *think* you'll be needed for the opening of the inquest,'

Vaynor said. 'But it's early days yet. Are you going to be around for a while?'

'I'm not sure. It depends on whether our programme goes ahead, and I'm guessing it probably won't, not yet. Everything's very uncertain at the moment, with all this… chaos.'

'If you go ahead, how long will you be here?'

She looked uncertain.

'We just need to know where to find you.'

'I like to think it depends on William Wordsworth,' Maya Madden told him. 'If *he* wants to help me unscramble some things about his time here. It's his two hundred and fiftieth anniversary, as I expect you know.'

'So I believe,' Vaynor said stiffly.

'But I imagine you know quite a lot about him, so perhaps you could talk to us, briefly, if we go ahead. Dr Vaynor?'

'Well, I don't think…'

'Just briefly. A police woman told me about your literary background.'

'I haven't got a literary background. Just a degree.'

'A *doctorate*,' Maya Madden amended.

Part Two

...And I have felt
A presence that disturbs me

William Wordsworth
On Revisiting the Banks of the Wye

11

Creeping erosion

It never used to happen, but these days you found screwed-up sandwich wrappers in the Cathedral gatehouse, and plastic cups left by the people who were using it on the days Sophie wasn't here. Which was most days now.

You sensed the nearness of the palace and the pale, flickering eyes of Bishop Innes. You felt somebody was trying to starve you out of here in the damp, dreary weeks before spring, if there was going to be one this year.

Sophie Hill, who 'worked for the Cathedral', reduced to a two-day week with the barely veiled implication that she should consider resigning quietly and melting away into unrecorded history. Merrily's old chair had been replaced by something made of mangled metal and foam rubber. She turned to the window, looking down at the thinning traffic through thickening rain.

Sophie wore a grey woollen jacket, its collar pulled up into her white hair and – *dear God* – a pair of those mittens with the fingers chopped off to enable her to type through the cold. Her smile was placid but somehow disfigured. It was like looking up at the tower and observing a creeping erosion in the stone.

'What I sometimes want to do now,' Merrily said, 'is stroll over to the palace, pick up the Bishop's crozier and...'

Sophie looked up patiently from her keyboard.

'I'd make it quick.' Rebelliously out of uniform, in jeans and a sweater, Merrily stretched out her legs under the desk, kicking off her shoes. 'Wouldn't want him suffering for *too* long.'

She shivered. Kill the Bishop? Was it possible she was turning into Jane?

Sophie's chained glasses had fallen into the folds of her white silk scarf. She replaced them. She seemed to have been typing formal letters on behalf of Innes. *Thank you, the Bishop would be pleased to... Regrettably, the Bishop has a prior appointment.* Et cetera. Mindless routine. Sophie was still, in theory, the Bishop's lay secretary, but no longer trusted with anything sensitive because she was too close to Merrily and, even worse, to Huw Owen, who had once planted a fist on Innes in this very office – an incident fully witnessed but then quickly forgotten by Sophie.

Rather than sack her, Innes would keep Sophie at this level until she disappeared. Letting her gradually shrink into shame at taking a wage from the diocese for doing nothing important.

Merrily pulled her bag on to her knees, found the vape stick.

'Sophie, I'm going to have to ask. What's the background with Ripley?'

'Oh,' Sophie said. 'You've heard from him, then.'

'He phoned me.'

Sophie didn't look up.

'Well... Although I can't say I cared for his TV drama, he seems an agreeable enough person. The Bishop, I think, was delighted to welcome him, as a priest, into his diocese. Especially to its premier holiday area.'

Merrily nodded. To Innes, Ripley would mean bums on pews. A TV face in the pulpit. It would be worth any tourist's twenty in the collection box to take home a selfie with the former Simon Wilding. And he wouldn't lose value too quickly. A successful cop series hung around for years on the repeat channels.

But was she right to take Ripley's ghost story on board? She didn't want to float the question directly until she knew how close this man was to the Bishop.

'He'll be getting a lot of requests to open summer fetes,' Sophie said, 'but if his main reason for getting out of Bristol was press attention, I imagine the last thing he'd want now would be a known connection with deliverance. If it was picked up by the press it would be rather more newsworthy than he probably needs.'

'Which is why he wants to unload it on me?'

'Especially if it's not true,' Sophie said. 'The woman works in television. You have to consider she might have a *professional* interest in him.'

'If she just wants to get close to him, I'd only be in the way,' Merrily said.

'If it's not genuine. I'm sorry to inflict it on you… as there's something else at Goodrich you may want to explore.'

'Oh?'

Sophie looked out of the window again.

'Look, as we both know, I may not be here long…'

'Sophie, I really…' A pause, then Merrily spoke very softly, but with insistence. 'I really don't intend to let that happen.'

Sophie snorted faintly.

'It'll be well out of your hands. The writing's been on the wall for some time. Merrily, please… please listen. If you're working in Goodrich, there are some things you need to know about. Relating to your predecessor, Canon Dobbs. Things about which I've been rather too reticent. But now you may benefit from knowing.'

Merrily was surprised, said nothing. It was true they hadn't talked in any depth about Thomas Dobbs who someone had once likened to Poe's doleful raven, with its repetitive call of *Nevermore, nevermore.* Her most significant memory of the late Dobbs was the brief, unsigned note he'd left for her, pinned to his door, just across the road in Gwynne Street, where she couldn't miss it.

Jesus Christ was the first exorcist, it had read. By which Dobbs had been emphasizing that Jesus was *not a woman*. As close as he'd ever come to raising the issue with her. At the end, he'd collapsed in the Cathedral in the middle of what could only be described as a final exorcism. He had not supported the bishop who'd appointed her. She guessed he would not support Innes, but for different reasons.

'Canon Dobbs was not, as you know, an advocate of women priests,' Sophie said.

'As he made fairly clear.'

She remembered feeling bad about replacing him. Wanting very much to discuss with him the job. The *night* job. But he'd never see her alone. She'd only been close enough to speak to him about exorcism in those last days when he was semi-conscious.

'If the canon had any spare time,' Sophie said, 'he'd devote it to research. I still have some of his notes, which were kept in box files in the cabinet here behind my desk. I would have shown the notes to you if they'd had any connection with something you were working on, but I always thought you had enough to think about.'

Merrily smiled. Dobbs would hardly have wanted to share his thoughts with a woman who thought she was a real priest, even after he was dead.

'I've seen his box,' she said. 'Didn't try to open it. I always thought that if he'd investigated something I was looking into… you'd tell me about it yourself when there was time.'

Sophie stood up.

'Now we have to *make* some time,' she said.

Sophie lived in a posh street behind the Cathedral, with her husband, a semi-retired architect. They had a big house and she'd often used a spare room there for office overflow.

'I concluded the gatehouse was no longer safe from prying eyes and duplicate keys,' she said now. 'In the canon's day, nothing was ever preserved digitally. The notes were for his own reference. There were some files he ordered me to destroy not long after he'd learned he was to be replaced. I kept them, regardless.' Sophie pulled on gloves to replace the ones with no fingers. 'These matters tend not to fade away with time. You might have need to consult them at some point. How well do you *know* the old village of Goodrich?'

'Not as well as I should, apparently. I've only driven through it. It's where—'

'And how much do you know about Sir Samuel Meyrick?'

'Sorry?'

'Sir Samuel Rush Meyrick?'

'I've think I've heard the name, but…'

Sophie said. 'Goodrich Court?'

'Is that another name for Goodrich Castle?'

The best-preserved medieval castle in the county. She and Jane had been once. It occupied a prime position above the River Wye. Ruined, but still impressive. As it had been in the poet Wordsworth's time when he'd met a little girl there.

'No,' Sophie said. 'It's not that one. Not the medieval castle.'

She crossed in front of Merrily's chair, making for the door.

'This virus madness makes me need to do everything *now* because I never know how much time's left,' Sophie said. 'But if there's an hour or so before dark… I can more or less show you what remains of Goodrich Court. And tell you what was bothering the canon. Can you bring your car round?'

12
Struck by lightning

When he put his head round the door, Jane could see his sauce-bottle glasses were crooked and one lens had a slight crack. When she pointed this out, he didn't seem too worried about it.

'En't no big problem,' Gomer Parry said. 'He's done that before and I had him fixed by… by that specs feller in town. Half an hour, all it took. He knows me, see, I done his ma's drains a year or two back.' He straightened his glasses. 'Don't fuss, girl, en't nothing. Shop'll be open again when this pandemonium's over.'

'They'll probably fix them right away, if it's an emergency, Gomer. I'll just call the shop, find out when I can take them in. And if you need a new pair, I'll see to that, too.'

'You're a good girl, Janey,' Gomer said, 'but it'll have to wait.'

He hadn't asked her in. There was a warm spray of sparks reflected on the wall behind the front door, a small stack of logs in the hall. Gomer shook his head, a new ciggy clenched between his improbably white front teeth. She and him, they were mates. Only in a place like Ledwardine could you look at somebody of the opposite sex, sixty years older than you, and realistically think, *Gomer… he's my mate.*

Sometimes he seemed younger than she was. Was it possible to be, like *eighty…* and still a teenager in spirit?

'It's cold out here on the path,' Jane said. 'Are you OK, Gomer?'

'Every bugger asses me that,' Gomer said. 'But it's a healthy place, this. Long as they don't let it get took over by the hestate.'

He waved a dismissive hand at the new houses. The nearest were a small field away. Some were empty – holiday homes, their owners supposed to stay in London or wherever until the virus was over. The lane outside Gomer's gate followed the river out of town – which, with its banks all sagging and sloppy, had seemed, up to a fortnight ago, to be the biggest current threat to the village if the water level continued to rise.

'Us'll be all right,' Gomer said. 'Be OK if we stays round yere, ennit?'

Nobody could forget the flood panic from just over a year ago, because the water had already been back. Nearly every other village hereabouts had got it again this January, only worse. But Gomer and Danny Thomas had had both JCBs out: the diggers Gomer was supposed to be too old to handle, and they'd be out again soon, finding new graves in the expanding churchyard if this virus did what the papers were predicting.

Busy time for Mum, when the funerals started building up. Except they wouldn't be big funerals, with all the new restrictions. Now a maximum of nine people – and did that include the vicar and the undertakers?

Gomer just stood there with the front door half-open, still didn't invite her in. Was he worried she might be carrying the virus? People Jane's age were supposed to survive it after a few hours' coughing and a temperature in flux. But they could always pass it on to vulnerable old people, who'd get the symptoms a whole lot worse. Old people like Gomer Parry himself, who now plucked the ciggy out of his mouth and began to cough.

Jane winced.

'Listen, I'll deal with the glasses,' she said. 'You need to get down to the surgery and get yourself checked out, just to be sure.'

'Aaaah.' Gomer waved a dismissive hand, scattering ash. 'If I gets him, I gets him. Anyway, they reckons you gotter be a beast to go down with him real bad.'

'A beast...?'

'Like a tubby bugger?'

'What?' Jane blinked. Thought she'd mastered all the local terms, but...

Then she grinned.

'Oh... you mean *obese*?'

'What I said, ennit? A beast. And I just yeard Danny's shelterin' now, see... cos his missus, her's got the virus now. So we won't get no heavy work done for a week or so.'

'Greta? Is she—?'

'Aaah, her en't sick but her's got it all right. Her works on the desk at the docs', so they spotted him right away, that ole virus. And Danny's place is a good few miles from yere, and he's gotter stay there for fourteen days before he can go out again.'

Bliss left the building and set off across the car park, ignoring the funeral directors.

When the footsteps behind him suddenly speeded up, he noticed and casually turned and blinked, capturing a quick snapshot of her with both eyes. Following him, no question.

She was on the tall side, slim, short-haired, blonde and pretty – but slightly stern-faced, he noticed when she couldn't help but draw level with him at the kerb.

'Are you Detective Inspector Bliss?'

'Yeh, I can't deny it. What can I do for yer?'

'Just spare a couple of minutes to hear me out, all right?'

'I can probably do that if it's not gonna take too long.'

'My name's Evelyn Eaton.'

He'd heard that name before. Where?

'One of your detectives is David Vaynor?'

Ah. Then this had to be…

'Eve?'

'We've never met, Mr Bliss, but David's talked about you.'

'Yeh. He's talked about you, too.'

She was a secondary school teacher, or worked at a college. In Worcester, somewhere like that.

'I presume he's told you we're no longer… spending time together.'

He waited for a lorry to grind past before replying.

'I didn't know that. I'm sorry.'

'It was just convenience really. We met at Oxford and were both from this area, so… Anyway we decided – *I* decided – there was no future in it and we should break up now.'

'Well, that's… sensible if…'

'If I can just unload something on you. Because he thinks a lot of you. Admires you professionally.'

'That's, er, very generous of him. He's the best young detective I've ever had. *And* he's a nice lad.'

'And gave up a brilliant academic career to follow your example.'

'Oh.'

'And when I say brilliant I know what I'm talking about.'

'Yeh, I'm sure you do, but…'

'And I think he's thrown himself away.'

'Oh. Do you?'

'I might not be spending my life with him, but I don't want to see *his* life wasted.'

'I don't wanna see that either, Eve, and I'm happy to—'

'Encourage him to think again?'

'Talk to him about his future prospects, I was gonna say.'

'I couldn't just walk away,' Eve said, 'and leave him to...'

'A copper's life, with other coppers?'

'Mr Bliss, we've been given... with this pandemic, we've all been given an opportunity to re-evaluate our lives and...'

'That's why you threw him over the side?'

'I suppose, yes. I certainly couldn't face a life waiting for someone who might end the night in hospital or...'

'I say this a lot. Things like that don't often happen to detectives.'

Eve said, 'Something once happened to you.'

'Aw, yeh, but that was—'

'And it happened in the beautiful, peaceful countryside, I was told.'

There was no answer to that. He didn't even try. He'd taken a long time to recover after stupidly walking into a rural cock-fight, and even now bright lights did his head in.

'OK, I'll talk to him,' he said after two empty buses had passed.

'Good. We probably won't see each other again. I'll be looking for somewhere to live around Worcester, where my sister is.'

'Good luck,' Bliss said.

Finding he liked her after all. Darth Vaynor didn't have bad taste.

'He gave me his thesis as a kind of farewell present,' Eve said. 'And to show how little it meant to him. Well, we'll see about that.' Walking away, she looked back at him. 'Thanks for listening, Mr Bliss. And always remember that tall people are the first to get struck by lightning.'

13

Apoplectic

In the rear-view mirror, Merrily saw traffic swishing past, under the two witches-hat stone towers and the darkening sky. Only a deep greenery lay behind the towers, the main road sliding in front.

'Hang on, Sophie… if this isn't the entrance, why did that signpost point to Goodrich Castle?'

She'd driven or been driven past this gatehouse a dozen times in the past few years. You could see where the portcullis used to be, between the towers. They'd travelled half an hour or so from Hereford, winding past more wooded hills until they hit the wide road with its industrial traffic, catching up with the maturing Wye and, unexpectedly, some late sunshine at the sandstone-arched Kerne Bridge.

The water below was like a smoky mirror, beyond which signs of antiquity had begun to appear: Flanesford, the former priory, later a hotel, Sophie said, and, above it on the near horizon, the actual Goodrich Castle, red stone against a foil-grey sky. Only half an hour from Hereford, and it seemed like a different county. No black and white houses before the warm-toned stone of the witches-hat gatehouse.

But it seemed that this wasn't what she'd thought.

'Admittedly, it *says* Goodrich Castle on the sign.' Sophie looked behind from the passenger seat. 'Because that's where this side road eventually leads. But this was never an *old* gatehouse.'

'Well, I can see that. But surely it's replaced the original Goodrich Castle portcullis…?'

'This is not the Goodrich Castle gate, this was for Goodrich *Court* – not far away, but a different place entirely and now blocked from traffic. Right, take the next turn, Merrily, left, here.'

Off the dual carriageway onto a minor road. No, she couldn't see a castle, only fields and a hill with mature trees growing out of it.

Sophie put on a thin smile.

'Goodrich Court was built in the 1820s, very much in the medieval style, by Sir Samuel Rush Meyrick, who was enormously wealthy.'

Merrily was looking down at a copy of a book cover depicting a man who resembled an early movie villain: fleshy lips, lavish black sideburns, early Victorian long jacket. His smile was on the edge of smug. He had a pen in hand, seemed to be autographing what could be a late-medieval breastplate.

'He was an early nineteenth-century lawyer and antiquarian,' Sophie said. '*Extremely* wealthy. Best known later as an expert on armour and weaponry. Becoming what amounted to Royal Armourer to William IV.'

'When was William IV?'

'He preceded Queen Victoria, and Sir Samuel Meyrick rearranged his armoury for display. At the same time building up his own huge personal collection.'

'Weapons?'

'*All* things martial, in fact – some items dating back to the Dark Ages and beyond. Quite a few Celtic relics. When Meyrick's collection outgrew his London home, he went looking for somewhere else to keep it all and put it on public display. Soon spotting, in this area, the perfect castle. Ruined but perhaps less so than it is today.'

'Goodrich Castle?' Merrily's eyes widened. 'But that would cost a fortune to restore and fortify—'

'And Meyrick *had* a fortune,' Sophie said.

And he'd been profoundly inspired by the extensive remains of Goodrich Castle. This was at the time when the lower Wye was at the centre of that early tourism boom – a Gothically-romantic place of woods and rocks and chasms, choked with history and legend. In fact, once the home of men who might have worn some of Meyrick's actual armour and slaughtered one another with his weaponry. Where better to give the wealthy tourists a preparatory frisson before they climbed back into the boats.

'The court was essentially a folly,' Sophie said. 'A hugely expensive imitation, far bigger than Goodrich Castle… and quite putting it in the shade… as it was meant to do.'

'Why? I'm not getting this, Sophie. Why did this guy want to put the old castle in the shade? And how was it possible? Compared to most others in this county it's still remarkably well preserved for the twelfth and thirteenth century.'

'*Why*?' Sophie leaned back. 'Because Sir Samuel Meyrick – for whom money was no object – had originally wanted to buy it – the original Goodrich Castle. Unfortunately, the owners of the castle didn't like Meyrick at all. Didn't trust him. Refused to sell the castle to him at any price. And Meyrick… well, he wasn't used to being treated that way. So…' Sophie smiled. 'In the end, he built his own castle on the next headland. Dominating the next viewpoint. No planning permission required in those days. If you had the land and the cash you could usually go ahead.'

'You mean he thought it would actually replace—?'

'And he thought the village could be made to support it.'

You couldn't see the castle from the village, but fragments of it seemed to have crumbled down the hill into the tight, wooded lanes, attaching themselves to existing buildings like the village pub, which had acquired turrets, and a deep window reaching from the forecourt almost to the roof. A village pub that was *olde* but not, it seemed, actually old. No pub these days called Ye Hostelrie could be genuinely historic. Sophie said she'd spent a whole day here in early autumn with Andrew, her husband – being educated about cruck-frames and quoins and learning what a broach-spire was.

This pub seemed to have them all. It might have been Dracula's local, with its long, pointed window, high turrets, Gothic gable and spires.

'Preserves some of the spirit of the court, according to Pevsner,' Sophie said as deep shadows rose up the masonry as if they'd been built-in. This was certainly a kind of hotel, but it should be in the centre of an established town.

'But it's still here. Unlike...'

'Unlike Goodrich Court. Previously, it was called the Meyrick Arms,' Sophie said.

Now, parked on the edge of Goodrich village, Merrily looked through the front and side windows and then back in the direction of the stone gatehouse facing the main commercial link between South Wales and the English Midlands.

She heard the grind and hum of industrial traffic, watched the first of tonight's headlights. Clearly, none of it had been here when Goodrich Court was conceived. But...

'But where is it?... I'm sorry, Sophie, I really don't know enough about the lower Wye Valley, but like...*where is it hidden?* I mean, if he was so keen on the court he must eventually have finished the main building to go behind the gatehouse?'

'Oh yes. And he had a talented young architect working for him, Edmund Blore. Many people saw what he would call Goodrich Court as a great asset to the area, and it went on to attract crowds of visitors over many years. It was a huge success. Very rapidly drew thousands of early tourists.'

'But—'

'But, you see, not everyone liked it.'

Sophie's face now wore a wintry smile.

Merrily said, 'You mean Canon Dobbs? Dobbs didn't like it?'

It was growing dark and she switched to dipped headlamps but kept the engine running, the old Freelander parked at the roadside.

Beside her, Sophie was shaking her head.

'I don't *know* what Canon Dobbs thought of it, but this was long before *his* time. I'm talking about the man who considered the original Goodrich Castle to be "the noblest ruin in the county".'

'That's the original medieval castle, not the new Goodrich *Court?*'

'And that, Merrily, is the point.'

'Sorry...' Merrily half-turned to face her. 'Sophie, I'm not getting this...'

'Nobody appreciated the spoiled grandeur of ancient castles more than the man still often widely acclaimed as the finest poet England ever produced,' Sophie said. 'Do I take it you haven't heard about Wordsworth's reaction to Meyrick's new castle?'

'I know he spent some time in this area in his twenties. With his doting sister sometimes.'

Remembering reading how the poet and his wife, Mary, used to stay with her brother at his farm at Brinsop, which she knew well, as it was only a few miles from Ledwardine.

No surprise, then, that he'd seen both the old Goodrich Castle and the new Goodrich Court. Even in a horse-drawn coach, this was surely no more than a day-trip along the Wye from Brinsop.

'He loved the area,' Sophie said. 'Picked up a famous poem near the ruins of Goodrich Castle. But when he arrived one day to find his view blocked by the newly built and vast Goodrich Court… on the next headland above the river where before there had been *nothing*…'

'Didn't immediately take to it?'

'The poet wasn't widely known for his displays of uncontrollable anger,' Sophie said. 'But he was what today we'd call a conservationist. One word used to describe his mood, on seeing the new building was "apoplectic".'

14

Joyless heart

THE FLAT WAS at the back of St Owen's Street, near the city centre, the ill-lit end. The five steps to the door were slippery. Vaynor moved along the dull brick wall. His key turned stiffly in the Yale lock and the door yielded.

No lights. He was alone here. He'd pulled back, waiting for a lamp to come on or the first hiss of the kettle. Waited in the silence for a few moments before finding the old metal switch in the hall, drenching the stained panelling in oily light.

It had been a good flat, but this end of the street was becoming a depressing place, sending grim messages with its closing-down shops and its desperate parking charges.

The morning post was on the mat. Never seen that before on a weeknight. Eve had always collected the mail before he got home.

Three envelopes, pastel-coloured, his name on them. He picked them up and carried them into the kitchen. The trace of a cooking smell. The oil lamp with the glass funnel standing on the window sill. It was out, but he could smell singed wick: the smell of warm light, bitterly extinguished.

He put the envelopes on the table. Knowing they'd be cards for his twenty-eighth birthday, and the last thing he wanted was to open them on his own. He went quietly back into the hall and along to the bedroom. Opened the door into darkness, became aware that the curtains were drawn. Not for privacy, he thought, not a sign of rage, but… *mourning* was the word that came to him, as he saw an edge of the Cathedral tower in an upper corner of the bedroom window and couldn't suppress it.

'Eve?'

Waiting too long for a reply. Her voice could be light and hopeful, like one of the first birds from the dawn chorus. Always reminded him of waking up on the first morning of his last expedition to the Wye Valley, before it all became forbidding.

He sank down on the side of the cold bed, unmade.

Alone. *His* flat again. *Through the abysses of a joyless heart, the heaviest plummet of despair can go.* Kept hearing that line. He'd come home on previous occasions, dragged by something he'd been dreading having to tell her. But he'd told her anyway and it was usually OK in the end. She'd once said that if they had a future together there should be nothing they couldn't tell one another and he'd decided, without much thought, that, on his part, there wouldn't be.

He closed his eyes, called on darkness…

…and midnight darkness seemed to take all objects from my sight.

No. Please, no.

Back in the cave, and he couldn't tell her about that. The deep cave that opened like a wound in the Doward. It was the first thing he couldn't tell her.

Or anybody.

He knew that nothing like that could possibly have happened outside of his head and she'd surely know that, too. Perhaps he'd been more physically tired than he'd realized in that cave. It had been raining outside, and he'd slid into oblivion between the ambered rocks that held him like a stone coffin.

... My brain
Work'd with a dim and undetermin'd sense
Of unknown modes of being; in my thoughts
There was a darkness...

And a dampness. He felt a dampness in his eyes. He was losing the woman he'd been with intermittently since student years. And also his job, the job he'd thought would save him.

Sometimes it befel
In these night wanderings, that a strong desire
O'erpowered my better reason...

The lines rushed at him through the gloom and he was back in the cave.

Vaynor rolled off the bed.

This had become *her* flat. He might be six and a half feet tall, but in a way, she was taller. Higher. She looked down on him. She was an already a senior academic and he was a low-ranking copper.

She was right. He'd thrown it all away.

It was barely eight p.m., and he wasn't qualified, as a human being, to stay here on his own.

15

In Agony

As a semi-rural darkness closed in on the car, Merrily learned that Goodrich Court had been nationally famous for a while. She read in the fading light that the great British architectural historian Nicholas Pevsner had called it 'a fantastic and enormous tower-bedecked house'.

'And it's all gone?'

Merrily gazed into the dusk through the windscreen hazed by a hint of rain.

The brash newness of Goodrich Court had apparently faded fairly quickly, leaving just over a century after it had been built, a gap on the skyline, and then empty fields and woodland directly opposite the darkening remains of medieval Goodrich Castle.

'It's gone? The entire building?'

'Never takes people long to cart debris away as building stone for farm buildings,' Sophie said. 'I'm told there are a few girders half-buried in the woods, but no masonry left.'

She said that none of Sir Samuel Meyrick's descendants had inherited his vision, and the court had been prematurely demolished. Having failed to bring good fortune to anyone.

'Leaving only the gatehouse to guard its memory,' Merrily said. 'But you said it attracted considerable tourism?'

'In its early years, yes. In the way that places like Alton Towers still do. More authentic than that, of course – it was opened in the 1830s and included a recreation of a medieval tournament, with imitation horses. And it was packed with weapons and armour dating back to the Dark Ages.'

'But it didn't bring Meyrick much luck.'

'He died at only sixty-four, having already lost his wife and son, Llewellyn. Its armour and various treasures were sold separately. In its later years, long after Meyrick's death, the court was sold as what apparently was a very unwieldy home – too big and impossible to heat. Finally, it became temporary accommodation for a school in wartime. Gradually, beams, flooring and panels were removed.'

'Did nobody think of turning it into a hotel?'

'If they did, it didn't happen. Finally, in 1950, with the help of explosives, it was brought down and the landscape healed over where it had been.'

Merrily dropped the torch on the dash. She felt cold. The village lights were coming on, but the horizon was dark. 'Am I feeling a ghost story developing, Sophie?'

'Not much of one.'

Sophie shrugged, cleared her throat, seemed almost embarrassed, although, outside the window, the weather was playing along. It was far gloomier than it should be at 4.30 p.m. not far short of spring.

'It's said that... when Goodrich Court was finally being brought down, part of the collapsing building is said to have roared in agony... like a large, dying animal.'

Merrily couldn't prevent a small shudder. She could almost hear it: a hollow, metallic tearing.

'It's actually a not-unfamiliar sound to demolition crews, according to my husband,' Sophie said. 'But apparently it was the source of considerable superstition around Goodrich at the time, and...'

'How long have you known about this?'

'Well... years, I suppose. A while before you came. I... I didn't think about it much, because it went no further. If Canon Dobbs ever returned, he didn't record it. He'd been persuaded to come out here in, I think, 1985. Early in the morning. In the mist. He was, I suspect, a little grumpy about it. Dismissive.'

'What was he originally told, do you know?'

'His notes say parishioners north of Goodrich claimed to have been awoken before dawn by what he described as... "an agony in the air".'

It was a strong phrase from someone Sophie had suggested was fairly sceptical.

'He was probably there before daylight. He records the presence of the morning star.' Sophie held up a page. 'I can't read it in this light, but if you take it home, you can find the details I've missed.'

Merrily pulled the car back into the middle of the street. There were no obvious parking places.

Sophie said suddenly, 'I remember onc phrase, near the end where the canon describes what he saw from where the court used to be. *Lucifer quite luridly apparent.* This is a reference to the star, not the Devil. The evening star, Venus, always starts to appear in the morning. Under a different name. Lucifer – I don't know why. But he saw the star where the court used to be.'

'In the new gap?'

'I'm not sure. Nothing to do with Satan... or exorcism. Although, in the end, the canon did apparently conduct a fairly ritualistic exorcism of place, walking three times around the site of Goodrich Court with holy water... and the vicar of Goodrich. Who was probably a little embarrassed, but the diocesan exorcist was respected, even then, for the work he did. I would have given you this file years ago if there was any suggestion it had carried on.'

'Who told you about Dobbs's exorcism of place?'

'It was Mrs Rees, his former housekeeper – still alive and coherent, if you ever need to confirm it. She said the canon rarely discussed his exorcisms, but she does remember hearing that on this occasion he'd assembled some of the people who had earlier been disturbed by the… death-throes of Goodrich Court.'

'The "death throes"? He actually used that phrase?'

'I don't…' Sophie was clearly distressed. 'There was a period of time between whatever happened that brought him here and the documents passing into my care.'

Merrily sighed.

'And the arrival of Innes. I'm sorry, Sophie, I— Did Dobbs hear it?'

'He doesn't say he did. Not everybody *did* hear it. Some people who were living here then say it's complete nonsense.'

'What did Dobbs think? I'm sorry, I'm trying to make up for knowing nothing about this.'

Sophie folded up the documents, looked as if she regretted mentioning any of it, then let her hands fall in her lap.

'I rather feel that, like other people, he disapproved of Meyrick and the way he'd imposed himself on this village.'

'Do *you* think that, Sophie?'

Sophie was quiet for a while, as if they were on the edge of something she wasn't sure should be disturbed.

'I think there's evidence that, despite all the money Meyrick poured into Goodrich, he isn't quite as highly regarded as you might expect.' She peered out of the right-hand window. 'It's a little too dark to visit his last resting place today, I'm afraid, but… I think the level of local esteem is reflected in his memorial.'

'Now we're here, I'd like to finish this story.' Merrily drove on slowly but with intent. 'The church, is it?'

'Yes, but…'

'Where *is* the church?'

Sophie laughed artificially.

'You wouldn't be the first person to ask that.'

'Goodrich doesn't have a proper church?'

'Oh, it does. Quite a large one. Thirteenth century. And well preserved – heavily Victorianized. But the thing is unless you've done some research, you won't find it. Even in full daylight you probably wouldn't. Are you sure you want to do this? There's a lot to understand.'

'Sorry, Sophie, we've come here now and I think I have to finish the story. There seems to be a whole slice of Herefordshire history I'm not really aware of. If this *is* Herefordshire. When the Wye gets wider it starts to seem like a different county.'

'Bear right,' Sophie said.

16

Undercurrents

MERRILY SQUEEZED THROUGH a gap between cast-iron railings near the church wall. One rail had been removed.

Full dusk now. It had closed in imperceptibly. She wasn't sure where they were or how they'd got here, but she could see the shape of a church steeple, as grey as the air, and no lights on or near it, no clock.

They'd walked through rough grass to get here, leaving the car near a footpath gate, house-lights not far away. They'd passed bent-over graves before reaching the railings.

'This is it?'

'If I'm remembering it correctly.' Sophie lowered her husband's golf-umbrella to get it between the railings. 'Yes, this is it.'

Merrily said, 'So he's still here, in the village?'

'His son, Llewellyn, was put in here first. He was going to be brought up as a medieval castle owner, learning to hunt in the grounds, but he didn't make it. That was the start of the Meyrick bad luck. You'd better have this.' Sophie bringing a small torch from her handbag. 'Keep the light down.'

The grave had not been cared for. The stone of the interior tomb was coated with mud and ivy. Sophie was hacking at it with the heel of her boot. Nobody was disturbing them. Few people seemed to live close to the church.

'No one seems to look after it any more,' Sophie said. 'If they ever did.'

As she lifted her foot, the torchlight showed

USH MEYRICK

And underneath

founder of Goodrich Cou

'When we first came here,' Sophie remembered, 'I asked four people where Meyrick was buried. None of them knew. Or were they claiming not to know? I wonder...'

Merrily bent down to brush more mud fragments away with a hand.

'I wonder why they didn't know. He certainly left his mark on Goodrich. Must have put an incredible amount of money into it. Did he do something they didn't like?'

'I wouldn't go that far, but...'

'What?'

'He's somehow managed not to be part of this area's history,' Sophie said. 'His castle was for tourists, not local people. And now it's gone. It doesn't exist any more. Its... its space is empty.'

Merrily stared roughly in the direction of the castellated gateway that apparently now led nowhere. Sophie told her that Meyrick had been born in North Herefordshire, though he always insisted he was Welsh. Married a Welsh woman who predeceased him, as did his son.

'He went on several expeditions in Wales in search of stone circles and cromlechs – which might be plundered for grave goods to go on display at Goodrich Court alongside the weaponry. He thought they were druid remains.'

'So people still believed, in those days, that the old stones and circles were erected by the druids?'

'They didn't know. They didn't know much about the druids. Anything mysterious was attributed to these obscure and dark Celtic priests. They were another of Meyrick's obsessions – a common one in the eighteenth and nineteenth centuries. He wanted to be recognized as an expert so he produced his own illustrated books about the druids.'

'Made him seem more Welsh?'

'And created the image of a druid we still accept today, though it may be entirely inaccurate.'

'Why did he want to be Welsh?' Merrily asked into the rain.

Sophie said, 'Perhaps he thought they were more exotic. Beyond that, I have no idea. He tried to master the language – with how much success I'm not sure.' She looked around. 'I think you've seen what there is to see. Perhaps we should make our way back to the car.'

They squeezed back between the gap in the railings, entering what could now be seen as an untidy graveyard with tilted stones leading to a small modern housing estate on the edge of the village. It gave them a full view of the church, like a quiet group of farm buildings set against a long hill. A few cottages on either side had lights coming on. Merrily stopped near the little footpath gate they'd used to get in. It wouldn't admit anything wider than a moped.

'Do congregations have to parachute in here, Sophie, or what?'

'This graveyard probably pre-dates parachutes by many centuries. And yet, when virtually all churches had entrances, this wasn't given one. Plenty of room for gates, yet you can't get a car near it. No road. Never has been.'

'What about funerals… the hearse?'

'I don't know. They must manage somehow – they probably have an agreement to use someone's land, someone's drive for the important vehicles. But I can't think of another substantial parish church unreachable by car, and I can't see anyone putting a road in now.'

'It's strange.'

Merrily unlocked the Freelander. Had this been a sign to Dobbs that something here was making it hard for the Church and always had? Did it go further than *undercurrents*?

'Erm...' She counted the bungalows overlooking the churchyard and the thought that had periodically bobbed in her brain since they'd arrived here arose again. 'The garden of the woman who contacted Arlo Ripley apparently is near the church.'

'That was what he told me: Goodrich church. I wondered if she lived near enough to the site of Goodrich Court for her to hear its... dying fall. If it really was heard again.'

It didn't sound too ridiculous. Not out here after dark, in the rain. Merrily pulled open the driver's door.

'Or perhaps she could hear Meyrick himself bemoaning the fate of his pride and joy,' Sophie said. 'Anyway, I thought you should know why Canon Dobbs had spent so much time in Goodrich.'

'Thank you. I always wondered if there were some things about Canon Dobbs that you hadn't told me. I never did have any reason to know that. What were his conclusions?'

'I'm not aware of any. He was working on this intermittently for... the rest of his life, I suppose. A year or two.'

Sophie stood by the Freelander, looking down at St Giles's Church, plain, its tower without buttresses. No adornments, no clock and not approached by any road.

'If Canon Dobbs reached any conclusions,' she said, 'I'm afraid he didn't live long enough to share them. Not with me, anyway.' She waited to get into the car. 'I don't think there's anything else we can see today. I'm sure you've already guessed why we came this afternoon. And why we're leaving now – I hope – before we lose *all* the light.'

'All right,' Merrily said. 'You'd better tell me how recently it was heard again.'

Sophie didn't reply until they were both in the Freelander, and its engine was running.

'I believe,' she fastened her seat belt and brought her window down a short way, 'that it was two days ago.'

17
Death's Dynamo

DC Vaynor was parked outside Starbucks, on the Ross bypass, wet snow now turning to rain on the windscreen. He didn't know why he'd come back here, unless he was hoping to encounter Maya Madden again.

This morning, not long before they'd gone their separate ways, she'd said, about William Wordsworth,

If he wants to stay around... to resolve some things... who am I to stop him?

And that had stayed with Vaynor. She regarded Wordsworth as a person, a human being, not just a literary figure. He'd been dead for a couple of centuries, but she knew there were emotions around him that still needed quenching.

Why should Vaynor conceal his study of the poet from this woman? She'd met him first as a copper. She had no reason to think he'd betrayed his roots.

Vaynor's mobile was on the passenger seat; he'd thought he might as well use it. Thinking how much he used to relish being at home with Eve on a wintry night like this, when snow could be a balm and an anaesthetic if you were in the warm. One day, perhaps, if she came back, they'd go to live in a house with an open fire and he'd be straight with her about why human motives were more important than literary techniques. But if that was all they had to talk about in front of an open fire in wintry weather...

Which was an illusion as well. According to Radio Hereford and Worcester, far higher temperatures were on the way, along with April.

In the flat, for special occasions like tonight could have been, they'd have the kitchen oil lamp alight on the window ledge, its glass funnel enclosing a shaky flame. Vaynor rang the flat again, from his mobile.

No answer. Again.

He saw there were not many customers in Starbucks. With this pandemic around, people were going home as soon as they could. The car park was down to five vehicles, including Vaynor's and one from which a woman was emerging. He made an abrupt decision to go in and get himself a coffee.

The lighting in Starbucks was what you found in waiting rooms or a low-energy factory canteen. Vaynor ordered an espresso and was looking around when the perfume reached him, along with a breathy murmur behind him.

It had to be.

'You walked right past me, Inspector.' Diana Portis was tall enough, in her high-heeled black boots, at least to get within whispering distance of his ear. 'I'm over there if you want to join me.'

He didn't correct her this time about his rank. A steaming cup and a handbag were on the table to the right of the door, a long, black umbrella leaning against a padded bench. Diana Portis's parka, black and shiny, was unzipped to show the smoky-pink suit jacket underneath. She looked up at him coyly.

'I feel a bit like a… what do they call them? Is it still a snout, or is that very last-millennium?'

'I'm not sure.' Vaynor picked up his coffee from the counter. 'I've never really had one of my own.'

Which wasn't quite true, but no informant liked being talked about over somebody else's coffee.

'Oh well, there you are then.' She took his arm. 'Should I be your *first snout*?'

The little smile, the breathy kitty purr and the border-country roll. She giggled and sat down at her table, crossed long legs in tight, dark jeans.

'I'm waiting for Royce. He's been out talking to funeral directors. Full burial, right next to the Wye, so he's treating it like an auction for the undertakers. Who'll get to plant Peter Portis?' She was flicking a would-you-believe-it? glance at the ceiling. 'I do actually quite enjoy these occasions.'

'Funerals?'

'Everyone in neutral black,' she said, 'but they're all quite naked underneath. Nowhere to hide at a big funeral.'

Cops still thought that, too. Standing at a murder victim's graveside, examining the faces of mourners for indications of guilt. A tradition dating back to long raincoats, hats and pipes. He wasn't sure that was what she meant in this case, though, there being nothing to say this was a murder or anything suspicious. Or was there?

Vaynor sat down opposite Mrs Portis, took a sip of his espresso.

'If you don't mind me saying this,' he said, 'you don't seem too grief-stricken.'

'Must improve my performance before the big day, whenever that is.' She sipped her coffee then looked at him over the cup, breaking out into laughter. 'Don't look so shocked, David, you're a detective. It's *death*. Part of life. Happens around us all the time, people losing their claw-grip on the twig. You *get over it*.'

He wasn't sure how to react.

'Well, I… I suppose you do. Sooner or later.'

'Royce doesn't want to be a suicide's son,' she said. 'Rather have it that his old man was murdered.' She hunched forward. 'No, listen, I got on well with Peter. Would I have preferred it if he'd hung around for another twenty or thirty years? Having to visit him in the nursing home, listening to the same climbing story he told me a few minutes ago? No, I would not. What does that make me?'

She sat back, observing his reaction but not with any great concern. Cold, thick rain wormed down the plate glass, swollen by headlight-glare, and they talked quietly but not in a confidential way, two professionals at the end of a long and complicated day. Slowly, he became aware of a muted excitement, the feeling of being suddenly taken close to something.

Well, close to her, obviously, in a curious first-date sort of way which he'd neither sought nor expected, but it might be telling him something. And if playing snout gave her a *frisson*...

'It was, after all, a lovely and appropriate way to go,' she said. 'The fitting end to his story. Would he really have wanted just to keel over in the office? Or collapse during a viewing, ruining the sale?'

'You... said this to your husband?'

'He didn't ask my opinion. But I meant what I said earlier about Peter. About the river rising to take him back. That's appropriate, isn't it?'

'Except that he didn't wind up in the river.'

'His *body* didn't.'

'The destination of the soul,' Vaynor said carefully, 'is not a police issue.'

She didn't reply. She sat back, her lips moist and slightly parted, her eyes dark and still. He was beginning to enjoy this surprise conversation. Challenging, in a way, but light and relaxed in another. How it used to be with Eve.

'Are you what policemen are like these days?' she said after a while. 'More educated? Am I sitting opposite the future?'

'If you are, I'm not sure that's a good thing.'

Diana was silent for a few moments, looking at him out of her dark-brown eyes.

'You got kids?'

'No.'

'Married?'

'I live with my p— person.'

Never liked referring to Eve as his *partner*. Too flat and prosaic. She was worth more than that, even if she was not, at present, a full part of his life.

'And is your "person",' Diana said, 'happy with you being a copper?'

He was startled. *He* was supposed to ask the questions. Was it possible she knew Eve from somewhere? He said nothing. Her eyes played knowledgeably with his. Although they weren't round, Diana Portis's eyes made him think of an owl's: wise, all-knowing. But penetrating. And she was even younger than he'd thought, which made things worse.

'Well, *is* she? Or he? Happy?'

'No,' he said. 'No, she isn't, actually. At least, not at the moment.'

The lights in here seemed significantly brighter, as if they were shining into his thoughts, illuminating Eve's words from last night. *Let's not forget you told me you'd be a bloody sergeant by Christmas.* Coming from anybody but Eve, it might have sounded like an embittered rebuke. Which he guessed it was.

It had been his own fault, a couple of years ago, passing on what he'd been quietly told after his first interview, about becoming a DI, or higher, before he was thirty. What he hadn't known then was that a DI worked mainly out of an office. It was the lower ranks who got to make the arrests and handle the interrogations. Who stacked up the first-hand experience, saw some segments of real life: the pace of it, the pungency of what remained of backstreet Hereford.

He was twenty-seven, now, and still loving all that. Passed his sergeant's exam and been strongly advised to put in immediately for any job that came up at headquarters. Hadn't gone for it because he felt he needed to stay on the front line for a while, not in his office directing cops twice his age who called him a fast-track twat behind his back.

Making the mistake of trying to explain all this to Eve.

How he'd wanted to be a detective even when he was told you had to serve time as a uniformed policeman first and maybe direct traffic – which was what a teacher had told him when he kept winning prizes for English but was always insisting he was going to try for the cops. And later, when he was informed by the most attractive girls that becoming a copper wasn't exactly cool.

Girls like Eve, the academic. And girls who, back when he was a student, looked like Diana Portis.

Snow pattered on the glass door behind them as Diana's face swam into ironic focus under hair that was suddenly like damp seaweed. And then he realized, with a tremor, that he hadn't just thought all that stuff, he'd might have *said* it. Poured it all out over this woman.

All of it? *Had* he? How long had he been here?

'Is she afraid you might, you know, die out on the street?' she said. 'Get stabbed or something? Shot?'

'Detectives don't often get hurt. Only on TV. No, it's not that.'

Not wanting to admit – even to himself, this time – that what depressed him most was the idea of Eve simply being too embarrassed to admit to her colleagues that he was still a detective constable. That he was in the police at all.

He'd started, even if he hadn't intended to come out with it all so quickly, and now he'd have to finish the story. For himself. To explain it.

He said, 'She found it quite exciting at first. I suppose because she thought it'd be temporary. Like a boy thing. Something I needed to get out of my system before settling into something that wouldn't look like a complete waste of a degree.'

He wasn't going to say *Oxford doctorate.*

'You're feeling under pressure, David?'

'To an extent.'

'But you're not married to her, are you?'

'No, but—'

'Or to your doctorate.'

Shit.

'What would you do, if not this job?'

'Haven't thought about it.'

Of course he'd thought about it. He'd met these guys, university lecturers, continually telling people how important it was for them to be teaching, passing on their learning as they acquired more. But that, in itself, wasn't exciting. All the time they were courting TV producers to try and grab a few weeks presenting some arts documentary on BBC 4.

Diana laughed lightly, and Vaynor laughed too, looking up to find her eyes full of amused disbelief, like they'd known one another half a lifetime.

Had they? Or was it more than that? Was it now time to find out?

'I first came up here to research my thesis,' he said. 'William Wordsworth. I became quite an expert on him. He learned a lot of stuff when he was young – when he was *here* – but then he stopped himself learning.'

'Why did he do that?' she asked, as if she really cared.

He felt disconnected, watching the traffic-lit snow melt into a bright river, like the one under the drone in that dizzying video in the shop in Corpse Cross Street.

Then she said, 'Learning wasn't experiencing, was it?'

'No,' he said, surprised at what she knew. Then, 'Are you happy in *your* work?' he asked. 'Dealing dreams?'

She raised her eyebrows.

'That's how you see it?'

'Well, it's how your father-in-law saw it. I read it on the Net. He said most of the people who came to live in the lower Wye Valley were chasing a dream. He prided himself on making the dreams reality.'

'He said that?'

Did he?

'I, on the other hand,' Diana said, 'having briefly trained as a surveyor, work more with sellers than buyers. The ones for whom the dream didn't come true. I can show them what's wrong with their homes and what they can do fairly quickly to make them more saleable. People value that, and it gets me into other lives and unexpected situations. Look at me now – I'm a snout.'

'Not yet,' he said.

She levelled a forefinger at Vaynor and her voice became lower.

'Before we start, David, you need to accept that whatever emerges about my father-in-law, none of it will have come from me. Snouts have immunity.'

'Which generally depends on the quality of the information,' Vaynor said.

'You've seen our window display. We only deal in quality. Individuality.'

She looked around. Five or six more people had come in out of the snow.

'I was expecting Royce, but he must have gone back to the office. You were at school with him, weren't you?'

'I, er…' He didn't look at her. 'Yes.'

'I think he'd rather talk to you. Not with the coroner's officer or anybody there. He could probably tell you things you had no reason to know about his old man.' Mrs Portis zipped up her parka. 'See you there, shall I? In about twenty minutes? If you want that. No one else will be there.'

She was calling the shots, which he thought he didn't mind. Something about the dense texture of her voice excited him.

The snow was still mildly falling, but it had not quite stuck. A watery yellow moon slid above the grey hulks of the old houses in the upper town.

Vaynor walked away from the small car park to where the street twisted into Old Maid's Walk. And then Corpse Cross Street, reflections in its windows of the tail-lights of vehicles creeping into town.

He stood there in the whitening road, thinking distantly how capably he'd been checked out. Perhaps Diana Portis did this with her clients to assess their worth. But she hadn't mentioned meeting him once before in King Arthur's Cave when he was in his very early twenties, and she was—

Don't think about it.

Vaynor stepped back onto the pavement to let a small car go by, its rear lights reflected in the long display window of PPP.

He stopped. The car had vanished into the town centre but the lights remained in the window.

Walking towards it, he saw movement. The carousel of house photos had gone, along with the spotlights. Now he saw a coil of pale rope, with clips and pulleys, below a pair of grey rubbery goggles. Resting on them, a dark safety helmet with straps and a lamp in the front. Switched on, angled down.

He'd seen this lamp before.

On a dead man's head.

Lolly and stick.

Couldn't be the same ones, obviously, but they were putting out the same signals. The window was darkening again, as the display rotated into shadows. If the headset hadn't been shining out through the trees last night, the upright body of Peter Portis might not have been found till morning.

The memorial display gathered a cold luminescence as it came back round into the window. Death's dynamo keeping the lamp alight.

The door began to open as Vaynor walked towards it.

18
Keys, please

SLIDING ON TO a very public bench, dead centre of Ross. He was feeling heavy but insubstantial, like vinegar-soaked fish and chip paper tossed from a passing car. The street was scabbed with wet litter. He was tired. So tired.

He'd come out of a pub. Blurry coloured lights and fire in the glass. *No, make it a double.* The once-familiar sting on his tongue. Had he really said that?

He didn't do that stuff any more. Very little he'd done tonight was anything he'd do any more. His head was expanding, his thoughts near hysteria. Had he fallen asleep on that bench?

Bewildered, he looked around. The old market hall at the top of town was behind him. Below it, Boots the chemist, long shut for the night. He sank back into the wooden seat, looking down through desultory traffic at the darkened shops sloping steeply away.

When he pulled out his phone, his car keys tumbled after it. His hands were numb… if these were *his* hands. The phone was switched off. He tried to activate it to check for messages, texts, missed calls, anything to connect him with real time.

It just got wet in his hands. He picked up the car keys. A man he'd once seen in a dark uniform was eyeballing him from a shop doorway: community support officer, plastic plod, obviously wondering if he'd nicked the phone and considering whether to make an approach.

He put away the phone and stood up, unsteady. It felt like the night itself had soaked through his clothes and also his skin, and suddenly his nerves were fizzing and crackling in the damp like stripped wires. He walked slowly past the plastic plod and the plod asked him if he was OK, and Vaynor nodded numbly.

He stood there, shivering. He'd gone into the pub shivering. Shivered over a double Scotch. *Through the abysses of a joyless heart, the heaviest plummet of despair can go.*

Wordsworth had written some wordy crap later in life, but while he was down here in the Wye Valley at the end of the eighteenth century he'd been blazing like a rocket and making every line count.

Vaynor walked away. He found his car more or less where he'd left it, in the little parking area near the church wall. Dragging out his keys, he let himself in, switching on the engine and the demister then backing up the car, too fast.

There was a parked van right behind him. Vaynor hit the brakes to avoid it and stalled the engine.

He leaned back, panting. What was he doing? Where was he? Maybe he needed to stay in the car all night, folding himself double. Punishment for what had happened. What he'd allowed to happen. *Had* he let that happen? Let that happen? What he'd done?

He restarted the engine, backed into a vacant space, sat up and pulled out his phone and found a missed call... from Bliss.

No message. Even as he was looking at the little screen, a text came in, and it was from...

Eve?

The print was swimming. He realized he was reading from halfway down the message which said, *Even though we're not together, it's still your birthday. So, happy birthday, David.*

He read the last line again. And again. Through possible tears.

Birthday... today... me...?

Letting the phone fall into the passenger seat, his mind still playing back things he'd done. Driving out of the parking space as another text came through, and he trod on the brake and his hands were unsteady as he lifted the phone.

The screen said the same thing again, plus

PS. I didn't tell you at the time, but I thought Al Fox needed a bigger audience, so a few months ago, I put his brilliant thesis on the Internet under his real name. A few people have already seen it and left comments.

The message ended.

Then there was another one

One day you'll thank me, it said. *Or not. Either way, it doesn't matter now.*

Vaynor sat there on the car park with the engine running and let it sink in, what she'd done: *she'd put his PhD thesis, now her property, online. Under his real name!*

Closing his eyes, he remembered how he'd come to give her the thesis. It was the night he'd learned he was going into CID. The night he'd told her he was definitely staying at Gaol Street. No question now of leaving the police to go back into academe.

He recalled she'd been beyond furious. She'd seriously thought that in Gaol Street he was just getting something out of his system. A boy's game. She'd been waiting for him to come back to the educated grown-up person's world. The *real* world.

'The thesis,' she'd screamed. 'What are you going to do with your fucking thesis? Abandon it?'

He remembered looking at her across the kitchen, and the space between them would now qualify as a good social distance.

'No, I'm giving it to *you*,' he'd said without thinking, the way you did in the middle of a row.

And he had. She'd been free to sell it, or…

…or… expose him online.

Now his eyes were blinking open to headlights in the car park entrance.

There was a car blocking it. Vaynor was stamping on his footbrake. He saw yellow and blue flashes. Two car doors opening simultaneously, two uniforms flapping up like cutouts. Vaynor was switching off the engine, snatching his keys from the ignition, flinging himself against the door which sprang open, and then he was rolling into the wet tarmac.

'*Stay there!*'

Man's voice. Policeman's voice. The breathalyser would already be out. And then there'd be, oh God, the handcuffs.

Or he could try to wing it.

Do you know who I am?

Yes, we do, you overeducated, fast-track twat.

A gloved hand was held out towards him.

'Keys, please, sir.'

Woman's voice this time. He knew it. Patti Calder from Traffic.

'Jesus Christ,' she said, 'it's bloody Darth.'

'Yes,' he said.

Pulling himself stiffly to his feet, finding the keys in his right hand. Feeling them slipping away but not hearing them clink on the ground.

Didn't matter. Wouldn't be needing them now. Not for at least eighteen months.

With his luck, they'd slid down a drain and into the grey fingers of one of those old, unremembered suicides.

19

Along the heart

Hereford Cathedral was no longer in the heart of the city which seemed to have grown away from it, possibly in search of new values. Driving home in the dark, Vaynor would glimpse the Cathedral tower out on its own by the River Wye. Sometimes there was a necklace of soft lights around it, and he'd felt welcome.

Tonight, in the last moments of his short journey home from Ross, he came out of his waking dream to see the necklace of lights and the river below it – only the building at the centre of the lights was not the Cathedral but the County hospital, and Vaynor came fully awake, his head loaded with what he thought at first must be the virus. He didn't know anybody who had it, but the virus was everywhere – people on TV attached to ventilators, people on the radio waiting for a vaccine that wouldn't be available this year even if they knew there was going to be one.

And no Eve. At her sister's, the answering machine was waiting to trap his message – his fifteenth message. It was his day off tomorrow, and he could spend it on her sister's doorstep if necessary. He had at least to persuade her to get that thesis offline.

When it first appeared, nobody knew who Al Fox was. Now it was online and they could find out he was a copper.

He left his car at Gaol Street. He'd been presented with the keys by Patti Calder's partner, Darryl Mills, who'd found them between his feet on the Ross car park and handed them over without a word.

Eventually, if unwillingly, in bed in the St Owen's Street flat, Vaynor fell asleep and slid back into his fever dream.

*

Wreathes of smoke sent up in silence…

No visible smoke, but this has to be the place.

…among the trees.

The nature-trust noticeboard at the top of the steep track tells him he's standing on a rocky hill encrusted in trees and reached by quaint-sounding old routes: May Bush lane, Leaping Stocks Road, Horse Pool Lane.

This rocky hill is actually the Doward: which always sounds heavy, solemn, sinister… and obviously very deeply haunted, in all senses of the word.

He's come here in an effort to bring his thesis to life.

It needs doing. Needs to be different from all the other theses online. Like William Wordsworth's plain-speak poetry was different, at the time, from all those pompous poems in the books.

It's taken him longer than he expected to make it up here through his end-of-day fatigue. He's used up too many hours searching for shady old sycamore trees close to the banks of the river, before the paths led him up to this wooded place, where his Ordnance Survey map identifies much older archaeology: **fort… well… tumulus… settlement.**

Mostly related to the Dark Ages and back into prehistory: *lines, circles, mounts,* Wordsworth wrote, *a mystery of shapes.*

He isn't any kind of archaeologist. It all just looks like grass and trees to him as he edges down the rubbly path, vaguely looking for signs of smoke drifting into the darkening salmon sky over *some Hermit's cave where by his fire the Hermit sits alone.* Not now, of course, although a fire would be welcome – somewhere to hang out for a while, as the day cools, decide if this is worth it.

He comes to a long-abandoned quarry, smoothed and mossed into a small, woodland amphitheatre, where the path turns to the right. Wondering how he'd have felt, more than two centuries ago, standing here in the poet's boots which have tramped hundreds of miles across western Europe, letting the juices of the earth lubricate him in the stifling city.

Sensations... felt in the blood and felt along the heart.

He's around the same age as Wordsworth was when he walked this way in the last decade of the eighteenth century, but he's feeling too tired to download the location into his bloodstream. Wishing he'd got here an hour or two earlier when he'd been more receptive. Wishing it could be morning, with sunlight hopping happily between the branches.

Wishing he'd found himself a different bloody thesis, had left Wordsworth alone. Far too many would-be PhDs have been here before him.

So he enters the amber quiet of King Arthur's Cave, and he slowly becomes aware that he's not alone in here, and then it starts to happen.

Again. He can't let it happen again.

He was awake. The bed was silent. Eve was at her sister's flat. Making it *her* flat. Eve was a presence, carrying her intellect before her. The intellect that no longer lived here, in St Owen's Street.

Vaynor thought about the cave and the woman he'd first encountered there.

Had he? Had he been in *that* cave with *that* woman?

And, tonight, had he been with her again?

Had they…?

Her hip bone was hard. He used to think he wasn't supposed to like that, but now he did. It told him she was ready.

'Annie?' Bliss murmured.

Annie went, 'Mmmrgh.'

'You awake?'

'Nrrrgh.'

'I've got something on me mind, Annie.'

The luminous alarm clock said it was coming up to three a.m. After a couple of minutes, the bedside lamp came on and Annie Howe's head was propped up on an elbow and she was looking down on him.

'Then you'd better tell me.'

He was amazed again.

Had she always been able to do that? Come fully awake, like she'd never even been to sleep, her mind flashing on as fast as the lamp.

'I'm sorry,' Bliss said.

'No, you're not. So tell me.'

'It's… Something *I'm* not gerrin' told.'

'By an underling?'

Bliss rolled over, couldn't help it.

'I read Vaynor's thesis tonight,' Annie said.

'*What?*'

'He'd sent it to CID. You'll see it on your laptop in the morning. Why's he done this, Francis? Is it just to show he's so much cleverer than the rest of us?'

20

Pious bitch

When the rain cleared it was not like the end of March. With all the trees still bare, Ledwardine looked brighter than most recent Julys and it wasn't cold, either.

Maybe it was the strange sun that had drawn Mum out. When she appeared at the shop door around 9.30 a.m., Jane's Ted Baker backpack was on the shop table crammed with books brought from home to join the new pile of vinyl LPs on the desk.

It was a good bag, stylish but functional. Eirion had bought it her for Christmas. He didn't do jewellery and perfume, perhaps still insecure about himself and Jane as some kind of item again. Possibly thinking a bag didn't carry any risky hints of long-term romance. Though actually it did. You could fit all your deeply important things into a backpack.

These books had been chosen with infinite care from the shelves in her apartment. Brought down, put back, down again and carried here in the bag before she could change her mind again. *You could start off by flogging some of your own*, the bookseller, Betty Thorogood, had told her in Hay-on-Wye. *Don't be afraid to part with some of the ones you loved. Buyers will grow to love them, too, and remember where they came from.* That was how they all got going, Betty said. It only hurt until you learned from experience that if it was a really important book another copy would soon turn up.

There was one she'd brought by mistake. One she wasn't ever going to offer for sale, although it would fetch really good money: the fifty-year-old hardback copy of *The Old Straight Track* by Alfred Watkins. Source-book for all followers of the prehistoric pathways between ancient monuments. It was coming up to the centenary of Alfred's discovery of ley-lines. And he was an ancestor… well, arguably. She'd once written to his grandson, the Rev. Felix Watkins, but she'd heard he'd died just as her letter arrived.

It really had seemed like a death in the family.

'Mum, it's open!'

Not wanting Mum to know yet that she was flogging so many of her own books – which made it all look too serious – Jane pushed them back into the pack and lowered it to the floor.

'Did you actually say it was open?'

'I meant the door, not the shop,' Jane said. 'Won't be long now, though, before we're in business. Just need to *expand* the business a bit.'

Mum came in. She had on her waxed-cotton jacket over the clerical clobber she seemed to feel obliged to wear around the village since the pandemic had arrived so nobody would forget what she was meant to be for.

'Dry cleaning?' Mum guessed, sitting on the stool. 'Body piercing?'

'Even more retro than that, as it happens.' Jane held up some 12-inch LPs in old but well-preserved covers: King Crimson, Nazareth, Captain Beefheart and his Magic Band. 'I'm installing a second-hand vinyl department. I've put up these shelves on bricks upstairs. The more rough it is, the more people think they're looking at a bargain. Incredible what these old folks will pay for something in a triple gatefold-sleeve.'

'But these…' Mum picking up Procol Harum's *Broken*

Barricades, which Jane had been surprised to find was actually too good to sell till she'd played it a few more times, but she'd still sell it if the money was on the counter. 'I thought you were just doing folk bands, mainly the ones appearing at the festival, but these are nearly all—'

'Vintage prog rock, I know. Despite my little note in the corner of the window, saying cash paid for folk.'

'Cash? How much cash have you *got*?'

'Eirion's helped. He knows he'll get it back, one way or another. No, see, what happened, yesterday, this guy comes in. His new girlfriend's moving in with him – she looks about thirty years younger and obviously not interested in dusting his old albums, so he's transferred his vinyl to digital. I take a look at what he's brought, and I'm like... hmm, not a lot of this is folk, is it? And he looks so pissed off, because he obviously needs the money and the space. And I'm going, *but I could take it off your hands, I suppose...*'

'You shark, Jane.'

'You think so?' Jane sat down at the table, stretching her arms out, pleased with herself. 'He got a good price. Well, not a *bad* price. And like one day some guy will show up, been looking everywhere for the complete works of Uriah Heap on vinyl, and when *that* happens—'

'Hang on...' Mum was frowning. 'When this venerable head-banger eventually shows up, you'll be long gone...'

'Gone where?'

'...and this shop will be a baby boutique or something. So I wouldn't take on *too* much stock. Because, after the festival, when you go off to Durham or wherever...'

They'd taken advice on this. Durham seemed to have one of the UK's most respected archaeology departments. Nowhere could actually guarantee you a job afterwards, but Durham came closer than most – or so it was claimed.

'No word yet, I take it.'

Jane said nothing, and then Mum was like,

'Do we need to discuss anything, flower?'

Insouciant.

Bugger. Not now, please.

But Mum was looking steadily at her like it *was* going to be now. Jane, praying silently to the Mother Goddess for someone else to come in and mumbling, 'Can't we just leave it?'

*

Bliss was in work early. The CID room, as usual since the virus, was almost empty.

He'd come in early because Big Patti Calder from Traffic wanted to talk to him. Patti, who'd been a mate for a good while, was smart, would have come to CID if she hadn't enjoyed fast driving so much. Car chases kept a lot of talented coppers in uniform these days.

'We both thought he was over the limit.' Patti had her back to the door. She was in dark jeans, not yet on duty. 'I mean well over. He was out there in the snow trying to sober up – I see a lot of that. He had his mobile out and I thought at first he was calling for a taxi. He'd been in the pub, where he apparently ordered a big whisky. He was like... all over the place. That was what we were told by the landlord.'

'Darth Vaynor?' Bliss leaned back in his office chair, incredulous. 'This was the tall lad, *Vaynor*, who you thought was drunk?'

'Look, I didn't believe it either. Obviously, I wouldn't normally do this... tell you. I mean, if it wasn't *you*...'

She turned to look out of the window into CID.

'Nobody's listening to us,' Bliss said. 'So let's get the whole story out. Off the record, if you like. Stay over there.'

'It's not what *I'd* like—'

'You're saying it was this plazzie who spotted him, right?'

'We were parked near the centre of town and the plastic plod came over. He'd recognized DC Vaynor behaving erratically and wasn't sure what he should do. To be honest, I wasn't either. It seemed so out of character I was wondering if he was working undercover or something.'

'In bloody Ross? Darth Vaynor?'

'Yeah, I know. So we decided to look for him, and that's how we wound up on the little car park near the church. When he started to move off, that was when we stopped him. Like we had an alternative?'

'No, all right. I *accept* that. What did he do then?'

'He stopped the car and got out and then he dropped his keys in the road. He was on his hands and knees, scrabbling around and not finding them, and it was Darryl who finally found the keys behind a wheel, and we… we invited him to take a breath test. How could we not?'

'Oh,' Bliss said.

And thought, *Oh shit.*

*

Mum said, 'Could you just acquaint me with the, erm, current position as regards Durham?'

'Let's just leave it, huh? Look, to celebrate the sunshine I was about to have some hot chocolate. Would you—?'

'"Leave it"?' Merrily said.

'There'll only be a row.'

'I promise there won't be a row.'

Jane brought down the chocolate tin.

'Basically, I'm thinking of a different university, that's all.'

Mum said, 'You're a smart person, flower, far too smart in many respects, but I don't see you getting into Oxford or Cambridge at this stage.'

'No. That wouldn't... that would be unlikely, as you say.'

Seconds passed. If there'd been an old clock in here, its ticks would have sounded slow and menacing.

Jane said, 'I was thinking, like... the University of Rural Life?'

She could see Mum working out if this was a joke.

'The University of Rural Life? And its campus would be... where?'

'Essentially, Mum...and I think you *will* see the sense in this eventually...' Please don't let this sound as rehearsed as it was. 'It would certainly save on, like, train fares and stuff. See, the last thing I want is to put us into debt working on a degree course that may never be any use... will not guarantee me a living wage, may not fully reflect my interests and... obsessions, and I'm not afraid to use that word.'

Meaning the Ledwardine henge, which only a handful of people were convinced existed, none of them on Herefordshire Council. Some possible sites needed at least to be investigated – sites which, by the time she was back from university, would be under dozens of *executive homes* for London retirees.

And... she became aware of Mum advancing on her.

'I may be wrong here,' Jane said, 'but I seem to recall you promising not too long ago that there wouldn't be a row.'

'Sometimes, I lie,' Mum said.

'Come on, *you* went to uni, and you didn't exactly finish the course. Look what that must've cost for—'

'Because of *you*. Because I got—'

'That was my *fault*?' Jane spinning round in a small cloud of chocolate powder. 'And does that mean you're sorry now that you dropped out of university? That you didn't qualify as a lawyer and maybe go into partnership with Dad and take on some of his bent clients?'

'Oh, for God's—'

'Yeah, God, too. What made you take Him on? *Her… It.* Did that seem like sanity at the time? No way. You followed some crazy instinct, right? Something deep in your—'

'Jane—'

'And I couldn't believe it for quite a long time. Embarrassed the hell out of me – a little kid – when you were in the clerical clobber for the first time. But did I once throw the dog collar in your face?'

'Jane, you only *stopped* throwing it in my face about a year ago.'

'I'll never forget walking into your bedroom, and you're kneeling by the window saying your prayers like in some really cheesy Victorian painting. And this is when you start seeing me becoming a pagan as like a… like some kind of test of your new faith?'

Mum didn't reply but she'd be remembering the teen-witch phase, Jane coming down in the night to arrange the breakfast cutlery into the shape of a pentagram. Which she now knew had been a bit childish, but…

'We both needed to mature,' Mum said surprisingly.

'And like… did we?'

Both?

'God knows…'

…if God exists.

She didn't say that, but she could be close. Closer than she'd ever been, Jane guessed.

'All right,' she said, 'I'm sorry – and I realize now that it was me that was usually wrong – but you seemed such a pious—'

Mum winced as if she'd been slapped.

Pious bitch. What Dad used to call her just as their almost-forced marriage was going terminal.

Mum was shaking her head.

'This is getting nowhere, Jane, never has, never will. It's about you throwing away a valid career for a romantic whim and the sense that your future is somehow tied to a village that we only wound up in because—'

'Because of *you.* And your *calling.* And I'm now unexpectedly happy here. *More* than that, it's given me a purpose and if I don't see it through, the years'll be all wasted. But now that it's all just collapsing because of a tosser in a pointy hat…'

See how I did that? Brought the argument back to the Bishop. Never fails.

Whatever Mum was going to say, she choked it off. Her face had become dark and smoky.

'And now I'm expected to toddle meekly off to uni,' Jane said, pushing it, because this was now the time to push it. 'And one day I'll get a call and it'll be like, Oh flower, don't bother coming back here at the end of term, I'm moving to, like, East Anglia or somewhere.'

'I wouldn't ever—'

'You might not have a choice. And me… archaeology? I mean that's not going away, is it? It just doesn't have to be this year. I have a few bloody good A-levels, I can be a mature student. In fact, give me a year running this little shop and I'll have enough money to pay my own fees.'

'Jane.' Mum, suddenly weary, sat down on the stool, bag at her feet. 'Vicars are still hard, if not impossible, to dislodge. Especially when the parish has a stake in this house. Uncle Ted won't let that go.'

'As long as he's still around and running the parish council.

He's not getting any younger. And with the Church you're dealing with an organization born out of politics, sex, greed and now—'

'And now fighting to hang on to everything it stole,' Mum said calmly. 'Maybe I should kick the whole lot into—'

Jane stared at her. She wouldn't have talked like this even a year ago. Certainly not in the days of the old bishop, Bernie Dunmore.

'What… abandon the Church?'

'It's a possibility. Congregations are on the slide.'

Jane's arms dropped to her sides.

'You're serious?'

'Why shouldn't I be?'

'Because…' a shock – don't let it show '…even if it's a crap organization it's still, like, the framework for the most significant things you've ever done?' Thinking of Mum practising deliverance rather than being a vicar. 'Mum, you've been closer to the edge of human experience than anyone I know who's still alive. And it's much bigger than…'

Much bigger than organized religion.

But was it? Grateful when Mum's mobile chimed in her bag and she was dragging it out, Jane was thinking, *Words mean nothing. I have to do something to show her that she can rely on me. That we're basically on the same side, hold the same values. That I'm, like… in this, too.*

'Merrily Watkins,' Mum said into the phone, and then, after quite a long pause, 'Siân, I didn't recognize your… No, I *am* at home, almost. I was just…'

This, Jane decided, was Siân Callaghan-Clarke, Archdeacon of Hereford. She was OK, basically. Mum listened. She said yes and no a few times, looking at first puzzled and then… just a bit suspicious?

And then she stood up suddenly.

'It was *you*?'

Jane didn't even pretend she wasn't paying attention.

'Yes, I probably can,' Mum said eventually. 'I suppose I can be there in about half an hour if the traffic's not too bad.'

Hereford, the Cathedral gatehouse, where she used to go at least once a week, for a meeting with Sophie. But those days were over.

Mum clicked off the phone and sat down in silence for a few seconds, not looking at Jane. She didn't exactly say, *Oh shit* or anything, but her expression came close.

21

Metaphysics

Patti Calder had been gone a while but Vaynor knew she'd been here, that much was clear to Bliss. Vaynor had come straight to Bliss's office; now Bliss had locked them in so they wouldn't be interrupted. Not that this was likely – since the virus, people stayed out of small rooms.

Neither of them spoke for what seemed over a minute. Bliss was still hearing Patti: *he was on his hands and knees… we did a breath test.*

It had to be explained sooner or later.

Eventually, Vaynor spoke.

'If it's better I just get out now, I'll do that.'

'Huh?'

'For good, if that's what you feel is right. I'll start again somewhere. There won't be a fuss about it. Some things I just can't discuss.'

Bliss nodded and sighed. It could turn out to be necessary, in the end, to go through some tedious bureaucratic shite but he didn't really want to see this lad's papers on the desk.

But he did want to know what was behind it, if Vaynor was seriously thinking he might be in the wrong job. Bliss rested his chin on his right fist.

'Darth, did you *know* when you blew in that bag last night that you were well under the limit?'

Silence. He saw Annie Howe gliding past the small window outside both his office and the CID room, let his eyes snap into a blink. *Stay out. Stay out, Annie.*

'No,' Vaynor said eventually. 'I thought I'd be well *over* the limit. And that's all that matters... what I thought.'

'Why? How much did you think you'd had?'

Vaynor said that all he could remember from Ross town centre was ordering himself a double whisky. He admitted it used to be his tipple for a decadent period in his last year at Oxford. When he joined the police, he said, he gave it up, switching to beer for a few weeks then losing the booze altogether. Couldn't explain why he'd bought that double, but guessed it was somehow related to a panic he'd rather not try to explain.

Annie looked into the window separating them from the CID room. Bliss turned his chair away to convey to her that this really was not a good time.

'And you think you knocked it all back?' he asked. 'The Scotch?'

'I'm not sure now. May have abandoned it.'

'You obviously *did*.'

'Yeah, I... I don't really drink any more. Didn't sleep much last night. Kept having this dream, couldn't get rid of it.'

'Kind of dream?'

Bliss thinking about what he'd read in one of the morning papers he'd found in the CID room, about isolation from the virus causing serial dreams. Because if that was all it had been...

'The kind you don't want,' Vaynor said. 'No, I don't think I did finish the drink.'

Calder had told Bliss that, because they couldn't believe the breath test had misfired, she and Mills had been back into that pub, where the landlord, who didn't know Vaynor, had said he'd found an abandoned whisky glass that was pretty damn full. It was probably still on the shelf under the bar and might be there until the pub came out of lockdown, because none of the regulars wanted to touch it last night in case it was contaminated.

Vaynor looked like he genuinely couldn't remember too much about that double whisky. Or what bloody day it was. He shook his head.

'I was confused. Boss, I'm really not in a good way. If I'm honest, I'd done something no decent copper ever does if he wants to stay in the job, and... Look, I don't want to talk about it. It came up in the dream, but also, it... something *happened*.'

There was a spare chair opposite the desk, and Bliss had nodded at it twice but Vaynor was passing up the opportunity to sit down and pour it all out; he was behaving like a frigging schoolboy in the headmaster's office.

Bliss said, 'Darth, listen, this is *not official*. I just wanna know what was happening in your head. I wanna hear it from *you*.'

Vaynor looked down at his shoes.

'Is this a police matter?' Bliss asked him.

'I don't know. It might be.'

'Meaning what?'

He was seeing puzzlement and a kind of anguish in Vaynor's eyes. Something had happened to this lad last night that he didn't understand and therefore couldn't unload. Smart guys like Darth Vaynor hated it when they couldn't get their heads around something. They'd failed, they were inadequate, couldn't do the job. Where other coppers would just roll over, Vaynor's first way of resolving it could be resignation. Getting out, moving on. Which would badly wound more than just his ego.

'Darth—'

'And I didn't send it.'

'What didn't you send?'

Vaynor coughed and looked down at his shoes.

'The thesis.'

'Thesis?'

'"The Wye in Wordsworth".'

'That's the title?'

Vaynor nodded. Bliss said nothing. He'd read it on his laptop as soon as he got in this morning. And he'd been in early.

'It was a good piece,' he said. 'We all thought that – at least them as could understand it did.'

'I'm embarrassed about that. As if I'd posted while I was drunk.'

'Except you weren't remotely drunk. Were you?'

'I'd better go,' Vaynor said.

But he didn't.

He looked into space and said, 'Boss, you remember… a year or so ago… there was a case that began with a storm, and the recovery of body parts underneath a tree behind the Cathedral?'

'Yeh, I remember, but why are we going back there?'

'And it all came back to a man who died in a private care home.'

'I remember, OK?'

'And it wasn't talked about much, even in here.'

Bliss nodded. He wanted to put more than social distance between them. It wasn't a case he or anybody in this building liked talking about outside of a very quiet pub. It wasn't strictly a police matter.

'You decided it was an issue that had only limited interest for us,' Vaynor said. 'I kind of realized that at the time.'

'I didn't think we'd ever find an explanation that meant we'd keep our jobs if we talked about it in the wrong company. You know what I'm saying?'

'Yes,' Vaynor said. 'I think so.'

Unhappily.

Bliss stared at him, feeling cold inside. No, he didn't understand a lot about that case, although he knew why he was always going to remember it late at night, until he could sleep. And why Anne Howe was never going to discuss it with him again, especially in her bed in Malvern.

'You did believe something happened, though, boss,' Vaynor stated quietly. 'Something that other people wouldn't consider strictly feasible. Didn't you?'

Bliss walked slowly round his desk, breaking all the social distance rules.

'I didn't necessarily *believe* it, Darth,' he said quietly, 'I… *accepted* it. Not quite the same thing. Sometimes you'll find stuff you don't believe but in the end you gorra accept it happened.'

'What you said at the time,' Vaynor said, 'was that while most of the villains we deal with are bad… some are evil. We talk about *pure evil*… It's something that exists outside of normal—'

'All right.' Bliss raised a hand. 'Let's not get too deep into this kind of stuff. Metaphysics, is that the word? Yeh, we all remember somebody like that. Somebody who… somebody to whom normal motives can't be applied.'

Vaynor stood up slowly, moved to the door, stood with his back to it.

'I'm sorry, boss. I don't like what this is telling me. I'm still trying to work out what happened, and I don't think there's a police answer. Metaphysics would get closer, and that's not a word you'd use in a thesis either. Not if you wanted to walk away with a PhD.'

'What did you tell Eve?' Bliss asked.

Vaynor said nothing.

'Look...' Bliss unlocked the office door '...there's norra lorra work for us right now, with the virus and all. Even burglars won't do places that might be infected with C-19. So... as it's your day off, why don't you go home? Think about it, decide how much you can tell me.'

'I...' In the doorway, Vaynor stopped, turned. 'I can't do that. Eve's not there. Eve left.'

Bliss let go of the doorknob.

'I don't know what's bothering you but if it falls into the box I'm thinking of, you need to talk to somebody. And norra copper, for once.' He paused. 'She'll be back? Eve?'

He wasn't going to tell Vaynor he'd spoken to someone who thought she'd already spent too much of her life with the lad.

'I don't know,' Vaynor said. 'And I don't want to waste your time, boss.'

Bliss moved towards him, taking over the doorway.

'The pure evil feller. You meant Kindley-Pryce, right? Was that the name?'

Vaynor might have nodded.

'If it's him then you'll know he died,' Bliss said. 'Which meant we didn't have to try and explain his strange behaviour. That's often the best way out with these people, who we don't encounter too often. Sometimes we need a middleman to quietly assist us.' He moved towards the window, his voice dropping. 'Or a middle-*woman*.'

22

Sealing the can of worms

THE SUNSHINE WAS getting absorbed by the tower of Hereford Cathedral, now closed down by the virus, with Reformation-era shadows fogged under the gatehouse arch, and Merrily walking into a dense new silence.

Every cathedral in the country was being closed the way they never had been before. Nobody knew when – or even if – they would open again. You couldn't avoid asking the big, scary question, the question that, until the virus had taken over, had only been whispered: was this *it*, as the Sunday broadsheets kept asking – the beginning of the end for the Church of England?

She moved quietly up the gatehouse steps to find the woman in Sophie's chair taking off a royal-blue cloche hat, turning it over in her hands and looking as though she wanted to put it right back on and get the hell out, with today's business, whatever it was, unloaded.

'I'm sorry we've had to meet in here,' the Archdeacon said. 'With the deliverance office open only two days a week, it's becoming rather dusty. But everywhere else here is shut because of the virus and it's getting warmer. Why hasn't Sophie complained?'

'Sophie doesn't complain.' Merrily shut the door. 'She endures.'

'Evidently.'

'But remembers.'

'Perhaps *I'd* better complain, then,' Siân Callaghan-Clarke said.

'Are you sure you want it to be known that you've even been in here lately? It's no longer the Bishop's favourite refuge. Not this bishop.'

Siân placed the cloche hat on the desk beside her leather briefcase. It was the same brass-cornered case she'd carried around when, as a canon, she'd been given the task of building a deliverance team around Merrily, including a psychiatrist. Getting, as it had turned out, a close view of the challenges of deliverance and why psychiatrists were not always in a position to address the problems that led to it.

It was fair to say that Siân now knew the score.

'If you've heard the whispers about the Bishop,' she said, 'there's nothing any of us here could do to stop that. It's far above our heads now. If Innes becomes special adviser on deliverance to the Archbishop of Canterbury we just have to assume that's the way deliverance is going.'

'Out of the highest window?'

'Not necessarily. Things like this are getting passed because everyone's attention is being diverted by the virus. And at worst… well, archbishops don't hold the job for ever, do they? I'd say your best policy might be just to keep quiet and see what transpires.'

'And the fact that the Bishop of Hereford is now monitoring all my cases and has managed to reduce Sophie to junior-typist level?'

'Things *change*, Merrily. Sometimes quite quickly. But getting new rules adopted is always a lengthy process in the Church.'

'Not if it's done by experts, with a series of small procedural tweaks, and at the right time. Now, for the first time, all the churches are closed, allowing the furniture to be subtly rearranged.'

Merrily went to her seat in the window. Siân was more sympathetic these days, but it was unwise to be lulled into indiscretion by the newly softened, untrimmed hairstyle, the hints of highlights, the smile that slid more easily into place. The Archdeacon was still a former barrister.

Siân reached over for her briefcase.

'The Bishop is someone with whom I have at least to pretend to rub along.' She unclipped the case. 'I'm glad you came, Merrily. I need your discretion.'

Extracting a small tin with a gold-leaf design on it, matches and – *bloody hell* – cigarettes. In an elegant, somehow old-fashioned way, Siân slowly lit one.

'*This...* is a very private vice, rarely indulged in outside my home. *Not* an addiction.'

Which sounded like the preliminary to an exchange of confidences.

'We all say that,' Merrily said.

Siân frowned.

'I invited... another addict to make an approach to you. Via Sophie.'

'Another...?' She thought of Arlo Ripley's character, Simon Wilding. 'I have to say I hadn't known the Rev. Ripley originally came from you. Maybe you can explain.'

'Yes, you need to hear it spelled out,' Siân said. 'Arlo's a man I've known for some years now. The Bishop didn't know him at all, except, possibly, as an actor. He'd looked at Arlo's application for Whitchurch and seen a man whose fame is almost guaranteed to triple a congregation.'

'That's as far as it goes?'

'As an actor, Arlo was, in his worn and wasted way, very appealing to women. British viewers love a damaged hero, someone who's suffered.'

Merrily said, 'But Arlo Ripley isn't Simon Wilding.'

The Archdeacon blew out smoke.

'Isn't he?'

'I'm sorry...?'

'The casting of Wilding was the result of an independent TV producer spotting Arlo looking vague and disconnected in a minor part. There was apparently a very good screenplay doing the rounds, which nobody wanted to take on because the central character was considered weak and unappealing. It's said the producer guessed Arlo would slip effortlessly into the role, generating sympathy rather than contempt, because... essentially, he'd be playing himself.'

Siân waved her cigarette in the air.

'I don't mean Arlo was an addict in the Wilding sense. He may have used cocaine for a while – as a few long-established clergy have been known to do before an important sermon – but this is different. Do you know much about something occasionally called addiction syndrome?'

Merrily thought about it.

'Is that when someone's kind of, erm, addicted to addiction?'

'In a way. But the roots of the condition are seen to be psychiatric, rather than a particular dependency,' Siân said. 'So it doesn't have to be drugs or gambling, or it can be both... and more.'

'The opium of the people?'

'Don't make light of it. I don't think this was addiction syndrome, but we were afraid it might not be far off. Arlo had read theology at university and, while studying hard for his degree, he'd been...' she paused, as if unsure whether to say it so bluntly '...self-harming.'

The phrase resounding in the unnatural silence as Merrily went rigid.

Siân said, 'If you want me to be more explicit, I'd have to say that he was inflicting what one might call Stanley-knife stigmata on various parts of his own body.'

'I...' Merrily sank back. 'I didn't know anything about this.'

'But you'll agree it sounds like a valid reason for keeping Arlo Ripley away from your particular discipline... exorcism, the paranormal. My first thought was that he was finding personal flaws that he could face directly and try to conquer... that he thought certain extreme redemptive processes would somehow deepen his faith. But...'

The Archdeacon pinched out her cigarette, half-smoked, and then dropped it in the tin.

'I needed to tell you this, because I want you to trust what else I may say.'

'I always have.'

Siân shook the tin, watching the stub roll around.

'Arlo and I were doing a post-graduate theological course together at a college in the West Country. We didn't see one another for a while after it ended, and I didn't know he'd applied for the parish of Whitchurch after his Bristol curacy. When he came here, we decided not to disclose to anyone that we'd met before. Although he occasionally rings me... for advice. Which is how he came to tell me about the woman at Goodrich and this supposed haunting he was being asked to address.'

She didn't seem aware of lighting another cigarette.

'I think we were both seeing warning lights. It wouldn't be long before it was out of his control.'

'Siân, can you clarify this a bit?'

'I'll tell you.' Siân tossed the tin back into her open bag. 'But if this ever gets out...' She shut the bag. 'The bottom line is, until I discovered the extent of his problem, Arlo and I became what you'd probably call... an item.'

Bloody hell.

'I do realize he's quite a few years younger than I am. To say I was flattered is using absolutely the wrong word. The fact is that we were only together, if you like, for a few intense weeks. After which, it was... just friendship. An increasingly cautious friendship on my part, I have to say.'

'Erm...'

'It was a mistake, of course it was,' Siân said. 'But these things happen at theological colleges, as you probably know. Something telling ordinands it's their last chance to behave... irresponsibly, if you like.'

Merrily sank back. Exploding revelations were becoming another feature of the current pandemic: people no longer concealing secret history.

'But what I've learned about Arlo Ripley,' Siân said, 'tells me that the lower Wye Valley is not the best place for him to function as a priest. And not only because *I'm* not far away and very much don't want him here. There are other reasons which you would understand.'

'I really...' Merrily's right hand squeezed her left wrist. 'I don't really know what to say. Can I take it the Bishop doesn't know any of this?'

'Not from me he doesn't!'

'You didn't need to tell me anything, either,' Merrily said. 'It's not my business.'

'Isn't it?' Siân's eyes glittered. 'You won't immediately thank me for saying this, Merrily, or fully understand what I'm saying, but... that valley is steeped in a history that somehow doesn't recede. As I've been discussing with Maya Madden, the young TV woman who approached Arlo Ripley.'

'Why did *you* see her? I'm a bit confused.'

'Maya is, of course, a producer with a TV company. And

very attractive. Both valid reasons for Arlo to keep his distance. Which I think he realized… and did the sensible thing, asking me if I thought her problem should be addressed. I told him it could be dealt with, if necessary, not by him but by someone like you. It's a deliverance issue.'

'You think she really has a problem?'

Siân uncoiled from Sophie's desk and wandered over to the window overlooking Gwynne Street, where Canon Dobbs used to live.

'Yes, I think she does. And I think you should look into it.'

'Without telling the Bishop?'

'I very much doubt you'll need to tell him.'

Having formally sealed the can of worms, the Archdeacon took a small, thick book from her bag and brought it over. It looked like a prayer book, but evidently wasn't.

'This includes the poem "We Are Seven", in which the Goodrich girl makes her appearance. You should read it before you talk to Maya.'

'I've read it.'

'Well, read it again.' She put the book on an arm of Merrily's metal chair. 'And there's something else. Perhaps I'll see you there myself later.'

She returned to Sophie's desk and sat down again.

'Go and see her now. I'll call her and say you're on your way. And I'll call you, later. Leave your mobile switched on.'

23

Intruder

A STARTLED BLUE tit was flapping up and away from the car. Startled because the black Freelander was the only mechanical device in sight on the road, the only visible vehicle in a landscape licked by the knotted river that seemed to rule everything in these parts.

Early wild flowers were glittering in the grass, including some which Merrily didn't think she'd seen before. Verges were ablaze with big new daffodils, all fluttering and dancing the way daffs had done in past centuries alongside the sprawling fields… fields which were conspicuously alive between trees stretching out their new boughs bristling with twitching twigs and bulging buds in an air-city of birds involved in family-planning, becoming louder and more insistent as if under the roving hands of some big sound-mixer in the sky.

Merrily slowed the old Freelander, letting its windows down, and nature in.

The unseasonally warm air helped her out of the car into a day that was not as dark as her thoughts. Inside the car, she'd become aware of church bells: the mobile phone on the passenger seat doing its familiar chimes, introducing a new call.

It hadn't stopped.

She put the phone on speaker and released the call.

'No number, just a name,' Siân said now. 'The house is called Churchyard Cottage. Park by the gate to the footpath leading to the church, where I believe you came with Sophie the other day, and you'll see it not far way. She should be in.'

'She knows I'm coming?'

'I gather you're going to be told about something,' Siân said. 'I can't say anything about it on the phone. The Bishop seems to have ways of monitoring calls.'

'Siân...' Merrily squeezed the phone. 'What the hell's happening?'

She stood on the grass verge and stared dumbly at the iPhone as if she was seeing it for the first time. It had no function here. It was ugly, unnatural. It had come out of the car which had come out of the future.

'She knows you're coming,' Siân said, 'but not when. Ripley thought it better we didn't make it too official. So you're starting from scratch, as an exorcist. But you should know the patter by now. Merrily, are you all right?'

'Yes, I'm...'

'You sound disconnected,' the Archdeacon's voice said out of the anachronism.

'I am. Suddenly, everything is.'

She looked down at the river, far more polluted now than it looked. *The whole valley is steeped in a history that remains with us,* Siân said in her head.

In spite of the closure of churches, she'd read that more people were thinking about spiritual issues, wondering if there was some vast plan behind this upsurge of mortality – this, in effect, was what some bishop had said on a radio breakfast programme a couple of days ago, with no suggestion of how lesser clerics might use it. He hadn't suggested why people like Merrily were waking in the dark hours of the morning, asking with bleak irreverence, what the *fuck* am I doing in this job?

Merrily ran a cold forefinger around the inside of her dog collar. It felt constrictive, wouldn't be required for this job. But she was stuck with it now. It was what she did.

She got back in the Freelander, let it roll downhill towards Goodrich, managing to remember how, with Sophie, she'd found the church.

She wedged the car in the grass verge leading to the footpath that provided access to the rough field bordering the graveyard and leading to the Meyrick tomb. It all looked very bright in the sunshine, actually cheerful.

She gathered up the mobile and rang Sophie at home.

'I'm going back to Goodrich,' she said. 'So I thought I'd ask if you'd heard anything else.'

It was Andrew, her husband, who'd learned about the anguished animal-roaring in the dawn on two consecutive days. He didn't believe it, Sophie had said. Well, of course he didn't. People heard noises, made connections.

Sophie coughed.

'And yet you thought I should be aware of it,' Merrily said.

'I'd thought – quite suddenly, I thought you should be aware of everything, no matter how unlikely I'd considered it.'

Merrily said nothing. This didn't sound like Sophie.

'So I… told you.'

No it *didn't* sound like Sophie.

'Sophie, are you…?'

'I've just got an annoying cough,' Sophie said.

'And your voice…'

'Sophie coughed then was silent.

'Sophie…'

'All right!'

A long silence, then…

'Andrew's rung the surgery,' Sophie said calmly.

And then Merrily was talking to Andrew Hill, who said unconvincingly that he wasn't too worried about Sophie, although she did appear to have symptoms and they'd know more this afternoon, when perhaps Merrily could…

Yes, yes, she'd call back this afternoon, as soon as…

Oh God.

While Merrily was still processing the flat, deadening news, another call came through on the mobile.

It was from Jane who was across the road at Lol's, both of them trying to interpret an eight-year-old girl's understanding of infant mortality.

24

A sleep and a forgetting

'BLOODY HELL, MUM,' Jane said on the phone. 'You're saying this kid had the Sight?'

Merrily switched the mobile to speaker and laid it on the passenger seat, next to the poetry book the Archdeacon had pressed on her.

'All the signs are here.' Jane's voice had gone lower, was more controlled. 'Is it only me who hears them? Look... If she's, like, actually seeing and talking to her dead siblings – at least, her brother – in the churchyard... and if she's chatting to them over her supper... like, what's all that telling us?'

It was the first time Jane had sounded this excited in weeks. Calling her in the car from Lol's cottage, energised by a borderline-mystical William Wordsworth poem from over two centuries ago. Ever since discovering that Wordsworth, as a young man, had been a near-pagan, Jane had felt obliged to enlighten Lol and Merrily about the unearthly secrets she was finding in his work.

Merrily pictured her standing by Lol's sunny sitting-room window, following the narrative in the book, as the poet recalled his conversation with the little girl he'd encountered walking down from the ruins of Goodrich Castle. The girl telling him about her family, not drawing a distinction between the ones she still saw, and the ones grown up and gone to sea, or wherever… and…

> *'Two of us in the church-yard lie,*
> *My sister and my brother;*
> *And, in the church-yard cottage, I*
> *Dwell near them with my mother.'*

'Don't you get it?' Jane said. 'She knows they're dead, but she isn't sad, because she knows exactly where they are.'

'Goodrich churchyard?'

Merrily looked through the car windscreen at the haphazard, sloping gravestones a few paces away, most of them with the names worn off.

It couldn't have changed much here since the late eighteenth century. Merrily summoned the image of a yellow-haired child skipping between the bent-over headstones in the untrimmed grass.

'…and knows how to get through to them,' Jane said.

> *My stockings there I often knit,*
> *My kerchief there I hem;*
> *And there upon the ground I sit,*
> *And sing a song to them.*

Lol had said he'd thought about what kind of song this kid might have sung to the dead… and found himself starting to write it. That sort of thing was what made him an interesting songwriter and might one day make him famous. One day.

> *And often after sun-set, Sir,*
> *When it is light and fair,*

I take my little porringer,
And eat my supper there.

Seeing these words on paper gave the poem a spooky sense of reality that hadn't emerged when Merrily had been checking it online for the name *Churchyard Cottage.*

'OK, they died, as we say,' Jane said. 'But the kid doesn't think of them as bodies rotting in the earth, because she's like… still communicating with them.'

The first that died was sister Jane;
In bed she moaning lay,
Till God released her of her pain;
And then she went away.

Merrily thought of Sophie, who would be in bed by now. She had all the symptoms. Her breath was getting weaker. Her sense of taste had been gone some time. She could be in hospital before long.

'And then she went away, but she didn't go far,' Jane said.

Hereford Hospital was five or ten minutes away in an ambulance with the siren turned on. Would they use the siren? *It's just precautionary,* Andrew Hill had told Merrily. But that was what they always said.

Merrily said, 'You're pushing it a bit, flower. It's just a poem about children's understanding of everyday mortality.'

'Exactly. The introductory verse of "We Are Seven" is generally seen as explaining everything. The child that "feels its life in every limb – what should it know of death?" Oh, it's about a little girl developing an understanding of mortality. But she's *eight years old* and a country kid! Her dad almost certainly keeps livestock and the fields and the woods are full of sheep bones. She doesn't wear pretty dresses and sleep in a nursery. She lives next to a graveyard and she knows lots of village families who've lost children. *Of course* she knows what death is.'

'Isn't Wordsworth – born and raised in rural Cumbria – just playing the part of the dim townie to get her talking?'

'Of course he is.'

'And the child's being literal, the way kids are,' Merrily said. 'Her sister and brother are in the churchyard. She goes to talk to them over her supper.'

'And don't you think they understand more than we can imagine?'

So in the church-yard she was laid;
And, when the grass was dry,
Together round her grave we played,
My brother John and I.

'"We *played*",' Jane said. 'Get it? They're having *fun*. The living and the dead. Having fun together. In those days, mortality in the average family was much more commonplace. And, as a young child she's closer to it. She's eight years old… just a few years away from… *not living.* Like… inhabiting the great void.'

And when the ground was white with snow,
And I could run and slide,
My brother John was forced to go,
And he lies by her side.

'You're seeing more than he wrote,' Merrily said carefully.

'The *great void*,' Jane said, 'which you can enter from either side. Now she's had a few years on *this* side. She isn't sad. She has a foot on each shore of the great divide. Young children do.'

'You remembered that?'

'I don't think I wanted to. Kids don't. Life's so exciting they want to seize the future. I can remember wanting that. And maybe that's what Wordsworth's trying to find out, the way he's questioning the kid: if she actually remembers! Interrogating her, approaching the same conundrum from different directions.'

'You run about, my little Maid,
Your limbs they are alive;
If two are in the church-yard laid,
Then ye are only five.'

'How many are you, then,' said I,
'If they two are in heaven?'
Quick was the little Maid's reply,
'O Master! we are seven.'

'Seven,' Jane said. 'The most mystical number in the old days – seven stars, seven days, seven sisters. I won't go on. But "We are *Seven*"? That's all I can say, Mum. Look, talk to Lol. He knows all the social background.'

A small clatter as the phone was transferred, then Lol's voice.

'Sorry about this. I really am.'

'How did Jane get involved?'

'I… borrowed a couple of books she'd taken to her shop. Including one that explores Wordsworth's early years as a poet. When his beliefs were closer to Jane's. And when he was living around here. You remember?'

'Yes. In full colour.'

Merrily thought back to when she and Lol had visited the ornate Brinsop church, a few miles from Ledwardine, which had a window devoted to Wordsworth, 'a frequent sojourner in this parish'. Wordsworth and Mary, his wife, had buried a faithful servant here, at considerable expense – with the most lavish stone in the churchyard. Jane Winder had died during one of their holidays at Brinsop, where Mary's brother had taken over a farm.

Lol said, 'Wordsworth and me... I was reading most of that stuff for the first time, and writing songs covering the same ground. In places that had hardly changed since he was wandering around them. I came to feel we were writing about some of the same things, from the same position. Words written against a background of the mysteries of nature. Wordsworth used to think of himself as a latent druid?'

Vaguely remembering, Merrily sighed. This would explain Jane's intermittent interest in the great poet, whose youthful near-paganism was glossed over in most of the biogs.

'I guess a lot of people messed with Druidism around the end of the eighteenth century,' she said. 'Pre-hippies, basically – Wordsworth's daffodil-children. A guy who called himself Iolo Morganwg started a kind of druid cult in east Wales in Wordsworth's time. I don't *think* they met but...'

'Then there was a scientific revolution,' Lol said, 'and an industrial surge that put spiritual stuff on the back-burner until the early years of the twentieth century.'

'And threatened Wordsworth's continuing reputation...' Jane was grabbing the phone from Lol '...if he stayed on his *sacred nature* path into the new era...'

'Yeah, that could be close,' Lol said. 'There was a lot of literary criticism of "We Are Seven" in the next century and most of it's predictable, lofty stuff about kids needing to get real and come to terms with mortality.'

Jane was audible in the background, sounding wistful.

'It's a simple, clockwork poem – a kid's poem – which is why some people didn't like it. But it's far from naive. This girl's outsmarting Wordsworth all the way, and he knows that, although he's not admitting it. And the religion… Like, I don't know whether a village kid would even've gone to school much in the 1790s… but she's throwing the orthodox religious stuff back at him.'

'He's going, Oh, their spirits are in heaven,' Lol said. 'And she's saying, Huh… that's all *you* know…'

Merrily could hear Lol beginning to side with Jane, and Jane identifying with the child, like she'd been there too.

Lol said, 'Wordsworth's subtext appears to be that the little maid has… or thinks she has…'

'The *Sight*.' Jane's voice was suddenly more alive. 'Sharing her supper with the dead in Goodrich churchyard? What's she really saying?'

'You might be pushing it a tiny bit,' Merrily said. 'Or more than a bit.'

'No, I'm not, Mum. The poem's pointing out that, as you get older, you gradually lose what you once instinctively understood although you were too young to put it into words: the knowledge that when your human body stiffens and rots and stuff, it's… actually *not the end*. Young children are closer to all this life and death stuff. They always have been.'

Or maybe they aren't.

Silence. A breeze was trying to awaken budded daffodils in the small field approaching the graves.

Lol said, 'Something was certainly making Wordsworth sit up. Throughout his life, he kept trying to find this girl again. He was in Goodrich nearly fifty years later and regretting he couldn't find any trace of someone he'd found so interesting.'

'If she was still round by then, she'd be in like late middle-age,' Jane said. 'As old as...'

Sophie, Merrily thought.

'She made a serious impression on him. You could have thought he'd made up this whole conversation to show that the facts about death and dying are something that all children have to come to in time, but...'

'But there was obviously more. This kid knew she could still communicate with the brother and sister who were said to be dead and buried in the churchyard at the bottom of the garden.'

That was Jane's expected interpretation, and it would actually be good to think it wasn't entirely baseless, if only to annoy the Bishop, who made no secret of his blanket dismissal of alleged paranormal phenomena.

Lol said, 'Wordsworth wrote a poem called "Ode: Intimations of Immortality". As close as he came to declaring an opinion on this issue. I remembered a couple of lines.'

'Yes...'

Merrily remembered them, too: *Our birth is but a sleep and a forgetting. The Soul that rises with us, our life's star, hath had elsewhere its setting and cometh from afar...*

Suggestions of reincarnation?

Don't go there. Don't fire Jane up.

'Listen...' She lowered her voice. 'I'll call you back later. I've someone to see about this. It shouldn't take long.'

As soon as she tossed the mobile onto the passenger seat, it chimed again.

'Yer all right, Merrily?'

'I hope so, Frannie. Listen, I'm in the car, but I swear to God it's not moving.'

'Yeh, but you're holding the phone, see. That's more than

borderline, vicar. Luckily… I need a bit of help. On the quiet. Very much so.'

He was calling on his mobile, which meant this was private.

'You've done this before for me – talked to somebody in a way I can't. I've gorra copper who's going through stuff they don't tell you about at police college. Or university, come to that.'

25

Husks

THE FRONT DOOR of Churchyard Cottage was oaken and studded, no more than fifty years old. When she began to tap on it, she saw that it was ajar, as if she was expected.

'Just leave them on the step, will you, Paula, hands are wet.'

The voice was educated English, smooth but airy. A professional voice. A moment later Merrily saw tight jeans and a nylon gilet over a chunky sweater with big pink stars on it. Dense, dark hair.

'Ms Madden?'

She was in her mid-twenties. A lecturer in English Lit at Southampton University when the Wikipedia entry Merrily had read last night had been submitted. Now apparently freelance, working mainly for TV, on programme research, occasional presentation.

'My apologies,' Maya Madden said. 'I thought you were the postperson.'

Merrily stayed outside the door.

'Sorry to just arrive like this. If you're busy...'

'No, it's fine.'

Ms Madden fully opened the front door, came down from the step. Her mother, according to Google, was an Indian nurse, her father from an English military family. Her voice suggested private school.

Behind her, Merrily saw St Giles's Church fully daylit for the first time. So close it might have been a garden feature, its steeple plain and straight, beyond the mid-twentieth century semi-bungalow with one tall chimney and its name on the frayed sign hanging from a rustic archway. To reach the door, Merrily had followed a light-green conifer hedge that wound into a turning circle divided by a projecting double garage.

She decided to give Ms Madden the opportunity to end this quickly.

'Arlo Ripley, the vicar at Whitchurch, asked me to come and see you, but yesterday I was with someone who's now believed to have the virus. We can talk outside or through an open window if you like. I'm not used to the pandemic rules yet. I'm Merrily, by the way.'

'Yes, I know who you are,' Maya Madden said. 'Found you online, under a rather blurred likeness, when the Reverend Ripley's archdeacon called to say she was bringing in an *expert*...' Hands on hips. That's a pure conceit, though, isn't it? There *are* no experts in this field, whatever the Church likes to claim.'

'The Church tends not to make any claims of that nature any more,' Merrily said. 'Most of us – the ones left – are just people who accept that unlikely things sometimes happen.'

'And your job is to exorcize them?'

'That's considered too spooky a word these days. We're usually just known as deliverance consultants.'

'Deliver us from evil,' Maya Madden said solemnly. 'You think the "unlikely things" that happen are actually evil?'

'Well...' Merrily stepped onto the edge of the lawn and said what she'd always wanted to say to Bishop Craig Innes. 'I think if we decide that everything we don't understand is evil, we'll never understand anything.'

A silence, then…

'I see.' Maya Madden stepped to one side, exposing the doorway. 'In that case, you'd better come in. Don't worry, I'll open windows.'

'Let the dogma get wafted away with the rest of the infection?' Merrily said.

*

'I met Mr Ripley when I was simply looking for someone with local knowledge,' Maya Madden said. 'I was told the nearest vicar could usually help.'

She drew back a floor-length velvet curtain, uncovering a French window framing a walled garden, the churchyard and the steeple, the long hill behind it topped by scrub, and a line of trees. On the other side of the glass was a narrow lawn.

'You particularly wanted *him* to remove it?' Merrily said.

'I wanted some advice. I was told he was minding this parish alongside his own.'

'If something psychically disturbing comes up, he's expected to report it. Deliverance then opens a file which usually stays open until we're satisfied nobody's in any distress, or likely to be. Which is why *I'm* here. Health and Safety. The Church of England has to cover itself.'

'I'm sorry…?'

'I expect the C of E would've warned Jesus not to walk on water,' Merrily said, 'if some impressionable little kids had been around.'

Maya Madden took some books off a sofa for Merrily to sit down.

'Look, I'm sorry…' Her hair had come unclipped. 'I *am* working for a TV company, but I'm probably not what you were starting to think. Would you like me to sign something to satisfy your people that I'm in no great distress?'

'You're not?'

'As you'll have heard I'm compiling an arts feature, to be made largely around this village.' She extended an arm along the window. 'It's no secret. This property might be on part of what used to be the parish churchyard. It's at least the third dwelling to occupy this spot, and many generations of people are thought to have been buried in what became its foundations.'

'I'm assuming that doesn't bother you a lot, because you think it's all rubbish?'

'You're actually wrong.' Maya Madden pushed the curtain back as far as it would go. 'When I agreed to rent this house, I did think it had something I might be able to use in the programme... as it supported the Wordsworth connection. I was taken on for the contract because of my knowledge of the romantic poets. William Wordsworth is believed to have had an encounter near here which he never forgot. It became the basis for a famous poem. With which – for my sins – I now live.'

'Here in Goodrich?'

'Possibly even in this house – or what was here before it. The encounter was with someone who may have lived long ago in a cottage on this site. I don't know her name and neither did he, and when they met she was only about eight years old.'

She reached out for a key emerging from the middle of the French window and turned it. When the long window swung open, she rose and pushed it and stepped outside onto the lawn, clearing her throat.

> '"Their graves are green, they may be seen,"
> The little Maid replied,
> "Twelve steps or more from my mother's door—"'

Merrily looked beyond her, over the patch of lawn. Was *this* the site of the little maid's mother's door... lawn weighed down with fat evergreens, the path snaking between them to a wooden gate set into a head-high stone wall. Over the gate, you could see a short, crooked corridor of graves, sloping towards the church. Maya Madden stepped back into the room, closing the French window behind her. Merrily said nothing.

Maya said, 'It's been suggested the girl was poetic invention, but I don't think so. I'm told there's considerable evidence that Wordsworth did actually meet someone like her. And I *think*... I think I actually saw something. Last week, not long after I moved in.' She sighed. 'I only wish it was someone else thinking they'd seen it.'

Merrily felt her eyes widening, her dog collar tightening.

'We always prefer a little distance, don't we?' Maya said. 'Academics *need* distance to establish a perspective.'

'They do?'

'Well, *I* do. I'll tell you what I may have seen, all right? As I would have told Mr Ripley. You're a priest, you've heard all this stuff before. You'll maintain a certain discretion? Accepting that I don't want to alarm the neighbours?'

'I always assume that. But... *may* have seen? You're not certain about it?'

'I'm trying to see the story from your point of view. How often do you listen to someone's story and think, yes, I fully accept that as the unvarnished truth?'

'It's happened,' Merrily said.

'All right then. I'll tell you what I was briefly convinced I'd seen.' Maya sat down again. 'Please... imagine that it's late afternoon. Approaching dusk.'

*

Through the dimming glass of the French window, it seemed you were hearing childish laughter, Maya Madden said, her voice holding a softness and yet also a precision.

'Shrill cackles and words you didn't recognize, although you understood what they were conveying. As if two kids out there were playing quite roughly, and one had pushed the other so hard it had torn a membrane in the air.'

A membrane in the air. Maya's actual phrase for it, as if this was part of a lecture she was giving. As if she'd already thought it out, choosing the right words to say something extra.

'Then,' she said, 'two or more voices were coalescing into the hollowness of… I don't know, let's just say *somewhere else* – I was looking at the garden, but the voices were not coming from it.'

She tried to laugh but quickly gave up, as if she was realizing this was not actually funny.

Merrily said, '*Are* there many children round here?'

'None of my immediate neighbours appears to have children. Well, one neighbour does get occasional visits from grandchildren, but never after dark, they're too young. On this occasion I leapt up at once and opened the French window to chase these two off. But, as soon as I opened it, the laughter just… stopped, along with all the other sounds in the atmosphere.'

It was as if the wind had been stifled, she said. All sounds of motion extracted from the atmosphere. Merrily understood what she meant by that – it was something that occasionally happened inside your ears – and now she was aware of an intelligent young woman, groping for rationality. Had begun to relate to her, as someone she might be able to work with. *Might.*

'I stood in the doorway in what seemed like complete silence for about a minute, then went out,' Maya said. 'I can't tell you how still it was. Normally you'll pick up the sound of distant cars or a door slamming somewhere. This night I realized the whole atmosphere had separated itself. At first I thought I could hear the river – which is not *that* far away, whichever direction you're facing, because it goes into loops. But this was in my head, like a child cups a curly seashell to an ear and listens to what sounds like the sea in its chambers, the ambience of a different area of time, filtering into ours. Is that something you've been told before?'

'Yes. Similar.'

Merrily was quietly excited, if not necessarily in a good way.

'Then there was a movement in the air,' Maya said. 'I remember it occurring to me that it might've been a late bird flying off to roost. I'm thinking, *silly bitch… only a bird*. And then… *oh God,* it was on the ground… a figure. Quite small. Moving towards me. But not in normal movements. In jump… jump-cuts. Like a badly-edited video, you know what I mean?'

'I think so.'

'Something hopping towards me, as a small bird does. Or a toad or something.' Maya swallowed. 'There were two of them. And they appeared basically human. Sidling up, half-shy but in a self-consciously amused… in a *grinning* way.'

'Children?'

'Didn't I say? You know the way, when you've wandered into some strange part of a town or a village where you've stopped to ask directions, and some children just come up and stand there, staring at you? Grinning inanely as if they know you.'

Merrily nodded. It had happened to her in small places, previously unknown to her: quiet villages, inner-city backstreets. Places that didn't get many strangers but always had kids of seven or eight, who were both curious and proprietorial. And you were unaccountably afraid, realizing that children could be a different kind of humanity.

'Rags,' Maya Madden said. 'They were like rags being blown. Grey cloth… clothing flapping about. One appeared to be wearing a cap of some kind and one had hair blowing out from its head. Like the husks of things.'

'Husks?'

'It's a good word, isn't it?' Maya said.

26

Other layers of time

MERRILY HAD FELT the beginnings of goosebumps, trying to picture this young woman relaying the experience to Arlo Ripley and perhaps shivering a little at the memory.

But they were only mild goosebumps, and she kept seeing Ripley fighting his syndromic urge to put a comforting, clergy-manly arm around Maya Madden, and take it from there.

'These… children… Were they… did they seem aware of you?'

'I'm not sure,' Maya said. 'I've heard of these things happening. People walking into other layers of time. Fragmented ghost stories lying around like torn-up newspapers, scattered. Perhaps I wasn't any more distinct to these… these spectral children… than they were to me.'

Merrily separated herself from the sofa as a book fell to the floor.

'Or perhaps you made them up?' she said, because she'd decided she had to. 'After reading the poem.'

It was the kind of poem you read quickly. And then thought about and discussed and read again.

*

When Maya came back into the room, both hands supported a cracked, grey-brown flat stone.

'"*Their graves are green*",' she said. '"*They may be seen*".'

She handed Merrily the stone and closed the French door behind her.

'We only know their first names from the poem. I've no idea – even here in Goodrich – what their family name might have been. And there are no suggestions here.'

Maya put down the stone on the sofa.

'I found this not far from the back door, in a flowerbed. It's the size of a small headstone. Maybe… or maybe not.'

Maya sat down in a chair across the room.

'I'm sorry for… dissing you.' She smiled. 'Is that term even used any more?'

'I've not heard it from my daughter for a while.' Merrily smiled. 'OK, let's spell this out. "We Are Seven" was written by William Wordsworth who said it had been told to him by an eight-year-old girl he met not far from here. Did she live where this house is?'

'Some neighbours think so. I don't know.'

She weighed the possible-gravestone in her hands.

Merrily said, 'These children. Did they appear to be approaching you?'

'They appeared to be getting closer… and hazier at the same time. By the time they reached me, they may have been only visible in my mind. I heard faint laughter a few times. Couldn't always see them but still… sensed them, I suppose. A moving dampness. The mustiness, the dead vegetation— It was that slightly rank churchyard smell, here in my garden. In winter. It was very wintry while they were here, increasingly cold.'

'What happened to them? Did they just fade away?'

'No. *I* did. I don't actually remember backing away from them, until I found myself sitting there, where you're sitting, with my ears kind of popping. Thinking I must have been having a mild stroke or a brain haemorrhage or something. That's what I was afraid of. We're no longer brought up to be actually scared of the supernatural, are we, as much as what our own bodies or our minds are doing to us, medically?'

'I've heard that.' Merrily realized she was now more than half believing Maya. 'What did Arlo Ripley say? You did tell him everything?'

'He was… the word would be "sympathetic", but I'm not sure he believed me. He asked if I wanted him to pray with me. I said I was uncomfortable with all that, and he said…'

She stopped speaking.

'He said what?'

'He said…' Maya Madden looked embarrassed, set down the stone at her feet. 'He asked how I thought William Wordsworth would feel, and I said, I thought he'd be slightly uncomfortable about it.'

Maya leaned back, half-smiling. She stood up, moved to a cupboard on the wall behind Merrily, opened it and backed away, holding a picture in a pine frame.

'Of course that would depend on when he was asked. If it was around the time he was in this area, he'd be less comfortable about accepting a blessing from you because – I'm sorry – as a young man, he didn't do God.'

'Who did he do?'

'Nature,' Maya said. 'He did Nature.'

'*Mother* Nature? We all do her, in our own ways.'

'He didn't mention Nature as maternal, but I do think he saw her as female.'

Merrily said, 'My… daughter goes that way. Nature as a female deity. She liked Wordsworth more when she saw him as a possible pagan, paying homage to an ancient goddess.'

'A *druid*, even?' Maya opened her arms. 'In an early version of *The Prelude*, the long poem which charts the development of Wordsworth's poetic mind, he refers to himself as a youthful druid taught primeval mysteries in shady groves. He got rid of that opinion later, but when he was a young man it seemed to suit his purposes.'

'Jane would lead you down these lanes and point out the actual shady groves where druids might have gathered,' Merrily said. 'She, erm… she accepts paganism. The kind that doesn't harm anybody. I hope.'

'But you're—'

Merrily felt herself blush.

'We've worked it out between us… to an extent. Things were a bit fraught for a while, when she was younger. But we came to an understanding.'

Why did she have to keep explaining this to people? Surely, all daughters gave you problems to overcome.

'I could probably do that, too,' Maya said. 'Find you some druid groves. This area in fact may be more druidic than Wordsworth's native Westmorland. The wooded hill up there – the Doward – was a significant ritual centre in the Dark Ages. With all these tight little lanes and ancient earthworks, I suppose it remains slightly sinister. And I want to convey that in my programme on Wordsworth at this crucial point in his life.'

'Crucial, why?'

'All the experts agree that it was the time when he was writing his most important work. What was empowering him then? A number of people have asked that in various books, but this will be the first time the connection has really been made visually – on TV. I'm excited. And I can show you why.'

She held the framed photo in front of Merrily. It was actually a reproduced engraving, a famous portrait of Wordsworth as a young man, with thin face and thinning hair. He was wearing a double-breasted jacket of the kind worn by some of the more stylish rock musicians in the 1960s.

'Are you going to bring him alive with an actor?' Merrily asked.

'Mmm... it's not really my decision.' Maya lowered the picture. 'Depends on what kind of budget we have. A drama-documentary would probably get us a better spot for the programme. We have some decisions to make... and time to make them.'

'With the pandemic?'

'It's on hold, of course. I'm using the time to plan a holding programme.'

'And deal with your... ?'

'Manifestation. How do *you* think it should be approached?'

'Depends on how much you believe,' Merrily said.

Maya looked uncertain.

'You mean if I believe I genuinely saw something...?'

'And – perhaps more importantly – if you believe there's some way you can deal with it. Possibly by using someone like me.'

'What do you feel?'

Merrily sighed, decided to be honest.

'I'm... not at my best, I have to say. A friend appears to have virus and may have to be taken into hospital, and I spent a lot of time with her yesterday. I *feel* all right, but...'

'Get yourself tested.'

'Yes. I'd better do that. And my daughter... and some other people.'

Then she remembered what Huw Owen often said about not leaving a possibly haunted house without doing *something* and offered Maya a blessing. Routine. Wasn't it?

Then she had a call on her mobile from the Archdeacon, and it wasn't.

27

Burial at sea

She looked downriver, towards a distant frill of rapids and then up at the steamy sky and the crag that reared behind the village like a chimney stack, taller than any church steeple and… oh *bugger*.

…this was the wrong place. This was surely Symonds Yat *East* and didn't have an obvious church. The minor road from Goodrich, where she'd been a few days ago, crossed a single-track metal-caged bridge that put Merrily in mind of some rural part of the USA. But this was British rich folks' country: pricey farmhouses projecting from the wooded hills rising in green tiers from a river racing towards weirs and cliffs and heart-stopping moments of pure spectacle. The river drew you into all that quite gently, the road diving into the trees, and a tight bend, and then the riverside village was below her under an emboldened summery sun.

This was the place where English sightseeing was born in the eighteenth century, according to Sophie.

In hospital with the virus? Which, you kept hearing – *oh God* – tended to have lethal designs on people of Mrs Hill's age. The doctors were convinced she needed to be within signing-in distance of Intensive Care.

There was a pub, the Saracen's Head, then a car park next to a place where you could hire canoes, and the *hand-ferrie* where you could cross the water in a flat-bottomed boat with the help of a pulley and a wire.

It was all here, only this was Symonds Yat *East* and if you were in a car, it was probably a dead-end. And it didn't have a church. Hell, she knew that. She needed Symonds Yat *West*, which was, as she recalled, a whole lot different.

Merrily slowed the Freelander to stalling-point.

Reversing into a cramped parking area, she sent it crawling back up to the bridge and then – no option, this time – onto the A40, the rumbling river of metal that brought tourists here at speed from the motorway network, dragged urban commerce through once-tranquil countryside and sliced the parish of Whitchurch brutally in two. The dual carriageway had also introduced urban ways. Merrily remembered reading about armed robbers holding up the High Noon services – with a name like that, you could be accused of inviting it – before burning rubber on the A40 and not getting caught.

If you didn't have a boat, a couple of minutes in the blast of traffic seemed to be the way into Symonds Yat West, where cultures continued to collide and Siân Callaghan-Clarke had said she'd be waiting.

'The church of St Dubricius at Whitchurch. Do you know it?'

'Erm... no.'

'It'll only take you a few minutes to get there.'

Merrily slowed. In the West, she saw an ancient inn and then a holiday caravan park, now entering its last weeks of out-of-season silence before this village was turned into Herefordshire's little Blackpool with its riverside bar and an amusement hall rattling with rides and gaming machines and rows of neon lights singeing the sky. As spring set in, a big wheel known as the Wye Eye would be erected to offer panoramic views of the valley. Until then, Symonds Yat West in the parish of Whitchurch would be sunk into its winter coma: flat, grey and mainly deserted. A small sign directed her away from the ranked caravans and into a narrow, tree-darkened lane. It led, sooner than expected, to a cluster of trees and a small church with a compact bell-tower, built of local stone and sitting like a fledgling cygnet at the river's edge.

The church of St Dubricius had a history close to legend, as she'd just read on her phone. Dubricius was the illegitimate son of the daughter of Peibio, the king of the early medieval Welsh kingdom of Ergyng. When he knew she was pregnant, his grandfather threw his mother into the Wye but she somehow escaped drowning, the unborn baby, too.

Dubricius was eventually born in Madley, the other side of Hereford. He and his mother were somehow reconciled with Peibio and the child became precociously brilliant. By the time he'd grown up he was already known as a scholar throughout Britain. Dubricius founded local monasteries, became the teacher of Welsh future saints, healed the sick through the laying on of hands and was appointed Bishop of Ergyng. At the end of his distinguished career, he retired to the sacred Bardsey Island in North Wales where, like many other saints, he was eventually buried, before his body was transferred to Llandaff Cathedral, Cardiff in 1120. According to legend, he'd crowned King Arthur who himself only existed according to legend.

If this was Dubricius's main church, appropriately alongside the River Wye, was this where his pregnant mother was said to have been thrown in? The crude barbarity of it came home to Merrily for the first time, standing between her car and the Archdeacon's red Mazda, empty and the only other vehicle in the church's small parking area.

'Merrily...' Siân Callaghan-Clarke walked down from the puddled church porch, pulling on her cloche hat. 'I can't get in, but the churchwarden told me the worst on the phone.'

'You're saying it's had a flood?'

Must have read about it in the *Hereford Times*, but there'd been no real relevance then.

'Worst in two hundred years,' Siân said. 'Won't be back in use for several months. That's why I wanted you to read the history.'

'Legend, surely?'

'In this area, it's all the same. History doesn't go away.'

'Let's not overreact.'

'Overreact?' Siân spun to face Merrily. 'Did that come from *you*?'

Lines in her face had suddenly deepened. As if to hold water, Merrily thought, saying nothing. She felt nervous, wondered what was coming.

'I realize that what I'm asking is irregular and possibly short-notice,' the Archdeacon said. 'Consider it a favour. These are not normal times, as we all keep saying...'

'Erm, does whatever it is involve breaking the lockdown?'

'Like all services that can't be postponed, it will be taking place outside the church. Because of the virus restrictions, there'll only be a handful of people attending. So, no, it won't be breaking the lockdown. I hope.'

'I... don't understand.' Merrily saw that Siân Callaghan-Clarke was dressed for work – not her current work, not a priest, more like the barrister she used to be.

'The funeral's next week. It would have been the biggest funeral this year in the diocese,' she said. 'But not now, with attendances limited to a handful of people, even in the countryside... and that includes a TV crew...'

Merrily backed away. *TV...?*

'They'll probably want just a short clip of video. He wasn't *that* famous outside the area.'

'Is this Peter Portis, the climber?'

'It is.'

'So why are you telling me?'

'There might eventually be a memorial service,' Siân said. 'When this pandemic is out of the way. You'll just have a short service at the graveside here with about half a dozen people.'

'*Me?* You want me do the funeral? I didn't know him.'

'Merrily, you're discreet and efficient. And you know the background.'

'No, I don't!'

There was nobody else here. No movement, no voices, no traffic sounds, although the A40 wasn't too far away. The houses nearby were probably holiday homes, empty. The Archdeacon leaned against the car door and lowered her voicc.

'The funeral would've been conducted here by Arlo Ripley. Maya Madden will tell you why it won't now be him. Why he'll be leaving this parish, quite abruptly.'

'He's *leaving*?'

'I wanted you to hear it first from Maya.'

'Maya?'

'They'll be working together when Arlo plays the part of William Wordsworth in her forthcoming TV production.'

'What?'

Siân frowned.

'It's not a conspiracy, Merrily. But I think we'd both prefer to see him resume his acting career. Which means he'll be leaving the Church quite quickly – which the pandemic will help. If we don't want a mass of press attention, it has to be done quickly and quietly.'

Siân looked around, patting her coat, as if in need of a cigarette.

'Personally, *I* just want him out of this diocese, but Maya's more specific. Very much wants him as her William Wordsworth – simply because he's perfect for the part. I'm not supposed to know this, but she's been after him since the first time she saw him in the next parish.'

'Which she's now admitting?'

'If she gets him, I suspect his career will soar and hers will... progress. And I myself... well, I shall feel a lot safer with what I know.'

Merrily said nothing. Felt she was in the middle of something that was suddenly drawing several unlikely people together.

The Archdeacon said, 'I'm also aware – and this troubles me considerably, even though my role in deliverance has receded – that the position of diocesan exorcist no longer exists for this bishop. And your only hope of survival here is for him to move out. Am I making sense?'

Unexpectedly she was, even if you accepted that the Welsh border was one of the few areas where deliverance, in the old sense, still appeared relevant.

'With the pandemic closing in,' Siân said, 'it's difficult for any major decisions to be taken and followed through. At the moment, you're the only person I can trust to quietly relieve the Rev. Ripley until it's too late for the Bishop to intervene. The funeral has been arranged for next Wednesday, late afternoon.'

Tap-tap. The ghost-briar in Merrily's head unaccountably sped up as another vehicle pulled into the car park, pulling a trailer carrying a cream canoe.

*

'Worshippers used to arrive by boat,' Adrian Fenn, the churchwarden, said. 'Essential in the days when flooding was almost routine.

'Even today, when the churchyard gets swallowed by the river, a funeral can be like a burial at sea.'

He was fresh-faced, with springy white hair, and, as he told Merrily, two canoes. He pointed to the grassy bank, which was neatly aligned with the silvery River Wye. He said he thought Peter Portis would have liked the idea of the river enlivening his last resting place.

They were standing outside the church porch at the foot of a preaching cross. The tufted grass around it looked squashy but not too flooded to cross.

'The service will take place around the prepared grave, close to the Wye,' Adrian Fenn said. 'They want to complete it fairly quickly. There could be more floodwater coming down, and they won't change the grave. Peter was very protective about the risk element. Estate agents are supposed to be keen on more and more development, but he relished the sense of danger here. Loved the rocks and the rapids, if not the, ah, candyfloss side.'

'This is where the word "picturesque" was first coined,' the Archdeacon said. 'But it didn't mean chocolate-box in those days, it meant awe-inspiring.'

Adrian Fenn sandwiched the view between his arms as if he was accepting control of it.

'Peter liked the valley to be respected, not treated as a side-show. Said it was a place to measure yourself against, physically and, ah...'

'Spiritually?' Merrily said.

'He did say that it challenged the spirit, but I'm inclined to think he meant that in an endurance sense.'

It seemed he knew the Archdeacon. He presented Merrily with an envelope.

'Copies of press reports about Peter Portis's climbing history.' He turned and pointed at a hill that was like a shadow on the sky beyond the village of Symonds Yat West. 'He lived privately up there, near the Seven Sisters. But his attitude wasn't just a not-in-my-backyard thing. He campaigned – sometimes behind the scenes – to prevent some of the more expensive housing projects, while supporting economic new housing for first-time buyers. He was well-liked for that, locally. And, of course, respected as a sportsman.'

'How long had you known him?' Siân asked.

'Since my wife and I came here. More than three years ago. Peter had always been a generous patron of this church. He…' a hesitant chuckle… 'he offered to give me basic climbing lessons. Said that would put me in touch with the area – hauling oneself up to crevices known only to peregrine falcons. Had to admit I just didn't have the head for it. I said would canoeing do? And he laughed and said it was the next best option.'

In the past few minutes two or three canoeists had gone gliding past, glimpsed between trees and bushes, the only sign of where the churchyard ended and the river began.

'He knew I wanted to be *useful* to the area,' Adrian Fenn was saying. 'I'd always wanted to retire while still physically fit enough to make a meaningful contribution. I was honoured to be asked to be churchwarden… feeling I could really help, as a former chartered accountant.'

Merrily nodded. So many people who retired to the country realized in dismay that they were regarded as no more than long-term tourists and searched around for a role.

'Peter understood,' he said. 'I'll miss him. In an area like this, one gets to know people surprisingly quickly, and when they die…'

'A death tends to echo in the countryside,' Merrily said.

'Indeed. All the way to the Far Hearkening Rock.'

'Sorry?'

'I was being whimsical.' He smiled ruefully. 'It's a natural rock across the river from the Seven Sisters, where Peter fell. Supposed to bounce sound back up the valley. Once used, apparently, as an alert for poachers or something. I always meant to go and find it. Perhaps I will now, though I suppose that part of the valley will always make me feel rather sad.'

Merrily said, 'Were you surprised to hear Mr Portis had died in a fall there? I gather it was near his home. He fell from rocks he probably knew rather well…'

'Or *thought* he did. Many people have made that mistake. And climbers probably accept that the most beautiful places can't always be trusted to be the most kind.' He looked at Merrily. 'Have you talked to the family yet?'

'May not be too necessary,' Siân said. 'This will be quite rudimentary. Think burial rather than funeral, as we all have to do in a pandemic.'

Keep social distance, Merrily thought. *Dig a hole, drop him in*. Wondering how it was being done in Huw Owen's parish, south of Brecon.

Part Three

'Men of taste' were beginning to lose their sense of disgust at the sight of barren, useless mountains and to experience them with a sense of pleasant horror.

Susan Peterken,
Landscapes of the Wye Tour
(Logaston Press, 2008)

28
Darth

OPENING THE FRONT door in the dark, Merrily was realizing that in the seventeenth century, all vicarage doorways must have been conspicuously lower. Even today, it was as if this visitor was stooping out of the future, half his head lopped off by the lintel.

'Who…?'

Oh God, she'd completely forgotten he was coming tonight and that he was so tall. She didn't know him well – had only seen him a couple of times, although she could hardly forget him; policemen weren't so obviously lofty any more.

Frannie Bliss had a name for him. A name from a popular film. Apart from his size, he didn't resemble the character at all.

'I'm David Vaynor.' The visitor put out a hand then swiftly snatched it back, remembering. 'Sorry. I think we've met before, briefly. But I realize this might be inconvenient… against government advice, even…'

'Nothing's convenient right now.' Merrily took a step back into the hallway. 'But Frannie Bliss thinks, for some reason, that we need to talk, so… please come in.'

He bobbed down, revealing the rest of his face in the light above the door. He was even younger than she remembered, and he looked more than a little unsure. She knew that Frannie Bliss liked him but, with a foot in height and a PhD between them, wasn't yet sure why.

'I suppose you know what I'm supposed to do in this diocese,' she said.

'Though I'm not sure I understand what it means.' He followed her into the kitchen, where she kept the length of the refectory table between them. 'I'm supposed to be a detective, but I accept there are things I can't detect.'

Her dog collar lay on the table in front of her. Not for the first time, she wished she could make it disappear. Or that she had an intelligent dog it would fit.

Vaynor said, 'The DI sometimes thinks people are responsible for certain things that are wrong but that we, as police, can't move against them in the normal way. Is that something you can get your head round, Mrs Watkins?'

She nodded because that was what Bliss would expect.

'Things happen… that we can't always explain. For some reason, Frannie thinks they don't happen for him, but occasionally do for me. Which may not be right, but… call me Merrily. We'll see how it goes.'

*

It was about seven p.m. and she'd been alone. Jane was up in her apartment, probably on the phone to Eirion, assuring him that a specialist had suggested on the radio tonight that both of them were in an age group too low to attract the virus. Vaynor clearly couldn't be even ten years older than Jane, but at an age where ten years was a long time. Merrily pulled out a chair for him.

'I've not had the virus, but… no obvious symptoms. I'm not coughing and I can still taste things. And the church is closed – most of my regular congregation seems to be isolating.'

The lamp on the dresser was mellowing the old room. She

sat down at the kitchen table. It would at least reduce the faintly ludicrous height difference between them.

'We've not really had much to do with each other before,' she said. 'Frannie Bliss phoned me a couple of hours ago. The arrangement is that I won't phone him back. Whatever you tell me stays in here, and he accepts that.'

'Church rules?'

'You won't get any unsolicited advice, prayers or offers of spiritual help from me,' Merrily said. 'I'd offer you a mug of tea, but I don't think I'm supposed to – Downing Street rules.'

*

Halfway across the scullery, Jane stopped.

Whoever this was, he must have parked in the street outside the gates and walked quietly to the front door, otherwise she'd have heard him from her apartment.

She always counted on creeping to the kitchen via the back stairs to the scullery. It was just that she didn't want Mum to know she was borrowing a Wordsworth book before they all went back to Lol tomorrow. Wordsworth – a bit tedious to her at school – was suddenly deeply interesting. Most of the teachers at Jane's school, if they thought he was any good, had probably decided that the young Wordsworth must have been quite a decent atheist. In fact – why was this always covered up at schools and colleges? – he'd been *a pagan*. Worshipping the gods of nature. *Her* kind of poet, and no damn teacher had ever told her.

Jane heard through the wall that Mum and the guy were talking about Frannie Bliss now, which suggested this visitor was another cop. Whatever that meant. Cops, like clergy-people, weren't widely respected any more. Last night Jane had watched one of those police actuality programmes, where the cops had been failing to impress these kids they'd taken pills away from. The kids inviting them to fuck off, no immediate arrests made. You were almost surprised the cops hadn't given them back the pills.

Jane sat quietly down at the scullery desk and began to listen closely. You never knew when overhearing these private discussions might be useful.

Still pleased that Lol had liked her suggestion that he should build a song around the little girl with the departed siblings who'd inspired Wordsworth. And, bloody hell, no wonder she'd inspired him. The kid was cool.

*

'I admit to checking you out, online,' Vaynor told Merrily. 'I'm not really sure what being an exorcist means these days, and I don't know why the DI wants me to talk to you. But I don't think there were clergy like you around when I was growing up here.'

Abruptly, Merrily stood up and drew the long curtains, concealing them both from the yard and any more possible visitors.

'There've always been clergy like me around places like Hereford, Mr Vaynor. Just not women... although we're not actually sure about that any more.'

She looked round the room a little nervously, as if she might glimpse the shade of her seventeenth-century Ledwardine predecessor, Wil Williams, who'd been more than a bit ahead of his time.

'You... talked to the DI about something our senior officers don't usually want to discuss,' Vaynor said hesitantly.

'Essentially…' Merrily leaned forward, spoke quietly but fast. 'Frannie Bliss doesn't want to know what you've done, in case he feels obliged to share it. But he thinks somebody *should* know. Somebody who understands certain things outside the box… and perhaps isn't a mate of the chief constable. Or the Bishop, come to that. Are you following me?'

Vaynor leaned back. He'd picked up a book from a small pile in the middle of the table left there by Jane. A thick book with a blue binding, no dust jacket, waiting to go back to Lol.

'You're reading Wordsworth?'

'I think my daughter's been reading him. How seriously I don't know.'

'I once studied him fairly seriously,' Vaynor said. 'He's further off the wall than most people realize.'

Merrily looked up.

'Jane's interested in a little girl who lived at Goodrich and met Wordsworth. The one in the poem called "We Are Seven". Which you'll know.'

'I once did some work on that child,' Vaynor said. 'Trying to find out who she was. There were a couple of families with seven children in that part of Goodrich at the time, but neither seemed quite right to me.'

'Jane thinks that, if she existed, the girl had psychic abilities. Would sometimes see her siblings.'

'After they'd died?"

'And talk to them. In the graveyard next to where she lived. Over supper. As, I'm afraid, Jane would've done herself. Or tried to.'

Vaynor produced a small smile.

'Psychic matters were not exactly in fashion in the early nineteenth century. Which didn't necessarily mean they didn't happen, but science, essentially, was taking over.'

Merrily said, 'I'm told Wordsworth was actually advised to drop the poem from a book that he and the Ancient Mariner guy were putting together.'

'Coleridge. *Lyrical Ballads*, it was called. One of his most significant collections. In Wordsworth's poems, ghost stories tended to be attributed to other people. He sits on the fence, usually, and so I'm afraid he was unlikely ever to have consulted someone like you.'

'I don't doubt that, Mr Vaynor.'

Vaynor was silent for a moment.

'I don't think he wanted to be thought of as someone who was completely open to that sort of thing,' he said eventually. 'Although he did come close to it when he spent time around here, as you probably know... or can imagine.'

Merrily said nothing. No, she didn't know but was starting to imagine. Vaynor tapped the complete poems.

'Have you read the one usually just called "Tintern Abbey", although the abbey's not in it? Perhaps he just wanted to obscure the *real* location.'

'No. Well... not since I was at school, when I expect I thought it was a bit mixed up. I guess I was too young then to make much of it.'

'It's usually said to be Wordsworth's best work,' Vaynor said. 'Written at the time when his genius was becoming evident. When I think something got into him, stimulating him in a way he hadn't known before.'

'I seem to remember it's actually set several miles upstream from Tintern Abbey. In fact, here in Herefordshire. You think something in this area stimulated him?'

'And would eventually scare him into toning down his poetry,' Vaynor said. 'My, um... my PhD thesis set out to find out what that was. But I don't think I managed it.'

The electrified oil lamp on the kitchen dresser seemed to go dimmer for a moment. Or perhaps she just thought it did because it had before when something uncanny was being tentatively approached. Like the way a briar used to scrape the outside wall of the scullery under the window. In this job, you noticed the recurrence of small things that meant nothing or perhaps hadn't happened at all.

'And *please*... don't call me Mr Vaynor,' he said.

Merrily smiled. She now remembered learning about Darth a year or so ago, before being asked by Bliss to watch some interview-room video of Vaynor looming over a suspect, probably not intending to appear menacing.

'I don't think it was meant to be flattery,' Vaynor said, 'but it doesn't matter. At least it doesn't sound like an academic.'

'You don't want to sound like an academic?'

'It hasn't helped me much in the police.'

She began to understand why his DI might have taken to him. Because he had this lurid Scouse accent, Bliss was regarded by colleagues as a hard man, but when you'd grown up surrounded by people who spoke like that and maybe used to a bit yourself, you saw another side of him.

'Frannie Bliss is very clever,' she said.

'Cleverest man in Gaol Street.' Vaynor nodding. 'By a mile.'

'Including you?'

He smiled, appeared to relax. Both had the same opinion of Bliss who probably hadn't progressed far beyond GCSE level.

'Darth, erm... do you have a copy of your thesis anywhere?'

She wanted to read it. Wanted know where he was coming from.

He shook his head.

'I gave it away. The rights to it. Gave it all to a girl who now seems to have dumped me for walking away from my qualifications.'

'You did that?'

'She thought I'd done the wrong thing, joining the police.'

'Does it matter?'

'Obviously did to her. And perhaps people in CID by now. You'll find it online. Under the pen name Al Fox.'

Vaynor gazed into the wood stove.

'All I know is that both of us have reasons to instinctively dislike the same man. With me that went back to schooldays. But I'm not sure that makes him a murderer.'

29
Finger

WANTED TO BE a detective for as long as he could remember, originally because his grandad said it was the best job in the world. A detective sergeant, up in Cheshire, Grandad was – one of the good guys committed to nailing the bad guys, but not necessarily with a hammer.

Vaynor's dad, who worked for the NatWest bank as a clerk, wasn't impressed and hadn't seen all that much of his old man. Got himself switched to the Hereford branch, and the family moved down-country and, though David didn't get to spend much time any more with his grandad, the stories didn't stop.

In the end, the main problem, Vaynor said, was that his parents were increasingly euphoric about him doing so well at school, and when he was accepted to read Eng Lit at Oxford... well, he could hardly puncture their pride at that stage, could he?

And he'd worked it out to his own satisfaction, how the two careers merged: a detective found and followed narratives in people's lives, which he infiltrated in periods of high drama, apprehension and sometimes naked fear.

Vaynor explained how the conflict didn't exactly go away in his last year at Oxford when he wound up renting two rooms in the suburban house of Eddie and Mary Masters. Eddie was a DCI coming to the end of his thirty with Thames Valley Police and already checking out cold-case openings for retired detectives on the basis that the brain *shouldn't* have to quit if it was still functioning to full capacity.

Merrily realized the wood stove was burning low and picked up a log. Vaynor said he'd never told anybody all this before. He edged to the front of his chair, said that for a long time he hadn't known which way to turn. Having nightmares about it. Analysing detailed crime reports in the papers and at the same time working on his PhD and remembering his last years at school and how, when you were six and a half feet tall, you didn't get bullied, just avoided.

He'd been new at the Cathedral school, a scholarship boy, from a less-affluent part of town than most of his class.

'Nobody knew me. I didn't know Royce Portis but I did learn quite soon that he was a bully who other boys didn't mess with. Had to do well for my dad, so I worked hard and got into Oxford.'

'Well done,' Merrily said carefully.

'Knowing there'd be a major row when I told them I wanted to go into the police, not education. And that I'd be putting out the wrong signals if I tried to finger Royce Portis.'

'Finger him for...?'

'For the money he was collecting from fellow pupils. For a few things. Like protection from another boy, who was a heroin dealer... and a violent kid on the side.'

'Was Royce protecting *you*?'

'He might have offered, and I turned it down. I didn't have any money then, anyway. And this guy... the police got him in the end – not because of me. He's off the hook again now, and back in business, I believe. But he's not clever, and we'll get him again...'

'You're saying you had a drug dealer at a private school?'

'No, not at the school,' Vaynor said. 'But Royce Portis had friends in town, connected with drug business. Small-time dealers. He did recreational… I didn't finger him, not wanting to be known as some kind of grass. Kept quiet. And then it was the end of term, and Royce left, went to join his dad's estate agency, as he was expected to – his career was mapped out. I wasn't aware of him again until I came to Gaol Street, but I guess he remembered we'd been at school together.'

Merrily said nothing.

'It's a small city,' Vaynor said. 'We were the two tallest boys at the school. *He* was the tallest until I turned up, and I was an inch higher despite being a year younger. And at the time he was *never* going to forgive me for that. No matter how mild and inoffensive I was… I had no idea at the time what he—'

He broke off. Merrily stared at him, wanting him to spell it out… about the indefinite thing at the core of this. So far, she couldn't see any reason Bliss might have seen for her to be involved.

'In most cases,' Vaynor said, 'a property is the most valuable item a man or woman will ever acquire. If you own property, you're on the way to owning people.'

'Some people do seem to think that.'

'*Some people* think he's on his way to owning much of the posh end of the Wye Valley,' Vaynor said. 'You can see all his signs on property and land. And an estate agent's not just a shopkeeper.'

'If his firm seems to have bought a lot of property there, does that suggest…?'

'It's not criminal. It's just… business.'

'So – can I ask? – what does Frannie Bliss find especially interesting?'

'He just doesn't like Portis. Thinks I know something about

him that I'm keeping to myself. Royce Portis once sold a house to the DI and his wife, and it wasn't a bargain.'

'*Former* wife now, I think.'

'Yes. I believe she persuaded the DI to buy it. He never liked it and maybe got into a negative-equity situation when his marriage ended.' He stared down at the flagged floor. 'I've heard of people Royce Portis is supposed to have ripped off on house deals.'

'Nobody closer to you than Bliss?'

'I… managed to avoid Royce at school, but years later I couldn't… And then there was Peter Portis's fall – odd things about it if it was accidental, and there was nothing to suggest it wasn't. Or suicide… for which there was no explanation.'

'Bliss thinks Peter Portis was murdered by his son?'

'He'd like to think that.'

'But…' Merrily was now hunched at the end of her seat, 'there's something else you're not telling me.'

'When I was sent to talk to him this week, his wife was there, too. Who, before they were married, was his colleague, his father – Peter – having given her a job at his new Whitchurch branch.' He leaned back, averting his eyes from Merrily's. 'Her name's Diana. And this is the difficult bit, Mrs…'

'Merrily.'

'Yes, I'm sorry. This is where it gets… onto another level. I knew her. I *think* I knew her well… had somehow known her… for years.' He kept on looking away from Merrily, as if he was searching for another door in the rooms, to give him a mercifully quick getaway. 'Maybe too well.'

30

Laid asleep in body

HAD HE ACTUALLY gone emotionally to pieces? In the kitchen? In front of Mum?

Jane couldn't be sure. But he was clearly getting to something he really didn't want to be talking about.

She put her ear so close to the scullery wall that the skin felt sore. She'd been growing to kind of like the guy. He was local; gradually the Hereford accent had let itself get unrolled. And if he'd had a thing going with the woman who would later become Mrs Portis, what did that matter? They'd both been young at the time, presumably. These things happened.

Then, as her hands coaxed a deeper purr out of Ethel, it became clear to her that this was not going to be so simple.

Vaynor was saying the thing had happened twice, the first time when he was developing his PhD thesis, visiting the places Wordsworth drew on to create his most profound poetry in the work known as "Tintern Abbey".

The first place where it happened was an old property, older than Tintern Abbey.

Much older.

Even with a map, it had taken Vaynor most of a day to find King Arthur's Cave. Jane had been there on a separate occasion, with Mum, about a year after they'd moved to Herefordshire.

A one-time Stone Age dwelling chewed out of a cliff above the River Wye. A real cave, like you found at the seaside. It went quite a long way back into the rock, had stalactites and water-drips and a smaller chamber off its main hall. The body of a huge man was said to have been found there a century or so ago, along with some prehistoric animal bones. Jane and Mum had been at Easter and expected to find dozens of tourists there. Almost anywhere else in England, it would be a major tourist attraction: a deep and quite lofty natural cavern linked to Britain's most famous mythical monarch.

King Arthur was usually said to be Welsh, as this cave probably had been for much of its history. As nobody knew whether he'd actually existed, nobody knew if he had any connection with the outsize skeleton discovered here, now a long time missing.

Jane remembered they'd been alone, and it was a bit eerie. Herefordshire Council treated the cave like it did most tourist attractions: no directions, no signs and parking space for no more than three vehicles on the edge of a narrow lane about half a mile away.

When Darth Vaynor described to Mum how he'd got there, Jane mentally followed him, observing the landscape after they turned the corner from a small quarry downhill from where they'd left the car. Ahead of her, to the right, was an empty green field and a soft hillside. To the left, the cliff face was pocked and pitted by deep cracks and fissures, rock-shelters rather than caves, although when you took a couple of steps back they looked more impressive in the dimness: like splintered front doors in a Stone Age tenement.

The ground rose ahead of them and the stones and ruts underfoot had collected layers of deep-pile dead leaves. A spoil heap of excavated earth and stone had made her look up and… she saw, just inside one of the adjacent stone entrances, a small circle of blackened bricks enclosing a now-cold, charred log.

'"Vagrant dwellers in the houseless woods",' Vaynor said on the other side of Jane's vision and the scullery wall.

*

'Who wrote that?' Merrily asked him.

She'd been thinking of King Arthur sitting at the entrance to his stone hall, gazing down towards the Wyeside church established by Dubricius, the Bishop of Ergyng, who had crowned him. All these interlinking legends – so many of them in this small, enchanted area of the Wales–England border.

'Wordsworth, of course,' Vaynor said. 'It's always Wordsworth with me. Studied him in depth for years. He mentions a cave, but there are no suitable ones near Tintern Abbey. King Arthur's Cave is a dozen or so miles upstream, near the top of the Doward.'

It was obvious that this area was where most of the poem was set. So he'd dumped his backpack and found his torch. The cave had two chambers, one almost circular and just about high enough for him to walk around. Him and the king. *Was* this him? Was this the mythical King Arthur's original natural-stone palace?

Jane spread out the OS map, which labelled **King Arthur's Cave/Hall**, although there was no solid evidence that the king (a) ever lived there or (b) ever lived at all.

But she knew his legend was connected, by some chroniclers, with the Wye Valley. He was usually linked with places like Tintagel in Cornwall and Glastonbury, Somerset. But then Arthur was also said to have been a descendant of Vortigern, the Celtic high-king whose last refuge was thought to actually have been here, on the Doward.

So who was it who'd first claimed the semi-historic Vortigern lived here? Surely it was the famous medieval scribe, Geoffrey of Monmouth... of *Monmouth* – the compact medieval town less than five miles downriver, less important now than it had been in Geoffrey's time.

So many stories. Jane wondered, had Vortigern existed? Was he killed here? Had Geoffrey of Monmouth made up his story of Vortigern's death, in flames after the sky opened up – above the hill fort on the Doward, above this actual cave, where archaeologists found bits of lion, hyena and woolly mammoth along with the anonymous human skeleton that disappeared. Wordsworth didn't refer to any of this, despite the famous fascination with prehistory which hugely increased his appeal to Jane.

She listened to Vaynor describing how he'd climbed over rubble, letting himself get sucked into the rock chamber where he shone his torch around. From a few metres in, the floor was, he said, quite dry and some internal rocks were arranged like old and petrified furniture. He'd found a gap in the stones at the back of the circular chamber, with rocks rising like the sides of an armchair. He'd abruptly lowered himself into the prehistoric world, switching off his torch and letting his eyes close.

It wasn't a perfect fit, and there were occasional plops of what he hoped was water from the ceiling. But he stayed there, passive, letting the poet's thoughts come to him – thoughts of the river, invisibly below him. Lying not in the warm grass under a sycamore tree, where he'd lain in a kind of trance to reach for the soul of nature, instead, almost encased in rock, he'd found himself pushing away dark imaginings from *The Prelude*, the book which followed the growth of Wordsworth's poet's mind.

...no pleasant images of trees... no colours of green fields...
...o'er my thoughts there hung a darkness, call it solitude
or blank desertion. No familiar shapes remained...

As a boy in his native Cumbria, led by her – and by *her* he meant Nature, his goddess – Wordsworth had recalled borrowing a small boat tied to a willow tree and rowing out into one of the lakes where all was tranquil... until he became aware of the black bulk of mountain above him and what it represented in the hidden world. She was modifying her mood. *She* – Nature – had exercised her power, released her darkness, and...

...huge and mighty forms, that do not live like living men, moved slowly through the mind by day, and were a trouble to my dreams.

*

Vaynor said a dark thrill had entered him as events from his thesis rewoke.

Merrily edged her chair back so that more of the amber lamplight could find Vaynor. He didn't look like a policeman. It was partly his hair – a bit too long because barbers' shops had been closing against the spread of the pandemic. DCI Annie Howe, old-fashioned and proper, like her father had become – in his case, to disguise his villainy – might not approve of David's appearance. It was as if the policeman had taken over and then briefly given way again to the untidy academic he thought he'd left behind. It occurred to Merrily that Vaynor had always been forced to hide some aspect of himself to fit in with his current situation. He wouldn't have made many friends at Oxford by disclosing his police ambitions.

'At the Wye Valley stage, Wordsworth didn't know what God was,' Vaynor said. 'The weight of it came down on him here, when he returned from France and found himself in the middle of all this *nature* – more intense even than the Lake District, where he grew up. He had no concept of a god outside of Nature.' Vaynor looked at Merrily. 'So you can imagine him being at his most intense, his most acutely sensitive, when he was here. It's all in "Tintern Abbey", partly written under a sycamore tree. Everybody who comes here instinctively looks for that tree after reading the poem. Lured back to Nature. Whatever moved him, people who know the poems all want to feel it too.'

Merrily said nothing. Since moving here she'd become familiar with a few of the poems, but how did this tie in with what Bliss had been forced to tell her about Vaynor being breathalysed and losing his car keys? What had he done that night that Bliss thought she might be able to uncover where he hadn't been able to?

'That poem,' Vaynor said, 'reads like it's going to be the start of something incredibly exciting... "The motion of our human blood almost suspended, we are laid asleep in body and become a living soul..."'

'That's quite sophisticated,' Merrily said. 'Ahead of its time. The kind of thing you hear from contemporary mystics.'

'Something got into him here.' Vaynor slowly sank back into his chair, as if the poetry had been draining out of him. 'Something he'd never felt so strongly before. My thesis tried to find out what it was, but...'

'But you didn't.'

'It didn't go any further. It all began to tail off. After Wordsworth left the Wye Valley that time, his poetry seemed gradually to lose its power, all its magic, if you like. I think the magic stayed here. I used to think I could feel it in the air. But he'd left it behind.'

Merrily asked softly, 'And when you say *magic*, what do you mean exactly?'

'Wordsworth was using nature poetry to try to open up some big mysteries that were partly inside himself. Why did he stop? Why did his poetry become gradually less exciting when he left here?

'Perhaps because he went on to become a middle-aged poet laureate,' Merrily said. 'And he found domestic bliss. Had children.'

'And let himself eventually get swallowed by the Establishment,' Vaynor said. He paused. 'Do *you* know King Arthur's Cave?'

'I went once.' Merrily saw a cliff facc, with jagged holes in it. 'Briefly, with Jane – my kid. It was getting a bit dark, so we didn't hang around. I don't remember too much about it.'

'It brought my thesis alive. I was very tired when I crawled in and I just fell asleep in there… which you'd think would be hard to do, but it wasn't, and…' his chin sank into his chest '…and I had this dream. At least, I *hope* it was a dream. I remember a woman, who… a young woman, this was. But then *I* was young, too. And she was…' He hesitated then was mumbling. 'I'm afraid she was all over me.'

Oh, hell.

She froze.

'"All over"? I'm sorry, do you mean she actually—?'

This was what Frannie Bliss hadn't known he was after. Not so much what his DC had actually done, as…

'I couldn't move,' Vaynor said. 'Didn't want to… I *assume* I didn't want to. And then afterwards I wasn't sure that anything had happened. All I knew was that I kept shivering because… because she was surprisingly c—'

He stopped, shaking his head in bewilderment. He looked young and naive in a way that cops rarely did after a few years in the job. Merrily opened the stove and pushed the apple log into the flames.

She – the woman in his dream or illusion or whatever it had been – was *cold*? Merrily made herself think calmly about this. Did he mean the woman had been physically cold somewhere she definitely should not have been, particularly in those circumstances?

Vaynor said he didn't know how long his shivering had gone on for that time. In fact he wasn't sure it had happened at all. Until it happened again.

'So how long before it happened again?'

He didn't look at her. As new yellow fire bulged in the stove, it felt colder than ever – *come on, apple log, burn, burn red.*

She heard him say it had been quite recently. The other night, in fact.

'In the cave again? You actually went back?'

'No, it—'

He didn't look at her. His voice had become a shaky whisper. 'No... it wasn't King Arthur's Cave. Not this time.'

But it had still been unnaturally cold. A drab night, he said, in an office in a place he called Corpse Cross Street in Ross-on-Wye. His eyes were wandering the room again, as if they weren't quite connected to his thoughts.

He went on to talk about how close this woman had been to him. How he'd felt her forming around him like gathering dust, as he settled with her into the night.

There was a word, he said, for a woman who came to men at night, giving them a dark, unmistakably erotic charge. This woman was a...

*

Jane scrawled it on the sermon pad. It was too dark to read back. But she'd remember tomorrow to check out this word. And this woman.

'It's not the kind of word I'd normally use,' Vaynor said tightly. 'It's a word out of fairytales.'

He coughed uneasily.

'Adult fairytales,' Merrily said. 'Don't you think?'

31

Mental-patient stuff

JANE HEARD THE sound of a wooden dining chair being pushed back along ridged and grainy stone flags.

'Thank you, Darth,' Mum said calmly into the unnatural quiet that followed.

Jane felt all of Vaynor's tightening embarrassment, couldn't imagine him recounting any of this in front of a couple of other cops in a police interview room. Answering all their questions, going through all the physical, anatomical details of something that nearly everybody would think had never happened outside his head, otherwise he wouldn't have been processing it like a policeman was supposed to.

But this was what his boss, Frannie Bliss, wanted to get at. Why he'd taken the gamble of involving Mum. Cops never tried to analyse this stuff. But it still must happen. Jane figured it happened to police more often than it did to other professions, apart from working clergy and people in the health service. It happened to people regularly exposed to terminal crises in late-night hospital wards, lonely old cells and long-deserted backstreets.

'I get the feeling it's the first time you've been told something quite like this,' Vaynor said.

'Actually, I've heard several slightly similar things,' Mum admitted cautiously. 'It's not all that uncommon in my world.'

But it was. It bloody *was*.

'I can't… I just can't accept that I was an active part of what I seemed to be aware was taking place,' Vaynor said. 'Obviously, I didn't want it to be happening at all.' He let his body sag. 'All right, at the time, some part of me apparently *did*, God forbid.'

Mum said, 'But you didn't actually *do* anything yourself, did you, Darth?'

This time, Vaynor said nothing, just drew a breath and quickly swallowed it. Jane thought he still couldn't be sure how much of it he'd actually done, if anything.

'If anything happened, then perhaps it was something *done* to you,' Mum said. 'Wherever it took place, even if only in your head.'

Jane listened, producing her own fast, shallow breaths. Heard Mum responding to Vaynor's tentative questions about whether or not she believed him. Did she? Could you ever be sure with this kind of thing, always in the foggy hinterland of Britain's fairytale history?

'*I* believe something happened,' Mum said surprisingly, 'on some level. Most people – in my limited experience – really don't make this sort of stuff up.'

'No,' Vaynor said. 'I mean, thank you.'

Jane would not have expected to be believed. She heard Vaynor's chair again being nervously scraped along the stone flags.

'Look, Mrs Watkins, I'm really sorry about this and I can't explain it at all, but it was like something overpowered my consciousness. It was just all so *fast*. And… I must've told her all kinds of things – before and since Corpse Cross Street – all kinds of things I didn't know I'd said until they were out. That's real mental-patient stuff…'

'No!'

'That's exactly what it is.'

Which was exactly what the Bishop and his pal Crowden would say because it seemed to explain everything quite rationally.

'When did you tell her all these things?'

'I'd... followed her into a coffee bar, and I was telling her things about myself— like about a relationship I had that was causing me some distress and people who... I mean if someone was telling *me* all this would I believe any of it?'

'I think you might,' Merrily said cautiously. 'But you said this was in a coffee bar?'

'Starbucks. Outside Ross, on the bypass. Seemed quite normal. She was there and I went in to join her. It seemed an obvious thing for me to do. Afterwards, I had the feeling of having been *invited* in.'

Merrily nodded. This made a kind of sense.

'And then there was the office in Corpse Cross Street,' Vaynor said. 'I remember going because she'd given me the impression her husband was likely to be there and I could find out from him some things the DI wanted to know.'

'You're saying you willingly told her... private things?'

There was the sound of the dining chair rocking back, as his body subsided into it. A long silence outside was interrupted by a woody thump, indicating a rising wind at work in the vicarage garden.

'I've told you what I know. I can't tell you any more. I haven't tried to find anything else because I know that if I get too close again... I— I only know what she did when... when she came down on me. What I think I *remember* her doing. In a hazy way... but also strangely urgent.'

He talked about some other irrational things that had happened that same night. How – shocked at what he might have done with the woman and fighting to restore calm and reason – he'd gone into a pub that looked warm and welcoming and bought himself a big drink, the way he hadn't done since Oxford nights, when he used to drink quite a bit because it was expected.

'You know what this sounds like?' Mum said. 'What you remember her doing with you?'

'I told you. Like mental imbalance.'

'*Can* a man be raped?' she asked suddenly.

Shocked, Jane clutched at her chair. Had Mum really asked that?

'It's late,' Vaynor said.

He stood up. Merrily also rose.

'What I meant, of course, is… by a woman. I didn't used to think that was possible. But that's a glib, thoughtless reaction, isn't it? Maybe I'm being naive. Just tell me what *you* think.'

Vaynor stared over her head.

'I could say a word that might fit,' he said. 'But… I can't.'

'Yes you can.'

'It's from a fairytale.'

'If it's an *adult* fairytale,' Merrily said, standing completely still, 'I think you'd better just tell it.'

32

Not just Mum's case

'THE KID.'

'My kid, Jane.'

She considered the number of times Mum had used that word, almost dismissively. There was a mere *nineteen years* between them. The older you got, the less that seemed. In years to come, when they both were the wrong side of thirty – Jane thirty-one, Mum an attractive fifty – it would seem minimal. Several people in the past year had commented, the way people always liked to, that they could be sisters, which Mum had appeared to find quite amusing. Jane remembering how, at the age of fifteen, she'd quite fancied Lol for herself until Mum had grabbed him.

They were now both grown women, but one day, in the distant future, while Jane was *still* a grown woman, Mum would be old and frail and ought now to be thinking about the implications of that. And how they needed to work together more easily to deal with the world.

Jane flopped back on her bed, listening to Vaynor's car backing out of the drive, watching its headlights carving out grey wedges in the air. She noticed there was still a light on upstairs in Lucy's cottage, where Lol lived.

If you could call this living, with the constant closeness of a pandemic death you couldn't see coming for you.

*

It didn't take long to find it online. Not when you had the author's pseudonym, Al Fox, derived from Alfoxden, the house in Somerset which Wordsworth had leased towards the end of the eighteenth century. From which base he'd discovered this area with his adoring sister, Dorothy, after spending time with his friend and fellow romantic poet, Samuel Taylor Coleridge.

'The Wye in Wordsworth' was the title of Vaynor's thesis, and Merrily found it compulsive. It opened up a side of the poet that people rarely heard about these days. Away from his home ground in Cumbria, according to Al Fox, an alternative figure had emerged: Wordsworth, the proto-hippie.

Merrily was still so alert after that originally unpromising session with the *thesist*, if that was how he thought of himself, that she was still awake after finishing her first reading.

'If you were a woman and she was a man,' Mum had told Vaynor, 'it would amount to something not far from rape.'

Jane's whole body jerked, remembering. Vaynor had said, 'It's one reason I can't say anything about this – especially telling anybody at Gaol Street.'

'You think a man can't be raped by a woman?'

Remember, Jane thought, that this, if it actually happened, was not in the back of a car. It was in King Arthur's Cave.

On the map, which couldn't easily convey height differences, the cave looked very close to the widening River Wye, but when you were there, no sign of the river was obvious, no sensation of its nearness. The only water was dripping from the stones in the ceiling. Outside, you could see only countryside. She'd been just the once, with Mum. An autumn evening, clambering over the rocks at the bottom of the cliff. There'd been two adjacent front entrances, leading into the same central chamber. And here, amid the ragged rocks in King Arthur's Cave up in the shorn-off hill called the Doward, this cop believed he'd lain and had *things* done to him by a woman. And done again, later, in an office in the streets of the town of Ross-on-Wye. Had King Arthur's Cave been carried there with him, in his head, or what?

She was going to try to believe it. Same things, same woman. Jane just couldn't imagine being that woman. Wasn't there a sense of intended invasion about what he reckoned had happened to him? Dominance? *Could* a man be raped by a woman? She thought back to when she was much younger and well into some lush guys on TV. That had been physical desire, no question, but didn't rape mean the victim was being in some way *passive*? That the victim didn't fancy it – quite the reverse? That he was getting no pleasure out of this, was actually very afraid of it?

This was a tough one. It couldn't have been easy for Vaynor coming out with all this to an attractive woman who was also an ordained priest.

She knew, from the thick silence following his crazy story, that Mum wouldn't be expressing a firm opinion on whether it had or hadn't happened. That wasn't how exorcists operated. You didn't ask the paranormally-challenged punter if he was *sure* he'd experienced it, or openly suggest he might've made it all up. You didn't get him to repeat the story to hear if his narration of it had changed in any way – this wasn't a police interview. Mum, the exorcist, would just be nodding silently, letting him finish in his own way.

Did she have the littlest sense that he was perhaps telling or *not* telling the truth?

Mum did not have an easy job.

*

After a patchy sleep, as the sun expanded, Jane blinked it in through the window and found Wordsworth's Goodrich girl in her head. In at least one of the books, a biographer had described the kid as one of the most inspiring people the poet had ever encountered. The way he kept returning to her insistence that those dead siblings had not actually gone away from Goodrich. The ghost story element in 'We Are Seven', *how* important had that been to the poet? Had he wanted to find out if the girl, by then probably middle-aged, still felt herself to be in contact with her dead brothers and sisters?

And were they still children? Before sliding into bed, she'd Googled *Wordsworth/death* on her laptop and discovered the lines:

> *Our birth is but a sleep and a forgetting*
> *The soul that rises with us, our life's star...*

Quite cool. Birth and death part of the same cycle. Wordsworth had connected with that but maybe didn't want the public to think he had. So he had it all coming from this little girl and had himself in there, too, questioning what she took for granted, being all adult and critical. Scared to admit wanting to believe in ghosts. No wonder his sceptical mate down in Bristol had said he'd regret publishing 'We Are Seven'.

One day, Jane decided, she and Eirion would take a drive down there and see if they could find the two kids' graves. It seemed that the village of Goodrich was hard to get away from, even when you died. It was one of *those* places.

Jane slid out of bed and, finding it pleasantly warm, moved across her apartment to the back wall with its large-scale map of the diocese and parts of the adjoining ones. Goodrich's thirteenth century church was marked with a cross – *twelve steps or more from my mother's door.*

The graves… were they still there? And how was she going to find out? If she asked him, Gomer Parry would take her over there.

She went back to bed, saw from the alarm clock that it was only five-forty-five, fell half-asleep and half-dreamed about the young William Wordsworth, who, in those sketches and engravings, looked surprisingly contemporary.

He wasn't *from* this area, but had spent significant time here. His brother-in-law, Tom Hutchinson, was at Brinsop and before that, at Hindwell Farm, right on the Welsh border, where William and his wife, Mary, stayed and loved it. On William's last visit, he was still trying to track down the spooky Goodrich girl… and that was nearly fifty years after he met her.

She'd be well into middle age, Jane thought as dawn crawled hesitantly into Ledwardine. Maybe a granny. How would he know her?

'It remains interesting,' Vaynor had said.

Why had he referred to the kid as spooky? One of his words. He'd also applied it to the Doward. Some very narrow roads up there. And steep. With long drops into the River Wye or its banks. Either way, a bad wrench of the wheel could put you into history. But there was next to nothing to be uncovered within the word doward; there appeared to be no other places with the same name, although it showed up very occasionally as a surname.

What, then, was the nearest sizeable community to the Doward, with its dense forestry and limestone caves? The nearest substantial town, four or five miles away, was Monmouth

– in Wales, just. In England, with the A40 dual carriageway crashing through it, was Whitchurch. And then – very haunted, it seemed to Jane – the medieval, or earlier, village of Goodrich.

It all came back to Goodrich. She had to go there. This was not just Mum's case. Not any more.

33

A decent horror film

THE FEW PAGES torn from the sermon pad were spread on Jane's shop table. On the last one, the felt-pen scrawl, done last night in near-complete darkness, was uneven, a name given serious emphasis.

Diana PORTIS

Now that Mum was unlikely to walk in on her, Jane made sure that nobody could, locking herself into the shop and activating her laptop. Wondering how she would react if she found nothing at all, if it all turned out to have been another vivid fever-dream.

However, Googling the name Portis she quickly landed on the recent report of a senior Hereford estate agent's death-fall in the Wye Valley which, it seemed, his firm now owned much of.

There were two or three pictures of Peter Portis's son, Royce, one of them including his recently acquired daughter-in-law, Diana Venus Portis. Register office wedding less than three years ago.

The photo showed a woman a few years older than Jane, with mid-length dark hair that was dense like seaweed, coming down to roundish but penetrating eyes like an owl's and then – not very city estate-agent, if she still wore it – a silver nose-ring with a little emerald in it. The face had a knowing humour and what Jane saw as a shaded sexuality.

Succubus

She hadn't put the word into the laptop until this morning. Here, at the shop.

a demon or supernatural entity in folklore, in female form, that appears in dreams to seduce men, usually through sexual activity. According to religious traditions, repeated sexual activity with a succubus can cause poor physical or mental health, even death.

It was the female version of the incubus, a priapic creature that introduced sex into nightmares.

That's mental-patient stuff—

Vaynor last night. What frightened her was that Mum also knew a fair bit about it.

She clicked succubus into oblivion, to bring up the website of the curious little store that was still in King Street, Hereford. She found the phone number and just hoped that the Pod shop hadn't completely closed for the duration of the pandemic as, sooner or later, it would have to. Even people like Jane didn't consider it an essential outlet.

Another triumphant morning for the virus, Lol Robinson was thinking. It would have been the fiftieth anniversary of the Glastonbury Festival. A significant milestone in music.

'I can get you maybe three tickets,' Lol's manager Prof Levin had said only yesterday. 'Merrily, Jane and… is it Irene? Jane's friend?'

'Eirion,' Lol had told him. 'He's Welsh. Jane calls him Irene. He hates it. But yeah, he'd probably love to go to Glasto. He was in a band at school. I expect he plays better than me, now.'

Now Lol sadly switched off the radio, unplugged the phone. He'd have to take a call from Prof sometime this morning, but please, not yet.

It was about a month since that first hint that he'd be playing Glasto this year. Then the realization about a week ago that he probably wouldn't. Waking this morning, *before* the abandoned festival announcement, feeling himself lying in a dull glow. Prof had promised a week ago that while he wouldn't be on the Pyramid Stage, he would still get noticed. The acoustic stage was easy to record from and still attracted TV coverage. *Always said I would fix it for you*, Prof had said.

Now Lol gazed hopelessly across at the Boswell guitar in his living room. At least he hadn't told anybody apart from Jane, whom he'd seen as needing cheering up by the tickets. He went over and turned the face of the Boswell into the corner. It wouldn't be heard in Glastonbury. Nobody would this year. It had been on the radio this morning that, because of the virus, the whole festival had been cancelled. It was like a semi-distant but sparkling light in the sky had turned itself off, maybe for ever.

A sign outside Ledwardine's Eight Till Late limited the number of customers at any one time to two.

*

Jane was remembering how, once, in high summer, she'd been out here at five a.m., with the shops all shut and a good feeling vibrating in the air: anticipation. She could hear no birds singing now, just a lot of noise in her head.

And she had work to do.

She had a missed call from Eirion to return; he'd phoned while she was dressing. She had told him last week that she'd get them both Glastonbury tickets. Saying nothing about Lol appearing there, of course.

But when she rang him back, Eirion picked up the phone and said he had bad news.

'It was on the radio. Thought I'd better tell you in case you'd missed it. The whole festival's been cancelled.'

Suppressing the shock and sadness, Jane said it had just been something special for them to look forward to, before the start of summer. Didn't tell him about this fantasy she'd had of Lol and Mum getting engaged under Glastonbury Tor, in the ambered afterglow of Lol's gig, which would include the weirdly magical new song he'd started working on about the child in Wordsworth's 'We Are Seven'. She'd heard the opening chord sequence yesterday afternoon. It would become immortal, she'd decided.

Meaning it couldn't die like the festival.

'...occurred to me this might happen,' Eirion was saying, 'that we might not see each other—'

'Ever again?'

'Jane, I wasn't thinking anything *that* bad...'

'I'm not joking, Irene,' Jane said grimly.

In fact she wondered if they were likely to joke about anything again. Kept remembering what Sorrel had said about the future pandemic when it was barely a sniff in the communal nose. *Nothing is going to be safe any more. There'll be violence and damage in the cities, even Hereford.*

Sorrel. There was someone she thought Sorrel might know or know *about*. So she rang the Hereford shop. Through her own shop window, she watched a woman pushing a pram and a man walking up the middle of the road in the slow traffic, as if to protect her social distance. The scene didn't speak of violence or damage but it was somehow a very medieval image: *unclean, unclean*, the new plague years.

How many plague years would there be before all this was over, if it ever was, or pushed into the background misery of ordinary life?

'Pod's.'

Sharp in her ear. Uncharacteristically impatient.

'Sorrel?'

'Jane? Is that Jane? Listen, I shouldn't be here. We're not supposed to be open, we—'

'Sorrel… I just need some information.' Jane was talking too fast and knew it. 'If you hadn't come into the shop that time when I was painting, I wouldn't've thought of asking you about this, but… am I right in thinking you have some long-time members in the lower Wye Valley? Say past Symonds Yat and towards the Forest of Dean?'

'We've always had members there,' Sorrel said. 'It's always been a pagan area. All kinds. Plenty of witches, for a start. Goes back centuries.'

Of course it did. It made sense, with all the moody forestry and the caves. She'd found some pictures on the Net, including one of King Arthur's Cave, accompanying a few paragraphs written by a guy who'd seen strange lights in there. Which also figured. You saw a reflection of somebody's torch and you put it down as a strange light because this was King Arthur's Cave where an outsize human skeleton had once been found and the detective, Vaynor, had somehow given himself to Diana Venus Portis, wife of Royce Portis.

For the first time. Was he at all worried about the implications of submitting to the image of a serial succubus?

According to religious traditions, repeated sexual activity with a succubus can cause poor physical or mental health, even death.

Religious traditions? Whose? Who would want a man

to think he might be risking his life messing with a spectral seductress?

Somehow, she didn't like this.

Having awoken early, feeling the same underlying excitement she'd felt over the eight-year-old girl at Goodrich. Only darker. If times were normal she and Irene would be planning a quick weekend trip there to find out what evidence remained of these people: who they were, where they lived, how you could find out about them while avoiding their attentions.

'Our members come and go,' Sorrel said now. 'Scores of them, including regular holidaymakers. There's always an element of pagan tourism that brings people back, feeling a mystical connection to the area. Somctimes they end up living here.'

Jane smiled. It was as if the Pod believed it qualified for an annual grant for boosting the local economy.

'You looking for anybody in particular?' Sorrel asked.

Jane hesitated, then thought *why not?* And shrugged.

'I suppose I'm looking for someone who might know a woman called Diana,' she said fairly casually. 'Diana Portis.'

Couldn't say that name now without feeling this dark thrill. She had the woman's wedding picture back on the screen, the copper's sexual fantasy – was it any more than that?

There was what seemed like a long break in the mobile signal before Sorrel came back to her.

'Jane… just give me that name again, will you?'

'Diana…' Jane peered at the laptop screen showing the newlywed estate agent. 'Diana Venus Portis.'

Sorrel echoed the name then paused again.

'*She* added the *Venus*.'

'She what?'

'Another goddess. After Diana, the huntress, comes Venus. More complex. And more dangerous. Venus can cast shadows, did you know that?'

'I... No.'

'I mean Venus the planet. Hotter than Mercury, though further from the sun. Named after the dark Roman goddess of love.'

'Yes, she...' Named after *two* Roman goddesses? Hmm. 'Sorrel, is Diana Portis in the Pod?'

'No.'

'But you do know her?'

'We *know* her.' Sorrel was sounding kind of reticent. 'As much as anyone is allowed to. She was once invited to join us but declined. We... don't actually invite many people to meetings, but we thought she'd fit our membership. Swell our collection of all the holders of ancient wisdom around here.' Sorrel hesitated. 'She comes from a family of established druids.'

'She does?'

'Going way back, I gather. To the days of Iolo Morganwg and Lady Llanover and all those people, if not before.'

'*Way* back? That was no more than a couple of hundred years ago, surely?'

After a pause, Sorrel said, 'Do *you* know much about Druidism, Jane?'

'Well, erm... I mean, it's like... it's Britain's... our oldest religion, isn't it?'

'Be honest,' Sorrel said. 'You don't know anything about Druidism.'

'Well, I—'

'There are no books or established druidic dogma. No gurus, famous priests, no rituals handed down. Because nothing was ever *written* down,' Sorrel said. 'We're told it was the religion of the Celts, before and during early Christianity. We think they carried out rituals in stone circles and we used to think they were involved in building them… and then the experts said the circles went back to the Bronze Age, which pre-dated the druids by a few thousand years. But yeah, the only druids we really know about were the eighteenth-century Welsh revivalists like Lady Llanover and Iolo Morganwg. Who *did* write stuff down, even if it wasn't authentic.'

'But surely they were just political – they were early Welsh nationalists.'

'And many of them were also English,' Sorrel said. 'More Welsh than the Welsh, the English, when they discover Wales – that's the kind of Wales *they* want to absorb, make a part of themselves. A heritage. Like the guy who built Goodrich Court. He used to hang out with neo-druids.'

Jane shut down the laptop. She was disappointed. She knew a bit about the eighteenth-century Welsh druids – who had made most of it up to give their country a mystical heritage that was probably phoney. They'd built all these new stone circles for their cultural ceremonies, the *eisteddfodau*, which were conducted entirely in the Welsh language and continued today only because they supported it. Druidism had begun to be about Welshness.

'You seem to be losing interest,' Sorrel observed.

'Because it's a different thing. That was just political.'

A silence.

'Was it, Jane?'

'Nothing wrong with Welsh nationalism, if you're Welsh, but linking it with the original druids is basically bollocks.'

'Oh?'

'My boyfriend's Welsh,' Jane said. 'He finds it all a bit unconvincing.'

She didn't want to offend the well-meaning Sorrel and what was left of the Pod but, as far as she could see, people had always been borrowing these unknown druids and getting them all wrong – hundreds of books attempting to glorify, sanitize and – like some Welsh people still did – even Christianize a bunch of barbarians whose only accepted legacy was the Wicker Man.

He at least had turned into a decent horror film.

34
Cold

THE SCULLERY: JANE had been in here.

Merrily slumped into the old captain's chair. No doubt about it. Jane was no tidier, no more discreet than she'd been at fifteen, when they'd first arrived at Ledwardine vicarage and she didn't yet have her own apartment upstairs. She left tracks, traces and debris everywhere.

The kid had clearly been in here last night for some time, writing in the sermon pad which Merrily had abandoned when the parish churches had been closed down by the pandemic. Pages from the pad had now been torn out and taken away. No discarded paper in the waste bin.

Jane had been making notes during a phone call? To whom? Had she been in here last night? Had she picked up any of the weird chat with Darth Vaynor?

Merrily held up the pad to the light from the window to try and read the impressions left on it by the pen. Only one word was distinct, letters deeply scrawled between lines.

SUCCUBUS

Oh God. She'd tried to avoid that word, precisely because she thought it would be familiar to Vaynor, and it wouldn't help him at all to know how it had been interpreted online. He was right to have suggested it could now be considered a psychological term for a woman's image appearing in the dreams of heterosexual men to arouse them. Nothing paranormal there. But what about the suggestion that 'according to religious traditions' it could, if it occurred too many times, become harmful, causing poor physical or mental health?

Possible. Again, there was nothing particularly paranormal in that, but…

Even death?

She thought hard about this, gazing out of the scullery window where the climbing rose used to swing, then slowly picked up the phone. She had a funeral looming, didn't have much time to try and get a few things clear.

'After what happened,' the unknown woman was saying into Jane's ear, 'everyone was being kind to her and indulgent. This probably went on for years afterwards, and they still don't like to bother her.'

When the phone call had come, Jane had been about to leave the shop, see how Gomer was doing. She hadn't sat down again, and kept the strap of her bag over her shoulder as she tried to balance the receiver.

'Sorry. Who are you, again? I'm not really thinking straight this morning.'

She'd picked up the phone and heard the unknown voice of a woman, older than her, maybe around Mum's age. But it wasn't Mum. It was local, well local*ish*.

'I had a call from Sorrel Podmore,' the woman said carefully. 'She thought I should let you know some things.'

Jane groaned to herself. What had she started?

'I admit I'm saying this for my benefit as much as yours,' the woman said. 'I need it to come out.'

Was this some member of the Pod who'd joined since Jane had stopped going to meetings? Also, when she asked them things, people – pagans, especially – were inclined to assume she was making enquiries on Mum's behalf. To pagans, Mum was considered to be the open, liberal face of the diocese, not too churchy, always accessible to fringe opinions. Sometimes, in the past, she'd used Jane as a conduit into pagan activities. Which Jane was beginning to regret.

'Sorrel says you've been asking questions.'

'It's what I do,' Jane said. 'I'm curious. And I like to help people. Sorry, I didn't catch your name.'

'Perhaps I didn't give you one.'

'Do I know you?'

'Evidently not. So I won't enlighten you. And I'll ask you not to be *too* curious about me. But I know about you and also a certain amount about Diana Portis who I think you were asking about.'

'Oh.'

Jane sat down, lowered her bag to the floor. This was someone Sorrel had persuaded to talk to her. Why?

'Diana Portis...' she had to choose her words carefully '...made a big impression on a... on a friend of mine.'

'Who would that be?'

'I can't tell you.'

'All right.' A very small laugh. 'Male or female?'

'It's a man.'

'I see. It was *that* kind of impression, was it?'

'I think you could say that.'

Sometimes you just had to go for it.

'All right,' the woman said. 'I grew up near Crocker's Ash, where her mother had a cottage and smallholding. Don't live there any more. Diana was younger than me, but all her friends were my age or older. When we started hanging out together at nights, I was fourteen, she was eleven. You see where I'm going with this?'

'I...'

She must be younger than Jane had first thought. Early thirties?

'Diana Portis taught me things. She *knew* all sorts of things. And places. Places we thought we were familiar with. It was interesting at first.'

'At first?'

'Then it became frightening. *Very* frightening. Soon afterwards I got married. I was only eighteen. I got married and left the area. I think that was one of the reasons I got married so young. To leave... I'm not sure why I'm telling you this. Except that I've known for a while that sooner or later I'd have to tell somebody, or she'd get somebody really damaged...'

Jane noticed that her speech had begun to get higher and faster.

'Damaged how?'

'Mentally. At least. If you're damaged mentally, you can hurt yourself, or somebody else...'

'Has she done that?'

'She likely has, but you didn't hear that from me. In fact you didn't hear anything from me.'

'And as I don't know who you are...'

'Nobody questioned her beliefs,' the woman said. 'Villages around the Doward have a very long tradition of it if you look in the right corners.'

'What?'

'People from South Wales settled here years ago and put down roots. And married into local families.'

'A long tradition of what?' Jane said.

'Sorrel said you would know.'

'No, listen, I—'

The phone suddenly was lifeless.

*

Huw Owen said, 'This is about the vicar in the Wye Valley? Tell me owt or nowt, lass. I'll help if I can. I won't be here for ever and I need to think deliverance'll still be in good hands when I've gone.'

'Come on, Huw. Don't start talking like that.'

'I mean when they force me to retire. As the bastards will, one day not too far off.'

Merrily pictured him, hunched in his leaking fireside chair in the Brecon Beacons vicarage. She told him, without naming names, about the two possible encounters between DC Vaynor and what he thought had been the woman, Diana Portis, or something connected to her.

'I don't know how much of this, if any, to believe, Huw. On one hand, the person who told me about it is intelligent, articulate and... somehow convinced it all happened as he described.'

'He saw this woman in a dream?'

'I didn't say that.'

'If a woman says she can be with a bloke after bedtime when they're apart, or the bloke says he's been having dreams about her and sometimes wakes up in need of fresh underpants—there are words for this. And you just used one.'

'Succubus? Did I say that?'

'A term out of myth, out of fairytales. A word we don't believe in, the way we once might have, as kids. But words like that were once used by folk as *did* believe. These were specialized words. I'm looking this one up now on t'computer. Looks like Latin, but it goes back to ancient Jewish mysticism – the Qabala. Describes a female spirit as appears to men in dreams, sometimes messing wi' blokes in intimate ways while they're asleep.'

Merrily sighed.

'You're right, of course – it's out of the fairytales. But do I now proceed as if it really exists? I've encountered things before that I only half believe in and—'

'Listen. I were once consulted by a feller, who had this very enthusiastic young woman as wanted to be his girlfriend. He wasn't sure about her himself. They worked together as teachers at the same school and he found he were dreaming about her a lot. Fancying her more in dreams than he did awake. At the time, he were engaged to a woman he genuinely liked – more than he liked this teacher who were throwing herself at him every night, in his own bed – or that's what he told me.'

'You believed him?'

'It don't matter.'

'You think this woman was producing something that could be described as a *succubus*? Or was it just his sexual fantasy?'

'Just let me finish, lass. One night it went further. He were with her – or dreaming he was – when he experienced what's known as… a nocturnal emission? In the middle of which, he woke up and it were… cold.'

'I'm sorry, you mean…?'

'Inside. Inside her, it were bloody cold. Normal sex, except entirely cold at the moment of… release. Listen, I'm not saying this to—'

'I know.'

In her head, she heard Vaynor: *All I knew was that I kept shivering because… because she was surprisingly c—'*

'And I'm not talking about a mutual thing born out of a close relationship,' Huw said. 'I'm not smoothing any of this up.'

'So it's usually a bad thing.'

'Course it's a bad thing. Owt unexpectedly cold is not usually a good sign in any faith. Cool is one thing, cold is summat else.'

'So what happened next?' Merrily asked. 'In real life.'

'He took my advice, I'm glad to say. Left the school. And the area. Got another job.'

'That worked?'

'And got married quick. I haven't seen him since, but I assume he's over her and whatever she were trying to do. Anyroad… that's my succubus story, for what it's worth. Somehow she found a way into his head and stayed there for a while.'

'In *my* succubus story, I don't personally know any of the people concerned, but…'

'But happen you're about to.' Huw made a small, faintly sinister laugh. 'It's one of them situations where things start to come together, and you're pulled into summat and, if you're doing this job proper, you're forced to keep asking questions and there might be more than one answer to the same question.'

'Huw…' She paused. 'Have I become one of those women who people go to when they want something done that may not…'

'Aye, I know.'

'And they know that if it's all wrong, I'll be there to take the crap?'

'Merrily…' He did the laugh again. 'You've *always* been one of them women. And this woman, who some people think can be seen as a succubus… if she doesn't exist, that's the last you'll hear. If she does, she'll happen be wondering if *you* exist. Then it might get interesting.'

35

Only the moon for light

IT UNLOCKED SOME sad history, that name.

Calling Sorrel back, Jane learned that Diana Portis's father, Sam, was the son of Pamela Farrowman, a divorcee who'd kept a smallholding near the Doward village of Crocker's Ash. Sam had worked in computers in the early years of the Internet and made quite a lot of money very quickly. He'd bought and extended the smallholding, which his mother had continued to rent and maintain on her own after her husband had left. They'd prospered.

Sam's new girlfriend, Mona, knew how to spend his spare money, and show him a good time with it. She knew about having good times, Sorrel said, and died in the middle of one.

This particular spring night, many years ago, it was very bright, and Mona, who Sam had brought over from South Wales, had taken all her clothes off and slipped into the river, as she'd done many times before. Naked, she was part of the night, revelling in the new season.

The truth was, Sorrel said, that they were both already well stoned, and he went in after her, even though he wasn't much of a swimmer and, in a fast flow of foliage, kept failing to reach her.

At some point, Pam Farrowman was alerted by a neighbour and called the police. The bodies were found at first light, some way down river, entangled in blown-down branches, near the rapids.

'Oh,' Jane said, dismayed. 'I didn't know about that.'

'It happens,' Sorrel said. 'Not often, but those of us born in this area all know of at least one fatal incident in the Wye. A famously beautiful river. But periodically it kills.'

'And the baby? Diana? She'd lost *both* parents to the river? She must've been seriously damaged by that.'

'Not damaged,' Sorrel said. 'Too young. But very much changed... perhaps changed is a better word. Although what happened to her wouldn't be known for some time.'

Sorrel said she'd cleared it with the woman on the phone that she could tell Jane what she knew of the back-story. The woman didn't live in the Wye Valley any more but was apparently a close relative of the smallholder, Pam Farrowman, who had moved away with her.

'Close how?' Jane asked, determined to get this unravelled.

'All right.' Sorrel released a taut breath. 'I'll tell you. I don't suppose it'll do any harm. Pam had two children: Sam... and Liz, who came along later. Another baby was probably Pam's attempt to rescue her failing marriage. But it didn't work. Pam was more successful as a mother than a wife. She adopted Sam and Mona's daughter, when they were drowned.'

'This was Diana?'

'Her orphaned granddaughter. Although they were different generations, Liz and Diana grew up like sisters, Liz the elder by just three years.'

'So...' Jane made some lightning connections. 'Liz is the woman who called me?'

'Yes.'

A complex family, Jane realized. The matriarch, Pam, was Liz's mother and Diana's gran? So where was Pam now?

'Living up in Shropshire with Liz.' Sorrel paused. 'Having left Diana behind. Diana, who's now grown-up and married to a wealthy estate agent. And about to live in a house that she believes was built by her own rich ancestor…'

'Who's that?'

'Have you heard of Sir Samuel Rush Meyrick?'

An image flared in Jane's head of the prominent gatehouse of an enormous castle that had completely vanished.

'Bloody hell!'

Jane was aware of her voice weakening.

'Mona's ancestor is believed to have been one of Meyrick's druid friends in Wales,' Sorrel told her. 'Nothing official, he must have made sure of that.'

'Things are…' Jane 's voice was down to a whisper '…coming out.'

'It's the pandemic,' Sorrel said. 'People are passing on old secrets…'

'Before they die?'

'Nobody is saying that.'

'Sorrel, they don't have to.'

After a silence, Sorrel said, 'Peter Portis's house is one of a number of properties built by Meyrick in the area to support his enormous new castle, Goodrich Court. This was originally a hunting lodge. Mr Portis bought it some years ago as his climbing base.'

'And now he's dead,' Jane said bleakly. 'Presumably leaving the house to his son… and his wife.'

And Mum would be the priest at his restricted funeral.

Jane felt cold. Through the shop window, the black and white buildings in Ledwardine high street seemed stilled in time. No traffic, no people… only nature moving: birds pecking among the budded trees.

Jane saw Gomer Parry, crossing the road from the Eight Till Late, unwrapping a pack of cigarette papers. A thought struck her.

'Where was Diana when her parents died in the Wye?'

Sorrel's reply was casual.

'Didn't I tell you?'

'No, you didn't.'

'Truth is, I don't know. Nobody knows for sure.'

'She wasn't at home?'

'No, she was with her parents. They often walked by the river at sunset before she was put to bed. Her mother seems to have made a sudden decision to take a quick dip, presumably leaving the child on the bank in full sight. But then, Diana could virtually swim before she could walk.'

'In the *river*?'

'I don't know. Why not? She was precocious in all kinds of ways. But I believe she stayed out of the water that night. The police eventually found her some distance away.'

'On the bank?'

'No. They found her somewhere it seemed unlikely she'd got to by herself. On the bank, where they deduced she'd been left, they found a few clothes. And small tracks where she'd... toddled away. Though how she finished up in the cave... I mean I've got kids and I—'

'*Cave?*'

'The big one. King Arthur's Cave. That part of it never came out,' Sorrel said. 'Not even at her parents' inquest. It couldn't be explained and probably many people didn't believe it. It's actually not that far to go. Up into the Doward, beyond the Seven Sisters rocks. Not far for an adult, perhaps, with a light. But a few people wondered how a child could get there on her own, with only the moon for light?'

Silence in the phone. Jane felt disturbingly alone here in Lucy's shop, burdened by too much information. She wanted to end this call, do some thinking. She just hadn't known about the drowning.

'Sorrel, somebody must know something. *Somebody* must've have carried her up to the cave. Did nobody ever talk about it?'

'No, and still nobody talks about it unless they have to.'

More silence. Jane felt she was separate, not part of all this, the mobile phone full of its own world. Gradually, she felt her mind moulding a question.

'I've been to that cave,' she was saying. 'Just the once. With my mum.'

'The exorcist?'

'Yes.'

And the copper, Vaynor, had been. And didn't think he'd been alone there.

Jane stared at the phone, on speaker. Last night's disclosures had already been swollen by this morning's revelations.

'It doesn't make sense,' she said. 'Is it *true*? Like, did it really happen? Did Diana remember *any* of it afterwards?'

'It's unlikely that she did.' Sorrel's voice came up from the speaker in the phone, now lying on the shop table. 'Probably not in any rational way. She didn't go in the water. And nobody local would ask her about it, this tragic child, growing up only yards from where her parents perished.'

'*...parents perished.*' The words shimmered in the silent shop. Jane didn't touch the phone. Had there been nothing in the papers about the miracle baby who'd lost both parents and survived?

'She must've said something to *somebody* at the time. Her gran – *she* must've learned something.'

'It was said that Diana, as she grew up,' Sorrel said, 'made a practice of going back to the big cave.'

'Like it had some special significance for her?'

'Her gran, Pam, didn't like her doing that... or some other things she did, other places she went. But she couldn't stop her. She was much younger, more agile and always fit. A good, sure climber.'

'Like her future father-in-law?'

'Exactly. Scaling the Seven Sisters and other places where climbing was forbidden. She was like a goat from the age of about seven, and probably far younger.'

'You remember her then?'

'I saw her occasionally. Flitting past our house. I...'

Jane waited. There was something Sorrel wasn't saying.

And she couldn't wait any longer.

'Sorrel, is she a direct descendant of Sir Samuel Meyrick?'

'I don't know. His family seems to have died away. His son died first, and there were no more children. Meyrick died nearly two hundred years ago and his enormous estate was divided between various nephews, and the court itself was finally demolished. Scattered buildings, like the pub in Goodrich and the stables and the gatehouse and this hunting lodge, kept changing hands and their origins were obscured.'

'Did Diana's family inherit any of the Meyrick estate?'

'I wouldn't think so. It all just got split up and—'

'Sorrel, is Diana some kind of genuine druid? Brought up in the religion, not just pursuing an interest, like members of the Pod.'

'Are you saying...' Something was hardening Sorrel's voice. 'Are you suggesting the Pod's not a serious group?'

'No, but—'

'We've been in existence for over fifteen years! We observe

all the local pagan festivals, we conserve the sacred stones and ancient holy wells, pass on the secret traditions to our children...'

Jane was detecting a growing outrage, not how she wanted things to go.

'Sorrel, I'm sorry. I didn't intend to demean the work of the Pod...'

'In which case...'

'I revere Lucy Devenish and all she stood for. I'm trying to revive her village shop. But living with Mum makes me aware of another side to all this, a deeper level of... of...'

'Evil?' Sorrel snapped out the word.

'With this pandemic, everything's going to pieces, coming apart. I'm just trying to find out where this Portis woman's coming from. Because if she inherited anything from Meyrick, maybe it was his religion.'

'We only know that, like a lot of people a couple of hundred years ago, he was fascinated by druids.' Sorrel was calming down. 'This has always been a strong druidic area and we were told Diana Portis was descended from a druid family.'

'But she wasn't a member of the Pod?'

'We thought that because all our members are pagans, that she'd be happy to join us... come and address one of our meetings. But...'

'But she didn't want to be associated with the Pod?'

'No. But also she was married by then, to the son of a well-off estate agent from Hereford. We thought maybe her new husband didn't want it broadcast among his posh friends about her family's druid past.'

'What does that *mean*? Druids are paganism-*lite* these days. You can dress up and prance around Stonehenge at the solstice, but you don't have to do anything risky. Calling yourself a druid isn't any more significant now than when William Wordsworth called himself one. Which was like calling yourself a hippy to show you weren't conventional. In Wordsworth's time it was about appreciating amorphous Nature rather than worshipping a personal God, wasn't it? It was… cool.'

'I suppose it was,' Sorrel said. 'We didn't know much about the druids so we made them what we wanted them to be. History actually records a good deal more about people who *opposed* the druids and fought against them than about the druids themselves. People like the Romans who put many druids to the sword. Julius Caesar had a lot to say about them, most of it bad. The Romans said they practised all kinds of cruelty.'

An unwanted image sprang into Jane's mind: the late actor Christopher Lee in a field near the sea in the film he'd always said he preferred to all those Dracula movies he'd starred in.

'They had the *wicker man*.'

'Exactly,' Sorrel said. 'The sacrificial wooden cage into which people and animals were herded and then burned to death. By the druids, according to the Romans. But *was* that the druids? Or was the celebrated wicker man invented to blacken the image of the ancient British healers and astronomers while the Roman invaders were busy killing them off?'

Jane had a picture of scores of people squashed in with farm animals, all squirming and screaming as the flames rose in the wooden cage. Obscene.

'All right, if the wicker man never existed…'

'That's what *you* think, Jane?'

'There aren't any left,' Jane said. 'So we'll never know. If the cages were made of wood, they'd have rotted away. Unless they were replaced by stone altars, and how would we know that?'

Sorrel said, 'Do you know the Queen Stone, for instance?'

'What?'

'The stone at Goodrich?'

Jane considered. It was the biggest standing stone in the Wye Valley. She'd seen old photographs of it, but...

'It's on private farmland,' she said. 'You can't get near it any more.'

'It's been on private land for over four hundred years,' Sorrel said. 'Sometimes it's hidden by tall crops. And visiting it would be trespass, so people don't. Have you ever been, Jane?'

'No. There are no signs to it or anything.'

'But a few local people know what used to happen there and remain a bit scared of it. And there's a photo in Alfred Watkins's book that hints at its history.'

'*The Old Straight Track*?'

'No, *Alfred Watkins' Herefordshire*. The book his biographer and his wife published quite recently, with loads of Watkins's old photos in it. Including the one where he's giving some kind of lecture near the Stone?'

Jane's gaze was suddenly on the bookshelf. There was the valuable Garnstone Press hardback of *The Old Straight Track*, published half a century ago. Jane had two copies, would sell one, if necessary. She hadn't looked at Watkins's famous work for years. But she desperately wanted to take it down. Now. And the soft-backed *Alfred Watkins' Herefordshire* next to it. She didn't remember the photo of his lecture there, though she must've seen it.

'Don't you think that's interesting, Jane? By the time that picture was taken, nobody was associating those Bronze Age stones with the druids any more. But here's Alfred Watkins with a recreated wicker man. Makes you think, doesn't it?'

'Think what?'

'What he knew.'

'What do you *think* he knew? I don't remember him actually saying anything about the Queen Stone and a wicker man.'

'He didn't,' Sorrel said. 'He let his picture say it all.'

'*What?*'

'I think,' Sorrel told her, 'that *I've* said enough.'

36

Wild surmise

JANE CLIMBED INTO the Land Rover, two books under her arm.

'I've got to tell you, Gomer, that we could be breaking the law here.'

Gomer nodded and drove them out of the village onto the bypass. Jane watched the last two cottages disappear into the left-hand wing-mirror.

'Is that OK with you, Gomer?'

'Sure t'be.'

'You don't want a police record at your age.'

Gomer had his flat cap on. It looked like his grin went all the way up to its brim.

'Ow you know I en't got a record already?'

'Because you're too smart ever to get caught trespassing,' Jane said.

'Dunno if that's true, Janey…'

'But you're not going to contradict me.'

'Sure to,' Gomer said. 'Where you say we're goin', again? Need to know I got enough diesel in yere, 'fore we gets past all the pumps where I got pals.'

'Goodrich, if that's not too far. Down past Ross?'

'Ent no problem at all, Janey.'

Gomer sucked on the stub of his ciggy. Jane would normally have felt unhappy about the number of cigs he was continuing to roll, but she'd heard on the radio that people in hospital with the virus tended *not* to be smokers. The world was a weird, contradictory place.

She said, 'You know the Queen Stone?'

Gomer thought about it. He wouldn't need to. There wasn't anywhere in this county he couldn't find driving blindfold through a snowstorm.

'That'd be the ole stone standin' up next to the river? Big grooves down him?'

Is there nothing he doesn't know?

'I think so, yes, though I've only seen pictures.'

'This feller...' Gomer tapped one of two books lying between Jane's knees '... I never met him. Before my time, see.'

'He died in 1935.'

'But his grandson... *he* rung me once.'

'He didn't really, did he?'

'Twenty or so years ago. He had this relation from down south wanted to come up and take photos of a few of the ole stones as was hard for some folks to find, so...'

'Alfred Watkins's grandson hired you to drive the guy around?'

'And findin' this yere Queen Stone, that meant driving across a few fields, but I reckon I done it.'

'Of course, you did,' Jane said. 'I never for a minute thought you wouldn't have.'

A great cure for scepticism was Gomer Parry.

She'd have persuaded him to take her a couple of years ago if she seen the picture in the book under her arm and made the druid connection that was now getting her so excited.

Bloody *hell.*

*

Lol would say that, seen from a distance, it looked like a very big stone guitar plectrum sticking out of the soil. And you *could* see it from a distance. It was the only standing stone in the lower valley, set in a wide field, in a deep curve of the Wye.

Inside her head, the music began. Then the words.

I am a simple trackway man
Who walks the lanes by ancient plan
Leading the people from beacon to steeple
And steeple to stone

And all the way home.

Lol Robinson's voice. His song. The one he'd written as Alfred Watkins.

She looked up and saw the middle-distant steeple of the village church at Goodrich. It was hardly Lol's finest song, but many people knew it now and sang along at gigs. Back in the day when you were allowed to hold gigs.

From moat to mound
We'll mark the ground
From barrow to camp
We'll carry the lamp

For some reason, Jane suddenly found all this slightly sinister. There was no path to the Queen Stone, no signs to it. You actually were not supposed to visit it.

An approaching vehicle could be seen only from a boat or canoe on the winding river.

Gomer had parked discreetly inside a field gate and followed Jane under a heavy dark-grey sky. You couldn't avoid the sensation of your progress across the grass being carefully watched by the monument.

‘The ole stone d’know we’re comin’,’ Gomer said.

‘You feel that, too?’

The stone was said to resemble, from some angles, the dumpy, middle-aged Queen Victoria, but Jane couldn’t see it. She stopped and opened *The Old Straight Track.*

Alfred Watkins had written,

The legend of this one was that it was a sacrificial stone of the Druids. The deep grooves make to me some grim suggestions connected with Caesar’s report of the Druids burning their victims in wicker cages.

But this is all wild surmise…

Jane closed *The Old Straight Track.* She, too, was good at wild surmise.

Her wildest had always been that she and Mum were actually descendants of Alfred Watkins, the Hereford man who, a hundred years ago, had either discovered or invented leys, the invisible straight lines he believed linked all those sacred stones and earthmounds dating back to the Bronze Age, along with the churches and castles that had been built around them. Joined together they would form ritual tracks across the countryside. Easily discernible in sparsely populated Herefordshire where Watkins had found dozens, taking hundreds of photos of them in the 1920s, using his early cameras and the exposure meter he’d invented. These precise black and white photos making it all so real when Lol had been writing *Simple Trackway Man*, which explained the Watkins philosophy.

‘See the grooves?’ Jane asked Gomer. She opened the hardback. ‘It’s over seven feet tall, it says here, and nearly as wide. “A sacrificial stone of the Druids”. There’s a kind of certainty about the way Alfred says that.’

Jane lifted the other book: *Alfred Watkins' Herefordshire*. There was the photograph of white-haired Watkins talking to a crowd gathered at this stone. A wooden cage had been constructed around it and there was a couple of figures inside, possibly kids.

'It's an actual wicker man,' she said. 'They made a druidic wicker man for Alfred so he could explain what happened here. Look at the size of that crowd!'

'When would that be, Janey?'

'Nineteen twenties.'

'Not long after World War One, then. Even afore my time.'

'But it happened, Gomer, even if it was way back. This stone could've been on the site of a wicker man... and then used as the base for one.'

She thoughts of the signs of fire that Alfred had found near the grooves in the stone and shut the book. It had disclosed that the photo was, in fact, a still from a length of primitive cine film shot in 1925. No wonder it had been missing for so long.

'See the significance of this?' Jane said. 'Everybody thought *The Wicker Man* was the first time a druid mass-sacrifice had been shown in a movie, but it wasn't. *This* was, even if it was mocked-up. I'm probably the first to actually see that but...'

She moved closer to the forbidden stone, feeling drawn in by its magnetism. She was tingling.

'...and how did Alfred know it was a *druid* sacrificial stone?'

Gomer just nodded. He didn't seem affected by the monument.

'Because he was *psychic*,' Jane hissed. 'Because he saw it all happening in his head, and he had it recreated. Bloody *hell*.'

Psychic? Alfred knew he was. His son pointed that out in his own book years later. Back then, it wasn't something you bragged about. Alfred was a businessman in Hereford and a magistrate. He had his reputation to protect. He didn't *want* to be known as psychic.

Jane looked slightly nervously around in case there were sceptics like the Bishop of Hereford listening.

But there was nobody in sight, and she'd reached the stone. Bigger than it had seemed. Also bulkier. Her phone chimed and she shook, thinking the sound was coming out of the stone.

'Hello?'

'Jane? It's only me.'

'Mum…'

She held the phone closer to her mouth so it wouldn't give away any *nature* sounds.

'Jane, I'm going out. Over to Goodrich and then I've got the Portis funeral. Back before dark.'

'Oh.'

The funeral was today?

There weren't many vehicles around in lockdown. The chances of Mum seeing Gomer and her were just too high today. They couldn't hang around.

'I've arranged to meet Arlo Ripley to pick up some stuff for the Portis funeral,' Mum said. 'And any other useful information I might need.'

Jane instinctively glanced up at Goodrich church then across at Gomer, backing away.

'What time are you leaving, Mum?'

'I guess in about five minutes? So I won't have time to see you till tonight. I'll leave you some stuff out for lunch. That OK?'

'Er… fine. Thanks. Have you had time to talk to the relatives?'

The succubus? Would she be there?

Mum said not, but it probably wouldn't matter. It wasn't much more than formality with only a few people allowed to attend and no hymns because that could mean breathing on one another.

Talk about panic…

*

Jane looked at the Queen Stone. It was sometimes said that the vertical grooves in it were for letting sacrificial blood drain into the earth. Artificial grooves weren't found on many stones. Some experts said they were natural but Alfred Watkins had found this unlikely. Jane remembered what he'd written in *The Old Straight Track:*

'A passing country-woman supplied this bit of local legend: "Do you know what they say about it? That if you prick it with a pin at midnight, it bleeds."

'This was Alfred getting what he called *a glimmer of folklore memory.*'

'What had he got there, Janey, in them ley lines?' Gomer asked.

Jane was silent for a while, considering. She looked at the stone and then at Gomer.

'I was told a while back that,' she said, 'that you knew all about leys. From when you were younger… back in Radnorshire.'

'I forgets these things,' Gomer said. 'All this yere psychic stuff with the ole stones.'

But she knew he hadn't. You didn't forget the stories you grew up with. She looked at the Queen Stone, imagined straight branches sprouting from its tight grooves, forming the uprights of a cage in which people were held. *Whoosh*, she heard – flames fiercely claiming twigs and then the slender branches, then dry clothing aflare, scorching skin, fizzing on crispening, blackening flesh.

Jane turned away.

'Gomer,' she said, 'I need to make a short phone call, is that all right?'

*

'I don't think Wordsworth ever mentions the Queen Stone in a poem,' Lol said in the mobile. 'But then, why would he? Although it's quite likely he saw it when he was here. He was always fascinated by old stones, and we know he spent time in Goodrich.'

'Looking for the little girl who talked to her dead siblings,' Jane said. 'She would definitely know this stone well, living so close. So Wordsworth himself was already into ancient sites?'

'Absolutely. All his life. He wrote about "Lines, circles, mounts, a mystery of shapes..."? So I think it's fair to say he and Alfred Watkins were coming from the same direction in consecutive centuries.'

'That's amazing, Lol. Would Alfred have known about Wordsworth's interest in leys even if he had different words for them?'

'Alfred Watkins died less than a hundred years after Wordsworth, who would've had a lot of things to ask him. We tend to forget that. Wordsworth was well aware of the power of stones.'

Jane was nodding seriously. Her phone call seemed to have enlivened Lol, who identified with both these guys and appeared to see a trail in this area crossing the landscape and the centuries. She'd collect all the pertinent references together and maybe go and see him and try to come to some conclusions.

'You do Wordsworth at school, Lol?'

'Not in any depth. Never got far beyond the host of golden daffs, anyway. Wasn't interested until a couple of years ago when your mum showed me Brinsop church and I found out he was well into ancient monuments and used to think of himself as a latent druid.'

'I wonder if he was in a semi-pagan period when he was living down here,' Jane said. 'His great Wye Valley works – none of them mention God, though he was clearly into something.'

'At school, we never learned about that side of him.' She felt that Lol was shrugging. 'See, Wordsworth, as a young guy, was essentially a hippy. A couple of hundred years before the word was known… and then widely sneered at.' He sighed. 'What we need is a *new* word for people who value places like this and think outside the box. And that word isn't going to be *green*.'

Heavier than that, Jane thought.

She said, 'You're not just a songwriter, are you?'

37

Called on darkness

FROM BEHIND THE rainy windscreen, it was like watching a watercolour painting slowly drying. You could see St Giles's slim steeple, spearing the trees, then pushing into low cloud – the last raincloud for quite a while, according to the Met Office weather forecast on Merrily's laptop.

Everything was seeping into stillness. Arlo Ripley was waiting at the top of the drive. He was dressed quietly, in dark, casual clothes, suede shoes, no dog collar. He carried a thick brown book spraying out page-markers of different primary colours: Wordsworth's complete poems, important lines highlighted, Merrily assumed.

She left the car outside Churchyard Cottage and joined him.

'It's a unique village, this,' he said. 'I'm starting to see that. Does the church still hold itself apart in its own circle of place and time? How many churches have ever been sealed off from traffic? Especially in a village this size. Do *you* know of any others?'

'People say several attempts have been made to provide vehicular access,' Merrily said. 'But the church seems to resist it. Perhaps it's not meant.'

Superstition. Time appeared to have fallen away at the end of a footpath paved with poems. Merrily stepped into the field which led to listing graves. Everything here was somehow coming back to Wordsworth. You could imagine the shade of an eight-year-old girl peering through the bushes.

When Maya joined them Merrily thought of the children *she'd* claimed to have seen. *Sometimes they swoop... and I realize they're all around me. Especially out here.* Merrily was surprised by a shiver. She had a book of Wordsworth's work in the poacher's pocket of her waxed jacket. She left it there.

Maya carried a cloth bag over a shoulder. As they wandered into Goodrich churchyard, a sliver of new sun was gilding the tip of the steeple. The church looked better preserved than most of the graves, on which lettering was often worn before its time, obscured by mud. Just below the oldest part of the graveyard, the village was subsiding into its nest of trees.

'Where's the river gone?' Merrily asked. 'I can't really tell from here. I'm disoriented.'

'Less than half a mile that way.' Maya extending an arm then swinging it round. 'And about the same distance *that* way. It keeps coming back on itself.' She walked into the grassy churchyard. 'The Wye seems to go mad here, forming great loops so that it's very nearly all around us. You just can't see it. But I get the feeling it can see you.'

Arlo Ripley had now wandered off on his own. He'd said he had a lot to think about, some lines to memorize. Maya said you could do that by connecting them with images of the places they might have been created. Pointing at the close horizon, she spun away, peeled dark hair back from eyes that were shining excitedly as Arlo sent serene verse sliding down the graveyard.

'"And I have felt a presence... a sense sublime of something far more deeply interfused, whose dwelling is the light of setting suns."'

'Wrong time of day, but it glows in your memory,' Merrily said. 'What do you think he meant by it?'

'I don't somehow think he meant God,' Maya said. 'Not yours, anyway. Not then. He was still half-pagan. And *I* have to say I think it meant stronger poetry.'

Merrily said nothing. Maya raised an arm towards the flank of Coppett Hill.

'He walked through nature and nature walked through him. It was a kind of god I never quite understood till I walked some of the valley for myself, quite recently.' She moved under the steeple. 'Walking, for Wordsworth, was itself a form of meditation. A spiritual exercise.'

'Didn't someone say the metre of his poems could be measured out in footsteps?'

Merrily looked around, realizing how little here must have changed since the poet had made the bootprints they were trying to follow. She watched Arlo Ripley's careful steps and heard appropriate lines find the rhythm as he brought his feet down.

'"Five *summers* with *the length*"' – a stride – '"of *five long winters*..."'

'He thought he was walking *into* something,' Maya said. 'By the time he met the little girl, I'm guessing he was rather high on all this scenery. So what she said about her dead siblings, who were not, for her, entirely gone, would have been so much more resonant. And become even more so, some years later, when he'd lost a couple of his own young children.'

This whole phase – perhaps the key phase in Wordsworth's entire poetic career, Maya told them – began with his return from France, a changed person: an adult, a father, but not a husband.

He'd been confused, she said, after coming back from France – now in the throes of the French Revolution, which, as a republican, he'd originally supported till he was exposed to all that blood. And then there was the rise of Napoleon – French imperialism. France at war with England.

'Wordsworth finally made it home – emotionally drained, disillusioned and out of cash,' Maya said. 'Leaving behind his French girlfriend, Annette, and their daughter, Caroline.'

'Must have been very difficult for them,' Merrily said, thinking of Jane when she was very young and her father had died on the motorway.

'William was thinking they'd join him in England when it was all over and they'd all live happily ever. Along with his beloved sister Dorothy, who was only a year or so younger than him and very much a part of his life.'

'And in a way, a driving force,' Merrily said, remembering now. 'But them all living together… it never got close to happening, did it?'

'No. When he got back… well, he had good friends, of course, and life went on. When he got back, an old schoolfriend, William Calvert, took him on a walking tour, from the Isle of Wight into the west of England.'

Maya opened up her case, took out an old brown book, opening it to a map showing the course of the lower Wye between Ross and Chepstow, down to where it came out into the Severn estuary, near Bristol.

'They moved up-country, travelling in this horse-drawn buggy… which unfortunately came apart on Salisbury Plain,' Maya said. 'Leaving Wordsworth walking solo. Calvert went off on the horse. You know about any of this?'

Merrily shook her head. 'I should do, but…'

'In a way, it was fate stepping in,' Maya said. 'Showing William important things… important for him. His enforced solo journey, on foot, took him across the plain, past Stonehenge. But he didn't immediately go past the monument. He actually wound up sleeping there.'

'On his own?' Merrily blinked. 'Among the old stones?'

'So we're told.'

'At night?'

'We don't know where exactly, or the time. But the henge was much lonelier then. No main roads, no traffic, no noise. We don't know how long he slept there, but we gather… that there were particular dreams.'

'Oh.'

There had to have been dreams.

'Vivid dreams,' Maya said. 'Possibly hallucinatory. And maybe he wasn't always asleep when they came to him. Arlo finds this a little disturbing, but Wordsworth was in a strange state of mind. Nobody knows how long it all lasted. But, because this was Wordsworth, there was, of course, poetry at the end.'

Maya moved to the side of the road, picking up the shadow of the church.

'"I called…"' Her voice rose. '"I called on Darkness – but before the word was uttered, midnight darkness seemed to take all objects from my sight".'

Maya closed her eyes. Merrily imagined her intoning this dramatically into clusters of students.

'"And… and dismal flames…"'

Maya's voice died back into her breath. She stopped, apparently unable to remember what came next, then began again.

'"It is the sacrificial altar, fed with living men",' a male voice picked up melodramatically. '"How deep the groans! The voice of those that crowd the giant wicker…"'

He'd walked around the church wall, Merrily recognizing the voice before he appeared, and the voice didn't seem to be taking it all that seriously,

'He'd been fascinated by druids since he was a boy,' Arlo said. 'Knew all the stone circles in the Lake District where he grew up. In his day, many people still thought the druids had built them, and druids were always connected with poetry.'

Even more so in this area,' Merrily said. 'Druids may have been the first Welsh bards and were said to have met up on the Doward. In an oak grove or whatever.'

'As far as I can gather,' Maya said, 'the druids left no evidence of their presence. People used to think they were responsible for stone circles and altars, but there's reason to believe they just worshipped in trees. All the temples were natural, which is why none are left.'

'And is that why they appealed to Wordsworth?' Merrily said. 'They worshipped nature, as he did, and they were doing it *inside* nature?'

'Well deduced,' Maya said. 'This issue is being developed in our programme – what I was telling you about, Arlo – the section where you lie in the long grass and enter a trance state?'

'I said yesterday that I didn't see him so easily relinquishing his senses.' Arlo Ripley's lips curving down in mild distaste. 'I still don't feel his intellect submitting to what you're calling call a "trance state".'

'Read it again, please,' Maya said. 'Slowly. And think that if you don't believe it, perhaps Wordsworth did. For a time. And *that*... is the time we're recreating.'

Arlo frowned.

38

Deep power of joy

'I CAN TAKE you down to the river, not far past Symonds Yat,' Maya said, 'and show you a sycamore tree where Wordsworth may well have got the idea for "Tintern Abbey".'

'How did he get the idea?' Merrily asked him. 'How did it come to him?'

Maya smiled.

'Maybe he had a dream?'

She knew what kind of dream. Or she knew what Vaynor's thesis said, and where Vaynor had found his Wordsworthian sycamore and lay down to enter an altered state of consciousness.

'The old druids would have called it something that we would call a trance,' Maya said. 'Druids have been said to habitually enter trance states at the climax of a ritual. Arlo doesn't want to think that Wordsworth also did; he's still something of an orthodox theologian.'

'Have you ever been in a deep trance state yourself?' Merrily asked.

'Perhaps, to an extent… and the druids, did they take drugs?'

Merrily shrugged. Darth Vaynor had thought so. Probably not chemical, but almost certainly the ones you still found growing around here: psilocybin – magic mushrooms. All in his thesis which, with using magic mushrooms being illegal, did not look good coming from a serving police officer.

She didn't elaborate. Arlo Ripley was examining Sir Samuel Meyrick's neglected burial place.

Maya whispered, 'Arlo's been trying to get into Wordsworth's rhythm. His walking pace. That's his secret, as you said: picking up the metre with his feet. It's how I see this programme coming together. Arlo feeling the crucial poetry in his legs as he passes through it. We're trying to find the places where the poetry reached for the poet and hope it reaches for him.'

When Arlo walked away Merrily decided to follow him and have a few words about Portis funeral.

'I did want to see you,' he said. 'And not only to give you some background on Peter Portis.'

Carefully distanced, they'd walked round the steeple to the front of the church.

'I'm sorry this all happened so quickly,' Arlo said. 'I'll be explaining in full to the relatives. I know them… rather well now.'

'I'll have to ring them, too.'

'No, it's my responsibility. I'll explain to them in full. I don't want them to have two versions. And I didn't intend to mislead you, either. When we first spoke, on the phone, I had absolutely no intention of leaving the Church. But there was, of course, another factor I wasn't fully aware of.'

They were approaching the main entrance. Merrily tried the door. Firmly locked.

'The virus?' she said.

Arlo Ripley stepped away among the graves, nodding grimly.

'None of us could have foreseen the extent of this horror. And it won't be forgotten or even over in the foreseeable future, will it?'

She said nothing. He leaned on a tall headstone.

'We don't know how many congregations will survive this pandemic, do we? Even whether the C of E itself will continue in the same way... or even continue at all. At St Dubricius and many other churches, there's been the flooding as well. Is it all connected, Merrily? Is the Church under attack from all sides?'

'It makes you think,' Merrily said. 'If congregations are drastically reduced, then the number of parish priests...'

'Beginning with me?' Concern shadowing his eyes. 'Yes, I know.'

'I hadn't meant to—'

'Who can blame you?' he said. You haven't been offered a life-changing contract.'

'Or life – *saving.* If I was, I might, right now, be feeling tempted.'

'I have to say, Merrily, that I'm grateful to Maya but I don't feel good about myself or what I'm doing. I'm throwing myself into this role, which isn't as solidly Christian as I thought it was going to be. I know I should be conducting this afternoon's micro-funeral for the Portis family, but obviously I can't now, and I can't very well come to the service and apologize to the family.'

Merrily felt his distress more powerfully than she'd expected to and put a tentative hand on his arm. He moved away.

'I won't be at the funeral, and it won't be an easy one. But I won't be far away. I intend to apologize to Him. Or Her. Offer a quiet prayer by the river – and I don't mean enter a *meditative state.*'

He took a cardboard folder from under his arm and handed it to her. It had a label, handwritten. *Peter Portis.*

'There could be a memorial service in the Cathedral later, which the Bishop may conduct himself. You'll just be at the small one to solemnize a burial in front of a close handful of people.'

'So I'm thinking a lengthy eulogy may not be required.'

'Nobody will expect that. I could, in theory, have carried on with it myself, but I think the Archdeacon would prefer it this way. I've... known her... a long time.'

Neither of them followed this up. She didn't look at him.

'So when you said this wouldn't be an easy one...'

'It has elements of uncertainty,' Arlo said. 'It might be a short service, but it needs dealing with professionally, so there are no awkward questions. Local people who knew him say he was too experienced a rock climber to fall like that. Especially from rocks he knew so well.'

'But he didn't leave a note, and so...'

'Perhaps he didn't want people to know that it wasn't an accident.'

'So *you* think it was...?'

'These are strange days,' Arlo said. 'If they found he'd had any virus symptoms, that's what it would say on the death certificate, simplifying things. As things are, I suspect a lot will need carefully covering up.'

On the other side of the parish church, she found Maya Madden was waiting alone, with her back to the wall, her cloth bag at her feet, opened up. She was making notes on a pad.

'Have you seen DC Vaynor again?' Merrily asked her. 'I'll explain why I need to know that.'

'No, but he phoned,' Maya said. 'To ask how I was feeling. He gave me his mobile number and told me to call him if... if I needed to. He seemed on edge about something. Uncertain. I felt he wanted to say something else to me, but he seemed to change his mind.'

Merrily frowned.

'How well do you know him?'

Maya shrugged.

'He was the police detective who came to see me because I was the first on the scene after Peter Portis died. And then I saw him again in Ross-on-Wye where I mentioned I was here to research a programme about William Wordsworth. Having found out by then that he probably knew more about Wordsworth than I did. Presumably you know about his Oxford doctorate.'

'And I've read...' Merrily tapped the manuscript, '...this.'

Maya began to look confused.

'"The Wye in Wordsworth"?'

Maya stood unsteadily, looking for a few moments as if she could barely breathe.

'You're actually saying *he* is responsible for this?'

'He didn't say?'

'"The Wye in..."' She held the typescript between both hands, shaking it. '"The Wye in Wordsworth"? Are you telling me honestly that this Al Fox, who I was directed to online is – or was – *DC Vaynor*?'

'You genuinely didn't know?'

'How long have *you* known?'

'I only read it last night,' Merrily said. 'A friend told me it was put online by someone who thought David Vaynor's decision to become a policeman was a mistake. A loss to literary studies. And other stuff.'

'Oh *God*. And now you probably realize it's... a surprising... and inspirational piece of scholarship.' Maya propped her back against the church wall again. 'No, he didn't own up to it. I wanted to interview him... ask him as the holder of a doctorate in English literature, how important he thought Wordsworth was to this area. And now here I am simplifying and rewriting most of it as a documentary script, without permission.'

'He wouldn't *give* you permission,' Merrily said. 'But he wouldn't refuse you, either. His thesis has some ideas which I don't think he can prove, and, as a working policeman, he wouldn't want to put his name to.'

Merrily looked up at the slim steeple, up to some cottage roofs, and then across to where she assumed the river flowed.

'Maya... you need to understand that Vaynor's been walking away from Wordsworth. He thinks he was treading too close. That there are some things he's been trying to get rid of... Things that he thinks originated in Wordsworth's time and should have stayed there, not floated up into ours. Things that have made Vaynor wonder what was happening back then, in the 1790s, to make this place so significant for Wordsworth... so spiritually powerful that it started to change the whole direction of his work.'

'Quite a few people have seen that.' Maya nodded. 'But it wasn't permanent, was it? After leaving here, he found a kind of peace. Became happily married. Stopped travelling around with his sister who always saw the genius in him... maybe too much genius. And people like the poet Coleridge, who was closer to...'

Merrily said, 'Closer to the paranormal edge?'

This time, Maya moved well away from the church wall. Arlo Ripley was walking around it from the other side, reading from his book of poems. Then he stopped, looked up.

'*I* don't think,' he said, a little irritably, 'that it happened like this. I think this is how he liked to imagine it happening, but I think he wrote these lines at his desk, with a clear head. And that's where I want the viewers to see him. Not rolling in the long grass under a hot sun...'

'So say it,' Maya said softly. 'Say it as if you're out of vision, and don't overdramatize.'

'What are you telling me to do?'

'I'm just suggesting you keep it casual.'

Arlo looked as if he might object, then slowly held the book out from his chest, stepped away from the church and spoke in a voice that Merrily quickly recognized.

'"...motion of our human blood almost suspended, we are laid asleep in body, and become a living soul..."'

The flattened voice of a semi-stoned Simon Wilding.

'"...while with an eye made quiet by the power of harmony, and the deep power of joy..."'

Maya pulled Merrily away, said softly, close to her ear, 'I keep getting the feeling I'm entering another country. And, although I realize you'll be the last to accept this, Merrily, I'm beginning to think it's *your* country.'

'"...we see..."' Arlo shut the book '"...into the life of things".'

He walked away, following the church wall.

'Close,' Maya murmured. 'But I think it needs more of a northern accent.'

39

Line through time

JANE PUT DOWN the book on Lol's desk under the living room window at Lucy's cottage.

The Old Straight Track by Alfred Watkins. An early hardback, its white cover yellowing, which looked appropriate framing the sepia photo of a path through a field.

Jane flattened out the book on its back, holding down the OS map.

'If we follow this particular ley, it's taking us to the heart of the mystery.'

'Mystery?'

Lol looked uncertain.

'A mystery which, if he'd been around a century earlier, Alfred could have solved for Wordsworth,' Jane said. 'Can you see them both walking this path in their separate eras, unaware of one another? I can.'

'Well, I'll try.'

Taking off his glasses, he leaned over the map and began to see, in a mist, the half-formed figures of William Wordsworth and Alfred Watkins gliding together across the blurry Herefordshire landscape, following the invisible line joining prehistoric stones, earth mounds and ancient churches. He couldn't see the symbols on the map, but he thought he could see the line. Without his glasses.

He said, 'How do you know this was the way Wordsworth came?'

'He *had* to,' Jane said emphatically. 'He was coming down from the Doward, heading for Goodrich Castle. It's obvious. Look, he goes past this old church, along the river bank…'

Making her forefinger follow the connected monuments. What would it do to her if some experienced archaeologist proved conclusively that leys did not exist, that it was all fantasy? OK, it was very unlikely that Alfred was actually among her Watkins ancestors, she knew that. But if his ideas produced enough of a buzz to light up this map for her…

'The odd thing is that, while Alfred indicates there *are* leys passing through the Queen Stone, they aren't identified here in his book,' Jane said. 'And this one's obvious, but he's keeping it a bit obscure, and hinting it's a dangerous area.'

'He didn't normally let that sort of thing get to him,' Lol said. 'And anyway, with a stone like this in the lower Wye Valley, surrounded by rolling fields, distant hills, a prominent steeple… all easy to find.'

Lol had never been there, but he'd seen pictures. He pointed with a red felt pen, drawing small circles on the map.

'It's interesting. The Queen Stone's been hidden away on private land for over four centuries. On the map, though, it's on a line joining other important places, including…' Lol slid his finger along the line. 'King Arthur's Cave! Bloody hell, Jane.'

Jane sat back, grinning. She clearly liked the idea of a grown man still getting excited about finding connections between magical places in the countryside and drawing circles round them with a red felt-pen.

'Take your time, Lol, I want us to get this very clear.'

It may not have been an exact alignment but it had to be

close. Lol didn't say anything, just kept following the line on the map, through the Queen Stone which had been sunk into a loop of river between Goodrich and Symonds Yat.

Before the stone, he saw a small cross + signifying the little riverside church of St Dubricius before the line dived into the base of the Doward, passing through King Arthur's Cave and the Seven Sisters rocks and ending up at something labelled...

'Far Hearkening Rock?' Jane jabbed it with a forefinger. 'I've *heard* of that, but it's a natural feature, not man-made.'

'Well, maybe but... I've never been there either but I've heard how it got that name. It's supposed to bounce sound back. And look, we're back at the river, no obvious crossing here, so I'm guessing it's the last point on the ley.' He looked across at Jane through half-closed eyes. 'Are you seeing it?'

'I'm seeing all kinds of things. If you pick up a vibe at Far Hearkening Rock, are you getting the same sensations at the Queen Stone and the church of St Dubricius?'

Jane looked up from the stone, at the river beyond it and then back at the map. Lol felt they were inside a moving organism.

'Tell me what *you* feel,' he said.

'OK... We *think* that leys were telling ancient people how they related to the countryside and how the countryside related to the world, and even the cosmos, through its sacred places. Alfred Watkins gave up his last good years to all this. And I don't think he wrote down all he sensed at these places.'

Jane was excited, and if you could excite someone of Jane's age with old rural magic, then it was still valid, Lol thought. Whether used for positive purposes or for the deepest, most voracious evil, the power was here.

He said, 'There could have been more to Alfred Watkins than any of them knew, even Watkins himself.'

'He was psychic,' Jane said.

'I've read that too.'

'He wouldn't have wanted people to know that. Didn't want to seem like a crank. Being accepted as a legitimate archaeologist was enough for him.'

'But, a century ago, leading archaeologists were refusing to accept him as one of them,' Lol said. 'They would have said that St Dubricius's Church and King Arthur's Cave came from entirely different eras and had no connection with each other so he must be a charlatan or deluding himself.'

'In which case they were missing things,' Jane tapped the map. 'Look at all these points in a straight line over a fairly short distance. A mysterious Stone Age cave linked to King Arthur, and an ancient riverside church dedicated to the man who's supposed to have *baptized* him.'

Lol nodded.

'They date back to different centuries… even different millennia, but they both connect to this one legendary person. If he existed…'

'Whether he existed or not…' Jane thumped the map '…it means *something*. They both draw on the same legends. Then we have the Doward, this traditionally mystical wooded hill crowded with signs of Bronze Age settlement and possible—*probable* – druidic worship…'

'And below the Doward, a stone with an alleged history of druidic blood-sacrifice.' Lol opened *Alfred Watkins' Herefordshire* at the Queen Stone pictures. 'Where did Watkins get the idea that the stone had supported its own small wicker man?'

Jane hugged herself. This was Druidism at its worst.

'Through the stories of local people. And through *his own psychic intuition*. This is an enchanted landscape, Lol! And it's still active.'

'Still *active*?'

'It started out as a real ancient Stone Age and then Bronze Age alignment before being taken over by the druids.'

'They didn't build it but they do seem to have used it,' Lol said.

'And it's still… Things *happen* on this alignment. Look at the other points – the Seven Sisters rocks, where the guy fell to his death, and the little church of Dubricius by the river is where Mum's suddenly going to be doing his funeral. And there's…'

She stopped. Lol didn't see how the death-fall fitted in and wondered where this was going, apart from along the archaeologically-untrustworthy straight line.

O
Far Hearkening Rock

DOWARD

*

King Arthur's Cave

*

St Dubricius's Church

Q
Queen Stone

< GOODRICH

A line through time? Lol looked down to the Queen Stone and raised his gaze towards Goodrich village and its steepled church which was not aligned with it. Then he followed the line the other way, towards the sometimes-ominous wooded hill housing King Arthur's Cave, which seemed to begin it.

'Listen,' Jane said, 'some of this I'm not supposed to know about, but… there are things I kind of happened to overhear at home. Through the scullery wall as it happens, but that doesn't matter. I heard it, and now I'm suggesting King Arthur's Cave was also used by druids… *and may still be.*'

'I can imagine it probably *used* to be used by them. But still? Would these be your friends in the Pod who usually go down to Stonehenge to watch the midsummer sunrise?'

'I'm not talking about a New Age thing. The Doward druids were the ancient kind.' Jane was not smiling. 'The ones who burned their enemies alive in the wicker man, and now seem to practise weird sexual rites in the dark.'

'Huh?' Lol shuffled out a smile. 'Sorry?'

Jane said nothing, waiting as three or four seconds passed in a hush.

Lol said, 'You did say weird sexual rites? Where's that come from?'

Silence. Jane pushed a bent knuckle into pursed lips as if she'd said something she maybe shouldn't have.

'Lol… have you,' she said eventually, 'ever heard of a succubus?'

It didn't take him too long to nod. He knew his folklore.

He said, 'An aggressive – a sexually aggressive – female spirit. Who seduces men in the dark?'

'Or when they're asleep.'

'That's a druidic thing?'

'In the old days, people would always find magic behind it, and if the magic in this area was druidic…'

'And are druids still around? In this area?'

Jane said nothing.

'It, uh… it was a serious question, Jane. All kinds of people end up in quiet places like this.'

Jane said, 'A guy came to talk to Mum, and said – this was what I overheard – that he'd been… attended to sexually, shall we say? By a woman who, like, meets the criteria.'

'Criteria.'

'Ticks all the boxes for manifesting as a… Shit, I don't know what words to use so as not to sound—'

'Spectral predator?'

'You already think I'm crazy, don't you?'

Part Four

To Gods delighting in remorseless deeds;
Gods which themselves had fashioned, to promote
Ill purposes, and flatter foul desires.
Then, in the bosom of yon mountain cove
To those inventions of corrupted Man
Mysterious rites were solemnized; and there,
Amid impending rocks and gloomy woods,
Of those dread Idols, some, perchance, received
Such dismal service, that the loudest voice
Of the swoln cataracts (which now are heard
Soft murmuring) was too weak to overcome,
Though aided by wild winds, the groans and shrieks
Of human Victims, offered up to appease
Or to propitiate.

William Wordsworth,
'The Excursion'

40
Prey

BLISS READ THE report again. It didn't take long. He tossed it dismissively across his table.

'Probably won't even make a friggin' open verdict.'

Vaynor had to nod. He'd read the report twice this morning as soon as he'd come in. What could he say?

'Slim Fiddler's team spent a lot of time on top of the rocks, boss. And Dr Grace himself appears to have done his best.'

Bliss snatched up the report as he came to his feet, flapping it at Vaynor.

'*This*... is his bleed'n *best*?'

'No sign of a struggle. No sign of anybody else going up there before Crime Scene arrived.'

When Bliss punched his left fist into his right palm, Vaynor stepped back as if he'd taken the blow.

'And you, uh, still need me at the funeral this afternoon?'

'We're still wairking, Darth. And it's an outside service. Couldn't be safer. Of *course* I need you at the friggin' funeral!'

'I might have a problem if there are too many people there,' Vaynor said. 'Restricting numbers seems to have become a serious rule.'

'You don't gerrout of it that easy. I've fixed it for you. Listen, I still think, for no valid reason except the kind of guy he is, that Royce killed his old man, and I want him for it. People with a lorra money think they're immune. So, for a start, I'd like evil rumours circulating at the posh end of town. Curb your natural discretion.'

'Boss, I was at school with him.'

'So you know what kind of kid he was,' Bliss said. 'And people don't change much, they just find ways of concealing what they are.'

Back at the shop, Jane called the Pod, where a recorded message told her that, for the foreseeable future, Sorrel was working from home. So Jane called her home at Walford near Ross.

She had to do this. She wasn't a kid any more. By the time this pandemic was over she'd be far beyond that stage. The virus had frozen time, especially in this area, where it wasn't infecting too many people medically but was still a stranglehold on normal life.

Sorrel answered the phone in seconds.

'Thank God you're in,' Jane said.

'Of course I'm in. This is lockdown. Nobody's allowed to go anywhere, except in a dire emergency.'

'And I know you're under all kinds of pressure. I promise this'll be the last time I bother you about...'

'Venus?'

'That's what we're calling her now, is it?'

'Especially over the telephone. Some people, as we both know, are rich and well-connected.'

'Sorrel, look, I just want to know what basis she has for calling herself a druid. Is it just an assumed religion like a lot of your members have?'

'As I've told you, Jane, Venus is not one of our members.'

'Then what kind of druid is she?'

Sorrel sighed.

'As near as you'll find round here to an authentic one. That's what she'd say, if she deigned to speak to you. Authentic is why we invited her to join the Pod. And why, you might say, she refused. Are you looking into Venus for your mother… the Christian priest?'

Had Sorrel added that slightly nastily?

'If you are,' Sorrel said, 'you didn't get anything from me.'

So Sorrel wanted the diocesan exorcist to know about Diana's form of druidism, which was well out of the Pod's league. Though not – *definitely* not – who'd been talking.

Time to go for it.

'Sorrel, is it true that her mother was descended from the druids who held the Doward in the Dark Ages… or Vortigern's time? Obviously, nobody today could legitimately trace their ancestry as far back as the seventh century, so how would she know any of that?'

'I don't know anything about that.'

'It makes sense. In Celtic society women at least had equality with men. The female druid was the prototype witch. Druidry was sexy and made you feel closer to nature. Made things happen.'

'In the Pod, most of us didn't *want* things to happen… not strong things we couldn't explain. We wanted to be excited, but not disturbed. We liked that motto "do what thou wilt, though it harm none". We didn't want to go deeper than that.'

'That didn't appeal to the early local druids, however.' Jane was aware of talking faster. 'For them, harming people was sometimes part of it, isn't that a fact?'

Pregnant pause.

'Does Venus Portis identify with the old local druids?' Jane said. 'The kind we don't really know anything about any more because they didn't write anything down… or do we? *Do* we?'

'I suppose she sees it as part of her tradition. Her mother, Mona... *her* ancestors were connected with Lady Llanover's group from Abergavenny. They revived druidry in the eighteenth and nineteenth centuries.'

'Yeah, but what kind of druidry? Are we looking at the old white-beards with wands snapped from the hedges, who studied the stars... or is this something else?'

Sorrel didn't reply for a few seconds. Then it was a different Sorrel, with a harder, more authoritative voice that shook Jane a little because it was more like the woman she'd known as a young teenager.

'You haven't been listening, Jane.'

'Yes, I have, I—'

'We're talking about *women*.' On this warm day, Sorrel's voice sounded suddenly almost icy. 'Angry women. *Young* women. Who still sometimes cross the Celtic border and... and *hunt*.'

'Huh?'

'You can watch them coming. Hovering under the clouds, carefully choosing a target and then dropping on it like a stone at two hundred miles a hour from the cliffs above Symonds Yat.'

Jane found she was blinking.

'Hunt?'

'Swooping hard on their prey.'

'Like... *birds* of prey?'

'People say that,' Sorrel said. 'How awesomely fast they are. The peregrine falcon, which lives and hunts in the Wye Valley, is the fastest creature in the world. The *fastest creature in the world*. Did you know that?'

'Well yeah, but...'

'And the female is considerably larger than the male.' Sorrel said. 'The dominant gender. Often living on high man-made structures, as well as natural ones like the Seven Sisters rocks.'

'I didn't know that.'

'A lot you don't know.'

'You're comparing female druids to certain rare birds?'

'I've said too much. I'm not involved in druidry at that level, much of it's beyond me, I'll admit that. The birds of prey, with their killing speed, is symbolic of what could happen here at another level.'

This was all getting out of hand. The phone was feeling wet.

Jane was scared. In the past years she'd been intrigued, faintly amused by local pagans. She'd never taken them too seriously. Now she wished there was someone like Lucy Devenish she could talk to again. Someone who understood how paganism could mingle facts with legends, turning your comprehension inside out. No wonder most people kept it entirely out of their lives, turned a blind eye to otherworldly mysteries, embraced scepticism. And also atheism because any kind of god was just confusing. Take all this stuff away and your life would slowly become rational.

But what if your life had also become endlessly tedious, what if it appeared to be going nowhere?

What if it *was* going nowhere?

The phone slid out of her hand, dropped to the floor. When she picked it up Sorrel had gone.

41

No hurry

MERRILY GLANCED OVER the swollen river which didn't seem to have much of a bank left and was near enough to the church porch to suggest a moat.

She stood alongside some dustbins on the edge of the churchyard, opened the envelope Arlo Ripley had given her and read about a man whose hobby had gradually overtaken his business career.

Peter Portis had closed down his Hereford office and opened one in Monmouth. His own farmhouse, up on the Doward, was between the two, with good access to the rocks he loved to climb. He was quoted, in a *Hereford Times* advertising feature, as saying he and the river and the rocks were family, protecting one another. And quoting Wordsworth. *How oft, in spirit, have I turned to thee, O sylvan Wye.*

Sentiments like this from a property dealer would be a source of derision. She folded the printouts and rejoined the path, as the churchyard's stone wall became a fence and the path gave way to a narrow, boarded footbridge over a stream.

'All congregations are rationed, now, because of the virus,' the Archdeacon said. 'I'll let Mr Fenn take it from here. He's spoken to everyone concerned.'

White-haired Adrian Fenn pocketed the church key then turned the stiff metal door handle and pushed hard, propelling himself into the church past a sentry-like DC Vaynor, who didn't acknowledge Merrily; she'd been to enough similar funerals to know why. Also knowing that, with a quarantined congregation, he'd hardly be able to maintain a low profile.

The church of St Dubricius was still unfit for normal use but would apparently do for storage. She followed Fenn inside. Even on a day like this, she knew that the interior, with its double nave, would be glowing, the stained glass supported by modern needlework in warm colours. It would feel welcoming in a *Merrie England* way.

Then she stopped.

'Oh.'

Sian said, 'You weren't told?'

'That the body would be spending a short time in the wet church before burial? No, I... I wasn't.'

She walked up to the stainless-steel bier, clearly awaiting a coffin. On it lay a sleeping snake of pale-blue nylon rope and a red helmet with a small lamp, switched off. A pair of black goggles gazed sightlessly up at the rafters.

Mr Fenn said, 'He won't be here for long and no flowers. Just the climbing equipment, as originally displayed in the window of the PPP agency, in Ross. Perhaps you saw them there?'

'No.' She was realizing she'd never been part of this. 'I've not seen any of this arrangement before. It's... fairly thoughtful, I suppose.'

At the top of the display, two pitons formed a cross. With the holes at the end, for the ropes, they looked like a pair of black scissors. She glanced at the churchwarden. He seemed unsettled, too, which made no immediate sense; he'd surely been in here many times with only a coffin for company.

She looked into the dark screens of the climber's goggles, which presumably would be positioned directly above where the body's eyes would be.

Fenn said, 'It'll look as if he's making sure he's equipped to make his own way to… wherever he's going.'

'Erm… was this the climbing equipment he was wearing when he was found? Had with him when he… fell?'

She glanced at David Vaynor who was clearly here in case it hadn't been as simple as a fall and something might give this away.

Fenn nodded at the tribute tackle.

'It's all supposed to go into the grave with him. Didn't his son explain that?'

Merrily slowly shook her head.

'Which could, as you said, be appearing to leave him with the means to *rise*.'

'That was how I saw it,' Mr Fenn said.

'Or, looking at it another way…' Merrily's head was still in motion '…it could be about burying the sport… putting climbing underground, with several feet of soil on top.'

'This is our first funeral since the lockdown,' Siân Callaghan-Clarke said. 'We can't overcomplicate it.'

The Archdeacon walked back outside. She was in plain clothes, a dark, waterproof coat, high black boots. The sun came through woolly cloud like a searchlight, turning the shaded river a smoky gold.

'There'll be a public announcement about the future of Whitchurch parish when this is over.' Siân had moved to the foot of the bier. 'Now, if you'd care to come with me… The funeral people are here.'

*

The waiting grave was down past a yew tree and no more than half a dozen paces from the riverbank: green baize, pile of earth, a gravedigger in waterproof trousers and, most surreal, a lone canoeist in an orange lifejacket passing in the mist as though he was paddling through the grass. Merrily was made aware that the river was *that* close, *that* high.

It wasn't raining, but she now knew enough about this river to be aware that even brilliant sunshine wouldn't affect what was coming down from the hills of Wales.

She said to Adrian Fenn, 'It's occurred to me you might not be kidding about a burial at sea. How many people are we expecting?'

'We were told we'd have a limit of nine. Including the undertakers... and you. We have a handful of relatives and a few fellow climbers of note. The TV presenter, Mr Gill, who had climbing instruction from Peter Portis.'

'*Smiffy* Gill from *The Octane Show*?'

'Indeed. And representing the property trade, the oldest person from Lang/Copper, the longest-established estate agency in Hereford—'

'Not Geoffrey Unsworth?'

'You know everybody, Mrs Watkins.'

'I know only one estate agent, but it's Mr Unsworth. He's usually very helpful.'

Get it right, Huw Owen would say. *If you get one thing right, make it the funeral.*

She'd asked Adrian Fenn for a glass of water and drunk all of it before slowing her breathing and going up the graveyard, head bowed. Her voice had still been croaky during the welcome and the opening prayers. Now she was telling the congregation how, since the beginning of recorded history, this most dramatic part of the Wye Valley had been very much *a place of legends*, implying that Peter Portis was the latest legend.

It had looked OK scribbled down on the back of a hymn sheet. Said out loud, it sounded like the kind of mock-heroic drivel you'd expect from Jane, who thought everything significant could be linked to the landscape.

She paused. In the shrinkage of time and space that you often experienced in the charged air in or around an active church, she could sense the nearness of the swollen Wye in which St Dubricius's grandfather had tried to drown his mother.

A hearse was parked between the open church door and a cross with steps. Smiffy Gill, middle-aged adolescent with his tufty grey hair and his diamond earring, was leaning against its bonnet looking like he was ready to deliver a piece to camera on *The Octane Show.*

He nodded at the coffin as she passed.

'Tell you one thing from the off, vicar. I'm not buying no accident.'

He grinned. On *The Octane Show*, he was famous for his grins which could switch from coy to full-on gleeful savagery. This one was unusually bleak and made him, for once, seem three-dimensional.

Mr Unsworth looked up, spoke mildly.

'Are you suggesting Peter Portis made away with himself, Mr Gill?'

'*Smiffy.*' Prising himself from the pew-end. 'I'm saying *nuffink* at all, Geoff, except that he was too good on the rocks for an accident. And too careful. I mean *clinically* careful.'

'Geoff*rey*, if you don't mind,' Mr Unsworth said.

There was a soft *thock* as the coffin was settled on its bier at the edge of the path. Merrily didn't glance at it. She'd sensed a current of curiosity passing through the small congregation, too separated for social distance to allow even low chatter. Why was this woman taking the service? people were asking. Where was the celebrity vicar of Whitchurch? The coil of rope, the empty goggles and the lightless lamp were now on the coffin, which she should have spent some time alone with, getting an impression of what the person would want her to say. If you knew about a possible source of unrest that could affect the transition, what you might do was work it into the service, carefully, in an oblique way which would embarrass nobody – not least you, if you'd got it wrong, which was not always unlikely.

Somehow she hadn't even had a chance to shake hands with the man who must be Royce Portis, now standing almost within touching distance, eyes lowered, not looking at her or the coffin while she talked briefly about his father. Pointing out that there were people far more qualified to discuss Peter's life and achievements, as they would have heard in the first hymn, on page three of the order of service, 'Oh God, Our Help in Ages Past'.

Time, like an ever-rolling stream,
Bears all its sons away…

But government rules forbade the singing of hymns because of the powerful – and possibly harmful – breathing they required. The word of God spreading infection. *Jesus.*

Royce Portis had thick near-black hair, finger-combed back from his broad face. He was looking down at something black between his hands that wasn't a prayer book. Maybe his phone. The woman next to Royce – long-sleeved black woollen dress, fairly low-cut for a funeral – caught her eye and smiled warmly. With sympathy, Merrily thought. Unlike Royce, she looked comfortable here.

Merrily pulled her eyes away, concentrating on the coffin, which didn't seem to have any connection with Peter Portis. She'd found a picture of him online, much younger, sitting on a backpack, relaxed, a cigarette between his fingers, smoke drifting up to the rocks. She'd imagined him scaling the misty cliffs over the river, smoky goggles shielding his eyes from an intense sky as he hauled himself up. She looked at the coil of nylon rope, the crossed pitons, the lamp.

And drew a tight breath. A nugget of light was aglow in the lamp on the coffin. Reflection surely.

She smiled quickly at Mr Unsworth, elder statesman of Hereford's property trade, watch-chain glinting between waistcoat buttons under his well-worn black jacket. She saw Smiffy Gill doing his naughty-little-kid grin, eyeing him warily. Was he in danger of losing his programme or something? Did he need to be in the public eye today?

'Erm… your eulogy, first, Smiffy?' she murmured, fearing that he was going to tell her not to let it worry her pretty little head.

But Smiffy Gill became serious again, explaining how Portis and two mates had been brought in to teach *The Octane Show* team how to look like real climbers for an edition they'd done in Snowdonia.

'It was faked but it had to look dangerous. Pete wasn't happy with that. Had a standup row with the producer. His steely side came out when he insisted on abandoning the SUV we were demonstrating. You… "did not diss the rocks".'

Merrily noticing Smiffy Gill had two voices, one giving away the private education he tended to disown on the show.

'That was always his catchphrase: "Do not ever diss the rocks". Wouldn't let me off the ground till he knew *I* knew what I was doing. No fakery, no camera tricks. He was firty years older than me and twice as fit. But I remember one of his team sayin' that if it ever came to him doing a piece sittin' there in his garden, lookin' up at the rocks and sayin' he was no longer... *equal to them*, you'd know...'

Merrily tensed. *God, Smiffy, not now...*

'...you'd know you were at his retirement party.'

Smiffy stepped back from the river. Out came the posh voice.

'If he'd suddenly been diagnosed with a debilitating heart-condition or something which would mean he'd never climb again, who knows? He was on his own. This was between him and the Seven Sisters. And they were *this* close.'

He crossed two fingers and held them up near Merrily's face.

'It might be unwise,' Mr Unsworth said, 'to suggest he committed suicide because he thought he might be unfit to climb or in danger of losing his skills. He told me last year that he was deriving even more satisfaction these days from his work with young miscreants, carried out on the lower rocks.'

Perhaps it was the combination of the tight congregation and the open air, but this was the first time she'd been aware of eulogies turning into chat. But she was inclined to trust Mr Unsworth – unexpectedly supportive in that difficult exorcism-of-place in the avenue of valuable homes at Aylestone Hill.

Smiffy backing down at once.

'Well, he found me a nice weekend cottage at a good price. People rip me off all the time, just because it's me. I'm not gonna start rumours, Geoffrey. Let's just give him a decent send-off, leave it at that.'

Mr Unsworth nodding, looking at Merrily.

'He was a capable and cautious man, with an uncommon integrity. With regard to his death, I would not disagree with Mr Gill and, like him, should hate to fuel rumour with no particular evidence…'

A flurry of breeze. Merrily stepped in front of the loose crowd and patted down her cassock. Smiffy Gill's eyes played with hers.

'There is nuffink I can fink of, Mrs Watkins, as indisputably erotic as what you might call "a woman of the rumpled cloth". Pete would've told you that.'

Mild, nervous laughter.

'He might have *thought* that, Mr Gill,' Geoffrey Unsworth said, 'but I doubt he'd have said it aloud.'

During the staggered shuffling sound of a congregation relaxing, Merrily gave Geoffrey Unsworth the nod and he stepped carefully forward and cleared his throat into the new silence.

'We estate agents nurture no illusions about our professional popularity. In the competition for public opprobrium, we used to jostle for base position between tabloid journalists and politicians.' He paused, smiled. 'Luckily, in recent years, the bankers have come to our rescue.'

Beyond the coffin, a man laughed sharply and smothered it. Royce Portis looked up, stroking his forehead as if brushing away an insect. Merrily managed to let her eyes do the laughing. She'd moved down to where she could see only a corner of the coffin. The light had gone. Mr Unsworth cleared his throat again.

'The property business is, as you realize, terribly aggressive, and Peter certainly *had* aggression, but he expended it, I think, on his physical contests with the rocks. "You cannot get to the top," he said, "without a respect for the rocks." Well, as he well knew, you can get to the top in this trade by climbing over more scrupulous chaps, but… it was about the standards he set for himself and what gave him the moral strength to keep to them. He was a good man, and in danger of earning his profession something approaching respect. He would invariably alert prospective purchasers to any potential problems with a property: if it was on a busy main road, for example, or close to a towering electricity pylon, this would be obvious from the photos in his window.'

He looked up in time to catch a few people nodding and a small ripple of support.

'In the decades I knew him, I never heard of him selling a house that would subsequently prove to have been far from the bargain it first seemed. Even by the standards of a small county like Herefordshire, his level of honesty was exceptional. I wish I could say that all his competitors would consider him a great loss.' He was silent for a moment. 'Unfortunately, in all honesty, I… I—'

He stumbled.

Quite hard.

Oh God, no… Merrily grabbing his arm before he slipped. Snatching up his stick and holding its shaft for him to grip the handle and fall forward. He looked confused.

'I think,' he whispered, 'that I need to sit down.'

'Relax a while, Geoff,' Smiffy Gill said. 'You may not die. Not quite yet.'

Two mourners walked either side of Mr Unsworth back towards the church. The season seemed to have regressed, the sky looking soggy and soiled, like a well-used dishcloth.

She watched his laboured moon-walk towards the parked cars. Everybody staring, not at him but her.

Because she hadn't finished.

'Better wrap this up, Merrily,' Smiffy Gill said.

Behind him, Peter Portis's trolleyed coffin looked like a wheelybin awaiting a refuse collection. When the bier was pushed away, there was no organized procession behind it, only the few mourners shuffling like a bus queue. Merrily was preparing to do the last business at the grave. She was at the head of the short procession, striving to keep up with Royce Portis and feeling like a cottage in the shadow of a tower block.

'Thank you... Mrs Watkins, is it?' Portis looked down at her, past the black stubble probably forming faster than his smile. 'I'm afraid I didn't have time, when you rang, to find out exactly why you were replacing Ripley.'

'But I thought you...'

She looked up uncertainly. *It's my responsibility*, Arlo had told her in the shadow of St Giles, Goodrich. *I'll explain to them in full.*

Maybe he *hadn't* explained. But he'd sounded so decisive about it. *I don't want them to have two versions*, he'd said.

It didn't make sense. Arlo didn't want her to explain why she was replacing him. But it seemed he hadn't offered his own explanation to Royce.

There were always dark secrets at funerals, and you could cause lasting damage to someone's memory of the occasion by allowing them to leak out.

'I'm sorry, Mrs Watkins, you were about to say something?'

Royce was still looking down at her.

'I... I was pleased to do it. Nobody should be buried without... prayer.'

A few minutes later, she was looking into the exposed shaft of the grave, a few yards from the new river bank.

'We have entrusted our brother Peter to God's mercy. We now

commit his body to the ground. Earth to earth, ashes to ashes, dust to...'

She lifted her head and turned to find the churchwarden holding a linen bag, which he raised above the wet shaft and shook. The contents drummed unevenly on the coffin, not sounding like soil, and she saw it had been a shower of small stones.

'Rock fragments. From the Seven Sisters,' Adrian Fenn revealed in her ear. 'I should've told you earlier. Someone collected them. It was felt, somehow, to be appropriate.'

Merrily was aware of a bird cruising over the waiting grave. It was the size of a crow, had a black head. She'd only ever seen one peregrine falcon before, briefly alighting on the high rock above Symonds Yat.

This one was in no hurry.

42

Heavy house

SHE WALKED OUT of the gate into the little car park and then the lane, where swollen trees dripped on her. Looking from side to side, she followed a track that led behind the churchyard wall. This suicide possibility? Where did that start? Smiffy Gill hadn't just dreamed it up, had he?

She was confused and anxious for Mr Unsworth. Her car was near the entrance. She hadn't heard an ambulance. Was one on its way?

He was leaning against her driver's door, with his back to her.

She stopped.

'Are you OK?'

He said, 'My old friend's safely in the ground?'

'Yes, he is. Thank you for what you said. Are you...?'

'I'm fine. Can we get in your vehicle and park somewhere out of sight in the village?'

Five minutes later she pulled into a space outside the caravan park, opened the door behind her seat for Mr Unsworth.

'Are you *really* all right?'

'I wanted to talk to you,' he said. 'And not small talk. No time for pleasantries, and I didn't want Royce around.'

'Oh?'

'Nor Diana. Definitely not Diana.'

She switched off the engine. He was now sitting in the far corner of the back seat – social distance, just about. He'd lowered his side window.

Merrily said, 'I didn't know you knew her.'

'Oh, she's a damn good surveyor,' Mr Unsworth said, 'for one so young.'

'Royce was lucky to find her.'

He laughed.

She said, 'Erm, you don't see it that way, do you?'

'Well, she's certainly good at property. Buying it. And buying it back when it doesn't live up to expectations, or… becomes difficult to inhabit.'

'Difficult?'

'The atmosphere of a house can change. Become less welcoming. You… must have encountered this phenomenon in your work.'

His eyes crinkled. He knew more or less what she did at work.

'I suppose I have,' she said. 'From time to time.'

'Diana Farrowman worked for me for a few months.'

'At Lang/Copper?'

'Until Peter poached her. I didn't mind too much at the time. I was a little insecure about her, and I didn't quite know why.'

'But then you did?'

'I wondered. Royce didn't suspect anything at all, and Peter didn't really know about these things. I tried to warn him, but… well, you know what that's like with your bishop, I believe.'

She smiled at him.

He said, 'The Portises and the Farrowmans were almost neighbours in the Wye Valley. And Peter knew how much his son desired the smouldering Diana. He also knew that she was good at her job, if not yet quite *how* good… or exactly why.'

Merrily said, 'Royce and Diana… when they got together, in a place as sparsely populated as this part of the Wye Valley, it must have seemed like destiny.'

'Yes,' he said. 'And destiny, of course, can be assisted. As can circumstance. One senses that strings are sometimes pulled. But by whom, in this case? Or by *what*?'

Didn't understand quite where his mind was going, but she knew him well enough to trust his judgement, however unlikely it appeared. Aware of the way he would study the history of properties he was buying, knowing at the start when he might be handling a *heavy* house.

'As a small child,' he said, 'Diana might easily have drowned at the same time as her parents, but instead she placidly went to sleep in a cave not far from the river. She was too young to understand what impact that particular cave might have on her subconscious mind. Of course, I don't know if it *did* have an effect, I'm just an old estate agent, but that cave—'

Merrily said, 'I agree that you don't know. You *can't* know, but you can *feel*. You can follow instinct and you're one of those people who senses when an instinct is genuine.'

'Thank you, Merrily.'

'Nothing to thank me for, just keep following your instincts. Now… King Arthur's Cave up in the Doward: what *is it* about this cave?'

He leaned back.

'It's a Stone Age residential cave. As an estate agent I've always said it's the oldest actual dwelling we know about along the course of the Wye. It was continually inhabited for thousands of years by… some significant people, I would suggest.'

'Druids?'

'I don't know a great deal about druids.'

'Nobody does. Except by instinct,' Merrily said. 'And inheritance, perhaps. Druids may have known how places can influence people. Places like, I'm guessing, this cave, used for hundreds even thousands of years.'

'Sometimes,' Mr Unsworth said, 'one wants to be influenced by places. Sometimes not.'

Merrily thought about this. It was silent in the Freelander for a while, until Mr Unsworth spoke again.

'I'd like to deal with Royce. The truth is I didn't particularly like him, although I understood him better than Diana. He once… well, he romanced a girl who worked at Lang/Copper, as a secretary. She subsequently asked for a confidential chat with me. We went out to a café but had to leave when she virtually broke down. We ended up talking in my car, with her offering to resign on the basis that she'd compromised the firm. He'd got her drunk and gone home with her. I don't think she even knew who he was but he charmed her, seduced her and was asking her all kinds of questions about her job.'

'He'd targeted her to find out about aspects of your firm's business?'

'Everything he did was easy for me to understand. He's an unscrupulous young man. One can only guess what he was after. I didn't accept the girl's resignation, and fortunately she didn't see him again. Peter Portis would've been appalled if he'd known.'

'This would've been before Royce's marriage?'

'No, no, afterwards. That was the worst of it. I think he told her he was ready to leave his wife.'

Mr Unsworth looked uncertain, telling her that when Peter and his wife, Royce's mother, had parted, he'd become a different man – showing a declining interest in the business. But he was said to be applying himself to the rocks with a new commitment. Soon afterwards, PPP had closed its Hereford office and

Peter Portis had opened a new office in Whitchurch and moved home, with Royce and his daughter, who'd soon marry, to that lonely house near the Seven Sisters rocks.

'Mr Unsworth,' Merrily said, 'would you say Royce had changed?'

He chuckled, but he was not amused.

'Not for the better, I'm afraid. They were never close, Peter and his boy. Royce has never been interested in climbing. Or finding the right house for someone, come to that. Property's not really in his soul, only his bank account.'

She stared at him. You didn't often hear the words *property* and *soul* in the same sentence, but this was an old-fashioned estate agent.

'Peter worked for us once. Must have been over thirty years ago now. We were sorry to lose him. Terrific energy. Worked all hours. Might've been his own company. Peter advised the diocese on glebe land, effective disposal of redundant Church property. Always undercharged for his services in that area, too, and was regarded as a good man by bishop after bishop. Disposal of glebe land is now to be handled by Royce, who will not undercharge. But Peter, as I said, was a good man and Royce, I regret to say, is less scrupulous.'

'Which the Bishop…'

'Is not expected to notice.'

'Is it hard for an estate agent to be a good man?' Merrily asked. 'Sorry, I didn't mean…'

Mr Unsworth chuckled, and this time he *was* amused.

'Of course you did. Peter Portis… essentially, he never liked to feel he might have exploited someone. To which you have every right to say, well, then, how come he lasted so long in a business where exploitation often is the name of the game?'

She looked at his three-piece black suit, with its shiny

patches, thinking he might have chosen not to replace it, not knowing how many more funerals, including his own, he'd be attending in it.

'When Royce told that girl he was thinking of leaving his wife,' Mr Unsworth said, 'he wasn't serious, but it showed how, while he might think himself obviously in control, he's actually very much the junior partner in that marriage. Have you observed that today?'

'No, I'm not sure I have.'

'Then she doesn't want you to,' he said.

'All right,' she said. 'Tell me about Diana Portis.'

He said nothing.

'You don't want to?'

'I don't think I'm able to,' he said.

43

Precocious

WHEN MERRILY SLUMPED into the kitchen, she thought Jane must have lit the woodstove. The air seemed dense as she peeled off her cassock. But the stove was unlit, summer-grey.

'I was going to light it earlier, but it seemed too warm.' Jane was in her old pale blue T-shirt, faded in places to near white. 'Even though it's barely April. Not long out of winter.'

'I was thinking it was just me.' Merrily was feeling all the weight of a humid evening in July. 'They were talking about an unseasonal heat on local radio. Another symptom of global warming. Time to start another panic.'

'The weather's kind of... precocious,' Jane said. '*Can* weather be precocious? Is that the right word for it?'

'I don't know. I'm always questioning things lately. Nothing this year seems to play by the book.'

Jane sagged in her chair at the kitchen table, throwing back her head in apparent relief.

'Thank God.'

'For what? What have I said?'

'You've said what I was thinking. That nothing is predictable any more, nothing is orthodox.' Jane sat up straight, gazing out of the window then suddenly switching her eyes back to Merrily. 'Listen, I've been thinking all day that we have to talk.

There are things you should know. And things I should know. Is that OK? We may not get another chance.'

'Jane, we live in the same house.'

'And we can die in it,' Jane said. 'Overnight. An invasion by the virus.'

The heavy, silent air seemed to have plummeted between them like a bag of cement.

'We could both catch this evil virus, and then we won't be talking about anything else except which one of us will go down with it first. And who'll feed Ethel, if we're wheeled out?'

'Jane, if kids get it – and you're still a kid in virus terms – they rarely die, unless they already have something else that's bad.'

'Mum, anybody can get it bad and, like, *die very quickly.* Even the bloody prime minister may not see the morning! When did *that* last happen?'

'All right.' Merrily put up her hands. 'Nothing happening just now has ever happened before, in my experience.'

She was weary, wishing she had an excuse to leave the explanations till tomorrow. But she knew the kid was right. The pandemic was in that cement bag; its dusk could come billowing out at any moment and they'd be choking. That was what you did, more or less: you choked, ran out of oxygen. That was how you died when the virus got you.

Merrily stifled a cough. 'This is one of the least affected counties in the UK.'

'And tomorrow it could be the most affected. We're *all* potentially in trouble.' Jane poured tea, pushed a mug in front of Merrily. 'Listen, because there should be no secrets between us, I'm going to tell you… I overheard a conversation between you and the detective, Darth… what's his name?'

'Vaynor?' Merrily sighed. She should be angry. Angrier than she was. Jane wasn't a kid any more. Keep reminding yourself. 'Were you by any chance in the scullery last night? Taking notes?'

'Well, I passed through there to pick up something to read, and overhead the cop saying he thought he was… molested?'

'He didn't quite say that.'

'By Mrs Portis. To whom he began to apply the word *succubus*.'

'We revive words that sound appropriate.' Merrily sighed again. 'Some women think they can control men through their dreams. By giving them private… erotic fantasies. Powerful fantasies.'

'A succubus.' Jane sat back, satisfied. 'Exactly.'

'That's the *old* word for it. Pre-psychiatry.'

'Thank you, Mum,' Jane said. 'And, in return, I'll tell *you* something I don't think you know. You went with Sophie to Goodrich to learn about one of your predecessor's cases that you hadn't been told about. Sir Samuel Meyrick?'

'That's not a secret.' Merrily carefully drank some tea. 'Just because *I* didn't know about Meyrick's attempt to acquire the whole valley through his enormous wealth.'

'And its ancient spiritual power…'

'*What?*'

'Or that he's thought to be an ancestor of Diana Portis? Did you know that?'

Merrily jerked, blinking, spilled tea. Another bag of cement had landed between them.

Jane said, 'This was something else you didn't know?'

Merrily said, '*Who told you that?*'

'Just somebody who…'

'*Who?*'

'Maybe somebody from that pagan WI we were on the edge of.'

'The Pod?'

'Lots of residual pagans live in the Wye Valley,' Jane said. 'And some of them know its secrets.'

'Including your friend, Sorrel? Look, I'm not pointing the finger. She's usually well-intentioned. But, Jane, just tell me, is this on the level? Have you honestly been told that Diana Portis is descended from Sir Samuel Rush Meyrick?'

'I don't *know.*' Jane threw up her arms, maybe floundering now. 'I don't know how many children Meyrick had, how many women there were in his past. He was only actually married once, according to his biography. But…'

'But he boasted about his continuing prowess with women – I've read that. And he hung around with a group of Welsh women who thought they were druids, just as he did.'

'*Welsh* women.' Jane smiled. 'That figures. Diana's late mother came over from Wales. And the night she drowned in the Wye, Diana was asleep in the cave where she… may have received a power that Meyrick knew about. And where, many years later, she and Vaynor—'

'Stop. Please.'

Merrily stood up and moved to the kitchen window, looked across the drive where, just days ago, she'd met Huw Owen as all this was only just beginning. How much of it would he believe now?

'Jane, I need… I need to think.'

'You need to think about one more thing,' Jane said. 'If Diana Portis has done all this and escaped retribution, she's only behaving like many people did all the time in the century before I was born. *And believe they will again.*'

Merrily began to feel threatened. She didn't want to be pulled into this. Not tonight.

'Don't go there, flower. And don't tune into other people's conversations.'

Silence. Then Jane's voice.

'Because I might be overhearing the future?'

44

Elohim

The domestication of the historic church of St Dubricius had involved the creation of a small lounge area in a corner of the nave, and that was where they seemed to have done it.

This area of the church was relatively dry. Vaynor perched on the end of a carved chair.

'How did you know what they'd been doing?' he asked.

It was quiet in here, and softly sunlit. The funeral was over, the riverside grave filled in, the undertakers and the few mourners gone. Adrian Fenn didn't touch anything.

'There are some noises you don't mistake,' he said. 'And certain smells. Gone now. Well, *I* can...'

'Still smell it?'

'Perhaps.'

The churchwarden turned away.

'I'm inclined to believe you, Mr Fenn,' Vaynor said, 'but... why did you wait so long to report it?'

Vaynor got to his feet. The churchwarden led the way out through the porch, shut the main doors and brought out his church keys.

'I was going to tell him what I knew and give him the opportunity to... explain.'

'You think he'd have an explanation?'

'Mr Vaynor, I know what I heard. But I thought he should be

given an opportunity to explain. It's a situation that could very much damage his… position.' Fenn jangled his keys together and put them away. 'But he didn't come to the service, and I didn't see him afterwards.'

'What about his, er, companion?'

'I was less certain about who *she* was. But the *main* reason I was rather reticent was…'

'The presence of the person in the coffin? You saw them both leave?'

'Unnatural, however urgent their… needs might have been. Unnatural and unsavoury. I could have made a fuss, but I decided to retire to the car park, conceal myself and consider what the next move should be. Somehow I didn't want to go back again. Don't get me wrong, I wouldn't be in this job if I was afraid of staying overnight in a dark church with a body in it but… *any* people having sex close to the dead… poses questions.'

'Are you going to see the vicar tonight?'

'If he'd broken in, things would be simpler, but as he seem to have used his own keys… Dear God, this just gets worse.'

It spooked Bliss that he was in full kit.

'That was how he was noticed,' the pathologist said. 'Flash of white on the water, like a swan with its wings spread.'

'Who found him, Billy?'

'Several people spotted him around the same time. Two men – canoeists – went in and hauled the remains, with some difficulty, to the bank.'

The body hadn't yet been moved from the water's edge. The soaking surplice was across the face, the nose making a small hump.

'*I* covered his face, by the way, Francis, after noticing one or two smartphones coming out in passing canoes. Everybody has one now, of course.'

'Who?'

'Just canoeists. I warned one of them off. Thing is, the corpse was… quite a well-known face, as you know. I didn't imagine any relatives – or you, for that matter, would want that face all over social media.'

'Quite right,' Bliss said, then summed up. 'Couple of miles from where Portis dies, here's the body of the briefly famous actor who should've been conducting his funeral. Had he been in the river since *before* the funeral – a few hours?'

'That's a possibility. No maceration, no sign of washerwoman's skin, as we used to call it in less politically correct days. So probably in the river for under five hours.'

'Could he've been dead before he went in?'

'Well, there are no obvious pre-immersion injuries. Messed up a bit through getting tangled in the branches in the water, but no obvious indications of him fending off a physical attack. But it's too early to say. And *that*, of course…'

'It's not boating rope, is it?'

'It was wound around his legs and knotted. Looks like the velvety kind that's used to isolate places in stately homes where the public isn't welcome – or churches, of course. You see it around a dead man's legs, all you can really rule out is an accident.'

'Any way of finding out if anyone else was involved?'

Billy sniffed.

'I'd be inclined to say he'd roped his own legs together before rolling into the river. Quite sad when a clergyman does something like this. Indicates his faith being well on the blink, don't you think?'

'Certainly not common among us Catholics,' Bliss said.

‘Really? I didn’t know you were RC, Francis.’

‘Lapsed. But I think suicide remains a mortal sin. Not for his lot, mind. How long before you can tell us something, doc? He have anything on him that we need to examine? Phone?’

‘Nothing significant in his pockets. No phone and probably not much in his wallet. Well, I *say* nothing significant in his pockets… except this.’

Billy Grace held up a small leather-bound book, its soaked pages mainly fused together.

‘I suppose, by the way he’s dressed,’ Billy said, ‘a pocket Bible *would* have some significance in this situation.’

Bliss noticed that some pages appeared extra creased, spread them out and saw some passages were underlined in biro. The word *Elohim* was handwritten vertically three times down separate pages.

Had this guy come out here purely to die, in some weird ceremonial way?

Bliss thought he could use an informed opinion on this. The name Merrily Watkins flashed in his head, just as his mobile quivered, but he thought he’d leave it a while.

When he walked up the bank, he could see the roofs of holiday caravans over the trees and bushes. Not fully dark yet, the lights still blinking on around the holiday village at Symonds Yat West. Within a few weeks the place’d be chocka. He stood looking down at the river and the group around the body under the lights, people with stale grass around their ankles.

45

Sour lights

MERRILY WENT TO bed early and hadn't been asleep for long – maybe an hour – when the first spadeful came down, bringing lumps of soil which exploded into fragments against the oak. Small stones came too, clinking together.

A second spadeful added substance as the fragments clung to one another and fused together. A third descending thud brought firmness. Airholes closed and then there was weight, a solid weight pressing down on her chest, and she was coughing. Rolling over, pushing up weakly, coughing painfully and unhooking the bedside phone.

To hear a distant voice.

'…help me?'

The duvet rose and the voice was imploring.

'Merrily, I'm sorry…'

'Maya?'

Merrily gulped hard, swallowing mouthfuls of night and finally was able to expel words.

'Is that you, Maya?'

'What? Oh God… Merrily, I didn't intend to ring you. It's just, I can't handle this. The police have been here for hours, on and off. They keep wanting to know things I can't tell them. I don't understand… don't see *why*.'

'Why what?'

'I didn't put any pressure on him. You know that. I wanted him for Wordsworth, but it was entirely his decision. Had to be.'

The duvet rolled off the bed, collecting in a heaving clump on the floor, and the bedside light blinked on.

'*Please*,' Maya said faintly. 'You're a vicar. Tell me why he did it?'

At the edge of the pavement, Lol's arms were around her. She fell against him. She couldn't remember how she got here, but she didn't want to move. Ever. Even if half of the population of Ledwardine was watching them from behind bedroom curtains.

He was backing away from her into Lucy's cottage, holding her up by the elbows.

'No!' Pulling away. Behind him, lights were coming on. 'I have to go. I just need you to...'

She said she needed him to come over the road and check that Jane was all right. Not now. In the morning, please. If she wasn't back by then. But she'd call him, anyway. She'd told him that, twice.

He was staring at her, his face creased into concern.

'Merrily, what's...' Gripping her arms, panic overflowing in his eyes. 'What's the matter with you? Have you noticed sympt—?'

'God, no. I wouldn't come near you if there were symptoms. I was dreaming about the funeral... and then it was my funeral and I was being buried. Normally, in a dream like that, you wake up, like when the first shovelful of dirt hits your coffin. And then the phone was ringing, and now I have to go somewhere because, what I think I've heard, it can't be right.'

'Wherever it is,' he said, holding her, 'you can't go on your own.'

She was fully but haphazardly dressed – jeans and an old black hoodie of Jane's with two holes in it. A metal cross on a chain was around her neck. She'd snatched it up on her way out. A worn canvas airline case – her exorcist bag – was slung over a shoulder.

'It… it was Maya, the TV producer working with Arlo Ripley… And she says he's *dead*.'

'*Ripley?*'

'Could be accidental, could be suicide. She wanted to talk to me, and I can't sleep now, so I'm going over there.'

'What's happened? Tell me what's happened.'

'I don't know, but she's very upset.'

She shook her head, noticing all the lamps along the street. It was as if people were reluctant to say goodnight, scared to register the end of another day.

'You need…' Lol held her close '…some kind of break.'

'I need answers.'

'You need some sleep.'

But he'd know it was not possible.

She said, 'I've had some sleep. I won't get any more tonight. Please just be there for Jane if she gets up. She's still young enough to feel abandoned if I'm not there.'

She saw sour lights burning into the early hours. Lights of people who, for weeks, you'd only be able to phone, not staying on the phone too long in case a doctor or nurse was trying to get through with urgent information.

His hands closed on her shoulders.

'Call me,' he said. 'And drive *bloody* carefully. And his voice faltering, 'we can't go on like this. We can't go on any longer.'

'You're right. Time we put somebody on standby.'

'*What?*'

'Huw won't do it, but we'll talk to Martin Longbeach. Or Abbie Folley over in Merthyr.'

'You're… serious?'

'That's if *you* can stand it. I need something strong and normal to happen in my life…'

'Strong and…?'

'Normal.'

Crossing the Ledwardine boundary, she broke the law, but not badly. With the phone on loud-speaker, she pushed it through the steering wheel onto the ledge below the illuminated dials and drove into the empty night.

'I'm on my way,' she said loudly at the phone when it was answered. 'Would you mind telling me again what you saw… where you saw it.'

'At the hospital,' Maya said. 'They just wanted somebody quickly who knew him and there are no relatives living within a hundred miles. They took me to… to where they take dead people. He was covered up. There'll be a proper identification but not tonight. I just… I saw his face. They… found him in the river. He… his body was wearing his church vestments, and they were all wet through. Soaked.'

Merrily's foot slipped from the accelerator pedal and the car almost stalled. It didn't matter; there was no other traffic, probably none this side of Hereford, except ambulances and police cars. She might get stopped, but what could she do about that, apart from keep trying to get through to Frannie Bliss and thinking about Arlo wearing his vestments for the river.

I don't feel good about myself or what I'm doing. I'm throwing myself into this role, but I know I should say no… and I should be conducting this afternoon's funeral. Obviously I can't now, and I can't come to the service and apologize to the family.

Said in Goodrich that he was going to find somewhere quiet

by this sacred river to make his apologies to God. Hadn't said what he was going to do then.

She took the Ross road out of town. He hadn't sounded *that* despairing. No element of finality had been there. Nothing to say he wouldn't be around in the morning.

But, with his ankles roped together, it could hardly be an accident.

They'd found him. And they'd...

Merrily didn't get stopped, not even in the city, where all the streets were so deserted and out-of-time that she kept expecting to hear horses' hooves alongside and was surprised that the lights above her car were electric.

Feeling disconnected from Hereford, she drove south across the river and down its valley.

46

Still, sad music

MAYA MADDEN, DRESSED in a brown cord tunic and jeans, looked dark-eyed and shaded with dark emotions. One small light was on in her downstairs office. The book on the sofa in the window was open at a photo of Tintern Abbey and the poem that took its title from the abbey but didn't mention it, not once.

'It's his day,' Maya said emptily.

Merrily nodded.

In all kinds of ways it was over.

'Exactly two hundred and fifty years since he was born,' Maya said. 'On the seventh of April. Does it matter anyway? I don't really think it does, but these coincidences occur, as if to underline things for us.'

'Maya.' Merrily closed the hall door behind her. 'I'm so very sorry. When you told me about Arlo, I didn't really believe it at first.'

'I shouldn't have asked you to come.'

'I'm glad you did. I feel I have to try and unscramble things while it's still possible. There has to be some sense here, some reason behind why the world's changed.'

'There's no logic any more,' Maya said. 'And my own feelings about Arlo and Wordsworth are mixed.'

After what she'd heard from Siân Callaghan-Clarke, Merrily had wondered about Maya's relationship with Arlo, whether there'd been another reason for his acceptance of the central role in this drama-documentary. But it wasn't her business, she admitted, and it had slumped from triumph to tragedy.

'Wordsworth considered a career in the Church,' Maya said. 'He thought he needed a safe income.'

It wasn't safe any more. In Wordsworth's day, the pandemic would have cemented faith, brought people fearfully together. Now it drove them further apart.

They're saying the clergy are here to help, not investigate, and shouldn't ask too many questions to which they know they won't get answers. Huw Owen's assessment of the C of E hierarchy's current policy on the night she'd first been drawn into this. Merrily felt a burst of anger. How did they know they wouldn't get answers?

Merrily accepted a mug of tea from Maya but didn't add sugar. The etching of Wordsworth in his 1960s rock star jacket was alone on the wall.

She was fed up with making excuses for senior clergy. *Fuck the bastards.*

Never thought she'd be talking/thinking this way. This really was it. Everything closing down.

'I've been a working exorcist in this diocese for several years.' She sank into the sofa, did not feel sleepy. 'But now it might soon be over.'

Had she said that aloud? She felt the night was now quietly alive around the grey village church you couldn't see from this window.

'Two of us in the church yard lie
My sister and my brother
And, in the church yard cottage, I
Dwell near them with my mother.'

She sat up.

'This house isn't actually called Churchyard Cottage, is it, Maya? You had that sign made as part of your plan to convince Arlo to take the job. Recreate Wordsworth.'

Maya said nothing, looked close to tears.

'But you didn't need to, really, did you?' Merrily said. 'Siân must have told you about his... problem.'

She wasn't enjoying this at all.

But it was time.

'It's this area,' Merrily said sadly. 'It somehow tells us to do things. I don't know if, in this job, I should be working for or against the area.'

Maya slowly came down on the sofa, sitting next to Merrily, wiping her swollen eyes. The area had much more power over her because of the way it had dominated William Wordsworth in perhaps the most vivid years of his life, messed with his consciousness.

But Arlo...

I still don't feel his intellect submitting to what you're calling call a 'trance state'.

There would have been discord. Arlo would have refused to accept that the energy of nature – no mention of God – was the power behind Wordsworth's greatest poetry.

Merrily said, 'This is a place where nature-worship, as famously practised by the twenty-something Wordsworth, is... somehow exciting – more exciting than Christianity, my daughter says. More British. And, in Wordsworth's case, not *quite* paganism. It involves the spirits of nature, rather than nature spirits, if you see what I mean.'

'I'm not sure.'

'Doesn't mean fairies with gossamer wings or big plants with faces.'

Merrily stopped and shrugged.

'But he stopped practising it, anyway, after it inspired some of his finest work,' Maya said. '"With an eye made quiet by the power of harmony and the deep power of joy, we see into the life of things".'

'Climactic lines.'

'That would have been explored in depth in my programme,' Maya said. 'I could hear Arlo breathing it out over the titles.' She looked at the picture of Wordsworth in his rock star jacket. 'If he'd still had breath. What can we do now?'

'Mourn him… then find another actor? I'm sorry but he… didn't really want to portray Wordsworth, did he? A half-pagan. A would-be druid, in a place where druidism lingers. People going into a trance state? Is that what that line's saying? Is it describing a form of meditation, but deeper?'

'I'm not sure,' Maya said. 'I might be half-Indian, but I've never got round to meditating.'

'And that poem… doesn't rule out a kind of spiritual possession. A surrender to the forces of nature. Going just a bit further than what he says in the poem about the power of harmony and the deep power of joy.'

'"An eye made quiet",' Maya repeated.

'It somehow has a soft echo,' Merrily said. 'An eye looking inward? What *things* did he see into the life of?'

'That's the big question,' Maya said. 'The question to which many people seek an answer in the Wye Valley.'

Merrily looked out into the night.

'Perhaps it *is* the Valley that enables people to see. Perhaps that's what you feel here when it all fuses together for you… the hills, the woods and the river which is joining them all together, with the missing element that finds… the sixth sense. He kept hinting at that.'

Maya gave in to a slow shiver.

'What's the missing element?'

'The human element.' Merrily smiled, relaxed. 'He was a hippy, two centuries too early. All he needed was love.'

Some people said that was where Wordsworth went next, after the nature-worship. Adding human feeling. Warmth, depth and what you could get from the vibrations of another person. Was *that* the life he picked up on?

'Near the end of the Wye poem,' Merrily said, 'he discovers his sister, Dorothy. His best friend. He realizes how close he is to her. Some people say he became *too* close. I don't think it came to anything incestuous, but if anything did happen here, on whatever level… In the poem he turns away from his adoring view of nature in "thoughtless youth" to tune into the… the, erm…'

'"Still, sad music of humanity",' Maya said.

'Yes.'

Merrily conjured the distant soft, moody chord-changing on the guitar she'd paid Al Boswell to make for Lol after someone had smashed his first one in the back of his truck. *Nor harsh, nor grating, though of ample power to chasten and subdue.* Wordsworth could hit the spot when he wanted to.

The mobile phone chimed its night chime. Softer than its day chime. More still, sad music.

'I'll make more tea.' Maya slid to her feet. 'Leave you alone with your call.'

'It won't be private.' Merrily took the phone from her poacher's pocket. 'Don't feel you have to go.'

'Merrily…' Bliss's scouse crackle. 'You hear about this feller we found in the river?'

'Yes,' she said.

'Mate of yours.'

'I wouldn't quite say that, but... our paths had crossed.'

'I was gonna ask you about it tomorrow, but it keeps coming back to me. Him and Mrs Portis. Did you know about them?'

'I... I'd been told about his condition.'

'Is it true he's a sex addict?'

'Who told you that?'

'Somebody who wouldn't want it talked about. Diana Portis, is she...?'

'A rather beautiful woman,' Merrily said. 'With a powerful magnetism that she likes to use. Mainly on men. I can see them both seizing an opportunity. She probably wouldn't let her marital status get in the way.'

'And one final point. Who's Elohim?'

'What?'

Bliss told her about a pocket Bible found on Arlo Ripley. About the word handwritten in it, down separate pages.

'What's it mean, Merrily?' he asked. 'Clearly it means something.'

'It's an old Hebrew name for God. I don't know much about it.'

'Why's this feller keep scrawling it in his Bible? The Bible he took with him to his...'

'To his death,' Merrily said. 'I don't know. Was his death accidental or...?'

'With his feet tied together?'

'His feet were *tied together*? Bloody hell, Frannie.'

'A way of making it harder to change your mind about suicide once you've thrown yourself in,' Bliss said.

When the call from Bliss ended, for Merrily, the night had gone shaky.

Either this was a courageous suicide, or...

She rang Siân Callaghan-Clarke.

'Look, I'm sorry. I know what time it is.'

'I was still up,' the Archdeacon said. 'I had an important call to the hospital…'

'Oh Christ…'

'Yes,' Siân said. 'Yes, it was. People kept telling me to call back in the morning, but I sensed something had changed and persisted…'

'Oh Jesus…'

'I'm glad I kept ringing,' Siân said. 'Sophie is said to be recovering.'

'*God…*'

'There aren't many holy names you haven't yet used, Merrily.'

'I'm sorry. Things are—'

'Things could be worse. Sophie faces a long recovery, I'm afraid, but I'm told she's unlikely to expire for some years. She may even be coming home quite soon. Merrily, are you still…?'

'Yes, I'm… thank you. So much. Best news I could have had.'

There was an uncomfortable pause.

'But there's clearly other news…' Siân's voice had sunk '… that isn't good.'

'Arlo Ripley?'

'The police told me. As his archdeacon.'

Merrily said, without really thinking about it, 'The name Elohim… was written in the small Bible found on his body.'

'I won't express surprise at that,' Sian said. 'A plural word implying more than one God is a concept I reject but…' sound of a cigarette being lit '…one that Arlo pondered at length during one of his possible addiction periods. Becoming obsessed by the idea of a plural God.'

'*Two* Gods? Or…'

'Or more. At theological college, people would laugh about it. Arlo never did. It interested him.'

'He thought there were two Gods?'

'And two ways of looking at a situation, both of which remain spiritually valid.'

'Theology is never a straight road, is it?' Merrily said. 'To me, two Gods looks close to no God. So… how do *you* feel about Arlo's death?'

'They say it might be suicide. Which didn't actually shock me as much as it should.' The Archdeacon was silent for a moment, as if deciding whether to say something else. And then… 'In this pandemic, lives seem to have become cheaper – even one's own. They're lost very quickly, whichever way it happens. Do you know what I'm saying?'

'I don't like to think about it.'

'Or think about what's happening to…?'

'What we do?' Merrily whispered.

She didn't like to spell it out. And didn't think Arlo's death – like Peter Portis's – was quite as simple as suicide.

*

Maya sat down and poured tea.

'I have to get back,' Merrily said. 'Someone's waiting for me.' She sugared her tea, stirred it. 'I don't actually mean Jane.'

It was time, she'd decided, to be entirely open, even when it didn't seem to matter.

'I've wondered,' Maya said.

'He's a songwriter. Even though they're all out of work, right now.' She drank her tea quickly. 'I'm not, yet.'

'*Yet?*'

'It's no secret that the Bishop wants me out. He thinks exorcists are unnecessary and possibly a liability to bishops who don't believe in…'

'While you know what you've seen…'

'No.' Merrily put down her mug on the table. 'And I certainly can't prove I've seen anything unearthly. I mean, I *may* have, and there are people who've convinced me that *they* have. But…' She picked up her bag and moved to the door. 'Are you going to be OK on your own?'

'I've a lot to think about. Thank you for coming, Merrily. I'll call you in the morning. The *real* morning.'

'Thanks for the tea.'

She slid out of the front door and moved up the drive to her car, briefly wondering why she couldn't see any stars above the hedge.

Then, as the Freelander crawled between the gateposts, she saw what was obscuring the night sky and trod heavily on the brake.

*

To Eirion Lewis

Cc

Bcc

From Jane Watkins.

Irene, love.

Listen.

(Or don't bother if I abandon this. I may have scrubbed it by the morning.)

Right now, it's late at night, and I'm supposed to be in bed. Only I'm not and won't be until either Mum comes back or

I find out what the score is. So I might as well tell you a few things.

Mum's 'gone to bed' as well, as she told me about an hour and a half ago. I don't think she went to sleep, though, as she was clearly in a bit of a state because of something I now wish I had decided not to tell her until tomorrow morning. Something about Sir Samuel Meyrick who I won't tell you about, but you'll find him online if you're interested.

Am I worried? Bloody right! The bishop's still a bastard and it looks like he always will be.

And yes, this IS another deliverance case, which, in the middle of this pandemic, is frankly not what we need. With the church closed down and the bishop off her back for a while, it should be a chance for her and Lol to get things together at last… except, as you know, Lol's lost Glasto and a bunch of small gigs because of the virus and I reckon he's on his uppers cash-wise. And now it's the middle of the night and… shit, she's getting the car out. I was thinking she'd just gone across the road on foot to bend Lol's ear about whoever was on the phone a short time ago. It was almost certainly Maya Madden, the TV producer (independent, not one of the big outfits but I suppose it's a living).

I watched her go, and she's on her own. Lol's still at home, and she's not left me a note.

Right. I'm giving her an hour then I'll go across to Lol and find out what's going on. This can be a risky job, and if Lol's going after her I'm going too.

And just as I was thinking I could actually make a serious concession.

University right? That's what I mean. I've told you about all the rows we've had about me saying I'm not going, and taking over Lucy's old shop – not just for the festival but forever. (I need to make a success of it, but I **will!**)

Would have.

Unless Mum deals with the bishop situation and doesn't have to move from Ledwardine.

And… solidifies this thing with Lol.

Like the big M…?

????

You yourself have said they need their arses kicking if they don't tie the knot. Bloody hell, it's an easy enough knot to **un**tie these days if it all goes wrong, and if I'm not here…

Yeah, I'd feel a whole lot better about going to uni, if I thought she wouldn't be on her own in the big old vicarage. OK, it's a kind of blackmail, but… let me know what you think. I mean if you can't blackmail your own mother…

Bloody hell, it's pushing midnight. Lol's lights are still on downstairs. I'm going across there. I'll send you this and do another one when (if) I get back.

Love, kisses and whatever else helps you get to sleep.

Jane

*

Merrily heard a car door opening.

'We need to talk.'

She didn't recognise the voice. But who else could it be?

'Mrs… Portis?'

'I drove past you a short time ago. There's next to no traffic on the roads, so I couldn't mistake you. I knew you'd be coming here.'

Merrily remembered a car passing her, a grey BMW.

'We should talk,' Diana Portis repeated. 'Which we couldn't do at Peter's funeral. Too many people about. But we can talk now, Druid to Christian.'

'I'll call you. Tomorrow?'

'Not on the phone. Get in.'

Merrily tensed.

'Now?'

'Unless you're afraid. In which case, you can bring your god with you. You're always safe with your god. Unless it…'

'My…?'

'Unless your god's afraid, too,' Mrs Portis said. 'Afraid it doesn't exist any more.'

47

A priest to nobody

IT WAS NOT huge but looked bigger in the bright night, dominating its immediate landscape, a sloping field, bending down to the quiet river.

A neolithic stone, once hot with blood and fire, it was said. After leaving the BMW they'd walked perhaps a quarter of a mile across the grass, down the side of Huntsham Hill, before the monument had come into view.

It had deep grooves cut into it, disappearing into the grass. These slits, which ended at ground level, were for blood to be drained into the soil, it was said.

Merrily had been expecting King Arthur's cave. Diana's spiritual base. Where she went to draw energy. But Diana had brought her here.

'Whether it is a sacrificial stone remains a surmise,' Alfred Watkins had written. This was before he used it as a base for his own small wicker man – a wooden cage, supported by the grooves cut out of it, with two children inside. The cage was long gone, but the stone remembered, Merrily thought, approaching it hesitantly.

This was all Jane-stuff, the stone laden with legend. It was important to Diana Portis and presumably to her like-minded ancestor, Sir Samuel Rush Meyrick. Both drawn to druidism, as potent to them, it seemed, as Christianity had been to her.

Trying to understand why this woman wanted to talk to her at a stone, to which she and the rest of the public was denied access, Merrily began to see it, see what Diane Portis saw.

She gripped the stone and saw, in the warm, velvet night, the three of them: the vicar, the druid priestess and the Queen Stone; three players in a vast cosmic tapestry reduced to the gently sloping hills and the low, knotted river.

She was trespassing. Diana Portis wanted her to be trespassing. As diocesan exorcist, Merrily could hardly wimp out of this.

It was suddenly hard to breathe, and she was somehow cold. She felt more alone, more separated from her surroundings than she'd been before the pandemic, when God began to be shut in the bottom drawer. Face it, *face it*: what kind of god would let millions of people lie there choking on their last breaths?

'Times have changed, very quickly.' A voice with a cool smile in it. 'You must be aware of what you're suddenly coming to… after just a couple of thousand years. This is the end, Merrily Watkins. *You're here, at the end.*'

*

Saw her now, side by side with the stone. Younger than Merrily, nearer to Jane's age. She had a rounded, possibly Gloucestershire accent and was standing two metres away from Merrily, against the Queen Stone. Almost touching it, but not quite, and somehow part of the same phenomenon, visible through a keyhole in the door of night, the sky around her a luminous pale grey.

Still wearing her funeral dress, but it wasn't for her father-in-law. Merrily couldn't suppress a mild shiver because Diana clearly wanted her to think it was going to be *her* funeral. She'd come out here to… gloat? Was that what druids still did, in high, cackling voices? *Was* Diana a druid, and what did that mean? Had it ever meant anything? Merrily straightened up, facing the stone, thinking about the illusion that there were three of them here, that maybe she was now counting the Queen Stone as another person.

Portis had slipped back into its squat shadow. Her voice seemed to be slithering out of its ominous cracks.

'You once tried to take us over, make your god our god. But it was never going to happen. We went underground for a while, but some people – people like your daughter – gradually came looking for us. Especially women, because Christianity had been run by men for two thousand years. Meanwhile, in druidry, in the days of the ancient Celts, women had full equality, as men had to recognize.'

Merrily – sole audience for a sermon that had been rehearsed many times, she thought – said nothing.

'For many centuries, women were not allowed to be Christian priests,' Portis said. 'Now it seems that you, a woman, are also a so-called exorcist.' She took a step towards Merrily, and a forefinger stabbed out. 'I *hate* that word,' she said mildly. 'Despise it.'

A sudden venom in the air spun Merrily back. She found herself thinking about her predecessor, Canon Dobbs, who'd left a message for her pinned to his front door: *The first exorcist was Jesus Christ.* She now realized he'd thought, as many clerics still did, that women were not ready even to be priests and would only muddy the water that men like Christ could walk on. But now…

'Now it seems that every new priest is a woman,' Diana Portis said. 'Until you realize that every new priest is a priest to…'

Merrily felt a thickening darkness around this woman and the Queen Stone. She tried to imagine a powerful light around herself and couldn't. She felt suddenly weak, a thin liquid seeping into her gut.

'A priest to *nobody*,' Portis said. 'Your congregations are dwindling… to just a few faded old people, most of whom, within five or ten years, will be lying dead.'

She smiled and stretched out a hand to the thick stone, with its deep cracks and grooves and its layers of lichen. By night, it rose to dominance in this otherwise featureless landscape. Merrily had the irrational impression that this woman believed herself linked to its continuing history.

'Much sooner, as this virus continues,' Diana Portis said. 'It preys on old people. Attacks your church congregations. Young people either don't get it or recover quickly. Old people… old people just *die*. The virus takes them together.'

She was using a small, sweet voice which did not reflect what Merrily had heard about her.

Or about women druids before a battle.

'You're still fairly young,' Diana said, 'but in the wrong way. Someone like you – a woman regarded by the new leaders of your church as a dabbler in Christian *magic* – has only a few priestly years to fall back on.'

Moving closer, she'd become more distinct. She had on a white cloth mask, which an increasing number of people were now wearing in public, to prevent the virus spreading. She hadn't worn one at Peter's funeral.

'Whereas *we* have a very ancient tradition to draw on,' she said. 'And we never lost touch with it. It lingers in places like the Doward. Where you can feel it all around, and *we* can call it down when we need it to come.'

Merrily stiffened.

'Call it down?' Aware that this was the first time she'd spoken, and it wasn't carrying like Diana's sweet little voice. 'Who have you called down? Who was it? Your father-in-law?'

No reply. Merrily tried again, but was unable to find the breath to power the words.

'Inviting him to jump from the seventh sister? Did you "call him down" from up there?'

Silence.

Then from Diana, there came a slow, quiet, slightly hoarse and more than slightly eerie…

…giggle.

48
Coming down

MERRILY WAS BACKING slowly away. The night around them did not have the texture of an ordinary night. Diana Portis was drifting into the swollen shadow of the Queen Stone.

She said, 'Peter's death happened. I was there, but I didn't touch him. Neither before, nor after it came for him.'

Merrily said carefully, 'Suicide? As some people have speculated.'

'It *happened*.'

Merrily was thinking this was becoming like a weird dream she wasn't quite attached to. She couldn't see the Wye, but knew it wasn't far away, doing its quiet curves through the agricultural fields. Flat and calm around the Queen Stone, making an easy, liquid loop, a…

'A noose,' she said. 'Like the noose around Arlo Ripley's ankles? The noose he couldn't loosen when he was drowning because he hadn't made it.'

'I didn't touch him either,' Diana Portis said. 'If we were… intimate earlier, that's not a crime.'

'*You and Arlo?*'

'Nothing there against the law. Except some law made by the Christian Church. In which case I'm glad to be against it.'

Merrily heard the smile.

'A man, with a woman, it's come and gone. For a woman it's

even less, although most women don't appear to realize that. In this case it was nothing to the woman – she was a druid. And this man was absorbing the essence of a famous poet. About to become the poet at his most potent, in the place where he was gifted with the most energy… young and strong and at his most receptive.'

'And now dead,' Merrily said. 'Doubly dead, now you've disposed of the man who was about to become him. In the Wye. A beautiful river that can also kill.'

'I didn't kill him, I gave him what he wanted.'

'Sex. You had sex with him.'

Merrily began to see. She heard the river.

'As a result of which, because you made sure he knew, your *husband* killed him.'

Diana Portis wandered close to Merrily and then stopped.

'You're stupidly brave, coming here with me in the dead of night. I've heard about you and how you sometimes interpret your role in the diocese.'

Merrily took a step back.

'Things get exaggerated. You knew I'd be scared. I'd been told you could move fast.'

As fast as a peregrine picking up small birds, Merrily thought, her abdomen tightening. She kept her social distance, mentally filing away everything the woman had said. Could anyone ever prove she did it? Killed her father-in-law? *Had* she done it?

There was a dense magic in the air around the stone. Merrily heard the close and yet distant sound of compacting masonry settling into moistened mortar. Was aware of disparate noises seeming to lift from the lofty ledges of the Seven Sisters and then descend to cluster around the sound-reversing Far Hearkening Rock which she'd never seen, only sensed.

'I've been finding out about you,' Diana Portis said. 'I realized I had to because of the way you kept showing up, or your daughter did, on your behalf. And because you're an exorcist and you think you can play with the dead.'

Compacting stone, masonry snuggling into soft mortar, grinding noises lifting from the lofty ledges of the Seven Sisters and around the unseen Far Hearkening Rock and then lowered into the volatile air above the Queen Stone.

'Your daughter asking questions about me, among the people who like to think of themselves as pagans. The Doward being given back to the druids. Like Sir Samuel wanted, by attracting thousands of tourists to his magnificent new castle.'

'Instead of the old ruins supported by the poet from Off?' Merrily finding a smile. 'Wasn't Meyrick just an incredibly rich man, for those days, a man who wanted to be even richer?'

'You haven't changed then, have you, Merrily Watkins?'

'Changed?'

'Exorcists,' Diana said. 'Always dropping in. From that early morning when the old man was standing on the court site with his black bag and his cross, sprinkling water he claimed was holy, calling on his god to deliver us from the bad spirit in the land, and the *bad spirit*, in his opinion... was my ancestor.'

The words of Diana Portis were absorbed into another noise that was growing out of the sky, with its few stars, above the Doward and possibly the dark throat of King Arthur's Cave. Merrily wondered why she'd come here alone. She felt very cold. There was no logic to it. It was an insane thing to do. She'd lost her footing. Her feet were no longer there. She could actually sense a space between the soles of her shoes and the grass, above which she was floating. She'd tripped, that was all. The night grass was slippery, and she'd lost her balance. She stumbled and fell. Toppled to the ground in front of the Queen Stone, where two hands caught her, seized her shoulders, preventing her from falling into the grass.

'Careful,' Diana Portis said. 'You're coming down.'

Coming down. It wasn't said as a warning.

More like a promise. The fall had propelled Merrily into the fat monolith. It felt shockingly cold. Her hood fell away. And then fingers slid into her shoulders.

She froze, close to the monument, her face forced upwards, her sight focused beyond the horizon above which she saw and heard a building site, a massive edifice taking shape.

Desperately trying to blink it back into the night, wanting to turn and run through the blurred visionary landscape to where she thought she'd left a real car. She was forced to accept, under a blanket of damp, that it had never been her car.

Fingers squeezed her shoulders, bringing her up and propelling her forwards into the monument, her nose and forehead connecting, *thuck* then *crunk*, into old stone. She tasted river. Acrid. Heard the chinking of stones that had been casually flung together into vast, newly formed walls, with sculpted towers and turrets, their foundations sunk into lush, lime-green lawns. Thinking how Diana Portis would be considered entirely innocent of at least two murders. And then Diana was only half there as the night clouds were darkening again over the river. Then not there at all.

Only an endless explosion of colour, blue and gold. And pain, as the building slowly collapsed, stones tumbling, and hands smashing Merrily's head into the dark blue night and the once-lamplit path.

49

Better come up

'You actually can't say?'

'Better if I don't.' The doctor flattened himself against a wall as a laden trolley was rushed past. 'It's not easy. And we're not badly affected here. And she's now at least getting oxygen. If we let you in, you'd see she was on a ventilator – endotracheal tube to deal with her breathing – and a nasogastric tube to keep her fed. Not conducive to discussion of any kind.'

'And she'll be staying here for the time being?'

'Almost certainly. Nobody's sure what's going to be required, but we're far from convinced she'll make it.'

'It seems to have advanced to this stage very rapidly,' Vaynor said hesitantly.

'Many of them do advance rapidly. And don't think she's too young for this; a few serious cases have actually been at primary school, and the national death-count is approaching ten thousand.'

'Well, please keep me informed. Any change at all. This could be nothing, as it were, from my point of view, but it could be…'

'I wouldn't advise you to try and talk to her, even from the doorway,' the doctor said.

*

On the floor below, another doctor was more forthcoming.

'It looks much worse than it is,' she said, 'but we'll keep her in for another few days, and change the bandages tomorrow. She'll be OK to talk in a couple of days, if you can follow what she's saying by then.'

She and Diana Portis had not been brought in at the same time, but Mrs Watkins obviously knew they were in the same hospital. She'd been unconscious for over a day, had no clear memory of what had happened, but Vaynor hoped for something. This was his second visit since she'd shown signs of coming round. Didn't want her talking about any of this to anyone else. Mrs Portis was upstairs, in a bad way, having been brought in by her husband who hadn't been seen again.

Merrily Watkins had been in here for nearly a week, after her near-neighbour, Laurence Robinson, and the old man, Mr Parry, had come rushing to find her, as her blood had dried on the Queen Stone.

Merrily's eyes had fallen closed. Vaynor thought she wouldn't hear him talking to the doctor again for a while.

On the hillside outside the County Hospital, Vaynor had been obliged to go the little guy, Robinson, who wouldn't be allowed in but kept coming back. He wasn't married or related to her in any obvious way. It seemed like he was a neighbour. But to Vaynor it seemed more like he was her dog.

'But, I've had another test!' Robinson insisted. 'I'm clean. That is, I've got… whatever they are, antibodies. Which means if I was going to get the virus I'd probably have it by now.'

'I'm sorry, I can't do anything,' Vaynor told him. 'Maybe you can still spread it. I don't know. It's early days, but we've been told to keep everybody out. I know it's three days since she was brought in, and, OK, that was with a head injury. Everybody who comes in here gets a test. Like a lot of people, she has no symptoms and she probably won't have any. But she's certainly carrying the virus.'

'Could be that we all are, but those of us not old enough to be at risk…'

'Look,' Vaynor said. 'We can't be sure of anything. There's another woman who only came in this morning, and she's only in her twenties, but in a bad way…'

It wasn't fair, but it was out of his hands. Robinson had been by the river that night, waiting for the ambulance with Mrs Watkins's young daughter and the old guy, Parry.

They'd come out of the night, the old man driving across a footpath and the grass. Mrs Watkins was more important to more people than she'd acknowledge. Including the DI, who Vaynor figured he'd be reporting to in a few minutes' time at Gaol Street.

The phone quivered in his left hip pocket and he switched it off as he loped back into the hospital.

He guessed it would be bad news for somebody.

'No,' he murmured unprofessionally. 'Please, no.'

Merrily's eyes were closed.

Her head felt numb. But her mind was moving.

In it she saw the virus.

It was yellow and it swirled.

And smiled.

It had a distinctly human smile, this virus. It knew exactly what it was doing.

She heard a mobile phone ring, then was hearing Darth Vaynor, in the ward entrance, saying, 'Yes.' Then his voice suddenly acquired a different tone. 'Oh,' he said, flat-voiced. 'Thanks for telling me. I think I'd better come up and confirm it.'

After a long pause, he said, 'Some other police and medical experts will be with you soon. Don't let anybody else into the ward... and please don't let anybody touch Mrs Portis's body.'

50

Work

It was the first time Vaynor had seen the DI with his feet up on the desk, his mouth and nose covered by one of the new NHS masks that it was rumoured would soon be compulsory to try and stop the spread of infection.

Bliss pulled his off with a snap of elastic.

'Not gonna make our job any easier, Darth, when every bugger in every bank's got one of these on.'

'Branches are being closed down so fast these days that there'll soon be none left to rob, anyway,' Vaynor said.

He started to say something else when Bliss held up a hand and lowered his shoes to the floor of the CID room.

'You seen Royce?'

'Not since last night. When I don't think they were exactly together, in the normal sense.'

'Complex situation,' Bliss said. 'But did it actually lead to another murder?'

'Do we have forensics, boss?'

'Nothing yet. But I got them techies focused as soon as you told me what the churchwarden had become aware of.' Bliss stood up. 'You're a clever lad. You know what I'm after. I want some evidence that his ankles were tied together *after* rather than before.'

'After he was dead?'

'That's it.'

'Something to prove he didn't tie his *own*...?'

'I'm not...' Bliss paced a slow circle. 'I'm not gerrin' *too* optimistic about this. Royce Portis has had a lorra luck since you and him were at school together. And there's no way we're gonna prove he arranged for his old man to come off that cliff. But one murder's all I need. If I *could* prove he had a hand in drowning the feller who frantically shafted Mrs P after Peter's funeral...'

'You don't think you will?'

Bliss sat down.

'Can't see it. What do you think?'

'Sorry, boss, but I don't think Royce Portis was as clever as *Mrs* Portis.'

'He's still alive, though.'

'Yes, there is *that* to consider...'

'And she was killed...'

Bliss smothered a smile.

'By the virus. She was killed by the virus,' Vaynor said.

Bliss thought about it, wiping his eyes, not looking at Vaynor.

'Unlike you,' he said. 'I'm norra doctor.' His voice intensified. 'And don't you ever friggin' *dare* repeat this to anybody. But I'd say she was also killed by Mrs Watkins.'

Bliss walked over to the window. A mist was thickening over Gaol Street.

'Inadvertently,' he said. 'But think about it.'

51

Learning to die

IT MUST HAVE been two weeks before Sophie told Merrily about her first visit to Hereford Cathedral after being discharged from hospital. She said she'd been standing close to one of the cylindrical cast-iron heaters in the cathedral's main aisle. They were monolithic, those heaters. They made a statement. They said, You *will* be warm. As if God had ordained it.

'I'd come to associate them with a comfort you could count on,' Sophie told Merrily. 'Reminds me of when I was a small child.'

In a thick, grey cardigan and two scarves, Sophie was hunched into her fireside chair. Then she was suddenly sitting up, stiffening, looking devastated. She said faintly that she'd always been aware of the cold even as a small girl, snuggling into her mother's long, woollen skirts in the winter. She remembered evening dropping like a cloth over the suburban village where she grew up under the blue glow of its first street-lamps.

It wasn't winter now, it was full spring, but the cylinders were full of the sort of dead cold that got into you permanently. The cathedral was still warm, Sophie said, but learning to die, because death was coming.

'I'm sorry...' Merrily said hesitantly to Sophie. 'This is about a bad dream you had?'

Her first visit since leaving the hospital. It was nearly dark in the street outside, and all the lamps in the room were out.

'And then, what I was seeing... Sophie reached out towards the faint redness in the grate. 'There were people all around me. Moving. Men in long overcoats. And women in—' She blinked. 'But women don't often wear hats any more, do they? Not like this. Not even twenty or thirty years ago. And they were steaming...'

'The hats?'

'The people. Cold was coming from them and drifting in the air... as if they were *made* of steam. Do you know what I—?'

Merrily didn't fight the shiver, didn't like the way this was going – Sophie didn't habitually do spooky except when she needed to convey something genuinely upsetting.

Merrily asked, 'Did you... touch any of them? Brush against them?'

'I should have, shouldn't I?' Sophie said. 'But I was repelled. And so kept my distance. I felt only this cold steam, as if I were reaching into a refrigerator where bodies are stored, and the people were...'

'Ghosts?'

'Not real. I prefer to say that.'

Merrily was beginning to wish she hadn't come. She might simply have accepted the Archdeacon's message that Sophie was *getting better,* was at least over the worst. Who knew how long her illness could last or what mental damage it could inflict? Sophie still hadn't admitted she'd only been having a bad dream. Or any kind of dream. She said she'd walked up the street, no more than a hundred yards, and passed through the Cathedral's rear entrance.

And she kept repeating details.

'These people... this congregation... came from the last long period when the cathedral was getting completely filled up as many times as there were services. When big congregations had gathered there in winter to find…'

'Warmth?' Merrily said. '*Spiritual* warmth?'

Leaning back into the heavy cushions of Sophie's sofa. She'd been into the cathedral this morning to dust the deliverance office because nobody else would be doing that. It had felt slightly cold up there and looked derelict.

'When was this?' She asked. 'The 1980s?'

'Seventies, I'd say. Or earlier. Do you understand what I'm telling you?'

'I… I'm not sure. This *was* a kind of… daydream?'

'It doesn't really matter,' Sophie said. 'It was happening then, in the seventies or whenever. The same kind of hats. The same… faces. And now it's happening again. The Cathedral returning to the old days. Remembering… before the end comes.'

'You knew these people… as individuals?'

'Not all of them.' Sophie stared into the growing greyness of the sitting room. 'Some of them,' she added falteringly, 'are actually still alive. Like the estate agent who sold Andrew this house. He became known as a rock-climber and now has a shop just round the corner.' She leaned back, as if she was pulling herself together. 'But I'm an old woman.'

'No,' Merrily said softly but desperately. 'No, you're *not*.'

The greyness hardened; Sophie had never talked this way before the virus. And whatever it was dragging behind it.

52

The fever

MERRILY FED ETHEL, the vicarage cat, then walked out into the village street. It was late afternoon, and Ledwardine was deserted. This was a Sunday outside the main holiday season, lockdown still in force and the church, like Hereford Cathedral, closed down. Its tower edged into view, an admonishing raised forefinger. Even empty, disused old buildings had to be maintained… or…

It hadn't taken long to replace Goodrich Court by the original green fields, the remains of its castellated walls rapidly snatched away by villagers with their wheelbarrows. Merrily envisaged them swarming like ants over the smoking ruins. The Court had only been a century old and starting to fit into its landscape when its time was up.

She saw the collapse, kept hearing its interminable groan.

How, in the end, would Meyrick feel? And Wordsworth, whose favourite castle survived? Wordsworth who won.

He *had* won, hadn't he?

She saw the poet walking the fields again, his consciousness seized by his surroundings then powerfully plucked away by a swooping peregrine falcon just as he was seeing into the life of things.

If this be but a vain belief, yet, oh! how oft—
In darkness and amid the many shapes
Of joyless daylight; when the fretful stir
Unprofitable, and the fever of the world,
Have hung upon the beating of my heart,
How oft, in spirit, have I turned to thee,
O sylvan Wye...

Greyness hardening on all sides. The Wye heavy with pollution. The fever of the world, inflicting a massive unbalance which might never be corrected.

Her memories of those moments down by the Wye and the QueenStone were increasingly confused. She didn't remember being driven to the field or walking to the stone. Had it been simple madness... or the onset of the fever of the world?

There were stories in the Sunday broadsheets about the damage to the Church hastened by the virus. Not huge, scary, prophetic stories, just inside-page leads hinting at the beginning of the end, indicating that the Second Millennium would be the last.

It had been forecast since the last century. Even in places like this, vicars who retired weren't being replaced. Villagers who'd do it for nothing were always around. Pretty soon they wouldn't remember the days when people got paid for leading appeals to an increasingly multi-gendered entity they couldn't be sure had ever listened. When there was at least one person in every parish who was paid to try and explain to people why it was worth maintaining an inner life... seeing into the life of things. What life?

The destruction had been speeded up by the pandemic. No better time to rid the collapsing Church of clerics who took the paranormal too seriously.

Took me back many years, to the days of Lampe and Cupitt. Huw Owen. *Long before your time, lass... Back in the 1970s, when understanding the Unseen and, when necessary, facing up to an active evil, were still accepted as part of the Church's job. Now t'Church is groping for credibility in an increasingly secular society by reducing what it admits to believing in. Demonic possession... that's become a mental health issue... They'll consign us to history.*

Then he'd asked her, *Can I take it you still want to go on peering into the Unknown? Listening to folk who think they're getting glimpses of the Unseen... I need to get this right. You've a decision to make and this is the time to make it.*

And she asked herself, Do *I* get to make that decision?

Huw said, *If the Church is reducing your role, prior to phasing it out, who's left to assist parish priests facing summat genuinely iffy?*

She didn't know. Upmarket news outlets claimed the Church was becoming more 'liberal', but it was the wrong word. In its attempt to save money the Church was only becoming more constrictive, run by a handful of centralised bureaucrats who looked out for themselves and their mates.

In the empty street, Merrily gave in to a slow shiver. Like most involuntary reactions, it made her head hurt and she again felt stone denting it and cold hands tight in her hair. She was finally avoiding mirrors reflecting the encrusted slash on the left cheek below the black tunnelled tracks to her eyes. But was still hearing Wordsworth's line about *the fever of the world,* as if the poet had been projected across the years to watch the 250th anniversary of his birth obliterated by a dark virus that crossed continents.

And had made Sophie think of herself as an old woman. She wasn't yet a link in the chain of death that may have begun with Peter Portis, whose memorial in the window of his shop in Ross's Corpse Cross Street had implied he'd not just gone but had been *taken...* by the rocks he thought he'd known, thought he'd conquered.

No inquest would ever reveal if his daughter-in-law *called him down* from them.

'This is out of our hands.' Lol was suddenly there beside her in his clean but very worn *Alien* sweatshirt, his left hand closing around her quivering shoulder. 'We just have to save what we can.'

She felt a warmth as they stopped at the church gate. It dissipated as she saw that two family graves had been opened ready for victims of the virus. That would be this week's work in Ledwardine for Merrily and Gomer Parry.

Gomer who, she'd now learned, had probably saved her life. Had kept going back to the QueenStone, four nights, then five, because he instinctively knew how important the stone was to young Janey.

He'd explained to Jane that the vicar had made him tell her about the long nights he'd spent down near the stone he'd first driven to for Alfred Watkins's grandson. Then with Janey, Gomer said. Then on his own, sitting, often sleeping, in the ole LandRover. Until one night he'd seen a grey car coming through the trees and felt *this was it*. And then – he wasn't stupid, he was an ole feller, no question, and he knew his limits – he pulled out his phone, which, like him, was too old to be all that *smart* as folks called them now, and he rang up, not Janey, but... young Laurence. And the boy had come out directly, bringing Janey with him – like he'd have a choice – and Gomer had seen a woman in his headlights and started his engine, and the woman had gone buggering off, fast.

He didn't know the vicar had been there, too. Not then.

*

'There's never really a satisfactory end to anything,' Lol said softly, as Venus – perhaps the year's last evening Venus – appeared between the chimneys of the Black Swan.

She spun to face him.

Why *not*?

But she stayed silent.

Everything in Ledwardine was silent.

An old woman across the street near Jane's shop lowered a red apple from her mouth and glanced at her.

'We'll just end up clinging to one another,' Merrily said to Lol. Or Lol said to Merrily; she didn't register which of them had spoken. She started thinking of the cathedral that would keep on raising money to hold its medieval masonry together and the Bishop who, like all other bastard bishops, would make sure he held on to his episcopal status.

The old woman's glance had become a stare. The face behind the apple was the pagan face of Lucy Devenish, who Jane would often claim to have seen.

But not the diocesan exorcist, who surely never saw these things. No sooner had she registered this illusion than the stare vanished with the rest of Lucy Devenish, leaving Merrily squeezing Lol's left hand with a hot urgency.

'And maybe we'll keep on clinging,' she said.

53

We are seven

MERRILY AWOKE IN the armchair, to find the stove burning low. The air was cold. Through the kitchen window she saw a black shadow under a familiar cloche hat.

In the hall, still half asleep, she was fumbling with the back door when the outside light showed her the Archdeacon of Hereford backing away.

'I know it's late,' Siân Callaghan-Clarke said. 'But I didn't want to be seen. And I won't be staying.'

'Erm…' Merrily shook her head, fuzzy. '… time is it?'

'Just gone midnight. I thought you'd have gone to bed. If you had, I was going to push this under the door and call you in the morning. I… somehow didn't want to take it home.'

'It…?'

'I could tell Sophie wanted to lock it away again, or…'

'What are you…?'

'Or at least, by tomorrow, have decided to ask me to bring it back… forget about it. But I didn't want her to have to live with that responsibility.'

Siân was holding, at a distance, a thick, brown envelope that Merrily thought she'd seen before. Maybe a week ago. Maybe in another life.

*

In the car, wasn't it? Parked in Goodrich village where Sophie had shown her some of the big envelope's contents. Merrily had half-expected to see everything Dobbs had left in Sophie's care – all the papers she'd kept at home rather than leave for the Bishop to explore during one of his paranoid investigations of the cupboards in the cathedral gatehouse. Why? What had been so important? What had Dobbs discovered that he didn't want to come out?

Merrily sat under the kitchen lamp, a thumb poised over the envelope. Why hadn't the Archdeacon stayed here to see it opened? Why had she slid so discreetly back?

Had she? Had she really slipped away, murmuring, *I didn't want her to have to live with the responsibility* – what did that mean? Was there something *Siân* didn't want to have to keep to herself?

I haven't seen the contents of this envelope. I don't know what they are. I don't know if I could be told. I didn't ask. I don't care to know.

Had she said that on her way out?

Now Merrily stood up – shakily, for some reason – and closed all the doors. She didn't want Jane to hear, even though she could trust her more than she'd felt able to a couple of years ago. But Jane was in bed anyway, almost certainly hadn't seen the Archdeacon arrive.

Returning to the table, Merrily felt a paperclip ridge under the envelope flap and found a typed note, unsigned but evidently from Sophie.

Canon Dobbs appears to have been in two minds about this. Was it imagination, conjecture, self-deception,

wishful thinking? I DON'T KNOW. I can't think. That is why I'm finally handing it to you. You'll realise that no one else must see it, or even know of it.

It appeared to be Dobbs's notes from September 1985, written on his return from a chilly early-morning deliverance exercise on the site of the demolished Goodrich Court outside the village.

Merrily weighed the brown envelope between her hands. It was not heavy, and yet *something* obviously was.

*

Dobbs:

I have been at home for less than an hour, have had two cups of coffee. As it is becoming light outside the window, although it is still cold, I have decided to write down what I remember from the fields above Goodrich.

This was shakily handwritten in black ink.

As I drove back into the city, with all its lights, I found the memories already beginning to curl at the corners like old photos. I do not know how much of all this, if anything, I am permitted to believe. These paragraphs are for myself, to be reread at a more rational time.

Merrily smiled. If he'd still been around, would he have found *this* a more rational time? The national lockdown was the least rational period she could think of.

She stared at Dobbs's words in the oaken light and tried to picture him, to see his severe face ingrained in the table's old polish. It was not *that* many years since she'd last seen him, but his head was now outlined by what appeared to be greying feathers.

A raven's head about to croak *Nevermore.*

Merrily shivered and pushed the paper away. It was as cold in here as it must have been when Dobbs had been writing his report all those years ago. Her dressing gown was upstairs and she didn't want to wake Jane, so she stood up and went into the hall, where she dragged her heavy funeral cape from the cupboard and pulled it around her shoulders.

When she went back to the table, she was feeling as though she was about to perform a rite of exorcism.

As Dobbs had done on that frigid morning.

I had been told that four people had heard the roar of agony and a splintering of timber. At first I did not believe it had been heard by anyone as an actual roar. I thought it must have been a gust of wind making its way through agricultural buildings that were old but still very much intact.

There had been seventeen silent spectators – Dobbs had counted them. Some had come from nearby farms, others had walked up from Goodrich village and a few had arrived in cars, parking close to the court's castle gatehouse. Dobbs said he'd recognised some people but he didn't name them. He was increasingly reticent, as if he wasn't sure who was a good witness.

Merrily thought she was beginning to see them, and stiffened. Had *she* been there?

No, Diana Portis would surely have been too young, back then. Were there, perhaps, others connected with the Meyrick tradition, bemoaning the gradual demolition of the Court, the slow dissolution of Sir Samuel's vision? Nurturing a resentment of Wordsworth who had hated the new castle which had stood where Dobbs had been standing.

Merrily, too. Back at the Queen Stone, she'd had a sensation of being there, feeling walls collapsing around her, the ground quaking under the weight of fallen stone. Hearing Diana Portis's ironic warning.

Careful. You're coming down.

She felt cold, hard stone meeting her forehead. Saw what Dobbs had written of semi-distant children's voices before scrubbing it out with hurried fountain-pen strokes among inkblots.

I thought I heard them, but there were no children amongst us.

What? Merrily clutched at a table leg to pull herself upright.

I heard another voice from someone who was not there.

*

A deeper voice, a man's voice, and it said, Let the moon shine on thee in thy solitary walk

Then, written probably minutes later, in a faster, less-measured hand:

Who said that? I don't know but feel I should. I was confused... Trying to pray to Almighty God and hearing these other voices... The children who weren't there, and the man, when all the men with me – five, at least – were silent!

How did I know it wasn't one of them? Because real voices in the open night air have a certain hollow vibration, usually accompanied by the sound of heavy breathing. And these voices were... somewhere else...

...these voices were... somewhere else.

As she read the words, Merrily heard, in her head, something similar in a different voice, a lighter voice, a woman's voice.

Whose?

Maya's.

And it was saying, *Two or more voices were coalescing into the hollowness of... I don't know, let's just say* somewhere else...Maya Madden talking about the voices she couldn't be sure she'd heard in the garden of her possibly – how could she know, how could she possibly be certain? – haunted cottage in Goodrich village, near the church. Had Thomas Dobbs heard the same children's voices, as if transmitted up here by the steeple?

And the man's voice. Possibly the voice of a man who *could not be here*. Whose only reason for being visible, to some, in Goodrich was to find a person who was only eight years old when he'd last seen her. Who had returned many times.

When they were both alive.

Oh God! Merrily found she'd let her head drop heavily to the table top, dislodging an untidy pile of books.

The first to land was old and small, in a fraying brown stiff cover on which 5p could still be seen, written in chalk flakes.

The poems of Wordsworth

With Memoir, Explanatory Notes, &c

Was it…?

She opened the book where a yellow tab marked page 116 and found

LINES COMPOSED A FEW MILES ABOVE
TINTERN ABBEY, ON REVISITING THE BANKS
OF THE WYE DURING A TOUR.
JULY 13, 1798

Not far from the bottom of the page, she read:

that neither evil tongues,
Rash judgments, nor the sneers of selfish men,
Nor greetings where no kindness is, nor all
The dreary intercourse of daily life
Shall e'er prevail against us, or disturb
Our cheerful faith, that all which we behold
Is full of blessings. Therefore let the moon
Shine on thee in thy solitary walk…

She wasn't quite sure when she had begun to sense Jane's voice in her head. The voice she'd often made a point of switching off…

…*too* often?

Switching off didn't seem as obvious a reaction as it had when Jane was fifteen or sixteen and talked mystical and pagan crap for effect.

Merrily leaned back in the kitchen armchair, closed her eyes.

Heard Jane's voice:

The Sight. *Sharing her supper with the dead in Goodrich churchyard? What's she really saying? ... Young children are closer to all this life and death stuff. They always have been.*[*]

Jane? Dobbs? Maya Madden? David Vaynor? William Wordsworth?

None of them could prove anything, even to themselves.

She resealed the report in its brown envelope in which she would return it to Sophie. She got up and walked across to the kitchen window, where she saw that the night sky had cleared.

And began to laugh.

NOTES

The following books were consulted.

Mary Andere, *Arthurian Links with Herefordshire* (Logaston Press, 1995)

Geoffrey Ashe, *The Ancient Wisdom* (Macmillan 1977)

Jonathan Bate, *Radical Wordsworth: The Poet Who Changed the World* (William Collins)

David Bentley-Taylor, *Wordsworth in the Wye Valley* (Logaston Press, 20021)

Jason Bray, *Deliverance* (Coronet)

Ronald Hutton, *Blood and Mistletoe: The History of the Druids in Britain* (Yale, 2009)

Rosalind Lowe, *Sir Samuel Meyrick and Goodrich Court* (Logaston Press, 2003) The only book on this character, who Ros *sometimes* admires.

Edmund J. Mason, *The Wye Valley* (Hale)

Arthur Mee, *The King's England: Herefordshire* (Hodder and Stoughton)

Mary Moorman, *William Wordsworth: the early years, 1770–1803* (Oxford, Clarendon Press)

Gary St Michael Nottingham, *Foundations of Practical Sorcery* (Avalonia, 2004)

George Peterken, *Wye Valley* (Collins)

Susan Peterken, *Landscapes of the Wye Tour* (Logaston Press)

Tamzin Powell, *The Witches Ways in the Welsh Borders* (Airheart)

Anne Ross, *Pagan Celtic Britain*
Ward Rutherford, *The Druids & Their Heritage* (Gordon & Cremonesi, 1978)
Elizabeth Rees, *Celtic Saints: Passionate Wanderers*
Graham Robb, *The Ancient Paths* (Picador)
Mithu Sanyal, *Rape: From Lucretia to #metoo* (Verso 2019)
R. H. Stavis, *Sister of Darkness*
Bryan Walters, *The Archaeology and History of Ancient Dean and the Wye Valley* (Thornhill Press)
Alfred Watkins, *The Old Straight Track*, *The Ley Hunter's Manual* and *Alfred Watkins' Herefordshire*, introduction by Ron and Jennifer Shoesmith, (Logaston, 2012)
Francis Young, *A History of Anglican Exorcism: Deliverance and Demonology in Church Ritual* (I. B. Tauris, 2018)

Stories in this novel are also covered in *Merrily's Border* (latest edition) by Phil Rickman, with photography by John Mason. Most locations and landscape features in the novel can be seen in this book.

The different attitudes to Wye Valley castles by Wordsworth and Sir Samuel Meyrick were explored in an excellent article by the playwright and TV writer Julian Mitchell – 'Goodrich Castle: antiquity and nature versus thingummies', which can be found online.

King Arthur's Cave is one of several holes in the Doward. The remains of prehistoric animals have been found there and – allegedly – a very big human skeleton.

On the subject of anomalous sightings around the Doward, during the recording of the BBC Radio 4 *Rambling* programme, the presenter, Claire Balding, revealed that a very large, apparently wild cat had just crossed her field of vision. Nobody else on the team saw it.

The Queen Stone also exists, and there is, at the time of writing, no official public access. Thanks are due to Richard Vaughan, whose family have owned the stone for over four centuries, for allowing me to sneak up on her. As the fields below Huntsham Hill are now used for specialized farming, I can understand the problem. There are, of course, several photographs in books and online and the Queen Stone can be glimpsed from the road linking Goodrich and the A40. Alfred Watkins's theories about it as a place of human sacrifice can be found in *The Old Straight Track* and that photograph of him with his own wicker man on the stone itself can be seen in *Alfred Watkins' Herefordshire, (in his own words and photographs, with a biographical introduction by Ron and Jennifer Shoesmith* (Logaston Press)). The Ordnance Survey map shows a line from the stone, through the ancient Wyeside church of St Dubricius, through Great Doward, the Doward caves and the Seven Sisters to the Far Hearkening Rock. The site of Goodrich Court also seems to be on this line. Thanks to the intrepid ex-soldier who passed on his own reactions to the Queen Stone, where he says he wouldn't want to spend a night.

St Giles's Church at Goodrich is, as noted, one of the few village churches inaccessible to vehicles.

Copse Cross Street starts at the top of Ross-on-Wye town centre and is sometimes said to have dropped its r. Some say, perhaps a touch queasily, that the burial of suicides there is pure conjecture. Some don't.

And closing credits: people who helped.

Mark Austin, forestry bushcraft
John Billingsley, Northern Earth
Rosalind Lowe, author of *Sir Samuel Meyrick and Goodrich*

Court for providing really useful information not in the book
The Revs, some of whom do deliverance
Ben Bentham
Jason Bray
Peter Brooks
Kevin Cecil
Petra Beresford-Webb
Liz Jump
Sir Diarmaid MacCulloch
Sir Richard 'Indiana' Heygate
Dr Mike Inglis, astronomer
Garth Lawson, pathfinder
Prof. Bernard Knight, pathologist and crime writer
Prof. Peter Mahoney, CBE, consultant anaesthetist
Anne Holt, astronomer
Graham 'Sven' Hassel, of Summit Mountaineering, Symonds Yat
Tracy Thursfield, astrologer and general esotericist
Dave from The Electric Shop in Ross
Andrea Collins
Sara Craig Lanier (on Lucy)
Richard Vaughan, of Huntsham Court
Marcus Buffrey, Hereford Archivist
Former Insp. Felicity Keane, of West Midlands Police
Former Hereford detective, West Mercia Police, Paul Matthews
Tamzin Powell
Peter Smith
Russell James
Andrew Jones
Pete Bibby
David Colohan

Dunstan-Maria, who's been sending me stuff for some years, but whose identity I still don't know
Rosalind Lowe
Prof. Peter Mahoney, ballistics
Doug Mason
Gary Nottingham
Ronal Ronsbury Fairweather
Trudy Williams

And a special thanks to Mairead Reidy who uncovered background information for virtually all these novels and died – very prematurely – during the final stages of this one. Thank you, Mairead, for years of help. Dream well.

Marcia Talley, novelist
Tom Young, techno-guru
Allan Watson, for Lol's music

Long-overdue appreciation to journalists Marla Williams and Andy Ryan in Seattle. Marla's help was essential in the final stages. So was Sarah de Souza, who took over as editor of Corvus in Fever's final week and immediately saw what it needed.

And Carol Rickman, who usually gets thanked for editing and seriously improving a book… this time, due to me being in gruelling recovery for two years, she had to unload much of that, due to the barely possible task of doing absolutely everything else.